THE FLORAL COMPANION

THE FLORAL COMPANION

Anthea Bell

St. Martin's Press
New York

Library of Congress Cataloging-in-Publication Data

Bell, Anthea.
      The floral companion.

      I. Title.
PR6052.E432F5   1989   823'.914   88-30566
ISBN 0-312-02578-5

First published in Great Britain by Souvenir Press Ltd.

First U.S. Edition

10 9 8 7 6 5 4 3 2 1

1

'Now I wonder,' mused Mrs Elliott, studying the unfamiliar signature of her letter, 'I wonder who my very affectionate Cousin Clarissa may be?'

Her father made no reply. It was not that he was deaf, or his mind not yet fully alert so early in the morning—for early it was: breakfast was taken in the handsome Russell Square residence of that fashionable physician Sir John Law at the decidedly unfashionable hour of half past eight, or sometimes even earlier. During the years when he held a senior appointment at one of London's largest hospitals, Sir John had got into the habit of walking there daily, rain or shine, and even now, when the many other calls upon his time had caused him to resign his hospital post, he still liked to take a constitutional before breakfast. At the age of fifty-five, Sir John had no intention of abandoning those habits of industry and energy which had brought him from Edinburgh and his father's modest apothecary's shop to an extensive London practice, recognition as a leading light in the medical profession, and even the social cachet conferred by Royal patronage and a knighthood.

He was, simply, too deeply absorbed in what he was reading to have heard his daughter's remarks at all. Guessing as much, she smiled indulgently across the table at him. Newly widowed, and just back from India after five years' absence, Caroline Elliott had been thankful to find her father as hale and hearty as ever. His fine head of hair might be iron-grey, but it was still thick, and his only concession to middle age seemed to be the eyeglasses he now wore to read small print, an activity upon which he was at this moment engaged. Having skimmed through his other correspondence, he had seized upon a journal which had

5

arrived with it, and was perusing it with the utmost interest.

Mrs Elliott was no late riser herself, and made a point of being up in time to preside over the shining tea urn and keep her father company. That, she felt, was the very least she could do when (to her own considerable distress) his usual and preferred companion had so provokingly insisted on absenting herself.

Father and daughter did not talk much during breakfast. Caroline Elliott was sure dear Hetty did not pester Sir John with inconsequential chatter at meals, and nor would she. But they were not entirely silent. A casual observer might have supposed that father and daughter were conducting a desultory conversation, but although they did speak from time to time, they were generally engaged in a couple of separate, abstracted monologues. Indeed, Mrs Elliott had addressed her question largely to herself, without much expecting any parental response.

Dear me, she reflected, hearing the echo of her own voice, what a shockingly bad habit that is! She remembered Hetty's gently taking her to task, many years ago. 'Carey, dear, I don't know if you are even quite aware that you do it, but I wish you would not talk aloud to yourself.'

'Papa does!' young Caroline had accurately pointed out, well aware that since neither she nor Mrs Pauling was going to admit that Sir John could ever do wrong, she was driving her governess into a corner.

'Yes, I dare say, but—well, in him it is just taken for eccentricity, you see. In a young lady, it is a very different matter,' said Mrs Pauling firmly. 'Young ladies ought not to be eccentric. It is not at all the thing. You might even be considered fast. What is more,' Henrietta Pauling shrewdly added, displaying, as she sometimes did, more worldly wisdom than anyone expected of her, 'what is more, I fancy your papa does it on purpose; so that when he wishes to tell one or other of his patients not to pursue some foolishly self-indulgent course of action, but he knows they will not like to hear his advice, he can be supposed to be merely thinking out loud, and thus he gives no offence.'

'As with the Duchess and the dog,' murmured Carey now, recollecting this exchange, and the day she herself had seen her father dealing summarily with one of the fat pug dogs kept by the most exalted of all his patients, the Duchess of York, whom he had treated efficaciously for years, until at last her case became hopeless and she was carried off by the dropsy in 1820. No doubt it was to his attendance on the Duchess that he owed his knighthood. In her lifetime, while a most amiable character, she had been fully a match for her physician in eccentricity, and unconventional enough, in an age when small children were strictly confined to the nursery, to have urged Sir John and his wife to bring their little girl with them to her residence of Oatlands, saying she knew the dear child would like to see the animals. For she lived surrounded by a positive menagerie of dogs, parrots and monkeys. Thus, Carey happened to be present when the Duchess thrust her wheezing pet at Sir John, desiring him to tell her what was wrong with it.

Even then, Carey knew that to consult an eminent physician on the ailments of lapdogs was a breach of medical etiquette. All the more so as the occasion upon which the Laws found themselves at Oatlands was social, not professional. She held her breath, wondering what her father would do.

In the event Sir John, taking the pug by the scruff of its neck, had remarked meditatively, 'Not a veterinary surgeon—no intention of becoming one, either,' but in such a tone that he might be thought to be addressing the dog rather than its owner. He had then opened a window and dropped the startled animal straight out, advising it: 'Go for a run in the park. Do you the world of good!'

The dog had meekly complied, probably from sheer surprise, and before the Laws returned to London Carey was able to see for herself that the novel experience had done it good. She rather fancied, however, that the Duchess had not tried consulting her physician on her pets' behalf again.

The memory made her chuckle, a sound which did briefly attract her parent's attention, for without raising his eyes from his journal he waved a large, well-tended hand at the covered silver dishes on the sideboard, and recommended her to try some porridge. 'Very good, this morning. I wouldn't exchange the excellent Mrs Mackenzie for the finest French chef in town. Remarkably clever of you to find her, my dear.'

By this Carey understood that her father thought himself to be speaking to Mrs Pauling, and her smile died away. Really, it was too bad of Hetty! Such scruples of conscience were most vexatious. And to take her mind off the matter, which had been troubling her own conscience a good deal of late, Mrs Elliott returned to her letter. 'Papa,' she said, addressing her father more directly this time, 'Papa, do tell me, who is my very affectionate Cousin Clarissa?'

But her question registered with him no more than before. 'Ha!' he exclaimed, turning a page. 'Used to wonder how long Tom Wakley would continue this publication. Used to wonder how long he would be allowed to continue it. Always thought it good rousing stuff, though. And he really seems to be making a go of it after all, don't you think, Hetty?'

'I can't say, as I am not Hetty,' said his daughter, her smile reviving. 'What publication, Papa? What sort of good, rousing stuff?'

'Eh? Oh, it's you, is it, Carey?' said Sir John, looking up at last and noticing that his daughter, not his much-loved mistress, sat across the table from him in the April sunlight. She made a charming picture, he thought, handsome rather than strictly speaking pretty in her elegant pelisse-robe of dove-grey, its fastenings concealed by ribbon bows of deeper grey satin, and with a spreading white lace pelerine setting off her fine neck and shoulders. She wore a becoming little white lace cap on her dark head, in token of widowhood. Sir John was glad she had gone into half-mourning even before her arrival in England, permitting herself shades of grey and white, lilac and lavender, instead of clothing herself wholly in funereal black. As Carey herself had said to him, 'It isn't that I mourn Andrew any the less, but you know, he wouldn't have wished me to go about in black crape all my life, and I thought how very hot it would be on the voyage home.' She grieved deeply for her diplomat husband, carried off by a fever during the tour of India on which she had accompanied him, but as she assured her father and Mrs Pauling, she had no intention of going into a decline, or anything stupid of that nature. Mrs Pauling was so pleased to hear this forthright declaration that, despite being a little shocked, she refrained from any mention of the grey and lilac gowns.

Sir John now observed that his daughter was still looking inquiringly at the journal he held. 'What's this? Oh, Tom Wakley's *Lancet*,' he informed her. 'He'd only just begun to publish it, I think, when you left England.'

'*The Lancet*, yes, now I remember. Of course, you wrote to me about it.' Searching her memory, Mrs Elliott dredged up several mentions, in her father's letters to India, of the crusading medical journal founded by his young friend the Radically-disposed surgeon Thomas Wakley. Her mind now running on medical matters, she sipped tea, her own letter momentarily forgotten, and added, 'I was sorry, by the way, to hear of the Duke of York's death when you wrote to me with news of that. So now he, for one, will never be King.'

'No, it looks like Clarence to succeed, and before very long, too.'

'Is the King himself not well?'

Sir John laid down his journal and favoured his daughter with a little more of his attention. 'Decidedly not. I doubt that he ever will be well again. Halford thinks he'll be lucky to last the year. He won't heed anything Halford or his other physicians say, but takes by far too much laudanum for his gout, and still eats and drinks to excess—no constitution could stand it!' Sir John leaned back in his chair, a handsome figure in the dressing gown his tailor had made from the heavy silk Carey had brought him back from India. His mind turned from the probable demise of King George IV to the welfare of a person whose interests both he and his daughter had more at heart. 'Calling upon Hetty today, my dear?'

'Yes, but first I am to see Mr Lindley—or no, I understand he is Professor Lindley now. It is about those seeds Andrew collected, and the plants we had picked and pressed together.' Mrs Elliott's voice briefly faltered. Apart from his diplomatic work, her late husband's great interest had been in botany and the collection of plants, and since she herself, even as a girl, had shown great talent for

9

botanical illustration—it was one of the things that had drawn them together—she had entered whole-heartedly into his enthusiasm. 'We were shipping material back to England for the Horticultural Society's Chiswick gardens all the time we were in India, of course, and what couldn't be sent I drew or painted in its natural surroundings; so I completed Andrew's collection as best I might before sailing home, and Lindley has been looking at the paintings I brought back and wants to talk to me about them. I'm to see him at the Society's offices this morning, and will then go on to Hetty in Chelsea. But now, Papa,' said Carey, returning to her letter, 'will you please tell me, who is my very affectionate Cousin Clarissa?'

'You haven't got one,' he immediately replied, and was returning to his journal when a thought seemed to strike him, and he looked up again. 'Well, not an affectionate one. Not unless she's changed mightily.'

'She certainly sounds affectionate,' said Carey, frowning a little as she began to read the letter itself, for she had looked at the signature first. 'Indeed, a trifle over-effusive. Ah, I see . . . a cousin of Mama's! That explains it.'

'Clarissa Gerard, eh? That's it,' confirmed Sir John, as she read on. 'One of your mother's grand relations.'

'And very grand she sounds, too,' agreed his daughter, chuckling. 'Listen to this! She may be found residing, she says, at Marchingham Priory, an historic seat set in pleasing and extensive grounds upon the borders of several of the eastern counties of England, with an estate of some fifteen thousand acres, an equal distance from the village of Little Marchingham and the country town of Great Marchingham, or Marchingham Magna, a vicinity having many advantages and offering genteel society sure to appeal to a lady of refinement—why,' concluded Carey, stopping to draw breath, 'anyone would think she was trying to sell me the place.'

'Are you sure she isn't?' inquired Sir John, drily. 'The Gerards are none too prosperous, as I remember—and you're a rich woman, my dear. Perhaps Clarissa's going into the real estate business.'

'No, no, this paragon of a place is obviously their ancestral home, and she is merely inviting me to stay with them.

That is to say, with herself, her husband Sir William and my Cousin Will, who is exactly my own age, as she is sure I must remember—though I confess I don't—and retains the happiest memories of our games together as children—did we play any games together as children?'

'Possibly—on one occasion, at least.'

'Well, I have not the slightest recollection of it.'

'Oh, you wouldn't have been more than five or six. We paid a visit, just one, as I said. Like the rest of Mary's family, Clarissa would have nothing to do with her when she married me—a mere physician, you see. Great sticklers, your mother's family, every last one of 'em. Well, so I got on in the world a bit, became Sir John, was noticed by folk even grander than themselves, and then they were ready to know us. Myself, I'd have had nothing to do with them; but there, your mother was the kindest soul alive, and couldn't bear to be at loggerheads with anyone.'

'I am sure she couldn't,' said Carey warmly, recollecting the gentle mother who had died of a wasting disease when she herself was only nine.

'Aye, well, so when her cousin Clarissa offered the olive branch, Mary was all for taking it, and off we went to Marchingham.'

'Wait!' said Carey, thinking. 'Yes, now you mention it, I believe I do remember the place—and being aware, as a child can be without quite knowing why, that you and Mama were not enjoying yourselves very much.'

'True, my dear. A patronising woman, Clarissa Gerard, and if there was one thing Mary never could bear it was to hear me patronised. I don't remember the husband a great deal—something of a nonentity, I fancy.'

'Oh no, you are quite mistaken,' said Carey, laughing, and referred to her letter again. 'A nonentity? No such thing: he's the thirteenth baronet in line, and all of them Sir Williams.'

'Aye, you'd have thought the Gerards sailed into Marchingham in Noah's Ark. All the same, it was Clarissa ruled the roost, not Sir William.'

'I believe I recollect him, too. Oh, he was not so bad, Papa. I remember that he put me on his knee, which I didn't particularly care for, and gave me a sip from his wineglass,

11

which I have to tell you I most reprehensibly did. And then he let me play with a pretty china dog which stood on the mantelpiece and had caught my eye, and which I liked best of all, but we had to put it back in a hurry when we heard somebody coming.'

'Clarissa, I expect,' said Sir John.

'As for my Cousin Will,' continued Carey, probing the recesses of her memory further, 'if he truly retains happy memories of our games together, then he must have grown into a singularly odious person. He was teasing and tormenting me the whole time, that I do remember, with the sole object of making me shed tears. And I was equally determined not to shed them. He won that contest, all the same, when he threw my doll into the middle of the farmyard, and I dared not fetch her out for fear of all the cattle trampling about the dirty straw, and their great long horns. Wasn't there another brother, too, though? An elder son?'

'No, I think not. Just the one lad, as I remember.'

'But there was another boy about the place, who went in among the cattle to rescue my doll for me, and told the insufferable Will to let me alone. I thought it very brave of him, even though he said it wasn't, because the creatures were only cows, not bulls, and wouldn't hurt me. But like the wary little Londoner that I was, I put no faith in such assurances.'

'Some farm lad, I suppose,' said Sir John.

'Yes, he must have been, since Lady Gerard mentions no other son here. So our visit was not altogether a success?'

'No; I fancy we were all happy enough to let the acquaintance drop. Mary found she didn't care for Clarissa Gerard's condescending ways. Well, so what has Clarissa to say, after all this time?' inquired Sir John, idly.

'Oh, she offers condolences on my loss. Rather flowery ones. Mentions her grief upon my mother's death sixteen years ago—'

'Failed to mention it at the time,' commented Sir John.

'Wonders if I have grown up, as she is sure I must have done, to resemble my dear mama.'

'You resemble me more closely, I'm afraid. Your misfortune.'

'And finally inquires whether I would care to see the country in high summer, though alas, she says, she fears she asks in vain, since the Season will beckon, and it is only natural that a woman still young must shake off melancholy and look to the future . . . however, should I not find the gaiety of Town to my taste just yet, I am assured of a welcome to Marchingham Priory, where she likes to think she herself might play the part of a mother to me. How curious!' Carey looked at her Cousin Clarissa's missive with a touch of distaste. 'And a little impertinent, too. She wants something of me, so much is clear. But what?'

'Hm. Married, is he, this Cousin Will of yours?' inquired her father, drily. 'Fellow with the happy memories, and so forth?'

'Oh,' said Mrs Elliott blankly. 'Oh dear! Do you think that is it?'

"More than likely. You must get accustomed to having suitors again, my dear.'

'But good gracious, these Gerards have not so much as set eyes on me since I was six. I might have grown into a perfect fright,' said Carey, with some indignation.

'Well, all things considered, your face isn't so bad,' said her fond father. 'All the same, your face isn't your fortune. That is large, and will be larger after my death, as you may be sure everyone knows.'

'And since you will certainly live to be a hundred, the matter need not concern them at all,' retorted Mrs Elliott, with spirit. 'How very disagreeable it is, to have people thinking of my marrying again already.'

'Only human nature,' said Sir John, mildly.

'Well, all I can say is, it makes me quite sorry I left off full mourning after all. That might have prevented our kind friend, your patient Lady Saye, from listing all the eligible *partis* she has in mind for me, while Hetty warns me against fortune-hunters, when I can look after myself very well in that respect. Really, it is too provoking!' said Mrs Elliott crossly, but then suddenly smiled. 'Although if I were to marry again, then of course Hetty could come back here with a clear conscience . . . no, no, don't scold!' she quickly cried, seeing her father's frown. 'I was only joking. You know very well I wouldn't marry anyone for such a reason.'

13

'If you did, all I can say is that Hetty's conscience would be far from clear. It would probably torment her ever after.'

'I know that well enough. Hetty's conscience,' said Hetty's erstwhile pupil, ruefully, 'is a most delicate, tender plant, and considering she had the charge of me from the age of ten, I marvel at it that mine is so much more flexible. I am sure it is not her fault.'

'Sometimes,' said her father, sighing, 'Hetty is more than I can fathom myself. Why she must insist upon moving out of the house just now, I do not know.'

'Yes, you do, Papa, because she told us, at length and several times,' Mrs Elliott corrected him. 'You mean that you don't understand her. I do. I don't partake of her sentiments, but I understand them. Though I must say, I certainly never expected this when I came home, and it was a great surprise to me.'

'Aye—she didn't do it before, when you came out and so forth. Didn't seem to think it was doing your reputation any harm then, living under the same roof with her,' said Sir John, with gloomy bafflement.

'No, but Hetty has explained all that: she believes that the connection between the two of you was not then widely known, in fact that she had taken good care it should not be widely known, whereas later—'

'I never cared a fig who knew!' interrupted Sir John.

'But Hetty did. And now that I look back—although I didn't notice it at the time—I can see she was being very discreet.'

Sir John nodded. 'May be something in what you say. It was only after you'd married Andrew she'd agree to appear with me in public.'

'Exactly so. You and I may think her notions utter nonsense, but as she sees them, they are not.' Going over to the window, Carey paused to look down into the square, where a small boy was bowling his hoop past urns full of spring flowers which she knew Hetty's clever fingers must have planted. 'I know it would be a most unusual step,' she said hesitantly, 'but could she not obtain a divorce, and then you could be married? After all, Mr Pauling is a hopeless lunatic, is he not? I suppose there is no likelihood of his ever recovering his wits?'

14

'None in the world, I am happy to say,' replied Sir John, with unfeeling briskness. 'For if he did, you may be bound she'd feel obliged to return to him, no matter how badly he had treated her in the past and might treat her again—and her feelings and my own could go hang. Divorce? Oh, I've thought of that myself, my dear, you may be sure. Asked legal advice, even. It would be possible, but difficult, and distressing, and in any event Hetty wouldn't hear of it. Regards herself as married in the sight of heaven, you see. The people who could help me to a divorce for her are the man's family,' he gloomily added. 'They could have her divorced for adultery . . . but only think of the distress of that to Hetty. And they won't: it's my belief we could commit adultery before those people's eyes and they wouldn't turn a hair. Not as long as they could keep their grasping hands on Hetty's property. Well, at least part of it goes to seeing that Pauling's comfortably cared for, and that gives her some satisfaction and peace of mind.'

Carey shivered slightly, remembering how once, at the age of fifteen or so, she had expressed a wish to accompany her father and Hetty on their weekly visit to the house in which the Honourable Thomas Pauling was confined. She had been reading a quantity of Gothick novels at the time, and had lurid expectations of dramatic Bedlam scenes. It had been nothing at all like that. The house was small and pleasant: whitewashed outside, spotlessly clean within, the keeper and his wife pleasant, kindly souls. No, a little to Carey's disappointment, there was nothing dreadful about it—until she saw Mr Pauling himself. Then Hetty, who had been anxiously watching for just such signs of distress as she now showed, quickly sent her off downstairs, to be regaled with cake and lemon barley water by the keeper's wife. She went home with an imagination much sobered, and never wished to go on that dutiful weekly visit again. That was over ten years ago, and still Mr Pauling lived on in the same place, no better and no worse.

She sighed. 'Oh dear. I am glad you were able to find the pretty Chelsea house for Hetty, at least, and she swears she is very comfortable there, but she would be much more comfortable here with you, Papa. How ridiculous it is: calling herself a Scarlet Woman, and saying she would ruin

15

my chances of a good second marriage. When if I can ever behave with reasonable propriety at all, it is Hetty's doing. Left to your sole upbringing, I'm sure I should have turned out a most shocking creature.'

'Very true,' agreed her father gravely, rising to change his dressing gown for a coat and go down to his consulting rooms on the ground floor of the house, while Carey herself prepared to fetch a mantle, for she saw clouds beginning to blow over the blue spring-time sky. Her eye falling again upon the spiky hand of her very affectionate Cousin Clarissa, she remarked out loud, as if addressing that lady: 'And why you should suppose I am in want of anyone to fill a mother's place I do not know. When I have had Hetty to supply that office these fifteen years past. Scarlet Woman, indeed! I haven't the remotest idea what such a creature even looks like, and I suppose Hetty has even less, but I'm very sure it can be nothing at all like her.'

2

Hetty herself certainly bore very little resemblance to a Scarlet Woman, however, one might suppose such a female to appear. She was a little woman, delicate of feature and still pretty at forty-five. Her fair hair might be faded from its original shining gold, but people meeting her for the first time generally reflected that Henrietta Pauling must have been an uncommonly attractive girl.

It was not the gold of her hair, however, but the gold of her father's guineas that had brought her to her disastrous marriage with the Honourable Mr Pauling. For his part, Miss Henrietta Holcroft's father had surely been dazzled by her suitor's rank. The brother of a Viscount, no less. Had Hetty's mother been alive, she might have prevented the match, for she was a shrewd woman who had been Henry Holcroft's staunch helpmeet during the years of his steady rise in the City. But she was not there to remonstrate when, as his own health failed, his usual acumen deserted him, and he jumped at an offer of marriage to his only child from a gambler of shady reputation and uncertain health, with nothing but his birth to recommend him.

It escaped Mr Holcroft's notice that the rest of the Paulings seemed suspiciously eager for the match as well. He did not move socially in their circles, or some well-wisher might have dropped a hint into his ear concerning the family's heredity. There was said to be instability there —actual insanity, some said. Indeed, Mr Pauling's whole deplorable career had been wildly mercurial, and by the time his conduct tipped over into certifiable lunacy, he had been married for three years to an increasingly distressed and terrified young woman. Henrietta, as dutiful a wife as she had been a daughter, fulfilled her marriage vow to obey, but loving and honouring were out of the question. When at last Mr Pauling had to be confined, she could not help feeling guiltily glad to see the back of him.

She had also seen the back of the large fortune that came to her on her father's death. Mr Pauling's family—frequently described by Sir John Law as sharks, vultures, and any other of the more rapacious members of the animal kingdom that sprang to his mind—had promptly appropriated it, or what Mr Pauling's excesses had left of it, as being legally still his property, explaining to his wife that it was required to keep the invalid in suitable comfort.

Henrietta herself had no quarrel with this notion, though it distressed her to find that he was not being kept in comfort at all, but was very poorly housed and nursed. Beyond protesting fruitlessly to her brother-in-law the Viscount, however, there was nothing she could do about that. And she had herself to provide for. A state of near-penury was something for which her upbringing had never prepared her, but she bravely set out to earn her own bread. She was fortunate enough to obtain a position in a school for young ladies, and remained there for nine years, until a pupil's father recommended her to his friend Sir John Law, who was then looking for a lady to act as governess and companion to his motherless daughter.

Mrs Pauling could scarcely believe her luck. Coming into her life like a particularly brisk and efficient *deus ex machina*, Sir John had utterly transformed it. Not only did he pay her what she thought a ridiculously high salary: he also, somehow or other, extracted from the Pauling family some small portion of her father's money, obliging them to disgorge enough of it to keep the Honourable Thomas in more seemly conditions.

No wonder Mrs Pauling had fallen in love with Sir John. And considering Hetty's sweet nature, thought Carey when she was old enough to understand such things, no wonder he had in due course fallen in love with her. Just when the closer relationship between her governess and her father began, Carey did not know. She had become aware of it only gradually, taking it as the most natural thing in the world. To be sure, she felt a little more curiosity when, as her marriage to Andrew Elliott approached, Hetty undertook to explain the physical aspect of the wedded state to her.

Carey was already tolerably well informed about those mysteries which Mrs Pauling proceeded to reveal to her, having found an interesting diagram in a book in her father's study years before. Putting two and two together, she had no difficulty at all in connecting it with some chance remarks made by a housemaid and her personal observations of the kitchen cat.

However, it wouldn't do to upset Hetty by revealing her unmaidenly knowledge of these matters, so Carey allowed Mrs Pauling to make her way through a speech so delicately phrased that had she really been ignorant, it would have told her very little, but from which one could gather that while Mrs Pauling must confess it was all dreadfully embarrassing, and not at all dignified, yet at the same time it somehow contrived to be the most delightful thing in the world. 'And not, not in the least what I once thought it was,' Hetty had involuntarily added, with a shudder which Carey accurately attributed to memories of Mr Pauling.

'It is a wonder,' she said to her father later, when she was married and had discovered the truth of Mrs Pauling's assertions for herself, 'that poor Hetty was not put off the thing for life. Quite providential!'

'Yes, well, very likely,' agreed her father, rather amused. 'Though you may give me a little of the credit, as well as Providence, I hope.'

The mere possibility of such an exchange between father and daughter was something that could still surprise Mrs Pauling. Even as a child, her charge had been inclined to say shocking things which she did not seem to realise were shocking. But Hetty had loved Caroline at once. So warm-hearted, even at ten—and so clever. The cleverness had rather dismayed Hetty, who knew that her own intellect was not superior, and yet it was her perceptive eye that first discerned Carey's unique talent, a couple of years after she first joined the household, and she who took the matter to the child's father. 'Sir John, she must have the best drawing master you can possibly find,' she told him earnestly, laying her pupil's most recent work in front of him. 'Do but look at these.'

'Aye, well enough, I dare say,' said Sir John indulgently. 'All young ladies like to sketch. An accomplishment, they call it. Well, well, no doubt she is accomplished.'

'Oh, better than that,' Mrs Pauling assured him. 'Yes, you are quite right, young ladies do frequently paint flowers; flowers are a very proper sort of subject for them. But their efforts are seldom of this quality, I do assure you. See the detail here, in the stem, and that leaf and bud.'

Sir John looked more closely, and now his eye, trained to the accuracy of an anatomical drawing, enabled him to understand what Mrs Pauling was talking about. Hetty had her way, to the gratification of all concerned (not least the drawing master who was in consequence engaged). And though she sometims had qualms about allowing a young girl to be so unconventional as to mingle, while still in the schoolroom, with the lively and learned circle of Sir John's acquaintances, she could not deny that Carey's talent throve on it. The interests of medical men and botanists so often seemed to overlap. In consequence, Miss Law met a number of the latter at her father's house, including that Mr Lindley, recently appointed the first Professor of Botany in the newly founded University College of London, whom Mrs Elliott was going to see this spring morning in 1830 before calling on her former governess.

Arriving at the Horticultural Society's premises in Regent Street just as Sir John's phaeton, driven by a groom and carrying Sir John's daughter, drew up outside them, Professor Lindley—still only thirty-one, but sole Assistant Secretary of the Society and the writer and editor of numerous botanical works—shook his visitor's hand and led her into the building.

'My dear Mrs Elliott, delighted to see you! I am sorry I haven't done so before—is it really two months since you came home? And I'm sorry for your husband's death, more sorry than I can say, but you know that, I wrote to you of that, so today we'll discuss other matters,' said he, bracingly. 'Here we are—come in!' He opened the door of a room, where the first thing to meet Carey's eyes was a pile of her own paintings spread about a large table. 'Well now, to business. Of course we have to possess our souls in patience and see how the seeds you brought us will do, but you'll be glad to hear that some of those your husband sent back previously germinated well, and we now have a number of exotic plants in quite a promising way. As for the pressed plants you brought us back—fine specimens, very fine indeed. We owe you a debt of gratitude.'

Carey smiled and demurred. 'Andrew was the one who knew what to look for. I only completed his work as best I might, making that last collection, before I left India, along the lines he had taught me.'

'Then he taught you very well, but of course you'll have been an apt pupil. I only wish we could send you back to the East to hunt more plants for us—but there, I suppose that as you are a female, it wouldn't do.'

Carey smiled. 'I suppose not, too. I have always found it rather lowering to reflect how many things won't do, just because one is a female! I did find Andrew's botanical collecting most interesting, and I shall certainly miss it. I only wish I could have brought you home live specimens, but it is so uncertain a business, when they are sure to meet with such extremes of climate and weather on shipboard, and one knows in advance that many will die, I couldn't reconcile it with my conscience to beg too much extra space of the ship's captain, when he had already been kind enough to find me a cabin on a decidedly crowded vessel.'

Lindley nodded. 'However, in the absence of living specimens, these paintings of yours, you know, are of the greatest assistance. Remarkable work! You won't—' and the Professor sounded quite anxious as he bent over the paintings on his table—'you won't be stopping such work now, will you, just because you are back in England?'

'Well,' said Carey, thinking rather ruefully of the plans for the Season already suggested by the helpful Lady Saye, 'I don't know precisely how much time I shall have at my own disposal. But I shan't give up painting altogether. I don't think I could.'

'Don't! Don't!' Lindley earnestly begged her. 'The native British flora are worthy of attention too, you know. There's always room for good botanical drawing, and you have the knack of the thing. You had it from a girl, as I remember.

21

Accuracy and detail, that's the *sine qua non*, and the fashionable mode of the moment can go hang. You don't care for fashionable modes, do you?' he inquired a trifle doubtfully.

Carey smiled, correctly interpreting the direction of his glance. 'Only in choosing what I put on my back,' she said, amused. 'As for the currently fashionable mode in painting, I don't even know what it may be, after so long abroad. In any case, I never could bring myself to depict anything but just what I saw before me. Even when kind friends besought me to paint a romantic crag, or a tempest or a ruined castle, or something truly grand, it was no use: I never could do it, hard as I might try.'

'You do much better not to try,' Lindley assured her. 'Your gifts can be used to better purpose. Now, tell me, will you let me see any work you do? I know of many periodicals crying out for work of such quality as yours. There's the *Botanical Magazine*, the *Gardener's Magazine*, and I myself am almost constantly revising the *Flora Londiniensis*. We can all do with contributing artists. Or how would it be,' he continued, a new idea striking him as he saw a decided gleam of interest in his companion's eyes, 'if you were to set about compiling a volume of your own? I am sure you'd have no difficulty in publishing. I'm in touch with a number of men who would be glad to reproduce such work. As to subjects, there are our own gardens at Chiswick, there's Kew, there is the Physic Garden—I can get you entry there whenever you wish, of course. Though myself, I own that after seeing your pictures of Indian subjects, done in all their natural surroundings, I would like to see your brush applied to the flowers of our own English countryside. But no doubt you don't get very much chance to go into the country—or not until later in the summer? I suppose,' said he, sounding slightly impatient with such frivolities, 'you'll be obliged to stay in London during the Season, tied to a round of sociability?'

Carey started slightly. 'You are the second person to say as much to me today. I had a letter to the same effect. But it is not,' she thoughtfully added, 'necessarily the case.' For an idea was germinating in her mind. 'A volume of wild flowers. I like the notion. Why not?'

'Why not indeed?' Lindley encouraged her. 'A series of

illustrations of the flowers of meadow, field and hedgerow —nor need you entirely exclude the cottage garden—oh yes, there is room for such a work! *The Ladies' Repository of Native English Flora*—how's that, for a title?'

'I don't think I care for repository,' Carey objected. 'It sounds so dry. And I don't know about ladies, either; it is not only ladies who take an interest in such subjects. Andrew did! So do you, and Mr Hooker, and a great number of other learned gentlemen besides.'

'You are right,' Lindley conceded.

She mused for a moment. '*The Floral Companion to the English Countryside*. What do you say to that?'

'Excellent! I say excellent!' said the botanist, warmly. 'The *Floral Companion* it shall be!'

'But what should I do, with publication in mind?' she wondered aloud. 'For I find water colour the easiest method when I am working out of doors—but will it serve, if the pictures are to be reproduced?

'Oh, do just as you normally do,' Lindley told her, 'and you may leave the rest to us. Stipple engraving, perhaps aquatint . . . part hand colouring, perhaps, part colour printing from plates—it is wonderful what various means of reproduction are available to us in this modern age. No, do just as you ordinarily would.'

'Very well, I will,' said Carey, and then caught herself up. 'But here I am speaking as if it were a settled thing, because I find the prospect so alluring. And I am not even sure if my father means to go into the country. However, there is another possibility,' she added half to herself, as her idea continued to grow. 'And I should like to proceed with such a work, indeed I should. I assure you I shall think about it.'

As indeed she did, most seriously, on her way through the London streets, and with certain considerations in mind which in no way concerned Professor Lindley or even the native English flora. About half way to Chelsea, she startled Simmonds the groom by exclaiming out loud, 'Yes, that settles it! I'll go!' And then, her mind made up, she sat back to enjoy the remainder of the drive.

'Dearest Hetty!' she cried, snatching off her chip straw hat, lavishly trimmed with the same grey satin ribbon that furnished the bows on her dress. 'There, that's better. Oh, these great wide brims—how can I kiss you with so much straw in the way? Well, I dare say I shall soon get accustomed to the new fashions. How pretty you are looking today, Hetty!'

She might truthfully have added that the house was pretty too, and made a charming setting for its occupant, but she was not going to say anything that might imply the least approval of Mrs Pauling's residence there. Pretty it was, however: whitewashed, neat and well-proportioned. Hetty had objected that she did not need a whole house, that lodgings would do very well, but Sir John would not hear of it. In the six weeks since he had rented it for her, Hetty had made both house and garden very much her own. A posy of fresh flowers stood on the polished table by the window, at which she had been seated awaiting her guest, looking anxiously at the sky and wondering if Carey would be caught in the rain.

But no. 'We're just in time!' cried Carey. 'Simmonds has taken the horses round to the mews, so they won't get wet, and neither will he or I. What luck! There is going to be a downpour at any moment.'

Sure enough, the trees were beginning to toss in the wind, the first heavy drops were falling, and rain was beating on the glass by the time Hetty and her guest were seated in the dining room across the little hall, addressing themselves to an elegant luncheon of early asparagus, cold chicken, and custard tartlets, served by a parlourmaid who then withdrew, leaving the two ladies free to talk privately.

This was the moment Carey had been waiting for, and as soon as they were alone she began, firmly: 'Now then, Hetty. I have been thinking, and there is something I have to say to you.'

'Oh dear!' remarked Mrs Pauling evasively, glancing at the rain outside. 'Just look—this storm will knock the tulips all to pieces.'

'Hetty, you are only pretending not to hear me,' said her former pupil, severely. 'Never mind the tulips.'

'But I do mind the tulips. They are very pretty. And oh, look! That climbing rose is being so badly buffeted by the wind that I am afraid it will come right away from the wall. I must ring for Jane to go and find Gully and tell him to pin it back more firmly.'

'You are still pretending,' observed Mrs Elliott. 'It is no use thinking you can persuade me that you would send Gully or anybody else out in this rain, just to knock nails into a garden wall.'

'Well, later, I meant,' said Mrs Pauling, defensively.

'You can leave it all till later,' said Carey. 'Hetty, I said I have something to say to you.'

'No!' said Mrs Pauling, fluttering a little in alarm. 'No! No, I won't! There!' And she looked at her determined ex-pupil with what defiance she could muster.

'No, you won't what?' inquired Carey.

'Won't do what you are going to say you want me to do.'

'You don't know what I am going to say yet.'

'I can guess. And we have been over all that before.'

'Dearest, I know how you feel.' Carey sighed. 'But, Hetty—'

'My mind is quite made up,' stated Mrs Pauling, nervously.

'What about my father, though? Ought you to make his mind up too, do you think, Hetty?' inquired Carey, shrewdly attacking her vulnerable point. 'Should you be making him unhappy, even if you don't mind it for yourself?'

'I do mind it! I mean . . . I mean I am not unhappy. Well, not very. There is the consolation of knowing that one has done right, and—oh, am I making him unhappy?' she added wretchedly, pushing aside her plate.

Carey felt a pang of compunction for spoiling Mrs Pauling's already birdlike appetite, but did not scruple to press her advantage home. 'Yes, you are. Very unhappy.'

For a moment, she thought she might actually have made some headway. But Mrs Pauling, though plainly distressed, summoned up her resolution and said more firmly, 'No, my dear, it would not do. He knows that as well as I do. Oh, I know it is early to be speaking of it yet, but the fact is that if you are to make as splendid a second marriage as I am sure you will, then we must make certain that not the slightest breath of indecorum comes anywhere near you. Dear Lady Saye says so too.'

25

'Hang dear Lady Saye!' said Carey impatiently. 'What's more,' she pointed out, 'I can think of many persons moving in the very first circles of society, who do so surrounded by positive gales of indecorum.'

'Yes, but that is quite different,' Mrs Pauling earnestly explained. 'Those born to such a position, you see, may do more or less as they like. But those of us born to a less exalted rank . . .'

'Had better mind our Ps and Qs if we want to be elevated to it?'

'Well, it may sound silly and—and even calculating,' said Mrs Pauling, still on the defensive, 'but it is true, and you know it.'

'I don't, Hetty. Indeed, I really don't know that I want to be married again at all, in which case all this delicacy of yours is for nothing. I suppose, although I cannot feel so now, I might in the course of time become sufficiently attached to some gentleman to marry him. On the other hand, I might just as easily not, and then I would do better to set up house on my own as soon as possible.'

'Set up house on your own?' echoed Hetty, horrified.

'Well, why not? There's nothing so very dreadful about the idea—and after all, it is exactly what you have just done yourself.'

'Oh, but that is quite different,' Mrs Pauling stated. 'I only wish I had expressed my—my desire to do so from the very first, instead . . .' Her voice trailed away.

'Instead of letting us see that you were really doing it only because you were afraid of ruining my reputation. Oh, Hetty, it is too bad of you. Or rather, it is too good of you.'

'I am not at all good. I am very wicked,' said Mrs Pauling sadly. 'Even though I cannot help loving your dear papa, I know how wicked it is. And if I were not wicked I dare say I could help it,' she added, a trifle obscurely. 'But we won't go into all that now. Have some of these Maids of Honour.' She pushed the dish of custard tartlets in Carey's direction, and endeavoured to change the subject. 'I wish you could grow plumper, dearest. You have filled out just a little around the neck and shoulders since you came home, I am glad to say, but you are still too thin.'

'Not thin. Slender?' suggested Carey. 'Willowy? Well, anyway, not thin.'

'Thin!' repeated Mrs Pauling. 'And it is the fashion to be plump now, you know. I am afraid you have not quite recovered from the voyage, and of course the dreadful shock of Andrew's death, and losing the baby not so very long before that . . . oh, how I wish you had never gone to India!'

'Well, we cannot tell what might or might not have happened to me if I had stayed at home,' said Carey quietly, 'so it is pointless to speculate on that now. As for my miscarriage, I suppose it was largely my own fault, and I ought not to have gone riding. The doctors told me, you know, that falling off a horse might easily cause it, and the fact that this particular horse was in India, so that the hole in the ground in which he caught his foot happened to be an Indian hole in Indian ground, had nothing to do with the case. And they assured me there was no reason why I shouldn't have plenty of other, healthy children. Except, of course, that we never had the time,' she rather wistfully finished.

'But you will have children. Though of course, you must be married first, for that. Now do you see the sense of what I am saying, and why it would be a good thing if you were plumper?' inquired Mrs Pauling, a certain measure of triumph in her tone. 'A plump arm shows to much better advantage in an evening dress than a thin one, and if you are to—'

'—to get myself a husband, then I had better fatten myself up like a prize pig? No, thank you!' said Carey, laughing, but she ate a custard tartlet all the same. 'And as you keep on warning me, there will be some who don't mind what sort of an arm I have, so long as there's a fortune dangling at the end of it. You know, you really can't have it both ways. In one breath you warn me of fortune hunters, in the next you suppose I must be wanting to hunt a husband for myself. Now, which is it to be?'

Thus caught in the tangles of her own contradictory reasoning, Mrs Pauling was momentarily at a loss. 'You ought not, my dear, to be quite so outspoken,' she

27

suggested at last, without much real hope of having her advice heeded. 'It scares gentlemen off.'

'And those who will be scared off are exactly those with whom I should lead a perfectly miserable life,' said Carey, laughing, 'so let us say good riddance to them, and I will tell you what I was going to say in the first place, which, as it happens, is not at all what you supposed. Now listen, and you will discover what an excellent plan mine is.'

And she proceeded to unfold it.

'Oh, but it would mean your going out of London just as the Season is really beginning!' exclaimed Mrs Pauling in dismay.

'Oh, but the flowers have seasons of their own, replied Carey, in smiling imitation of Hetty's dismay. 'I see nothing but advantages in the scheme. You cannot possibly tell me there is anything improper in such a book as John Lindley suggests. Nothing could be more respectable than botanical illustration, now could it?'

'Well, no,' Mrs Pauling was forced to admit.

'Or more conventional, even? Or less eccentric?'

'N-no,' agreed Hetty, but guardedly.

'And then again,' offered Carey, demurely, 'wouldn't it, conversely, be a little improper of me to stay in London attending parties, when I have been a widow for only just over a year? Kindly observe,' she primly added, 'that I have taken to heart all you say about decorum. Oh, dear me, yes. Wouldn't I do better to observe the very utmost decorum this Season, by withdrawing from society, in order to stand an even better chance of social success next year?'

Mrs Pauling eyed her former charge most suspiciously, and said, 'You don't care a pin for any of that.'

'Lady Saye would, though. You just ask her. She may regret, a little, the amiable plans she has been making on my behalf, but I am sure she will agree with me, and postpone them. Also—and you will certainly see the force of this argument, since it comes from my father, so pray listen carefully—also, it is quite likely the King may be taken mortally ill at any time, which would have a most deleterious effect upon the Season altogether, wouldn't it?'

'Well, of course. If the King is ill, and dies, a great many social events must be cancelled,' said Hetty, nodding wisely.

'So then it won't be much of a Season in any case, and I might as well miss it. I make that three good reasons, so far, for my going to stay at Marchingham,' said Carey, counting off points on her fingers. 'Then there is Reason Number Four: my Cousin Clarissa earnestly wishes me to see the countryside in high summer. Besides Reason Number Five: I earnestly wish to see the countryside in high summer. Not to mention Reason Number Six: John Lindley earnestly wishes me to see the countryside in high summer, too. What could be more fortunate and convenient for all of us?' she concluded. And seeing Mrs Pauling open her mouth to offer some other objection, she forestalled her by adding, mendaciously, 'I've already written a letter to Lady Gerard, accepting her kind offer, so it is all a settled thing, and there is no more to be said on the subject!'

Unless, she thought, driving home to make good her words by writing and dispatching that letter, unless one were to mention Reason Number Seven, unspoken but uppermost in her mind: an extended visit to her very affectionate Cousin Clarissa would surely allow Hetty to move back to Russell Square and Sir John, at least for the duration of that visit, to the mutual comfort of them both and the considerable easing of her own conscience.

3

Breakfast at Marchingham Priory was taken later than in Russell Square, at the more elegant hour of ten o'clock. Or rather, it was taken at that time by a majority of three of the Gerard family, the fourth having breakfasted and gone out a good deal earlier, as was his wont. Of the remaining members of the family, one attended the meal unwillingly. Mr William Gerard would much rather have stayed longer in his bed, especially when he had not got into that bed until the small hours and was tenderly nursing a headache, as was the case on the morning when Caroline Elliott's reply to his mother's letter arrived. Only the certainty that if he proffered the headache as an excuse, his shrewd mama would immediately guess its true cause, prevented him from ignoring the manservant who brought him his hot shaving water at half past nine.

Mr Gerard did, however, assert himself to the extent of appearing at the breakfast table in all the glory of a voluminously cut crimson banyan, at the sight of which his mother winced slightly. But she had common sense enough to recognise that her son could not be reprimanded like a child any longer. He had always been such a tractable boy, she reflected—at least, with her! (It scarcely occurred to her that this was because she seldom denied him anything.) But recently there had been a distinct inclination to rebel. Well, thought Clarissa Gerard, a certain wildness was natural enough in a fine young man like Will. Although there was no doubt that he had gone rather beyond the line in London last year, and was thus obliged to stay kicking his heels at home this Season.

Which was Benedict's doing, of course, thought Will's fond mama. One might have supposed anyone would see

30

that being barred from Town did Will no good whatsoever, and only made him resentful. For her own part, she was sure the money could have been found somehow—but of course, Benedict would make no effort to help his step-brother, nor could one really wonder at it. Clarissa Gerard conceded that it was natural enough for him to envy Will's looks and easy charm. His refusal to budge over the matter of Will's allowance, however, was mere pettiness.

'Do you really mean to tell me,' she had inquired, with heavy irony, 'we are reduced to such straits that we cannot afford board and lodging for one young man in London, for three months or so during the Season?'

Her stepson had smiled a little ruefully, saying only, 'Board and lodging . . . if that were all . . .' And Clarissa really had no answer. The sum of Will's debts in London last year had come as a considerable shock to her; it would have startled the most indulgent of mothers. However, she could understand his present discontent, and would not object to such comparatively harmless excesses as the wearing of a crimson dressing-gown to breakfast.

In any event, her letter from London swiftly banished all minor irritations from her mind. She had to go to the window-seat to read it, for the dining room was extremely dark, even on a summer's morning. The Old Refectory was all that now remained of the original Priory, largely demolished in the reign of King Henry VIII and reconstructed as a handsome brick-built manor house, which came into the possession of the first Sir William Gerard when its builder's son, an otherwise inoffensive Puritan gentleman, fell foul of authority for his ill-timed loyalty to the Parliamentarian cause at the time of the Restoration.

Taking in the gist of her letter, Lady Gerard exclaimed aloud with satisfaction. 'Excellent! Will,' she announced, 'your cousin Caroline is to visit us!'

Will, wondering whether tea or coffee would do his throbbing head more good, or anyway prove least nauseating to his delicate stomach, received this news with perfect indifference.

'She tells me a great deal of stuff,' Lady Gerard continued, 'all about botanical drawings or some such thing. Well, I am sure the countryside here is full of flowers, she

31

will find no shortage of them. But never mind that—it doesn't signify. She is coming to visit us, that is the thing, and I must confess it is more than I dared to hope for.'

For Lady Gerard was a realist in her way. She did not suppose that a widow as rich as Caroline Elliott could really lack friends in London, and she was aware it was rather late in the day for her to be making a great show of affection for a motherless girl. Her invitation had been in the nature of bread cast upon the waters, something that at least could do no harm—and lo, it had returned to her, not even after many days, in the most gratifying way imaginable. A prompt acceptance! She was jubilant.

'The dear child,' said she, fondly. 'You remember her, of course, Sir William. My cousin Mary's little girl—the most delightful creature!'

Her husband was indeed vaguely trying to identify the subject of her raptures in his mind. But that mind was never very clear at this hour of the morning; indeed, if the truth were told, it was seldom very clear at all nowadays. Some thought Sir William had never fully recovered from his first wife's death all those years go. Some considered his decline the result of enforced inactivity; once a fine sportsman, he was now afflicted with gout that led him to dull his wits as well as the pain of the disease with claret. The claret, of course, did the gout no good at all, so it was a vicious circle, particularly when Sir William administered the additional nostrums of port and brandy to his protesting system.

He had been gazing out of the window at the park beyond. The sight was an agreeable one. Sir William's grandfather, besides having some rather good notions of landscape gardening, had possessed the financial means to realise them. The notions of the same subject entertained by Sir William's father had been rather wilder and more Gothick, but the agricultural boom of the French wars enabled him, too, to give his fancy rein. This he did, lavishly, with the consequence that in the fifteen years of depression since the war had ended Sir William himself, whose mind was encumbered by no notions of landscape gardening whatsoever, had been left with a number of interesting views to survey from the windows of his house, but no money to keep the Priory in good repair. Seating herself at the breakfast table again, Lady Gerard automatically, as one used to it by long habit, averted her eyes from the threadbare brocade of the curtains and chair seats. Instead, she let her gaze rest again upon the more pleasing sight of Mrs Elliott's letter, now lying folded beside her plate.

'How happy this makes me!' she said, sincerely.

Sir William started, wondering whether any comment were expected of him, and what had become of the bottle of brandy he kept in a little cupboard in the library. He had looked for it there just now, before coming in to breakfast, and found it mysteriously absent. Had one of the servants discovered its hiding place and made off with it? Or had Clarissa herself done so? In which case, he might be unwise to mention his suspicion of the servants. Might be unwise to mention the matter at all . . .

'How very, very glad I shall be to see Caroline!' continued Lady Gerard.

'Fond of her, are you, my dear?' Sir William ventured.

His wife was honest enough to hesitate before replying. 'I would have been fond of her—very fond—had I been given the chance,' she said. 'But of course, there was her father. Poor Mary's uncouth Scotsman. *Quite* impossible! I am sure I cannot account for his having become such a favourite in high places. Nor can I be blamed for failing to foresee it, when poor dear Mary married. I am sure, it would be a very odd thing if every obscure Scottish physician were to be so lucky,' she added, in a vein of some indignation, as if either her husband or her son had reproached her for her failure to ingratiate herself with Sir John Law.

But her remarks had jolted Sir William's memory. He brightened momentarily. 'Ah, now I remember! Caroline, to be sure! Taking little thing.'

'Yes, indeed,' agreed Lady Gerard. 'I am sure you remember your cousin too, Will.'

Will merely shook his head, and wished he hadn't.

'Glad to see the child again myself,' offered Sir William.

'My dear Sir William, she is no child now,' his wife corrected him. 'Five and twenty years of age, just back from India—and widowed. I dare say that is why she feels she would like to come into the country, poor creature. No doubt she is a young woman of sense who doesn't care for the rackety life in London.' This with a brief, sidelong glance at her son, who was now unenthusiastically tackling a cup of tea. 'And I do hear that that father of hers openly keeps a mistress. No wonder, then, if she feels the need of a refuge. Well, she shall certainly have one here. Such a situation must be most distasteful to her. She says she will come next week if that is not too early. No, indeed it is not. Nothing could be better than to have dear Cousin Caroline here. I will tell Mrs Jackson to make the Blue Room ready for her.'

And so saying, Lady Gerard pressed down the pretty china handle of the modern bell anachronistically installed in the Old Refectory, with the object of summoning a parlourmaid to fetch the housekeeper. Nothing happened. Young Mr Gerard was heard to mutter something morose, to the effect that he didn't see what there was about this female to cast his mama into ecstasies. Then, sipping his tea cautiously, he decided that it was doing him good after all, and cheered up slightly.

'You may care to bear in mind,' said his mama, a little tartly—for indulgent she might be, but it was galling to have her best efforts go thus unappreciated—'you may care to bear in mind that she is extremely rich.'

Will's hand hovered above the dishes on the table: would it be tempting Providence too far to consume a buttered muffin? A tentative bite suggested it would not. 'What about it? Ain't going to hand us her fortune on a platter, is she?' he remarked, and as he was now feeling distinctly better, he laughed a good deal at this witty sally.

Lady Gerard sighed and thought, looking at her son, that it was a pity one had to explain so much to Will. However, if his mind was not particularly quick, his looks made up for it. In fact, she reflected, they were a good-looking family. Without personal vanity on that score, she knew herself to be a handsome woman, with the pronounced bone structure that had enabled her to keep her looks into middle age. Sir William might now be only the wreck of a fine man, but vague as his gaze often was, at least he had not run to fat. Ah, what a catch she had thought him when she married him, twenty-seven years ago! It hardly seemed fair that in the end, her cousin Mary had made what some would consider the better match. Some, but not Clarissa Gerard. Even in reaping the rewards of success, Sir John had only a knighthood, not to be compared with the Gerards' baronetcy. And unlike Mary, she, Clarissa, had borne a son.

It was a pity, perhaps, that that son had not inherited her own firm mouth and resolute chin. About Will's mouth and chin there was, instead, a certain fullness, just now accentuated by the puffiness resulting from a late night. Apart from this, however, Will's regular features were a pleasing sight: his silky brown locks were stylishly cut, his figure tall and well proportioned, and he set it off with a wardrobe in the latest fashion. As for his speaking hazel eyes—well, his mother was sure they could not fail to melt the heart of any woman, Caroline Elliott included.

Benedict, naturally, was the odd one out in the Gerard family where looks were concerned, but equally naturally, that could not signify. Will was the one who would marry. How fortunate that while the family name of William was one of her stepson's names too, he had never used it, his late mother preferring 'Benedict'—and Sir William, it was said, could deny his first wife nothing. That at least left 'William' for Clarissa's son—and a grandson of hers would eventually inherit the title and the Priory. She had been thinking for quite a while now that it was time Will settled down and produced that grandson. Cousin Caroline's return to England was most timely. She, Clarissa, had managed to obviate the disadvantage of Will's not being in Town this Season by inviting an heiress to come to Marchingham instead. And the heiress had accepted! A rich, biddable girl, thought Clarissa, delicately nibbling bread and butter. The very thing for Will.

Here a tiny doubt entered her mind. *Would* Caroline prove biddable? Mary had always been meek and gentle to a fault, but suppose the girl took after her father instead?

Realising that no parlourmaid had yet appeared, Clarissa pressed the handle of the bell down once more. Again, nothing happened.

As to Caroline's nature, time would tell, but perhaps she should start preparing her son's mind. Subtlety, she knew, was wasted on him. 'Will, do you never think of marrying?' she bluntly inquired.

This did not go down at all well. Lady Gerard could hardly have known that her son's surly temper this morning was the result of a great quantity of brandy consumed last night, the consumption of that brandy being the direct consequence of a trying episode earlier in the evening. Will had had in view a pleasant couple of hours spent in dalliance, when a chance remark from the girl with whom he was dallying quite spoiled all his enjoyment. 'And when we are married', she had casually said, going on to prattle of he couldn't now remember what, so unpleasantly had those five words fallen on his ear. Could he ever have been fool enough to mention marriage? No, surely not! Well, perhaps in the heat of the moment, he just might have said: '*What a lark to be married and doing this all the time!*' Or something stupid of that nature, simply to please the girl. But she couldn't have taken him seriously . . . could she?

In any event, marriage was a sore subject with Will just now. 'Don't mean this cousin, do you?' he ungraciously inquired. 'Oh, come, Mama—me, marry a widow?'

'A young widow, Will, handsome if she takes after either parent,' Lady Gerard allowed, 'and very rich, if all I hear is true.' But she saw that she had said quite enough for the time being, and uttered what she meant to be a light laugh, not something that came naturally to her. 'Well, don't take me too seriously, Will. The thing is, I so look forward to welcoming dear Caroline as a member of the family, I am sure I shall wish she might stay here for ever. I only meant that if you and she should like each other . . . think what such a wealthy match would mean for the Priory.'

'Ben would like it, I am sure,' offered Sir William, believing himself to be making a helpful contribution to the family discussion.

Lady Gerard had some difficulty in concealing her irritation at this utterly irrelevant remark. It also occurred to her that still no one had answered the bell. She had first rung over ten minutes ago, and while they certainly could not afford a large staff at the Priory, someone in all that time ought to have noticed the quivering indicator by the door into the servants' quarters, and come hurrying to the Refectory in response.

'Where *is* the girl?' she said crossly, and pressed the bell for the third time, hard. The little china handle came away from the wall, showing a loose, ineffectual wire dangling, broken and no longer connecting with the indicator at all. She looked at the little device in sheer exasperation. It represented everything that needed doing to set Marchingham Priory to rights. Everything that couldn't be done for lack of funds.

'Very well,' said she, addressing herself more to the broken bell than to her husband and son. 'I will seek out Mrs Jackson myself, and tell her to expect my cousin next week.'

The news that an interesting visitor was soon to arrive at the Priory spread rapidly not only through the household, but a good deal farther afield as well. This was in consequence of Mrs Jackson's hearing from Cook that her stock of butter muslin was running low, so that the housekeeper was happy to accept the coachman's offer of a lift in the family's travelling chaise into Great Marchingham, whither he was taking that vehicle to have a couple of springs attended to. It was only natural that Mrs Jackson should repair to her friend, Mrs Eliza Pacey, for the butter muslin, a length for a new stuff gown, certain minor items in the way of braid and tape and trimmings, and a good chat over a nice cup of tea.

Mrs Pacey—Milliner, Straw Hat Maker and Linen-Draper—kept her shop in Riverside Road. This thoroughfare was not in fact beside, but rather above the river Marching, a waterway flowing below the hill on which the market town of Great Marchingham had grown out of a former manorial village. Shops and houses stood on one side only of Riverside Road, with a fine view down the hill itself to the marshes and water-meadows beyond.

Mrs Pacey's was a flourishing emporium, far more prosperous and better patronised than her husband's little cobbler's shop beside it. But then James Pacey, though a good craftsman, was inclined to lay down his hammer and dream for minutes on end, gazing out of the window at the great cloudy sky above the marshes, while his mind roved with delight along those byways of thought to be discovered in his precious shelf of books. What ideas you could find on the printed page! Ideas such as those of Tom Paine, about the Rights of Man! It was just as well, perhaps, for Mrs Pacey's peace of mind, that she knew nothing of her husband's interest in such radical notions. She was considerably more practical: a bustling woman was Eliza Pacey, good at business and good with her needle. Their only child, Susan, took after her mother, who was training her up in the dressmaking line, for which she had shown an early aptitude.

While her mother drank tea with Mrs Jackson, Susan served in the shop, and though she attended dutifully to the occasional customer, she was still well able to lend an ear to the conversation in the next room. She was an amiable girl: even those who thought it pretentious of the Paceys to have sent their daughter to Mrs and Miss Gage's school allowed that Susan was not proud, and she numbered many girls in service in Marchingham among her large circle of friends. Somehow it seemed these girls could always find time to drop in for a gossip as they went about their employers' errands, and thus the Vicar's Hester, the Gages' Cicely, even Mrs Carmichael's Betsy, all bore home their nuggets of information, embellished first by the surmises of Mrs Jackson, and then by Susan's imperfect understanding of them.

Grace Hodson too called at the draper's when her eldest brother Hugh brought her into town with butter and eggs from Brook End Farm's dairy to be left with the woman who sold them for Mrs Hodson on her market stall. Hugh was courting Susan, who had been Grace's particular friend at school, where they were drawn together by a common fear that the other pupils would look down on them for their relatively humble origins. Grace had a little more leisure for conversation than the rest of Susan's cronies, so that when she came into the shop, young Miss Pacey was particularly pleased with this opportunity to tell her the news. Although she owned to herself, later, that Grace's reception of it was disappointing. Why, you would have thought she was hardly interested at all, so absently did she reply when Susan wanted to know whether this was not an amazing thing to happen in Marchingham.

Grace seemed altogether disinclined to gossip that day, although by no means cross-tempered; indeed, she had a kind of smile in her eyes, as if she were thinking of something private and very delightful.

But Susan had no cause to complain of the rest of her friends, who received her news with the most gratifying interest, and proceeded to add their own flights of fancy, so that by the time it reached their employers' ears it was often remarkably changed. India, however was the constant theme: India the magical, exotic word that caught the fancy of everyone, including Mr Tiberius Taylor, the Vicar's brother-in-law, who remarked to his sister and her husband, when the tea tray was carried in after dinner, 'So I hear there is an Indian lady coming to stay at the Priory.'

'An Indian lady?' repeated the Reverend Theodore Whittier, his scholarly and in general abstracted eye lighting up. 'Indian! How extremely interesting!'

'Where did you hear it, Tiberius?' inquired Mr Taylor's sister.

'Where? Oh—oh, from Hester, I believe,' said he, avoiding her steely blue gaze.

'I wish, Tiberius,' said Mrs Whittier, austerely, 'oh, how I wish you would not be familiar with the servants. Really, it is most improper!'

And she continued staring at him, so steadily that he felt guilt must be writ large on his pinkly cherubic countenance, or visibly hovering above his crown of white curls. 'Familiar with Hester? Oh, I wasn't familiar at all, Augusta, I promise you. Oh, dear me, no! Nothing of the kind! Nothing improper about it, no, no, no!'

'Hm!' was Augusta's only reply, and the Vicar, who had been pursuing a fascinating reverie of his own, took advantage of this pause to remark, 'She would not actually speak it, I suppose? No, no, of course not.'

'Speak what?' inquired his lady, this time turning her suppressed irritation against her spouse. She was sometimes tempted to think no woman alive had more to bear, living with two persons so unworldly (in their different ways) as her husband and her brother. Not that worldliness was to be thought a virtue—but someone had to manage the affairs of daily life. 'Speak what, Mr Whittier?' she repeated.

'Why, Sanskrit, to be sure!' replied her husband, a little surprised to find his private train of thought not immediately clear to everyone else. Mr Whittier had come to take tea in the drawing room with some reluctance, for matters of greater moment awaited him in his study, to which he was anxious to return. Chief among these matters, it must be confessed, was not the composition of his Sunday sermon, but the perusal of a learned article upon ancient Oriental languages in a periodical devoted to antiquities, to which Mr Whittier was an enthusiastic subscriber. 'Sanskrit, the language of the ancient Hindus,' he explained. 'But no—I must not nourish vain hopes. It is not at all likely that she can speak it, for as I am sure you know, my dear Augusta, Sanskrit, a language which has only recently come to the attention of European scholars, is a dead tongue, standing in much the same relation to the dialects of modern India as does Latin to the languages of Italy, France and Spain.'

Mrs Whittier assumed a dutifully interested expression, as of one who believed her husband's intellect to be superior.

'It is possible, however,' he continued hopefully, 'that she may *read* Sanskrit.'

'Possible that who may read Sanskrit?' asked his wife, rather shortly, having forgotten the original remark that gave rise to these speculations.

'Why, the Indian lady, Augusta! The Indian lady who is coming to the Priory, if Hester's report of the matter to Tiberius is correct. What conversations might I not have with her, concerning India and its ancient history!'

'The wonders of India!' Mr Taylor murmured to himself, a gleam in his eye. 'The scene of Alexander's farthest conquests! You will recollect your Herodotus, my dear Augusta, the Herodotus we read at our mother's knee!'

It was true that the late Dr and Mrs Taylor had both been notable classical scholars, as witness the names they had bestowed upon their offspring; Mrs Whittier did not, however, pause to recollect her Herodotus.

'Ah, now I know what you are talking about,' she briskly

informed both gentlemen. 'Not an Indian lady, if by the term you mean a lady born in that country. It is Clarissa Gerard's cousin's daughter, who has lived in India, and is coming to stay with Clarissa and Sir William. I hear this,' she added, lest anyone accuse her of gossip, 'from Clarissa herself, who called on me today. She has been expecting the visit for some time, and tells me that Mrs Elliott—her cousin's name, for she is widowed young, poor soul—is the most delightful creature alive. So I do not suppose it likely, Mr Whittier, that she is in the least acquainted with Sanskrit. Clarissa says that besides being delightful, she is very pretty-behaved. She wrote Clarissa an extremely proper letter, charmingly expressed. Also, she is left extremely rich. Clarissa would like her to marry young Will.'

Lady Gerard might have been rather disconcerted to find her intentions so easily divined and bluntly expressed, but as the Whittiers themselves were childless, and very well to do in the world besides, Augusta Whittier made her report without malice, and even with a fair amount of goodwill.

'I am sure,' she added, 'we shall find Mrs Elliott very pleasant company. And it is only to be hoped,' she darkly concluded, 'that when Clarissa brings her to call, no objectionable persons will be seen coming out of Number Nineteen.'

Both gentlemen seemed to understand this obscure remark well enough, for the occupation by its present owner of Number Nineteen, New Road, was a source of constant annoyance to the Vicar's wife, and as she was unable to vent that annoyance on its proper object, she was in the habit of complaining at length to those about her. The Vicarage itself stood in the pleasant street called Petergate, named for the Church of St Peter and St Paul (or at least for half of it). Petergate skirted one side of the churchyard; New Road, prosaically so called by the builder who speculated in a row of very pretty houses there in the reign of Queen Anne, ran along the other. The triangular piece of land upon which church and churchyard stood tapered towards its far end, so that the Vicarage, at the end of Petergate, was almost facing the windows of Number Nineteen, the last house in New Road. This was the root of the trouble.

'It is a wonder to me,' reflected Mrs Whittier out loud, 'that people will tolerate the presence of such a person as Mrs Carmichael, as she likes to call herself, living within sight of a church. And with gentlemen—if they may be so termed—for ever going in and out. I must say, Mr Whittier, it does amaze me.'

Mr Whittier had heard all this so many times before that while he understood the force of his wife's objections, he heaved an inner, weary sigh as he ventured, 'I suppose, my dear, Mrs Carmichael bought Number Nineteen in the usual way, which could hardly have been prevented—I mean, one could not have foreseen—well, at any rate, you must admit that she and her—the young ladies—well, they appear to behave quite properly.'

'Appearances, as you very well know, Mr Whittier, are not everything,' declared his wife. 'And how she can bring herself, sinner as her life proclaims her, to live in such a place as this, I do not know.'

'I fancy,' offered Mr Whittier, with a gleam of humour, 'that even sinners must live somewhere, and in that case, perhaps better here than elsewhere. After all, the Lord himself mingled with sinners.' But he did not sound much as if he expected to bring his wife round to his own way of thinking.

He was right. 'With the proviso,' said she, caustically, 'that they repent and amend their life.'

Mr Whittier was answered, and knew it. For the household at Number Nineteen showed no signs of any inclination to repent and amend its life. Not that anyone had actually *seen* Mrs Carmichael conspicuously sinning, but then some sins are, of their very nature, committed in private. And privacy, indeed propriety, was certainly the order of the day at Mrs Carmichael's; not even Mrs Whittier's eagle eye could detect the gentlemen 'for ever going in and out' of whom she complained, but that did not stop her complaining. It stood to reason that they would use the back door.

Armoured in conscious virtue, Mrs Whittier had actually bearded Mrs Carmichael some eighteen months ago, when they chanced to pass in Petergate, and Mrs Carmichael gave her a civil nod and smile. Almost but not quite drawing aside her skirts, Mrs Whittier had glanced at the lady's companion, and frostily remarked, 'Another of your charming nieces, Mrs Carmichael? What a great number of them you have!'

'Yes, haven't I?' agreed Mrs Carmichael affably. 'Now that I am so pleasantly situated out here in the country, the girls are quite glad to come and keep me company from time to time. So kind of them.'

There were many possible replies to this bland speech, indicative of Mrs Whittier's disbelief, disapproval, and moral superiority in general, but the trouble was that she thought of them only later, which had been a grievance with her ever since.

'As for Mrs Carmichael's household,' she now added, unable to drop the fascinating, maddening subject once she had embarked upon it, 'that is only your Christian charity speaking, Theodore. You have a mind above such matters,' she futher informed her husband, 'and quite right too.' Mrs Whittier sipped her tea, sniffing slightly, before winding up her own sermon for the evening. 'And if the information Hester gleaned came from That House, I am all the more astonished that you should credit it. It is most undesirable for Hester to associate with the girl Betsy, as I fear she still does. I shall speak to her about it. As for you, Tiberius, I will merely observe that I am amazed you should listen to the vulgar gossip of maidservants. It is not,' finished Mrs Whittier, in majestic anti-climax, 'it is not the thing.'

4

Mrs Whittier might have been surprised to learn that at this very moment Mrs Carmichael's nieces, sitting around a tea tray of their own just across the churchyard in Number Nineteen, were themselves being reproved for gossip in similar terms. Contrary to public opinion, it was not so very often, certainly not every night of the week, that the young ladies entertained those gentlemen whom, on account of their presumed use of the back door, the Vicar's wife failed to see.

'It's a Indian lady what's coming,' Dolly, the most recently arrived niece, confided to her companions. 'Did you ever hear the like?'

'*An* Indian lady *who* is coming, Dorothea,' Mrs Carmichael automatically corrected her. 'You really must mind your speech more, my dear, if you truly wish to establish a liaison with a gentleman of rank and fortune.'

For it could not be denied, despite the propriety of the young ladies' conduct on this particular evening, that public opinion was correct enough in its assessment of the establishment's true nature.

There were never more than four of Mrs Carmichael's nieces in residence at any one time, nor did a niece, having left, ever return. So much, said respectable Marchingham society, for the fiction of a family relationship. Everyone *now*, of course, had suspected Mrs Carmichael all along. Yet on her first appearance in the town as the new owner of Number Nineteen, New Road, she had seemed respectable enough. Several ladies had been rash enough to call, and must now own, if only to themselves, that they had been most shockingly taken in.

Mrs Carmichael herself was a lady—or had seemed to be a lady—perhaps in her late thirties, of elegant appearance

44

and deceptively distinguished manners and bearing. She wore her pale fair hair neatly dressed, and her clothes spoke of Paris rather than London, whence she had come: so much she freely admitted, but that was all anyone really knew about her. And little more might be gleaned from conversation with the awesomely respectable married couple she had brought with her to run her household. They intimated that they had been with Mrs Carmichael a long time, but otherwise preserved total discretion concerning her affairs. Mr Thompson, or John as he allowed a few cronies to call him when he occasionally unbent over a pint at the Rose and Crown, in build resembled the pugilist he let it slip he had been in his youth, and had many another talent besides: even the local countrymen would admit that he was good with a horse. His wife Nell ran Number Nineteen's domestic concerns with the utmost efficiency; the whole of the more professional side of the undertaking, so to speak, was conducted by Mrs Carmichael herself, but it was Mrs Thompson who had picked out young Betsy for the post of housemaid, with an unerring eye for the girl's native sharpness. Betsy fully vindicated Mrs Thompson's judgment. Despite the dire warnings of the neighbours in the poor street where her rather feckless parents lived, Betsy thought herself lucky to have such a good place. She had soon discovered the value of discretion, and when meeting certain gentlemen out in the street, would gaze at them in an unsettlingly thoughtful, *recognising* sort of way, calculated to arouse justifiable nervousness, so that they were as like as not to press a small consideration into her hand, adjuring her to be a good girl and keep quiet.

And a good girl, in the popularly accepted sense of that term, Betsy was and remained. She was also disappointingly unforthcoming about the young ladies at Number Nineteen. She did, however, let her mother know—and her mother made sure the information went further—that no one had attempted to persuade *her* to make up one of their number by becoming an adoptive niece, so to speak, of her employer.

As for the nieces themselves, no one could now remember just how or when they began to arrive, or even when and how it gradually became known that they occasionally received gentlemen. But not all gentlemen: while respectable Marchingham society was obliged to revise its first impressions of Mrs Carmichael pretty rapidly, Mrs Carmichael herself turned out to have some curiously arbitrary standards of her own. It was almost a case of visiting Number Nineteen by invitation. A request to call there was not always granted, and certain visitors, having called once, were indignant to find themselves courteously but firmly refused a second visit to the house. Among these visitors had been Mr William Gerard. It was not a circumstance Will broadcast to the world, yet somehow, and most irritatingly, his acquaintance Davy Leigh, son by her first marriage of that Mrs Gage who kept the girls' school, had heard of it.

Davy, one of the local lads over whom Will had lorded it in their childhood, had later become his crony and drinking companion, at least on those occasions when business brought him to Great Marchingham from his own land, some thirty miles away, and the horses he kept there. On this particular occasion, he had sold a couple of good hunters, before going on to the billiards room of the Rose and Crown, a house frequented by the more fashionable and well-to-do young fellows of Great Marchingham, and thus generally esteemed a cut above the town's other hostelries. Leigh was not, therefore, surprised to find Mr Gerard there.

'So you ain't welcome at Number Nineteen any more, eh, Will?' said he by way of greeting, slapping his friend companionably on the shoulder. Several other people turned to look curiously at them.

Will did not care for this remark, but at least he could afford to laugh it off. 'Pooh, who cares for that?' For he had a better conquest to boast of, and no scruples in doing so at some length either. 'Mind, I name no names,' said he finally, with a great show of discretion. 'Pretty little thing, though, head over ears in love with me—and a maid at that!'

'Or was a maid?' suggested Mr Leigh, his smile a knowing one.

'That's about it.' Will smiled back, with becoming modesty.

'Careful now, my boy—she'll kick up more fuss and tantrums than any of the little beauties at Number Nineteen, y'know,' Davy warned. But Will merely laughed again, for at this time he was feeling on top of the world. Adoration was pleasant, and no doubt of it, he'd swept his little sweetheart off her feet. This, as he later ruefully reflected, was before any ridiculous notions of marriage had so much as entered the chit's head.

'Tell you the truth,' he now further confided to Mr Leigh, 'Number Nineteen's not all it's cracked up to be. You'd almost take it for a girls' boarding school, though that it most decidedly ain't. With the Carmichael woman as schoolmistress . . . don't she remind you of some of your more formidable female relatives, eh, Davy?'

'Hm. Reminds me of my own sister, now you come to mention schoolmistresses,' said Mr Leigh, and eyed Will Gerard slightly askance, something that Will failed to notice. 'You don't care for such ladies?'

'Well, I suppose a girls' school wouldn't be without its charms,' said Will playfully, ignoring Mr Leigh's last remark. 'But without a schoolmistress to spoil the fun, don't you think, Davy?' And he laughed immoderately, being in high good humour and liable to be overcome by his own wit.

It was certainly true that, in indicating politely to a young gentleman (or sometimes even an older one) that his notions of 'fun' did not come up to those standards of behaviour expected by herself and her nieces, Mrs Carmichael could adopt an extraordinarily effective air of hauteur, calculated to quell such a gentleman's natural indignation until later, when he had recollected who and what she really was, and thought of some very good remarks he would have made if they had occurred to him at the time. But by then he was no longer in her presence, so the joke was generally held to be against him. If the circumstance became known it did the reputation of Number Nineteen more good than harm, and thus there was really nothing much a gentleman with a grievance, however legitimate, could do.

Mrs Carmichael might be shunned by the gentry of Great Marchingham, but the town's tradespeople knew her chiefly as a good customer who paid her bills promptly. She purchased a great deal from Mrs Pacey, and had even looked judiciously at some specimens of Susan's dressmaking work and then ordered a gown for one of her nieces. Mrs Pacey, a woman of strict moral principle, was in a quandary. Should she righteously spurn custom for Susan from so tainted a source, or take the order as a compliment, coming from a woman every stitch of whose own gowns showed Parisian elegance? The businesswoman in Mrs Pacey won without too much of a struggle, though she strictly charged Susan not to chatter to the niece herself during fittings. However, the niece, Polly Brignold by name, had already learned discretion, one of the very first lessons Mrs Carmichael taught, and rather to Susan's disappointment was not disposed to chatter at all.

And here was another circumstance which puzzled the good people of Marchingham: when the nieces came to stay with their aunt they were certainly no better than they should have been—and it showed. By the time they left again, however, they had changed out of all recognition. It was common knowledge, for instance, that during her sojourn at Number Nineteen Louise Vine, who used to go with sailors in the fishing port of Lowestoft, had so taken the fancy of an elderly Norwich lawyer that he was now actually keeping her in a neat little terraced house in that city, where she went about calling herself Miss Louisa Delavine. In general, the girls left not only better dressed than before, but infinitely better behaved and better spoken than suited their station in life. It was decidedly odd, and to some provoking.

Yes, and how, it was asked, did they come to Mrs Carmichael's in the first place? What criteria did she employ in picking them? Why, in short, did she do it at all, when she seemed to have ample private means, and the sums which passed from the gentlemen callers into her hands were known not to be excessively high? (They were, in fact, nicely judged so as to convey a notion of the exclusive nature of the establishment, while not pricing it beyond the reach of gentlemanly persons of reasonable if not lavish means, such as were likely to be found in the neighbourhood of Great Marchingham.)

Nobody knew all the answers, although Polly, a handsome, dark-haired girl, could have supplied some of them (but for those strict lessons in discretion); for Polly was an early recruit and had become a particular favourite of Mrs Carmichael. She was quick-witted and instinctively ambitious, and promised to do extremely well in the kind of life for which Mrs Carmichael was educating her nieces. For Marie Carmichael did not like to see a girl waste her talents, so that when she met a girl like Polly Brignold, who could benefit, she felt, from her own experience, she strove to endow her with all the social habits and graces necessary for advancement. And Polly was undoubtedly an able and willing pupil. The other nieces of the moment were good girls in their way, but it was Mrs Carmichael's opinion that though they might do well for themselves, Polly could go farthest. It was Polly who successfully insisted on keeping her own name when, doubtfully considering the rather ridiculous circumstance that her three present nieces were called Polly, Molly and Dolly, Mrs Carmichael declared that these diminutives should be jettisoned: Polly Brignold she had always been, said the bearer of that name, and Polly Brignold she would stay, besides which she and Molly couldn't both become Maria without fear of confusion, and no, she didn't fancy being Mary either. So Polly she remained.

She also learned to keep a proper distance between herself and the respectable servant class whose ranks she had long ago determined not to join: no fortunes, she saw, were ever made in service. But pretty, blonde Dolly (or Dorothea), and red-haired Molly (Maria when she could remember) were not averse to a little gossip with Betsy in the kitchen now and then—Mrs Thompson herself being far above that kind of thing. It was through Betsy that Dolly had learned of the imminent arrival of the Indian lady.

'She'll have a jewel in her nose, I dare say, and one of them turbans!' continued Dolly, excitedly.

'No, no: one of *those* turbans, Dorothea, not *them* turbans,' her mentor said, sighing, and docile Dolly repeated the correction, trying to commit it to memory. It had been uttered in Mrs Carmichael's own impeccable tones, unfailingly elegant in diction and flawless in grammar. There was, nevertheless, just the faintest trace of something else underlying her beautiful pronunciation. Mrs Whittier, in those early days when she was so shockingly taken in as to suppose her new neighbour a lady, had thought it Scottish, going partly upon the evidence of the surname, and was in fact correct. But now that Mrs Carmichael had shown herself in her true colours, the general opinion was that she could have no real right to a respectable Scottish name; the occasional slight trace of accent was more likely to be French, and thus as disreputable as anyone cared to surmise.

'And I should doubt, in any case, that a real Indian lady is meant,' she rather dampeningly told the three nieces. 'It is more likely some English lady who has lived in India. In any case, if she is staying at the Priory, it is most unlikely that she will cross the paths of any of us. Thus,' concluded Mrs Carmichael, 'it is of no consequence to us, and even were it not so, my dears, gossip is very vulgar, and quite beneath you.'

Even the Vicar's wife could hardly have found fault with this precept, and the girls tried to look as if they were convinced of it.

At about the same time, the same item of news was also made known at the Hodsons' great oak table in the handsome, big kitchen of Brook End Farm. It was reported not by Grace but by her brother Hugh, Susan Pacey having found him a more appreciative audience than his sister. He had been happy enough to linger a while and talk to his sweetheart when he called to pick up Grace again, and now, having delivered his brother Sam a parcel which Sam eagerly received, to Hugh's wonder—'That's only a book Mr Pacey say he said he'd lend you, Sam,' he warned—he delivered Susan's news as well, telling his family about the Indian lady.

'Not that I reckon much on that,' he added, and his father George and his brothers, with the exception of Sam, who was already immersed in the book, all nodded, more concerned with getting Peggy Hodson's good bread and home-cured ham inside themselves after a day's work in the fields

50

than with bothering their heads about exotic visitors to the Priory.

Mrs Hodson, however, looked at her daughter Grace with concern. She would have expected Grace to be full of such news. Little as she herself was given to gossip, Peggy Hodson knew Grace for a flibberty-gibbet sort of creature, over-indulged, goodness knew, by George and the boys, just because she was the youngest child and the only girl, and in the ordinary way the greatest chatterbox alive.

But these days, Grace went about with a happy, abstracted smile on her face, and her mother only wished she did not guess why. Or at least, having guessed, she wished she knew more about it. With every passing day, she felt her grounds for anxiety increase. Didn't the child herself worry at all? If only she would confide in her mother.

Grace, however, seemed perfectly happy, caught up in a private, golden world of content that was all her own.

'Oh, and Susan do say,' added Hugh as an afterthought, carving himself another mighty slice of ham, 'that Mr Will's to marry this Indian lady, but I don't go for to believe that neither.'

Grace's smile did not alter, but deepened a little as she sat absorbed in her own thoughts. Her mother, watching, and with all her mind on her daughter, had failed to catch Hugh's last remark, for she was busy thinking that at least there was one mercy: thank God that George, and the boys, and men in general, were habitually so blind to what was before their very eyes.

5

'My dear Papa, my dear Hetty,' wrote Carey, making it plain, in addressing the same letter to them both, that she assumed they were now together again. And if not, she thought, I shall have something rather severe to say to them when I return to London. I trust I have not delivered myself over to Cousin Clarissa to no purpose. Well, not to no purpose, she reminded herself, since there were wild flowers to be captured on paper, so in any case the visit would not be wasted—but surely by now her father would have descended on the pretty Chelsea house and borne Hetty off again, willy-nilly.

She dipped her pen in the elegant inkstand of white, gilt and violet china, frowned slightly at her sheet of notepaper and then continued:

'So here I am at the Priory, where I have had a kind welcome and am very comfortable.' She decided she could reconcile this version of events with her conscience, which had pricked her a little at first, for taking advantage of the Gerards' invitation for her own ends. Now, however, her qualms were largely set at rest: she was comfortable enough, and yes, the welcome *had* been kind, but she sensed calculation behind it. It had taken her a very short time indeed to find, in Cousin Clarissa's little hints, confirmation of Sir John's guess: she had been invited largely for Will's benefit. Fortunately for Carey, who was considerably less dazzled by his charms than his mother plainly expected, Will himself did not seem to share Clarissa's notions concerning his future. She was thankful for this indifference, and supposed that if Clarissa noticed her thankfulness, she must find it something of a puzzle to account for her ready acceptance of the invitation to

Marchingham Priory. For carefully as she had explained the scientific, indeed scholarly nature of the project she and John Lindley had devised, her cousin obviously thought nothing at all of botanical illustration as a serious pursuit, particularly for a young woman of fortune. She would have liked to share her amusement at this with her father and Hetty . . . but it couldn't be done without giving her own game away to them, and she didn't intend to drop the least hint that she had *their* interests chiefly at heart in removing herself to the country.

You will have heard news of my safe arrival, of course, when Timothy Jenkins came back with the travelling chaise (she continued), so I won't weary you with an account of our journey. The Priory is a handsome kind of a manor house in a state of some disrepair. I understand that much money was spent upon the laying out of grounds and improvement of the house towards the end of the last century, and now there is no way to maintain the place as it should be maintained. But you may well imagine that after some of the hovels where Andrew and I put up during our Indian travels, the sight of a faded curtain at my bedroom window does not trouble me. From that window I have a fine view of the grounds, with sheep and some cattle grazing in the distance—very picturesque. A little way off, one may see a cluster of farm buildings, belonging, I am told, to the Priory's own Home Farm.

So now, you may be wondering, what have I been doing? Oh, all manner of things. I have been driven out to call on a number of local families, and into the market town of Great Marchingham, where we took luncheon with the Vicar and his wife after morning service on Sunday. The Reverend Mr Whittier, a pleasant, learned sort of a man, could not refrain from telling me (when he had had a glass of wine) that with a surname like his, he had often thought it a pity his sermons were not *wittier*. His wife, good lady, looked as if she had heard this 'Whitticism' many a time before, but bore it well. She is a rather formidable person, who might, I fancy, be bosom friends with my cousin Clarissa did they not resemble each other a good deal. As it is, a state of mutual respect appears to exist between them. And Mrs Whittier has much to bear, poor soul, for one of her neighbours, living only just across the churchyard . . .

Here, however, Carey caught herself up, and stopped writing. No, this would not do. The tale of Number Nineteen, New Road, the nature of that establishment, its location just opposite the Vicarage and the consequent indignation of the Vicar's wife, would probably amuse her father a great deal, just as it had amused her when she at last discovered the reason for the hushed, horrified whispers in which the Marchingham ladies referred to the pretty house at the end of the row. But nothing must be said that could possibly upset Hetty, peculiarly sensitive as she was to anything touching the subject of feminine virtue.

'. . . for one of her neighbours, living only just across the churchyard, is the kind of lady with whom the Vicar's wife has nothing in common,' she tamely finished her sentence, and changed the subject.

But besides these mild sociabilities, you will be glad to hear I have done a good deal of drawing and painting, and that was my object in coming here. I have material almost complete for plates to illustrate a number of flowers and grasses in the *Floral Companion* already, so if you see John Lindley, Papa, would you tell him so? I will send him news of my progress shortly. I was just in time for the late cowslips, and have made a sketch of the first furled rosebuds; I will return to the same spot in a little while, when the buds break and come fully into bloom. I find there are a number of old hedgerows on the farms here—by which I mean not just made in this century, but dating from enclosures that took place a couple of hundred years or more ago. It is where such hedgerows still stand that the botanical specimens are most interesting, so that is a piece of good fortune for me.

Oh, and in the course of exploring my hedgerows, I have made a friend: a delightful woman called Peggy

Hodson, married to one of the largest of the Priory's tenant farmers. His father leased the same farm before him, so the family has been here some forty years. I called at Mrs Hodson's door to beg a fresh bottle of water for my dirty brushes, and she provided liquid refreshment for myself as well—new milk from her dairy, poured by her very pretty daughter, who acts as dairymaid and looks charmingly in the part, although I rather think it is the mother who does the real work. Mrs Hodson's family is large: she and her husband have four sons as well as the pretty girl Grace. Thus they can farm their acres without needing to employ much other labour, apart from casual workers at the busier times of the year, so Mrs Hodson tells me. She gave me leave to walk anywhere I liked upon their land, and laughed a good deal on first learning of my identity, saying, 'Oh, so you are the Indian lady!' It seems that the people of Marchingham were all expecting an exotic beauty in a saree, and I have brought none of my own with me, which is a pity, but I was not to know what a sad disappointment I should be without them.

During a pleasant hour passed in her comfortable kitchen, I learned from Mrs Hodson a good deal I never knew before, which I am pretty sure you, inveterate townsfolk both, do not know either. Mr Hodson's fields, and indeed the Home Farm of the Priory itself, both look to my admittedly inexpert eye models of good management, so that I would never have guessed, had I not been told, that there is a great deal of trouble among the country labourers just now. The nature of this trouble, Peggy Hodson told me, is that many farmers will not pay their men a reasonable wage, knowing that in law wages must be made up, by way of the poor-rate, to a certain level fixed according to the price of bread at any given time . . . I think I have that right. At any event, the arrangement, though charitably intended, does not answer. And then there has been the recent introduction of new machines, which take away the men's usual winter work by threshing mechanically, instead of with flails, so that what with one thing and another the farm workers' families often find it difficult to make ends meet, particularly in the winter-time. I haven't told you this as well as it was explained to me, but I can see that it is hard on the labouring men. We scarcely think of such things as we consume our daily bread in London.

There are some members of the more notable local families whom I have not yet met: Mrs Whittier's brother, for one, who lives at the Vicarage too. He is an artist, I am told, and I expect I should have liked to make his acquaintance, but I understand that he is rather an invalid and was obliged to keep to his bed on Sunday. Oh, by the way, Papa, Sir William has got another son as well as my cousin Will—an elder son by his first marriage, but I have not yet met this son either, and perhaps shall not. I collect that there is something the matter with him, since Cousin Clarissa habitually refers to him pityingly, and with a deep sigh, as 'poor Benedict'. So it is not likely that he is the boy I remembered from my earlier visit to Marchingham as a child, since that lad had nothing wrong with him, and indeed appeared very fearless and active in rescuing my poor doll. (Carey reached for a second sheet of paper, and continued.) Clarissa is at some pains to let me understand, in the most delicate manner imaginable, that 'poor Benedict' is unlikely to marry, and therefore Will is in effect his father's heir and will continue the line—something which plainly means much to her, though it is a matter of indifference to me, as I have not the least intention of being married to Will. I find Papa was correct in supposing this to be Lady Gerard's amiable plan. However, I listen to her with perfect civility, Hetty, so you need not fear for my conduct. I tell you this only so that Papa may have the satisfaction of knowing he was right, and I am not ashamed to own it when someone else is in the right.

Well, I am unlikely to meet the unfortunate, or afflicted, elder son, since he is away from home, and Cousin Clarissa says nothing of any imminent return. From the melancholy tenor of her remarks, I am inclined to believe that the poor fellow has to be kept out of ordinary society; perhaps he requires a keeper, or some such thing.

Here Mrs Elliott broke off again, scanned the sheet with her last few sentences on it, crumpled it up and tossed it away. That won't do either, she thought. I meant it light-heartedly, but such flights of fancy are *not* for Hetty's eyes, considering the state of the wretched Pauling's health.

She took up another fresh sheet, re-wrote that part of its predecessor which seemed innocuous, and then resumed:

Well, enough of all this, or it will cost you a fortune to receive my idle tittle-tattle. However, I must tell you one more intriguing thing: I have made an enemy. Now how can I have done that, when I have never been in this part of the country before, and have certainly never set eyes upon the person in question? It is a great puzzle to me. This enemy is a small, neat, dark little lady, I suppose about my own age, with bright, snapping eyes and a rosy complexion. The Vicar introduced me to her and her mother; they are a Mrs and Miss Gage, who keep a well regarded girls' school in the town. Miss Gage was civil enough, to be sure, but plainly did not care for me at all. Perhaps it was merely the look of me she disliked. Yet I am vain enough to say I did not think my appearance so very disagreeable. It was after church we met and I had put on that pretty lavender-coloured challis pelisse over my gown, the one dear Hetty helped me to choose, because May mornings, even late in the month, can be so chilly—and really I don't think that it was un-becoming. The mother, *Mrs* Gage, a very pleasant middle-aged woman, was at pains to make up for her daughter's lack of warmth (I had almost said, in-civility), and talked most agreeably to me about their school, and its pupils . . . when up comes Miss Gage again, says something into her mother's ear which causes Mrs Gage to go quite pink, and become flustered, and then little Miss Gage sweeps the good lady away, with the curtest of nods to myself.

I suppose it is quite a salutory thing (Carey concluded, coming to the bottom of her sheet and preparing to cross it with her loving salutations), to meet people who don't like one, but in this case, and upon such brief acquaintance, I really am at a loss to account for it. Well, enough of that, or I shall never have this letter ready to go off with the post to London. I think of you both daily—believe me, my dears, your loving

Caroline

* * *

Miss Gage's dislike was easily enough explained, and might have been largely dissipated could she have read the first part of Carey's letter. The fact was that Roberta Gage had recently suffered a disappointment: it could not have been called a disappointment in love, precisely, for love had very little to do with the case, but on the surface it bore all the appearance of such a thing, and Miss Gage's tender-hearted mother, interpreting it thus, made every allowance for the sharpness of tongue her daughter was inclined to display just now.

And it had been a disappointment, felt as keenly in its way as if a genuine affair of the heart had been at stake. When Roberta had worked so hard to achieve her ends, which would surely have been in the best interests of all concerned, it hardly seemed fair, she resentfully thought, to have her best efforts thwarted by another person's sheer stupidity. (For it was in such affectionate terms that she thought of the gentleman she had been hoping to marry, Mr William Gerard of Marchingham Priory.)

Her resentment was exacerbated by the sight, in church, of that rich Mrs Elliott who was to marry young Mr Gerard, or so rumour had it. Carey's exquisitely cut lavender pelisse, her ready smile, her easy manner, all fed Miss Gage's natural inclination to dislike her. To make matters worse, Roberta gathered that Mrs Elliot was not even of particularly distinguished origins. Her father was a mere physician. How had she come by her wealth and social standing? Only married a rich husband who then conveniently died.

Whereas she, Roberta Gage, had worked to earn every-thing she had, quite unaided. She had exercised her abilities, her industry, her strength of character—even to the point of prudently disguising this last quality. And yet the good things of life had not been showered on *her*. Miss Gage had made it her business to find out a good deal about Caroline Elliott. Money, she gloomily concluded, was the crucial difference between them. What was the use of being clever, and working hard, if you had no money in the first place? As for birth, she rather thought they were on an equal footing there, each with one, but only one, parent of very good family.

The late Mr Gage, Roberta's father, had been an attorney in Marchingham. Not a particularly successful one, but, as his widow fondly remembered, very much the gentleman. This wonderful gentility arose from the circumstance of his being a younger son of a cadet branch of the Gage family, great landowners up in Norfolk. Roberta had few distinct memories of her ineffectual father, who had died when she was only ten, leaving his widow, stepson and young daughter almost penniless. But as she grew older, and understood that her education at a select Norwich boarding school was paid for by the grand Gages of Dullerton Hall, doing their family duty, she learned to think better of him—or at least of his undoubted status as a man of gentle birth.

Nobody could have claimed such status for Mrs Gage's first husband. Herself the daughter of a gentleman farmer, Elizabeth Dering had decidedly gone down in the world when she fell in love with a handsome young fellow whom her father suspected to be something of a rogue. But no actual harm was known of Frank Leigh, and since the girl's heart was set on him, her father was indulgent, and in the end the wedding was celebrated—despite the dire foreboding expressed by the bride's affectionate relatives. Frank Leigh was only a younger son, had gypsy blood in his veins—and his dark good looks, and his thinking more of horses and horse-dealing than his own small farm, only went to prove it. When Frank broke his neck steeplechasing, and his now ramshackle property had to be sold to pay his debts, these same well-wishers were prompt to assure everyone that while they sincerely pitied poor Elizabeth,

59

left with her little boy, they had known something of the kind was bound to happen.

The child had inherited his father's love of horseflesh, and was lucky enough to be able to indulge it. For a stroke of luck came his way when his mother was left a widow in financial straits for the second time. Seeing the Dullerton Gages come to the widow's aid, at least in providing Roberta with an education, the Leighs at last roused themselves to do their duty by young David, then a boy of thirteen, rather wild, but with engaging, cheerful ways. The main part of the Leigh land belonged to Davy's paternal uncle, who happened to be childless and whose wife took a great fancy to the lively lad; young Davy went to live with them, showed great aptitude for managing horses, and when in due course he inherited the farm himself he sold off part of the land and then set up as a horse-dealer.

Horse-dealing turned out a pretty profitable line (for Davy was shrewder than his father), but no one could have called it a genteel profession, a circumstance which irked his half-sister. Roberta was fond enough of Davy, but she didn't want him spoiling her own chances.

For Roberta hankered after a grander way of life than any she had known. As a schoolgirl, she rather prided herself on these hankerings. Were they not the natural consequence of her gentle blood? The Gages were a cut above the Leighs—several cuts, in fact. They were a cut above the Derings, too. Relieved of immediate financial responsibility for her children by their respective fathers' families, Mrs Gage continued to live quietly in Marchingham, eking out her own tiny income with the sale of her exquisitely fine needlework. Roberta wondered how her mother could be content with such an existence. It was certainly not for her.

She might feel proud of her Gage blood, but she felt no particular gratitude to the family for sending her to school; it was only her due. She worked hard at her lessons, with a view to improving her prospects. She also learned to make herself agreeable, so as to be invited to the homes of her fellow pupils. And invited she was, yet just as she reached the age when those invitations would have come in really useful—for she might now reasonably have hoped for some of those fellow pupils' brothers to take an interest in her—they began to taper off. It was provoking.

The reason was not far to seek. Her friends were bound for the heady joys of society and the Season, maybe even a trip to London, though it would be provincial society only for most of them. Roberta had had hopes of the Dullerton Gages in this respect, but nothing came of them. Duty was evidently felt to have been done: the Dullerton family suggested she make use of the education she had now acquired as a governess or schoolmistress.

Such employment was easily enough obtained, and in the very school where she had been a pupil. Its proprietress was glad enough to accept the diligent Miss Gage as a teacher. The work, however, was dull and without prospects: Roberta felt sure she could do better for herself.

She was delivered from the dullness of the Norwich school by a stroke of luck: an unexpected legacy to her mother from an old Dering aunt, who had always had a soft spot for 'poor, good Lizzie'. Elizabeth Gage did not object when Roberta made it plain that she was going to decide what use should be made of this windfall. She herself had thought of opening a small millinery business in Great Marchingham, but Roberta shrewdly pointed out that she stood little chance of rivalling Mrs Pacey's well-established shop. 'Whereas a seminary for girls,' said the twenty-year-old girl sagely, 'is one thing that Great Marchingham *does* lack.'

'Seminary?' said her mother, a little faintly.

'Hm . . . I wonder,' mused Roberta, frowning, 'if Seminary is a good name after all? Academy?' She pondered. 'No, I believe simply *school* will be best. School for the Daughters of Gentlemen? Although that might frighten off some of the kind of parents I have in mind . . .'

'Wh . . . what kind did you have in mind, dearest?' faltered Mrs Gage.

'Well, we can't hope for the daughters of the very *best* families in this part of the country,' said Roberta, thinking aloud—and speaking, to her mother's alarm, as if her plan were quite a settled thing. 'Or not yet. No: at first we must aim for the better sort of farmers and tradespeople in and around Marchingham: people who can pay our moderate fees—moderate, but not *too* low. And we must not scare them away by suggesting that if they themselves lack gentility, our school is no place for their daughters. Do you follow me, Mama?'

'I—I hardly know,' confessed poor Mrs Gage. 'People who can pay our fees? Roberta, my dear, do you really mean to open a school? Why?'

'Why not?' said her daughter briskly. 'I have not been slaving away these last three years to no purpose, Mama. I know just how to run a school, and you and I will contrive to teach it very well between us. Don't look so alarmed—I only mean you to teach needlework, and that, you will own, you are very well able to do.'

Mrs Gage did brighten a little at this prospect, but stipulated nervously that she should not be required to instruct anyone in such terrifyingly abstruse subjects as French, or Italian, or the use of the globes.

Accordingly, the Gages, mother and daughter, spent Aunt Amelia's money on the purchase of a neat house in the street known as Saltgate, and put up a plate describing it, in Roberta's final choice of wording, simply as a School for Young Ladies. The young ladies came: as Roberta had calculated, there were plenty of farmers and tradesmen willing to pay her fees. The prosperity that the French wars had brought to such market towns as Great Marchingham and the farming country round about was now in the past; aspirations to gentility, however, did not fade along with the means to indulge them.

So the little place prospered in a modest way. But the hoped-for influx of really ladylike pupils from the *best* Marchingham families had not yet materialised, in its five years of existence. Roberta's chief prize, and not a particularly dazzling one, was Mr Meadows the apothecary's daughter. The school was well enough, Roberta thought, but now she must see if she could use it as a stepping stone to better things. And casting a shrewd eye around her, she soon fixed it on those better things to which she might step.

She had not, she reasoned, demeaned herself by opening a school. It was a perfectly ladylike occupation. The Dullerton Gages need not be ashamed of her. Indeed, they should be proud of the good use she had made of her education.

'You may write to them with perfect propriety, Mama, just delicately mentioning these things, you know,' she had told her mother, one day in the autumn of 1829, at about the time when Caroline Elliott was making her final preparations to leave India.

'Write to them?' Mrs Gage was instantly in a flutter of alarm, for she was decidedly afraid of her late husband's family. 'Write to them? What for?'

'Well, they are sure to attend the Assemblies in Norwich this winter, and I should like to go too. In fact, I am surprised they have not thought of asking me to join their party before. I am sure they ought to , aren't you?'

'Oh, my dear, yes, of course! Such a good, hard-working girl as you are, and I am sure it is only natural for you to want to go to parties,' cried Mrs Gage, full of mingled sympathy and doubt. 'Only . . . only the fact is, dearest, they have not asked you.' But she trembled with apprehension.

'No, so they may as well do it now,' said Roberta briskly. 'You can write to them and suggest it.'

'I? No, no! How could I?'

'Very easily, Mama,' said Roberta, smiling a little. 'I will compose the letter, and all you have to do is hold the pen.'

The letter, once written, was such that Mrs Gage marvelled at her daughter's cleverness. Roberta caused her mother to dwell, very properly but not over-effusively, upon Roberta's own gratitude to the Gages, and the success of her school. And now, wrote Mrs Gage at Roberta's dictation, although she penned this note with some diffidence (a massive understatement, considering her dire misgivings), she wondered if Roberta might not join their party at the Assemblies this year? Roberta—so that young woman blithely dictated—had not the least notion that her mama was writing this letter, but seeing how hard her dear child worked, and feeling that the innocent diversions of youth were passing her by, she, Elizabeth Gage, ventured to ask the favour. Of course there was no question but that Roberta would pay her own subscription. All that was required was chaperonage of a sort which she, Mrs Gage, felt unable to provide, having been so long out of society.

That part at least was true, reflected Elizabeth Gage,

scribbling away obediently. She was not sure that she had ever really been *in* society, and would certainly tremble at the thought of going into it now.

She waited several days for a reply, in great trepidation, fearing the snub of a refusal. But a graciously phrased invitation came instead, as Roberta had been confident that it would; the tone of the request had been such as to ensure that a refusal would sound churlish. She replied in her own person, expressing suitable gratitude.

'Oh, but my dear!' cried her mother, suddenly seeing a snag. 'How will you *get* to Norwich? Why, we are miles and miles away—and Dullerton almost as many miles again, on the other side of the city. You cannot expect them to send a carriage all this way for you.'

'No, of course I don't,' said Roberta calmly. 'The Gerards always go to the Norwich Assemblies, so they may as well take me too.'

'But my dear—you can't ask—you cannot suggest it yourself.'

'I don't really see why not,' had said Roberta. 'But I take your point, Mama: it would look better if the idea came from another quarter.'

'Not me again,' begged Mrs Gage. Sheer alarm made her bold enough to protest quite vehemently. 'Not again! In any case, it wouldn't answer. Why, if Lady Gerard so much as nods to me in church, I promise you that is all the notice she takes of me.'

'No, but the Dullerton connection will serve,' said Roberta. 'The families are friends. You may write to Lady Gage again—or no, wait, I will mention the matter in the letter I am now writing her myself.' Mrs Gage heaved a heartfelt sigh of relief. 'And then *she* will write to Lady Gerard at Marchingham, and that should do the trick nicely.'

Just what Roberta was putting in her letter Mrs Gage did not feel strong enough to inquire, but it certainly *did* do the trick. A seat for their cousin in the Gerards' carriage was duly begged by the Gages and offered by the Gerards. Roberta had made the suggestion so properly that Lady Gage of Dullerton Hall was perfectly ready to write the required note, and if Lady Gerard was not quite so willing to grant the request, there was no civil way she could say so to her old acquaintance, even if she felt rather ill-used, and feared Miss Gage would put herself forward unbecomingly.

She was pleasantly surprised. Miss Gage did no such thing. She was a Gage, after all, and seemed a quiet, obliging little creature. 'Not in the least encroaching,' Clarissa graciously observed to Sir William after the first Assembly, when Roberta had made up a fourth in the carriage with herself, her husband and her son. 'I fancy,' she added, doing Mrs Gage a grave injustice, 'that any boldness in suggesting the notion in the first place was due to her mother, who of course is not quite the thing. As to the daughter, however,' she concluded, cheerfully committing another error of judgment, 'I am sure there is no harm in her at all.'

What Roberta had really wanted, and got, was the opportunity for conversation with Mr William Gerard on the long drives to and from Norwich. For this was to be her start, her foot in the door of Marchingham Priory. She made sure that the flattering attention she paid to every word young Mr Gerard uttered was obvious enough to please him, but not so obvious as to alarm his mother.

And Will Gerard did find Miss Gage's presence a pleasant addition to the company. He expected the winter Assemblies to be as much of a dead bore as usual, but his mother *would* have him go, and for once even his father took a firm stand, saying young Will must learn to make himself agreeable to the other county families. Privately, Will considered these families a set of dull sticks—and if there did happen to be a pretty girl among them, it only made him wary. He knew his mother would like to see him married, and had no plans of his own in that line. His amorous forays were made among the pretty daughters of the lower classes, where he could not be expected to mean marriage, and he intended to continue in the same carefree way for some while yet.

Miss Gage was not easy to place; she belonged to neither the county families nor the lower orders, and at first Will did not even think her pretty. But she listened to all he had to say with interest, and with such a sparkle in her eyes, and so taking a smile. Will found he did not wish to lose her company once the carriage reached the Assembly Rooms. In the circumstances, it was the most natural thing in the world for the Gerards and Gages to make up a single party, and Will thought himself very clever to contrive it, unaware that the contrivance was largely Roberta's. And as he and she were the only unattached young people in either group, what more natural, again, than for them to dance together a good deal? Moreover, if he fetched her a cup of tea, or a glass of ratafia, he need not be hovering around some young lady forced upon his notice by his mama.

So far, so good. Roberta had high hopes, and was therefore particularly disappointed when those hopes were dashed, as it turned out that Mr Gerard's own plans, though they ran parallel with hers up to a certain point, by no means led to the same end.

For there came a day, towards the end of the winter Assembly season, when Mr Gerard called at the school after the pupils had gone home, and while Mrs Gage was out. With a pretty, bashful smile, Roberta confessed that she must receive him alone, and waited to hear what he had to say.

To her chagrin, it was not at all what she had expected. She was obliged to express herself quite forcefully, and with genuine indignation. She could not imagine what had led Mr Gerard to think her *that* sort of a female. She very well knew that no fault could be found with her conduct towards him, and she said so, roundly.

Mr Gerard went away in a huff, and Roberta waited hopefully for him to come to his senses. There was no question of his getting what he wanted without marriage. However, she thought she had said enough to bring him back to her. Her indignant rejection of his proposals ought, she calculated, to sharpen his desire. But Roberta had underestimated Will's wariness. She and he were not playing the same game; he liked his conquests easy, and had no difficulty in shrugging off the whole incident. At the final Assembly, she could not help noticing that his manner had markedly cooled; in fact, he was barely civil to her. It was mortifying.

This might have been supposed the end of the matter,

66

but Roberta Gage would not give up yet. She had few illusions about the man she wanted to marry, and would not have been in the least surprised to know that he had found a new rustic mistress in the spring. Such creatures could easily be ignored. The arrival of the 'Indian lady' was another thing altogether. The news that this rich lady was to marry Mr Will was delivered to Mrs and Miss Gage by Cicely, and Roberta could not even have the pleasure of rebuking the girl for credulous gossip, since Cicely added immediately that for her part she didn't believe a word of it.

Roberta did, though. It seemed all too likely, particularly when she had met Mrs Elliott at church, and seen the way Lady Gerard smiled fondly on her. A hopeful thought did cross her mind . . . surely a rich widow could do better for herself than Will Gerard? However, Roberta dismissed this as too easy a consolation. What was Mrs Elliott doing here at all if she did not mean to marry him?

Thus, Miss Gage was in no very sunny mood as she and her mother, back from church and their encounter with Mrs Elliott, sat down to a light luncheon of coddled eggs, prepared by the invaluable Cicely. Guessing what lay behind her daughter's frown, Mrs Gage unwisely tried to divert her thoughts by telling her how Mrs Saunders, after church, had expressed pleasure at her daughter Ellen's progress. 'So good of her to say so, don't you think, dear? Considering that Ellen is not . . . well, clever, I fancy she is doing as well as could have been expected.'

'*Better* than could have been expected,' said Roberta tartly. 'I know who finished that sampler for her!'

'Oh . . . oh dear!' Poor Mrs Gage, found out again in this mild misdemeanour, was flustered. 'I'm sure there was no harm in it, Roberta, and Ellen may learn by watching me, and do her own work better next time.'

'Or more likely, she may not.' Roberta took no such charitable view. 'That child is naturally awkward, and Mrs Saunders would do better not to delude herself about Ellen's prospects of becoming lady's maid in some great household, which is her ambition for the girl.'

Mrs Gage vaguely felt that her daughter would have been

more indulgent to, say, the apothecary's daughter, ham-fisted as Jane Meadows might be. In fact, she had heard Roberta compliment Mr Meadows on the child's perform-ance of a piano sonatina, at a little concert the school had given, saying pleasing things which Mrs Gage was sure she had not meant . . . well, nobody *could* mean them, unless they were tone-deaf. But she still persisted in her defence of little Ellen Saunders. 'She may improve, dear. She is so willing, and eager to please.'

'Willingness,' said Roberta, shortly, 'is no substitute for ability.'

'No, to be sure, but then of course Ellen will very likely marry, and what I always tell myself, dear, is that our girls may marry the better for having learnt at our school, and if she were to marry well—I mean, well for a farmer's daughter—why, I am sure a willing, pliable disposition is a very comfortable thing in a wife.'

Mrs Gage could have bitten her tongue off. Her own ramblings echoed distressingly in her ears. How could she have spoken so, to her far from pliable daughter? Not that she meant any criticism; but she knew how poor Roberta still suffered from her disappointment over Mr Gerard, even if she was too proud to confide in her mother her feelings when she saw his interest wane. Mrs Gage's heart bled for her. Casting around for some change of subject, she was doubly pleased to glance out of the window and see a familiar figure jauntily turning the corner of Saltgate.

'Oh, do look, Roberta! Why, here comes Davy! What a delightful surprise!'

She was on her feet in an instant, about to run to the door and greet her son. Roberta showed no such enthusiasm. 'Oh, pray, Mama, don't jump up like that in the middle of your luncheon. It is not the thing, and Cicely can perfectly well show him in. I wonder what he is doing here?'

Daunted, Mrs Gage sat down again, but her son was no stickler for formal ceremony either, and was soon striding briskly into the room unannounced. 'Well, Mama—well, Bertie—and how do the pair of *you* do?'

'Davy, how nice!' cried his mother, happily receiving his kiss. She regarded him with fond pride. Young Mr Leigh was certainly a good-looking man in his way: dark, wiry, of medium height and slightly raffish demeanour. His sister thought there seemed to be an air of the stables for ever hanging about him—only metaphorically, since, she reflected as he turned to bestow a second hearty salute on herself, at least Davy was scrupulous about his person. Whether his business dealings would stand up to such close examination she was not at all sure.

He was now holding her away from him to scan her face, smiling a little mockingly. 'Bearing up well in adversity, Bertie, as usual! Sorry to see you've had another blow!'

'I have no idea,' said Roberta stiffly, 'what you can mean.'

'Why, the wealthy widow, to be sure! You'll have seen her in church, I'll be bound. Handsome woman too, I'm told. Tell you what—shall I try to cut Will Gerard out with her? Anything to oblige a sister!'

'Oh, Davy, pray . . . !' exclaimed Mrs Gage, distressfully. But Mr Leigh took a more realistic view than hers of his sister's recent disappointment, having a pretty good idea of its exact nature. He therefore heartlessly continued, 'Mind, I don't think Will's the man for you at all. You'd make just two mouthfuls of the poor fellow, Bertie.'

'Davy, you should not talk to your sister so.'

'Oh, Bertie don't mind—do you, Bertie?'

'I certainly pay no attention to your nonsense, if that's what you mean,' retorted Roberta, with spirit. The fact was, though she was reluctant to admit it, that Davy cheered her up. She might disapprove of him, but privately she recognised that they were two of a kind, with a shrewd grasp of practicalities deriving, she could only conclude, from some distant Dering ancestor, since neither of their respective feckless fathers had shown much sign of such a thing. 'What's more,' she added, 'I wish you will not call me Bertie. It sounds like a boy's name.'

'And you should have been a boy, m'dear! Then you could have made the running with anyone you fancied—awkward thing for a female to do, though, ain't it?'

'*Davy!*' protested his mother.

'Anyway, how do you know whom we met at church?' inquired Roberta, shifting her ground. 'I didn't see *you* there, did I?'

'No, no, but one can pick up the latest Marchingham gossip anywhere! As the pair of you are dying to know to what you owe the pleasure of my company—now wait, for this will astonish you—I came . . . I came to sell a horse! There, are you not astonished?'

'Hardly,' said Roberta, suppressing a smile.

Mrs Gage could not help laughing at her son's nonsense either, but said, with gentle reproof, 'Oh, and on a Sunday too, Davy!'

Davy had the grace to cast her a slightly apologetic glance. 'Yes, well, the only time that suited my buyer, but never mind all that. I saw you from afar, coming out of church, so feeling peckish I said to myself, there'll be luncheon for a hungry man in Saltgate! Though what . . .' he added, lifting the lid of the serving dish and viewing its contents with comical dismay, 'Good God! What have we here?'

'Oh, coddled eggs, Davy,' his mother earnestly informed him.

'Yes, I can see that.' Mr Leigh reached out an arm to the bell that summoned Cicely. 'Coddled eggs! No wonder you're down in the dumps, Bertie, my love—I beg your pardon—sister Roberta! Coddled eggs won't put you in good heart for the chase! Ah, Cicely—dear Cicely, Cecilia, Ceciliest—do see if you can find me a nice piece of rare beef, won't you? There's a good girl! Or a pie if there's nothing better in the house. Wait a moment, what's this?' He was investigating the jug of barley water that stood on the table. 'Orgeat, eh? And Cicely, while we're about it, send out for a pint of porter, too. Another for yourself, Roberta? No? Very well, just the one then, if you please, dear Cicely.'

'Cicely,' observed Roberta, as the maidservant left the room, 'made this herself, and it is very good!' She helped herself to the despised barley water, setting the jug down with a slight thump. 'So what brings you here besides the horse?'

70

'Why, family affection, of course!' Davy grinned at her. 'And also—oh, well, this, that and t'other. Nothing that need concern you.'

'I'm not so sure of that,' said Roberta, slowly. 'We *are* your family, you may recollect. And we, at least, are respectable.'

'You mean to say that I'm not?' Mr Leigh mimicked exaggerated horror. 'You fear I'll bring dishonour on the family name? My dear girl, have I ever, ever, set foot on the wrong side of the law?'

Roberta pursed her lips, said nothing, and looked at him. Her look spoke volumes. Indeed you have, it said, and you are lucky not to have been caught at it, that's all. She was thinking of the consignment of poached game found in the luggage compartment of a gentleman's travelling carriage, half-way between Newmarket and London; a carriage which mysteriously disappeared while the confiscated game was being stowed away in a cold larder to await the attention of the magistrates. From a description of the horses drawing the vehicle, given her at second hand, Roberta strongly suspected them to have been her brother's.

Not that she and her mother were averse to the occasional gift of a couple of pounds of best tea. Smuggling, after all, was a flourishing trade here in the eastern counties, and few thought any the worse of those who engaged in it, as long as they had the sense not to get caught. Still, Sir William Gerard was one of the local Justices of the Peace, and it would not do herself, Roberta Gage, any good with the Gerard family if her half-brother were known to be involved with poaching, smuggling, and the less reputable side of the horse-dealing business.

As if reading her thoughts, Davy, gratefully accepting the heaped plate of cold meats and the tankard Cicely brought him, said, 'But don't you worry, m'dear. I'm old friends with Will Gerard, remember.'

'*Friends?*' Roberta lifted her brows with as much hauteur as Will's mother herself might have done. The only effect upon Davy was to elicit from him a shout of appreciative laughter.

'My dear, you're wonderful! You should be mistress of

Marchingham Priory, I swear you should. I'll put my mind to helping you, and that's a promise.'

'Davy, Davy,' his mother pleaded. 'You really must not distress poor Roberta so.'

'"Poor Roberta" will thank you not to meddle in her business, Davy,' said that lady, not in any noticeably distressed tone.

Glancing at his mother, and seeing that she really was upset, Mr Leigh dropped his bantering manner. 'Well, I'm sorry—about Will, I mean. But seriously, Bertie, you're too good for him. He always did have a taste for low company, you know.'

'Which you supplied!'

'Oh, exactly so, dear Bertie. I still do, from time to time. He wasn't above calling me a gypsy when we were lads —but after I'd knocked him down a couple of times, we heard no more of that.' Mr Leigh fell momentarily silent, looking more thoughtfully at his sister than was his wont. 'And low company he *did* like, yes, even as a lad: mine, and that of the other Marchingham boys, and nowadays . . .' But he thought better of what he had been going to say; hints about Will's preference for girls beneath his station were superfluous if, as it appeared, Roberta's designs had come to nothing. 'He had the unfortunate knack of setting other children's backs up, though, did Will—playing the young master—not like Ben, who's a different kettle of fish, always was. Can't think why you don't set your cap at him.'

'At Benedict Gerard?' Roberta was plainly astonished.

'Why not? He's the heir, ain't he?'

'Well, to the baronetcy, yes . . . but only a small part of the estate itself is entailed, and . . . well, in any case Lady Gerard believes him unlikely to marry.'

'Parroting Lady Gerard now, are we?' Davy Leigh regarded his sister with some amusement over the rim of his tankard. 'I dare say that's what she'd like to think—all the more for her precious Will to inherit some day, or at least his sons. But *why*, now, d'you suppose Ben wouldn't marry? Come along, Bertie, use that sharp little mind of yours. Why?'

Nettled, Roberta set herself to answer this question seriously. 'Well, he does not mix in Society, does he? I

suppose he is of a naturally misanthropic disposition.'
Davy snorted somewhat derisively, but offered no other
comment, merely cocking a questioning eyebrow at his
sister. 'It is not to be wondered at, with that mark on his
face, you know,' she added, and realised as soon as
the words were out that she was indeed parroting something she had heard Lady Gerard say on the way to an
Assembly—not that she was going to give Davy the
satisfaction of admitting it.

'It's only an ordinary birthmark, after all,' he remarked.
'In my opinion—from one or two hints I picked up, and the
rest's mere conjecture—some silly chit years ago decided
she didn't fancy the look of it, which gave him a dislike of
girls in what you'd call Society. Nothing *else* the matter with
Ben, you know.' Mr Leigh tilted back on his chair. 'Well, no
accounting for you females! Here am I offering you my
advice, free, gratis and for nothing—and mark you, there's
many a man glad to take it in the matter of a horse, so why
wouldn't you take it in the matter of a husband?'

But here Mrs Gage spoke up, more firmly than usual.
'Davy, I must ask you not to say such things! Do you not see
how very mortifying they are to Roberta? And—and they
are improper, too!'

Being genuinely fond of his mother, Davy was finally
quelled. 'Then I won't speak of them any more. Well, I must
be on my way. Just thought I'd look in and see how you
both did . . . you've not heard any talk, have you, of trouble
in the countryside?' he asked, in a casual manner that made
Roberta look at him rather sharply.

'Trouble? Dear me, no,' said Mrs Gage apprehensively.
'What sort of trouble?'

'Oh, rioting and so forth, such as they had hereabouts in
'16.'

'Oh no, no! Nothing like that, I am thankful to say. Have
you heard of any such terrible things, Davy?' inquired Mrs
Gage, in some alarm.

'Not here, no, though there's talk of trouble brewing in
the south of the country.' But seeing his mother's face, Mr
Leigh made haste to reassure her. 'Nothing I know of
for certain—and nothing that need trouble you, Mama.
Such things may be bad for business—for my kind of

73

business—or then again, they may not . . . Well, thank you for the luncheon. Bertie will see me out, so don't you move.'

Roberta had no object to this; she had been watching her brother's face, and said curiously as they stood by the front door, 'What kind of business are you up to, Davy?'

'I'm up to buying and selling horses, my dear,' he said blandly. 'It's a respectable calling, you know.'

'I think there's something else besides—something that brought you to Marchingham today. In fact, I am convinced of it.'

'Well, what of it?' Provokingly, Davy merely smiled at her.

'Only that I'll thank you not to disgrace your family.'

'Now when have I ever done that? Afraid I'll thrust a spoke into the wheel of your matrimonial plans? No, no, never mind what you were going to say—I can see you're mortified, but not just in the way that Mama thinks, eh? So, I suppose I may say I don't think anything I do will make a bit of difference.'

Roberta did not deign to reply to this, but something in the set of her firm jaw made her brother pause.

'Is your mind really set on Will Gerard, then? Hm . . . well, little sister, who knows but that I may try if I can't be useful to you after all?'

'I beg you won't try anything of the sort!' said Roberta, in such lively alarm that Mr Leigh could not help laughing.

'Don't you trust my tact? My delicacy?'

'Not for a moment!'

'Then you should. Don't fear, I won't put you to shame—but I might see what I can contrive for you. How's that for a brotherly act, then?' And so saying, he turned and went off down the street, whistling.

Roberta watched him go, caught between exasperation and amusement. There was no denying it—as usual, he had raised her spirits. Not that she had the least faith in his ability to 'contrive' anything for her, yet somehow their conversation had stiffened her resolve not to give up. Not yet. After all, it was Lady Gerard who was said to be so anxious for Will to marry the rich widow; Will himself, at least in church, had not appeared particularly besotted.

74

She, Roberta, had once attracted him and might do so again—only she must bide her time, be careful and clever, and be sure any arrangement was made upon her own terms . . .

If she had known of Will's present disinclination to pay attention to any female, rich or otherwise, her mind might have been easier. Bent as she was on her chances of rivalling Mrs Elliott, she would not, even if she had known all, have seen her former pupil Grace Hodson as a rival. Nor would she have wasted a moment's pity on a simple miss who had been foolish enough not to hold out for a ring, and whose world of magical contentment had just been brutally shattered.

6

Peggy Hodson supposed, bleakly, that her daughter took her for a fool. And I dare say I have been a fool too, she told herself, thumping dough down fiercely on her well-scrubbed kitchen table. Why did I never stand up to George more over Grace? Why did I let him spoil her so?

Well, she knew the answer to that. It would have been different if Grace had been the first child. George would have regarded her as something of a disappointment, for a man needs sons to help him on the land, and he hoped to see one of his boys take over Brook End Farm in due course. Mr Ben, Peggy knew, would like nothing better than for the Hodsons to continue as tenants there; he often said it was seeing what George had made of the place, cleansing and fertilising the soil, introducing a good four-course rotation, that had shown him what could be done on the rest of the Marchingham estate, and gave him heart to begin doing it. Mr Ben had been to George often enough for advice in those early days, and very willing George had been to give it. Well, there was Hugh, or Jack, or Bob, or even Sam, to step into George's shoes when he grew old.

Yes, if Grace had been the first child it would have been different, but coming fifth as she did, she was her father's pride and joy and still the family pet, at an age when Peggy herself had long been in service as under-nursemaid at the Priory and was used to standing on her own two feet.

There was no denying that Grace had been an enchanting baby. At eighteen, George fondly said, she was like a flower—and George was not a man generally given to flights of poetic fancy. Peggy had to admit he was right. Their Grace didn't look like a farmer's daughter: she was slender and fair, with a milk-and-roses complexion that never took on a really deep sunburn, and was only faintly tinged with gold even when she had been working in the fields. Not that Grace was ever required to work in the fields except at the very busiest times of the year. Her mother was training her in all the crafts of the dairy—or so, at least, her mother hoped. At any rate she made a charming picture there, against the background of shelves of wood and cool stone, surrounded by shining cream pans and scrubbed butter churns.

In fact, as Peggy Hodson sometimes reflected, not altogether approvingly, Grace looked rather like a lady playing at dairymaid, and was inclined to leave her work when she tired of it, just as a lady might. Peggy used to shrug her shoulders and complete Grace's tasks without fuss; that was the easiest thing to do, but she now regretted it. Better for the child to have finished churning the butter that was so reluctant to come, instead of wandering off to the parlour to tinkle idly away on the piano, striking what anyone (except, apparently, George) could hear was an excessive number of wrong notes.

That piano! A deeper frown furrowed Peggy Hodson's broad brow as she pummelled the dough again. What real good had it done Grace to go to the Gages' school? If *any* of her children was to get book learning, Peggy reckoned it should have been Sam, her third. A clever lad, Sam, always good with figures, and handy with his pen as well. And George *had* sent him to school as a boy, and would have let him go on with the schooling, even seen him articled to Mr Ridley the attorney or some such thing, if that was what Sam had wanted. But Sam did not want. He saw that only hard work and good management kept the farm thriving in these difficult times, and protested that he wasn't going to leave his father short-handed now that he was big enough to do almost a man's job about the place. Yes, a good lad, Sam. It wasn't long before he had taken over the farm accounts entirely, and now, at twenty-two, his cleverness with figures was the wonder of his father and brothers. 'Many's the penny young Sam saves me,' George would boast. 'Many's the pound, come to that!'

But of course, you didn't send a girl to school for book learning. What you sent her for, so far as Peggy could see, was to pick up silly, fanciful notions from her fellow pupils. The piano had been provided after Grace informed her family, wistfully, 'Janey Meadows hev a pianny . . . *has a pianoforte,*' she had carefully corrected herself, Miss Gage's remembered reproofs ringing in her ears. So what must George do but buy his darling one as well? And if sitting in the parlour playing that genteel instrument led to *this* sort of thing, Peggy knew what *she* thought of pianos!

No, that was absurd! She pulled herself up short in her train of thought, sprinkled her dough with a little more flour and kneaded away. As the yeast began to work, the dough grew to a smooth, creamy puffiness under her capable hands, and the vigorous action helped to clear her mind. Blaming it all on a thing made of wood and wires and ivory—ridiculous! She was just looking for excuses. If a girl was going to do as Grace had done, it didn't make a bit of difference *how* she spent the rest of her time.

Better not to be so pretty, Peggy dismally supposed. With her looks, it wasn't surprising Grace had half the young men of the Marchinghams at her feet, but so far as her mother could tell, she wanted nothing to do with any of them. It was only some six weeks earlier that Mrs Hodson had begun, with a dreadful sinking of the heart, to suspect a change in this state of affairs.

She had gone to the bucket, kept decently hidden away in a closet, where she expected to find the cloths Grace wore during her monthly courses soaking, and found it empty. She stood there counting on her fingers. The girl's late for once, that's all, she told herself—although she was usually regular as clockwork. But Grace had a fastidious nature and didn't like to mention such matters, so Mrs Hodson, respecting her daughter's modesty, told herself not to pry —not yet.

She waited another couple of weeks, resolutely not prying, and then went again to take the rinsed, soaking cloths and wash them with her own. This time, the results of her finger counting appalled her.

Two months gone at least, she suspected. Possibly, even probably, longer. Could Grace herself tell? Had it been just one occasion, or more? Peggy thought very likely more. That would explain the daft, dreamy radiance which had surrounded her daughter for some weeks past. That would explain the times when Grace neglected the dairy even more than usual, and went off to visit former schoolmates in Great Marchingham (so she said), or to pick primroses in the woods, coming home after quite a long absence with a curiously sparse bunch of flowers, which had all the appearance of having been plucked in great haste.

Taxed with the empty bucket, Grace was not at all abashed.

'Oh, that,' she said airily. 'I did them myself, Ma. Didn't want to give you the trouble.'

Didn't want to give me the trouble! It was all Peggy could do not to snap her silly daughter's head off. That girl has got no sense at all, she thought. For the bucket had been not just empty, but dry as a bone. In her shoes, she thought, infuriated by Grace's transparent stupidity, I'd have had the wit to swill the thing out, make it look as if it *had* been used, to back my story up. Then she reproved herself; did she really wish her daughter a better liar? If only Grace would confide in her. She knew very well what effect the eventual, inevitable revelation would have on George, and Grace would need her mother to stand by her then.

Once she was sure she did Grace no injustice, and the matter was as serious as she feared, she had begun watching her daughter in good earnest, frustrating Grace's efforts to slip away on her own—though goodness only knew that was a case of shutting the stable door after the horse had gone. And then, three days ago, Grace managed to make her escape, without a word to anyone to say where she was going. Peggy went into her poultry yard to collect eggs, and on glancing into the dairy found the butter half churned, bowls of cream standing about all anyhow—and no Grace; only her apron, flung carelessly over her chair, as if she had been just waiting for her opportunity to run off the moment her mother's back was turned. Peggy had thought she was dressed rather fine for butter-making, with one of her prettiest print gowns on under the apron.

Gone to meet her lover of course. But where? And who was he? Mrs Hodson would dearly have liked to know.

When Grace came home, the dreamy light in her eyes was quenched. Peggy asked one or two sharp questions, but soon saw she was getting nowhere. Grace could be as obstinate as a donkey. Peggy's exasperation and anxiety were soon mitigated by concern, for everything about her daughter seemed sad and drooping, even to the natural waves and curls of her fair hair and the pretty pink ribbons on her gown.

That was three days ago, and Grace hadn't recovered her spirits since. Peggy paused in her kneading for a moment and went to the foot of the staircase. Unusually, mother and daughter were alone in the big farmhouse, for the hay harvest was being brought in. The weather had been fine for some while and the grass was in good condition: some fields were still to be mown, while others were ready for turning, or building into haycocks, or carting. George Hodson glanced at the sky and thought the fine spell wouldn't last much longer, so all hands were needed. But when Grace pleaded a headache, her father looked at her with loving solicitude.

'You do look peaky, my girl, and that's a fact.'

Mrs Hodson had glanced up from the big baskets of provisions she was packing for George, the boys and the two men hired to help them, so that no time need be wasted coming home to eat in the middle of the day. 'I'll be here to keep an eye on her, George. With all the boys to help, you won't be needing me, and I've baking to do.'

Thinking of Grace's wan face, she could well believe in the headache that now had her upstairs in bed. Not a peep out of her! It wasn't a sick headache, either, thought Peggy rather grimly. No, if Grace had been obliging enough to suffer from morning sickness in the common way, she could have been sure of her suspicions that much earlier. However, some women escaped the affliction. Peggy had never felt nausea in the mornings with her own five babies, and plainly her daughter took after her.

The busy activity of her hands was stilled. She covered the dough and set it to rise by the hearth in two large, brown earthenware basins. Hungry haymakers ate plenty of bread, and it had given her an excuse to stay at home with Grace. I'll let her be a little longer, thought Peggy, but then I *must* go up and speak to her.

She had fervently hoped that Grace would seize the

chance to confide in her mother of her own free will, that her frozen silence of the last few days would break and her defences come down at last. Because she must know I know, thought Peggy. She must know she'll soon begin to show her condition, and then she'll want help. It's all too plain the man has left her in the lurch—married, I suppose. Perhaps she thinks George will take it less to heart because she's always been his favourite? If so, little does she know her own father! Oh, dear goodness, what are we going to do?

And then, at last, she heard Grace upstairs. Not quietly tearful, or breaking into a storm of violent weeping, as she had half expected all morning. Instead, there came a cry of pain and terror from Grace's little bedroom; a sound of panic fear.

Carey had been at work, she thought, for at least three hours, though it didn't seem so long. With George Hodson's ready permission, she had been painting and drawing subjects from this hedgerow for the last two days. She was elated when she found the spot while exploring Brook End Farm for likely places: this was the best yet! Oh yes, said George, this hedge was an old 'un, and Carey nodded, unsurprised. One need not be a countrywoman to see that the hedgerow had nothing to do with modern enclosures, but had been standing for decades, even centuries, and harboured a rich variety of botanical specimens. Carey set to work with a will.

The haymakers, turning the grass in the field next to the place where she sat, were inclined to gape at first, as if she were some sideshow at a fair, but a brisk word from the farmer recalled them to their own tasks, and now they had gone on to mow the field on the other side of the hedgerow, out of her sight.

'Off sketching again?' her Cousin Clarissa had inquired, encountering her as she set out purposefully with her little folding stool, her painting and drawing materials, a broad-brimmed hat to shade her face, and a scarf in case the sun should beat down too strongly on the back of her neck.

'You must think I take it to extremes,' said Carey, smiling. 'But I can't tell you, cousin, how grateful I am for your

81

hospitality to me, with all my untidy painter's habits! I am so sorry if I put you out at all.'

'I had thought,' continued Lady Gerard, ignoring the fact that this apology obviously did not mean Carey was about to change her plans, 'I had thought we would drive into Great Marchingham and call upon some very agreeable acquaintances of mine whom you have not yet met.'

And be paraded before them with the implicit assumption that I'm Cousin Will's future bride, thought Carey, now the wiser for several calls upon Lady Gerard's very agreeable acquaintances. 'How very happy I shall be to meet your friends,' she said warmly, adding at once, 'but another time, please, not today, I beg you, for if I were to neglect such weather as this I really couldn't reconcile it with my conscience—or my undertaking to Professor Lindley.'

And she made her escape, leaving her cousin to reflect on two irritating circumstances: first, that Caroline had actually meant what she said about wishing to spend her time painting, and second, that Will showed not the least interest in diverting her from that occupation.

Brook End Farm was only a couple of miles from the Priory, its land adjoining the Home Farm, and a broad green lane led there. Sir William had kindly given Carey the use of a little dog-cart, but she thought she would go to her hedgerow on foot today: it was not so very far to carry her things. Passing the Home Farm by a route which cut a corner off her journey, she saw the cowman just emerging from one of the farm buildings. She had met the man before; he touched his cap and wished her good morning, and she stopped for a civil word. 'What a very handsome barn that is, Mr Fowler. I don't think I really noticed it until now.'

Fowler the cowman nodded. 'That want new thatch, though, when Mr Ben think we can run to that.'

She had previously heard him and some of the other men about the place mention this name, and said idly, 'He is the farm manager, I suppose?'

'He do manage the farm, yes,' agreed Fowler.

'But you, I am sure, manage the cattle.' Among those in the yard, she recognised a beast whose virtues he had been describing to her the other day, and greeted it. 'Good morning, Buttercup!' The creature's soft nose snuffled gently at her through the yard fence: it was evidently the cowman's favourite. As Carey listened with every appearance of interest to further details concerning Buttercup's calving prowess and phenomenal milk yield, she let her eyes wander around the farm buildings, and noticed for the first time that while some were in good repair, others were sadly dilapidated. The cowhouse and the carthorse stable, however, had been very neatly renovated, and given new thatch, and she could see that if the barn received similar treatment it would be an impressive building. 'Aye, we're sprucing the place up, bit by bit,' said Fowler, noticing the direction of her gaze.

Taking her leave of him, she was soon back at her hedgerow, to greet George Hodson and his haymakers and go on where she had left off the previous day. She spied a small clump of wild strawberry plants just beginning to flower—but they were in the shade, and could wait. The sun was rising higher, and if she wanted to capture the spray of briar roses in bud, which she had picked out yesterday as a good subject, she had better lose no time. Then she could return to paint the same spray later, when the flowers were fully open.

She worked fast, with concentration, and was surprised to see how high the sun had climbed when she sat back to examine her painting with a critical eye. It would do. The sound of scythes in the hayfield beyond the hedgerow had ceased, and she supposed the haymakers had stopped for rest and refreshment. She could do with refreshment herself but had not thought to bring anything with her. If she were to walk down to the farmhouse and beg a cup of tea from Mrs Hodson, would she find her new friend at home? She had not seen either Peggy or Grace at work in the hayfields, so she might as well try.

She gathered up her things and set off for the house. Skirting two fields, she reached the farmyard. Between yard and house were the long, low, whitewashed dairy and Mrs Hodson's well stocked poultry yard. A few pet guinea-fowl and bantams were pecking about, and scuttled out of her way, clucking, as she unlatched a white gate and went down the garden path, but otherwise the stillness and heat of midsummer held everything in a spell of silence. Tall lupins grew in Mrs Hodson's flowerbeds, with stocks and pansies, and beyond the garden, Carey knew, lay a paddock and an orchard of apple, pear and plum trees, with beehives standing among them.

On previous visits to the farmhouse, she had realised that the front door with its gleaming brass knocker was seldom used, so she went on along the gravel path around the house to the kitchen door, whose upper half stood open. Leaning in over the half-door, she called cheerfully, 'Mrs Hodson, are you there? It's only me—Mrs Elliott. May I come in?'

Next moment, the illusion of midsummer tranquillity was shattered.

It was as if the house briefly held its breath. Then came the sound of voices from upstairs: someone moaning in fright, and another alarmed voice trying to soothe those moans.

'Oh, don't go—don't you go down! Don't leave me!' Surely that was Grace? What could be the matter?

'Hush now, I must, there's someone at the door—oh, do lie still, Grace, just you lie still and I'll be back directly!' And Mrs Hodson came running downstairs, remarkably flustered for so calm a woman, even wild-eyed, her hair coming loose under her neat cap. She halted half-way down the staircase, trying to make out her visitor's face against the dazzling sun behind it, and Carey leaned over to undo the latch of the bottom half of the door and let herself in.

'Mrs Hodson—what is it?' She stepped into the room, laying down her folder of paintings on the broad sill of the big kitchen window. 'Can I help? What is the matter?' For plainly, something was very wrong indeed.

Mrs Hodson's first instinct was to get rid of her unwanted visitor by any means in her power, but seeing that Mrs Elliott appeared bent on coming in, she resigned herself to making the best of this new complication—after all, it might have been worse. She had taken a liking to Mrs Elliott, and thought she would be discreet, if asked. Besides, the lady didn't live in Marchingham, and would be gone again soon. 'Well, thank the Lord it's only you!' she said, letting out a small sigh.

Carey took this as the compliment it was. 'Is Grace ill? Surely I heard her voice, didn't I?'

'Ill?' With an effort, Mrs Hodson calmed herself. 'Whether you'd call it *ill* I don't know,' she said grimly, hurrying the rest of the way downstairs. She bent to lift a great pot of water to heat over the fire.

'Here, let me help,' said Carey, moving to do so, for the full pot was too heavy for one woman. 'Then Grace is not unwell?'

'Miscarrying. Miscarrying, that's what Grace is doing,' said Grace's mother, bluntly. 'Thank you, Mrs Elliott; I reckon I'll be needing hot water before long.'

'Miscarrying? Oh, dear me!' said Carey, dismayed, thinking of the pretty girl she had met in the dairy, and in this very kitchen with the rest of the family. 'Did you—does her father—that is to say, who knows?' For she was sure enough, from her brief greetings exchanged with George Hodson a couple of hours ago, that he for one did not.

Little, frightened whimpering sounds drifted down the stairs. 'I'm coming, just coming—I won't be a moment!' called Mrs Hodson. She bent to tend her fire. 'Who knows? Well, not George. I had my suspicions—and now I suppose it can't be hid from anyone,' she added bleakly. 'I dare say it's a mercy in its way, but—but she don't seem right to me, ma'am.' She was busy all the time she talked, fetching a pail, testing the temperature of the water as it heated, snatching a bundle of clean rags from a drawer. 'I never miscarried, you see,' she added, half to herself, 'so I don't rightly know how that should be. None of my family ever did, neither. We carry our children to full term—never any trouble. But—well, seems to me there's a deal too much blood,' she said, panic creeping into her voice as Grace's whimpering upstairs grew more distressing.

'It will be easier if we tip that water in the pail together,' said Carey, suiting the action to the words again. 'And then I'll come up with you.' Seeing Mrs Hodson about to protest, she continued, in matter-of-fact tones: 'You see, I *have* miscarried. It was while I was in India. And of course, I'm no physician myself, but my father is, so that I know just a little about such things. May I look at Grace, Mrs Hodson? Then perhaps I could tell you how much cause there is for alarm.'

Peggy Hodson's first impulse was still horrified refusal, but Carey, brushing her protests briskly aside, was on her way upstairs already. One glance at Grace, lying terrified on her bed, her flower-like face marred with misery, was enough to show that there was indeed cause for concern. A great deal of blood, as the child's mother had said; more than Carey would have expected, far more, she was almost sure, than there should have been. Casting her mind back to her own miscarriage, she tried to remember whether she had bled quite so much, or so fast. She rather thought not, though of course she had been in no state to notice details at the time. But she did remember helping the young wife of one of the Indian servants, when she too lost a baby, and soothing Meera as best she might until a quantity of the girl's female relatives arrived, clucking busily, to take over. She did not recollect that Meera's condition had been quite so bad; the poor girl's distress had been largely for what her mother-in-law would say. And Carey felt something else nagging at her mind: could Grace's present panic be ascribed solely to ignorance? She was a farmer's daughter, after all, and must have some notion of what was happening to her.

It was at this point that Carey's glance fell upon an object lying discarded on the floor. She would have pushed it out of sight somewhere, but Peggy Hodson, following the direction of her gaze, was too quick for her. She bent and picked up the sharp-pointed, narrow-bowled spoon.

'Oh, you wicked girl! To do such a terrible thing to yourself!' cried Mrs Hodson, but Grace only wailed in fresh grief and pain.

'I didn't, Ma, I never did! I didn't!' And more blood flowed, soaking into the rags Carey had wrung out in water and was gently applying as she did her best to assess the situation.

'She must have a doctor,' she said presently, straightening up. 'How far gone was she, do you know?' Poor Peggy could only shake her head. 'Grace, listen to me, please!'

86

Carey continued firmly. 'Grace, how long have you been expecting this child? The doctor will need to know.'

There was another piteous wail from Grace. 'I don't want no doctor!' she cried, Roberta Gage's carefully inculcated lessons in grammar forsaking her. 'I want my *baby!*'

'Too late to think of that now,' said her mother grimly. 'You went the right way about getting rid of it, didn't you, then?'

And perhaps herself, too, if we can't get a doctor to her quickly, thought Carey, but left that unspoken as she drew Peggy over to the window, and said quietly, 'Mrs Hodson, I don't want to alarm you unduly, and I hope all will be well, but as you said yourself, there can be no hiding this now. She *is* bleeding too much, just as you thought—which is not to be wondered at. The thing is to get a doctor to her as soon as possible.'

'I *won't* have no doctor!' wept Grace mutinously.

'Oh, do be quiet, you bad girl!' cried her exasperated and terrified mother. 'Supposing you should die—oh, dear Lord, don't let her die!' Then, sensible woman that she was, she pulled herself together and spoke more calmly. 'Yes, of course, the doctor—oh, Mrs Elliott, if you would go to the field and find one of the boys? Ask him to run up here, quick as he may, and I'll send him for Dr Goodwin. Get Sam, if you can . . .'

But here she paused, for they could both hear the steady sound of a horse's hooves approaching the farmhouse. Looking out of the window, Carey saw a serviceable cob rounding the corner of the path. Its rider hitched the horse to a post and walked to the kitchen door. Now here, thought Carey apprehensively, is a complication. Mrs Hodson, in tones of relief, cried, 'Oh, thank God! It's Mr Ben—he will go for the doctor, I'm sure!'

The name seemed familiar: yes, Carey remembered, the manager of the Home Farm. Peggy Hodson moved towards the door, but Grace caught her hand as she passed, clung to it, sobbing, and would not let go. Mrs Hodson awkwardly patted her daughter's head with her other hand and tried to pull away, but Grace clung all the harder.

'It's all right, Mrs Hodson—you stay here with her, and I'll go down,' said Carey quickly. She was half-way to the kitchen already as the newcomer leaned in over the half-door, as she herself had done, calling out, 'Peggy? Is there anyone at home?'

This was no time for anything but the most rapid of explanations. 'Mrs Hodson is upstairs, sir,' said Carey, 'And if you please, would you go for a doctor? I was about to run to the fields to find one of the young men, but then we heard you coming and Mrs Hodson thought—you will go, won't you? It's Grace—you know Grace? The daughter. She is very ill, and I believe the matter is urgent.'

'Yes, of course I'll go.' He glanced around the kitchen, seeing the dough rising unheeded in its bowls and the huge pot of water hissing over the fire. 'Grace is ill? What's the matter? Dr Goodwin will ask me.'

Carey hesitated. However, this was plainly someone Peggy Hodson trusted, 'Well, after all, he will have to know. She's miscarrying. We've been trying to find out how far gone she was, but to no avail. To be blunt—well, you had better tell the doctor she tried to get rid of the baby and something seems to have gone wrong. She's bleeding heavily—far more than she ought—so if you could go, and at once . . . ?'

Mercifully, the farm manager was evidently not a man to stand about uttering useless exclamations in an emergency. He turned to leave. 'Tell Peggy I'll have Dr Goodwin here as soon as I possibly can,' he called, and was gone, riding his cob away up the lane again very much faster than he had come.

Three hours later a midsummer calm lay over the farm-house once more. It was hard to believe, thought Carey, coming downstairs as the doctor drove away in his neat little gig, that it had ever been shattered. After all the drama of midday, she felt quite weak, but was thankful for the sake of both Grace and Peggy that matters were no worse. Dr Goodwin had certainly looked grave at first, but by the time he arrived Carey had managed to calm his patient a little and make her lie still, and when she could finally be induced to say exactly what she had done to herself, he seemed relieved; *that* accounted for the excessive bleeding, he said, and fortunately it had already begun to slacken, thanks to the sensible treatment of Grace by this lady (with a brisk nod at Carey). As she had thrust no further in, no permanent harm should be done. Yes, she'd live, the doctor assured Mrs Hodson, as tears of thankfulness ran down the mother's cheeks. He left her some medicaments. 'And Grace had better take this now, to make her sleep,' he added before leaving.

Exhausted and miserable, Grace obediently swallowed the laudanum, but seemed ready to shed more tears when her mother made as if to leave the bedroom.

'You stay with her until she falls asleep, Mrs Hodson,' said Carey quietly. 'I know what would do *you* good now, and that's a cup of tea.' It seemed much more than some three hours ago that she had walked into the farmhouse, hoping to request just such a thing for herself, and now she realised how very welcome it would be. 'I expect I shall find tea in the kitchen? Good, then I will bring you some soon.'

She had quite forgotten the farm manager, and indeed had not realised that he had accompanied the doctor back to Brook End Farm, but there he was, rather unexpectedly closing the iron door of the brick oven upon a quantity of burning faggots. 'I think your dough's risen.' he announced, and added, looking up, 'Oh, I beg your pardon. I thought it was Peggy.'

'She's upstairs, waiting for Grace to fall asleep. What *are* you doing?'

'Firing her oven for her. If she's to have any hope of keeping this wretched business from George Hodson, she'll want some semblance of normality here when he and the boys come home. With the fine weather holding, they won't be back till near dusk, so there's a reasonable chance.'

'Goodness me,' said Carey, taking in this speech. 'Do you think it *might* be kept from poor Mr Hodson? Surely there could be no harm in that—only good, if it's possible. Yes, why not? I believe Grace said she had a headache —and the doctor has both been *and* gone. I suppose he won't trouble George Hodson with information, unless he's asked? Here,' said Carey, pushing up the sleeves of her lilac chintz walking dress, 'I'd better shape that dough, then.'

It was lucky that Mrs Hodson had been conducting the

identical operation when Carey visited the farm before. She set to work to form the dough into cottage loaves, trying to remember just how the thing was done if the topknot was to stick properly to the main part of the loaf, and frowning slightly with concentration. She then placed the loaves on the large, flat wooden shovel which Mrs Hodson had told her was called a 'peel', and stood back to look at them, feeling quite pleased with her novice handiwork. Glancing up, she saw that the farm manager was still there, seated in a chair at the window, and regarding her with a trace of amusement.

'Very creditable! Your first effort in the bakery line, is it?'

'I suppose that's all too obvious . . . very well, so they are *not* perfectly regular,' she ruefully confessed. 'But I don't suppose it will matter very much.'

'No, the Hodsons will be too hungry from haymaking to examine them for perfection of form,' he agreed. Then she saw that he had her folder of work open on the window seat beside him. Uttering a swift exclamation of dismay, she moved to snatch it up.

'Forgive me,' he said, a little guiltily. 'These must be yours—the folder lay open, and when I had seen the painting of the wild rosebuds here, I own I couldn't resist looking at the others. They are remarkable! I hope you don't mind.'

In the normal way Carey *would* have minded, a great deal. She did not like anyone to see her work before it was finished. But her new acquaintance was examining the flower sketches with such genuine interest that she felt it would be ungracious to take offence. She looked at him properly for the first time: a pleasant, gentleman-like man in his early thirties, quite tall, with a lean, spare look about him, like one who spent much of his time out of doors, and plainly dressed as befitted his calling, though his speech and manner were those of an educated man, as no doubt he was. Estate management, she knew, was a respectable occupation for the younger sons of the gentry, and goodness knows the Priory can do with some management, she thought.

'No, look if you like,' she said. 'After all, the pictures are eventually intended for other people's eyes. I think it is time we introduced ourselves, don't you?'

'On the evidence,' said the gentleman, civilly handing her back her folder, 'I conclude you must be that Mrs Elliott who paints the flowers.'

'A reasonable deduction,' she agreed, smiling, and then —'Dear me, why are you looking at me like that? Have I got flour on my nose, or what?'

'No,—was I staring? I must ask your pardon again. It's just that you are not at all what one had expected.' .

'Ah, I see! I collect I was previously known by repute in this locality as "the Indian lady", and have occasioned general disappointment by leaving all my more exotic finery at home. I'm staying at the Priory, by the way, with my cousins the Gerards.'

'Yes, I know.'

'And you, I believe,' Carey pursued, 'are Mr Benn—is it spelt with two "n"s? But I don't know your first name.' He was looking a little amused. 'Haven't I guessed right? I was talking to Fowler the cowman as I walked through the Home Farm this morning, and I took it you were the farm manager he mentioned. Oh, good heavens, the tea!' she suddenly exclaimed. 'I almost forgot! Do you know where Mrs Hodson keeps it?'

'On the shelf there—here you are. Yes, you have my name right, but it is my first name. I'm Benedict Gerard.'

'Good God!' said Carey blankly, and really, as she thought too late, rather impolitely. Tea caddy in hand, she swung round to look at him with frank curiosity. So this was poor Benedict, the object of Clarissa's sympathy. Carey could not for the life of her see why he deserved it. He did not look at all as if he needed to be pitied—a man who had been an unobtrusive tower of strength that afternoon, and even now, in a very practical way, was opening the door of the bread oven to rake out the ashes. The brick cavity gave off a fierce heat as he picked up the peel and placed the loaves inside. Readjusting a number of her ideas as she made the pot of tea, Carey was relieved from the necessity of any immediate comment by Mrs Hodson, who now came downstairs.

'She's asleep. Well, thank the Lord, is what I say!' Peggy

dropped gratefully into the chair Mr Gerard pulled out for her. 'And thank *you* too, Mrs Elliott, and Mr Ben—I don't know what I'd have done without the two of you today. It's bad enough as it is, but I feared worse. Though what George will say, I dread to think.'

Understandably, she seemed on the verge of tears and Carey was quick to set a cup of tea in front of her. Pouring tea for herself and Mr Gerard she said matter-of-factly, 'Mrs Hodson, Mr Gerard and I have been thinking. Since Grace is going to be all right, we believe Mr Hodson may not need to know about this after all.'

Mrs Hodson, sipping hot tea, revived a little. 'Do you know, well, I'm half ashamed to say it, but I was almost wondering the same myself,' she said slowly. 'I can pay Dr Goodwin out of my egg money—George would never know—and he's no tale-bearer, not the doctor.'

'No, indeed. I'll have a word with him myself,' said Mr Gerard. 'Leave that to me—and then, why shouldn't it be kept between the four of us? Five, if we count Grace herself.'

'Aye, she knows all about it, to be sure,' said her mother drily. 'But will she tell me who the man was? Not Grace! Poor silly girl, it seems she thought he'd marry her. Oh, I wish,' said Mrs Hodson, with some venom, 'I wish I could get my hands on him! Who may *he* be to interfere with the daughter of a respected man like my George, and not think her good enough to marry? Mind, Grace is much to blame too. But at least she'll live!' She heaved a great sigh of relief and reached up to press the soothing hand Mr Gerard placed on her shoulder. 'No, I don't deny she did very wrong, but what's the good in poor George knowing? Lord knows, Grace is punished enough. But I blame myself too,' she fiercely concluded. 'To think she wouldn't tell her own mother when she was in such trouble!'

'Don't distress yourself, Mrs Hodson,' begged Carey, seeing tears start to the poor woman's eyes again, and Mr Gerard said in the same moment, 'Hush, Peggy, there was nothing you could have done, as I'm sure your own good sense tells you.'

Mrs Hodson drank her tea, stifled her tears, and tried bravely to smile. 'Only, I don't know that it can be kept between us. Dr Goodwin said Grace is to lie abed for some days and do no heavy kind of work for a while, and how am I to explain that?'

'She must do just as the doctor says, of course,' Carey instantly agreed, remembering her exhaustion after her own miscarriage.

'I *could* tell George she has her courses very badly. For one thing,' said George's devoted wife, thinking aloud, 'that will embarrass him, so he won't ask too many questions, particularly if it seems I'm about to tell him all the details.' She managed a wan smile.

Mr Gerard was evidently pleased to see it. 'Very true,' he solemnly agreed. 'But I suppose that won't serve for more than a few days? No, I thought not—and she can hardly go out working in the fields with her brothers as she usually does at this time of year.'

'Does she? She has so delicate an appearance,' said Carey, surprised.

'Appearance is as appearance does. Strong as a horse, our Grace, in the general way, and able to turn hay with the best if she likes,' said Mrs Hodson briskly, 'as George well knows, and the boys too. Yes, what's to be done? I can give her work in the dairy, of course, in a few days' time, and then do it for her when no one's about to notice. But what she ought to do is sit idle in the parlour—and I never thought the day would come I'd say *that!*'

'Wait!' said Carey suddenly. 'I have an idea. Might she not just as well sit idle in the *garden*? Or not entirely idle, but sitting to me for her portrait. I told you of my book of flowers, Mrs Hodson, didn't I? My *Floral Companion*?'

'Is that it?' inquired Mr Gerard, his gaze straying back to the folder on the window-sill.

'Part of it, yes. It's a project I am executing at the suggestion of John Lindley of the Horticultural Society; but never mind that just now. I am sure it was in your husband's hearing I complimented you on your pretty garden the other day, wasn't it, Mrs Hodson?'

The farmer's wife nodded.

'So suppose I take a fancy to have a picture of a lovely young country girl, surrounded by flowers, for a frontispiece? Flora herself, as it were? And once that notion comes into my head, of course I see Grace as the perfect subject for my brush. She would be, too! So I have asked you to let me paint her, sitting in the garden. We should thus have an excuse to move into the parlour, taking a few flowers with us, if the weather was inclement. And you, Mrs Hodson,' said Carey, warming to her theme, 'did not like to refuse me! I shall pay, of course; you may tell Mr Hodson that models are always paid. As she is such a favourite with him, I expect he'll like the idea of her picture being painted, won't he?'

'Yes, but with the hay harvest, and all . . .'' ventured Mrs Hodson, doubtfully. 'Some other time, he'll likely say.'

'Ah, and that is just what *you* said to me yourself, but my work must be done now and can't be delayed because . . . because the flowers are at their very best, and so is the light, and—oh, you don't know what else I said to you, but it was a great deal, even if you did not perfectly understand it all, and I was so pressing you didn't like to say me nay. And Grace must wait in for me, you know, even if I can't come every day, and no, I cannot say just when that will be, so she will not be able to work on the farm, or I shall be provoked. I am a very capricious lady.'

'Are you, indeed?' remarked Mr Gerard, with some scepticism.

'Yes, *exceedingly* capricious!' replied Carey firmly. 'I have always been used to getting my own way, you see. It comes of being rich and spoilt. I have whims, and fancies, which make me inconsiderate of others.'

'Now that I will *not* say!' protested Mrs Hodson indignantly. 'But for you, Mrs Elliott, I don't know how I'd have managed today.'

'How long would the picture take you?' Mr Gerard was bending his mind to practicalities again.

'Oh, as long as it's necessary for Grace to be convalescent. Mr Hodson won't know how long such a picture ought to take. I can always undo some of my work in the evening if it seems to be getting on too fast, like Penelope with her web, and begin again next day. And you needn't be thinking it's any sacrifice on my part, Mrs Hodson,' she added swiftly, 'because I can import my own models, my field and hedgerow flowers, into your garden, and paint some cottage garden flowers too, as Professor Lindley himself suggested; so it will all be very useful to me. Besides, you know, Grace *is* enchantingly lovely and, true to her name, would grace any book. And I *shall* require a frontispiece, after all! So let us agree it's an innocent device for Mr Hodson's own peace of mind, and that's all settled.'

7

'Was there any truth in that—the last part of it, I mean?'
inquired Mr Gerard, walking his horse up the lane beside
Carey, who had protested that she really needed no escorting back to the Priory, but did not demur when he pointed
out that he was going that way in any case. The fact was
that, now she had time to think of it, she was intrigued to
meet this last member of the Gerard family, who was so
very unlike anything she had been led to expect. On the
evidence of their short but eventful acquaintance, Cousin
Clarissa's 'poor Benedict' seemed a distinctly resourceful
gentleman, of pleasing appearance and manner, even if he
had not Will's striking good looks—but then, neither was
his face marred by Will's habitual expression of boredom
and discontent.

'What was that you said?' She heard the echo of his
question still ringing in her ears. 'Any truth in it? You
mean, do I really require a frontispiece showing Grace in
the character of rustic maiden? Good heavens, no! It's a
botanical book I am engaged upon, not an album of pictures
of pretty country girls. But then I thought I might just as
well let Mrs Hodson think I genuinely did wish for such a
picture, because it would make her feel less beholden
to me. I'm afraid my friend Hetty, who used to be my
governess, would say one should not practise such little
deceptions.'

'I hope she would agree that this one was both kind and
thoughtful,' said Mr Gerard, which Carey found silenced
her, and they went on up the lane together in a mutual but
companionable silence. She was carrying the greater part of
her painting equipment, but had left the rest behind at
Brook End farmhouse, by way of helping Peggy Hodson

break the news of Grace's new career as artist's model to her husband. Also left behind was a kitchen in its accustomed state of spotless order, the cottage loaves deliciously scenting the air, while Grace slept quietly upstairs, pale and drained, but with a faint flush of pink returning to her cheeks beneath her still swollen eyelids.

Remembering this picture, glimpsed just before they left, Carey said, 'Poor Grace. I wonder who the wretched man is who got the poor child into such a situation?'

'I own I am surprised by the whole affair,' said Mr Gerard thoughtfully. 'It's not what I would have expected of Grace; she may be a featherheaded little thing, but Peggy had the rearing of her, after all.'

'You are very fond of Mrs Hodson, I think?'

'Very fond: she was nurserymaid at the Priory when I was a small child, serving her apprenticeship under a fierce dragon of a nurse from London. Peggy was very good to me when my mother died. You must have seen how well she manages her house and family, and I need hardly tell you she's a woman of the strictest principles, which she has certainly tried to teach Grace.'

'I am not sure,' said Carey, 'that we are doing poor silly Grace justice. Of course she did wrong, but I rather think, from what little she would say, that the man either promised to marry her, or let her assume the promise was as good as made; and so, loving him, she forsook those strict principles of Peggy's. You'll say it's a hackneyed story, and I agree, but I dare say it seems new to every girl who wants to believe a man's protestations of love. Oh dear! I do most sincerely pity Grace.'

'She must indeed have been desperate to do such a thing to herself.'

'Try to abort the child, you mean? Well, the sad fact is that she *wasn't* trying to do so. It seems that when this man abandoned her she was much distressed, but all the more determined to have the baby. That's how I know she did love him, you see, and it was not just thoughtless indiscretion. Perhaps, too, she thought the coming child might bring her lover back to her—nothing less likely, of course, but girls in love are apt to take such illogical notions into their heads. So, though I dare say you will scarcely credit this, when the miscarriage began, she started trying to do quite the opposite of what Mrs Hodson and I at once supposed. Did you see that spoon? I believe Dr Goodwin brought it downstairs.'

Mr Gerard nodded, looking at her rather curiously.

'Having little knowledge of her own anatomy or physiology,' Carey continued, 'she thought it might be possible to use the thing to stop the flow when she felt herself begin to bleed, or even return it to the place whence it came; to spoon it back, so to speak. You might well expect more common sense in a farmer's daughter, but poor Grace was in a panic.'

'Poor Grace, indeed! There's not much common sense in her to start with, I'm afraid.'

'So of course she made matters much worse: in her frantic state she must have done some injury to the neck of the womb, tearing the tissues around it,' said Carey, in practical tones. 'But she had *not*, as I at once assumed, tried to dilate it, or thrust anything up inside the uterus, you see. Dr Goodwin believes that although the damage she did to the cervical tissues accounts for the great blood loss which so alarmed us, it was not too serious and will soon heal up. Why are you staring at me again? I am a physician's daughter, you know, so you needn't be surprised by my knowing these things.'

'Not surprised—impressed!' said Mr Gerard, leading his horse on again, for they had come almost to a standstill as Carey told her tale.

'So now,' she said, 'let us change the subject, and you may tell me how it is that I have not met you before when I have been here above a week.'

'I have been in Norwich for some days, on estate business, and then—'

But here Carey interrupted him. They were taking the same short cut as she had employed that morning, and had reached the farmyard. 'Why, of course! It *was* you!' she exclaimed. 'In this very yard! Oh, I beg your pardon, I interrupted you. But we have in fact met before, and there *were* two boys, just as I told my father. However, I see you don't remember *me*!'

'Should I?' He sounded civil, but puzzled.

'No, I suppose not. At least, I was a scrubby little thing of five or six years old at the time, and tearful into the bargain. But you rescued my doll for me, didn't you? She was no beauty, but I was greatly attached to that doll.'

'Good God, were you *that* little girl?' Their walk was proceeding very much by fits and starts, for Mr Gerard stopped again to look harder at her, and Carey, returning this scrutiny, was interested to see a quite unusually attractive smile spread over his features. She had received hints of it before, she now realised, but the stress of the afternoon's events had scarcely allowed for much smiling. 'No, I wouldn't have known you again. Scrubby and tearful, did you say?'

'Well, yes, but I wasn't fishing for compliments.'

'I didn't suppose so. But I *do* remember the incident very well; indeed, it is engraved upon my memory by the circumstance of my having been thrashed for it.' Mr Gerard threw his head back and laughed heartily.

Carey did not feel at all disposed to laugh, but was retrospectively indignant. 'What, for rescuing my doll? Why, it was excessively kind of you! Brave too, I am sure, for the cattle appeared to me very large beasts, and there was a bull in one pen—no one else dared go near him. I suppose you were thrashed for foolhardiness.'

'No, for knocking down my little brother, as I recollect.'

'Did you?'

'I didn't, though I might well have been tempted to!' He clicked his tongue to the horse, and they moved on again.

'Oh!' Carey pondered this. 'You mean Cousin Will said you did. Well, he was an odious child, and it is just what one might have expected of him. Still, what a shameful fib.' For the first time during the conversation, she found herself shaken out of her good humour, and said, with vexation in her voice, 'Oh dear! It is rather late to apologise to you. I hardly know what to say.'

Mr Gerard seemed surprised. 'Why, it was of no importance at all. I wouldn't have mentioned it, Mrs Elliott, if I hadn't thought it would amuse you.'

'Then you have a very odd notion of my sense of humour. And please don't call me Mrs Elliott in that formal way. We may not be flesh and blood relations, Cousin

Benedict—no, we can't be, can we, when you are Sir William's son by his first wife?—but it is near enough, and anyway I should like you for my cousin, so let's adopt each other, as it were.'

A suggestion of the smile showed again. 'Are you always so direct, Cousin Caroline?'

'I believe so,' said Carey, a little ruefully. 'The governess I mentioned to you used to reprove me for it. But we had no time for the social graces this afternoon, and I really cannot bring myself to feel we are strangers now. You will just have to forgive me—oh, and my name is commonly shortened to Carey. Goodness, here we are at the Priory already! I take it we say nothing at dinner but that we chanced to meet at Brook End Farm?'

'At dinner?'

'Why, yes. I shall see you at dinner, shan't I?'

'I don't always . . .' Mr Gerard hesitated. 'That is, I frequently keep different hours from the rest of the family; I have a couple of rooms of my own, so that I need disturb no one coming or going.' But as she glanced at him in some surprise the smile returned with a spark of mischief in it. 'Oh yes,' said Mr Gerard firmly. 'I shall be at dinner tonight.'

My dearest Papa, my dearest Hetty (wrote Carey), I hope you both go on as well in London as I do here. The *Floral Companion* continues, I think, to make reasonable progress. The weather has been kind and the flowers very patient—so much more obliging, as sitters, than the human variety! You will point out, correctly enough, that I say so only because I have no true talent for depicting the human figure. Unfortunately, I have committed myself, perforce, to sketching a positive gallery of my hosts here—but I shall come to that soon.

As for Marchingham itself, it proves a most interesting place. In your last letter, Papa, you thought I must find it tame after India. Not a bit of it! Take today, for instance, which was full of stirring events . . .

Here Carey paused, laid down her pen, walked to her bedroom window, opened it, and leaned a little way out to

100

breathe the cool night air. She almost fancied she could catch the fragrance of hay drifting over the fields from Brook End Farm. An eventful day indeed. So much so that she found her mind far too active to allow her to sleep just yet, although the Whittiers, after dining at the Priory, had left, and the Gerards themselves had gone to bed. Now, however, she found herself on the point of telling Grace's story, and on sober reflection she thought she had better not. It was not hers to tell, even though her father and Hetty were unknown to the Hodson family and never likely to meet them. She must make do with the other incidents of her day.

She sat down again at the little writing desk in her room, moved the lamp so that its light fell directly on her paper, and wrote on:

> . . . full of stirring events, involving cows, and haymakers, and a visit to my friend Mrs Hodson. And I must tell you that I have now met the one remaining member of the Gerard family: my cousin Benedict. That is to say, of course he is not really my cousin, but as I find him better company than the younger Mr Gerard, who *is*, I have therefore adopted him in that capacity. It is plain enough that no great degree of liking exists between him and his stepmama, although why she is in the habit of referring to him as 'poor Benedict' I still have not discovered.

Laying her pen down again, Carey fell to musing: could it be that the elder Mr Gerard had suffered some accident or illness as a child, rendering it impossible for him to produce an heir to the Priory? Cousin Clarissa seemed so certain of that. Such unfortunate things did happen; she would rather have liked to ask her father about it. Then she chided herself for vulgar curiosity. What business was it of hers? Sir John could hardly make a diagnosis at a distance of a hundred miles, and how shocked Hetty would be by her even speculating on such subjects!

There are unforeseen problems in writing to the two of them at once, thought Carey. But I think, after all, I can answer my own question: no, it is not likely Benedict has suffered any misfortune so conclusive, or I fancy Cousin Clarissa would not scruple to tell me all about it.

She resumed writing:

> At all events, we had the pleasure of the elder Mr Gerard's company at dinner, as well as that of Mr and Mrs Whittier. I believe we all passed an agreeable evening. It seems that Benedict does not always dine with the family when he is at home, but Sir William was evidently pleased to see him back from estate business in Norfolk, so tonight's was a pleasant gathering . . .

She had not, of course, witnessed the degree of astonishment displayed by her Cousin Clarissa on hearing that her stepson would be eating his dinner with them, or her vulgar curiosity might have been yet further aroused. The information was conveyed by Miss Howlett the lady's maid, after a whispered conversation with Long the butler and a discreet knock on her ladyship's door. One did not show displeasure in front of the servants, so it fell to Sir William to bear the weight of his wife's annoyance, and his own reception of the news made it no better. For when she walked through the communicating door between her husband's dressing room and her own, to pass the butler's message on to him, he perceptibly brightened, saying with rather less than his usual vagueness, 'Ben coming for dinner, eh? Good! Glad to hear it! Haven't seen him since he got home from Norfolk . . . have I? No, don't think so. Dare say he'll like to tell me how matters went there.'

It had taken some time for the full force of Clarissa's austere gaze to make itself felt, but at this point her husband did become aware of it, and his voice trailed away.

'Not, however, at dinner!' pronounced Lady Gerard. 'I will not have agricultural matters discussed at my table, if you please, Sir William. My intention in inviting the Whittiers to dine was to provide dear Caroline with an evening of cultured conversation; she will not care for tedious discussion of the merits of various breeds of cattle.'

It passed fleetingly through Sir William's mind that only the cattle made it possible for his wife to set a good dinner before her guests. Hadn't Ben and that cowman of his taken prizes at some show or other with the herd they were building up? He was pretty sure it was something like that. Still, he didn't feel equal to reminding Clarissa of the circumstance. His mind wandered back to another of her remarks and he inquired, 'Didn't tell me before that the Whittiers were coming, did you?'

'Yes, I told you so yesterday,' said Lady Gerard patiently. 'And the day before, and if my memory serves me correctly, this morning too.'

'Taylor coming as well?' asked Sir William hopefully.

'He is not!' said Lady Gerard, and shut her mouth very tight.

'Ah. Pity,' ventured Sir William. 'Good company, Tiberius Taylor.'

'That,' said Lady Gerard, preserving her patience only with difficulty, 'that may be your opinion, Sir William. Only too well do I remember the last occasion upon which Mr Taylor came to dine. And Augusta, who then assured me that it *would* be the last occasion, has not, I am glad to say, forgotten her promise.'

'Livened things up a bit, did he?' Sir William searched his memory for any details of this dinner party, which he had quite forgotten.

'One can hardly deny that!'

'Entertaining fellow, Taylor, I've always thought.'

'If you consider it entertaining to hear Mr Taylor address highflown sentiments of the most extravagant nature to every female present, not excluding the parlourmaid, I can only tell you, Sir William, that I beg to differ. Extravagant, did I say? Worse! They were positively suggestive!'

'Apt to put 'em in Latin, though, ain't he? The sentiments, I mean. Which the parlourmaid don't understand. Don't recollect the lingo too well myself, these days,' said Sir William, a trifle wistfully. 'Still, I suppose you're right. I mean, of course you're right, my dear,' he hastily added. 'And Caroline might understand the Latin, eh? Had a deal of education for a girl; too much of it for Will's liking, I'd say. If you were to ask me, I'd say she ain't in his style. I thought not, all along. More in Ben's style, if you were to ask me.'

Although he might have delivered this entire speech, unusually long and coherent as it was, on purpose to provoke Clarissa, she was a fair-minded woman and absolved him of any such deliberate intention. She knew the amiable vacuity of her husband's mind all too well. His oldest friends privately considered him only half the man he had been before the death of his beloved first wife, believing he had never quite got over it, even when he became enamoured of the handsome and determined Clarissa. After marriage, that infatuation had passed over, as infatuations do, to be replaced by habit and a certain wariness of his wife's temper, for Sir William liked a quiet life, and would do much to avoid trouble.

He could not but see, however, that Benedict did not get on with his stepmother, and went in no particular awe of her either. He supposed—regretfully, since it meant he saw less of the son who reminded him so much of his dear, dead Anne—that it was better for two such strong-minded characters to keep out of one another's way. There had been trouble of some sort between them during one of Ben's Oxford vacations, that much Sir William *did* know, although he had preferred not to inquire too closely into its precise nature. Something to do with a girl, he fancied . . .

However, he could not help being aware of the cause of their violent disagreement when Ben came down from Oxford, and insisted, whatever anyone said, on looking at the accounts and all the other business records of the estate. He could not help being aware of it because Ben had appealed to him for support, which he had really been obliged to give, and it was most distressing. For upon emerging from a morning's study of the documents he had demanded to see, the young man immediately proposed the dismissal of the inefficient estate manager who had brought things to such a pass.

This manager, one Mr Doddington, owed his place to Lady Gerard's kind offices, and never ceased to make it plain that he regarded her as his generous patroness, so it was decidedly awkward all round. Lady Gerard had opposed Benedict, claiming that he was far too young and inexperienced to know anything about it, and saw only surface appearances.

'I can tell when surface appearances are all that there is to be seen,' had said Benedict, rather grimly, 'and as for experience, ma'am, I'm plainly about to acquire plenty of that!'

'And don't you spare a thought for poor Mr Doddington?' inquired his stepmother. 'Mr Doddington, who has done his best for us all these years? It is not his fault if there are such charges on the estate as must be necessary, with two young gentlemen to be maintained in a proper style. And I am sure,' said Lady Gerard, with the air of one producing her trump card, 'that we shall never find another manager for the Home Farm and all the estate affairs willing to work for so moderate a salary.'

Benedict's perusal of the accounts had in fact caused him to think a little remorsefully of some of his own Oxford expenses; reasonable enough in all conscience, but there were things, he told himself, he would have gone without, had he known how matters really stood at home. Slightly stung, therefore, by the justice of Lady Gerard's first point, he had said, 'We'll leave Will to maintain the character of a young gentleman in a proper style. Now he's left school I'm sure he will do it admirably. As for finding a replacement for Doddington, I intend to manage the place myself.'

He had wondered, since, whether it would not have been better for everyone if he had placed the full facts before his half-brother at that time, and urged him to share in the attempt to retrieve the family fortunes. But it seemed hard on the lad. He himself had known nothing of all this at Will's age: no, let Will enjoy a few of those youthful follies to which he already seemed much inclined, and he'd settle down later, thought Benedict—too optimistically, he now acknowledged. The result was that with half a dozen years between them, and very dissimilar natures, the brothers had grown yet farther apart, the more so as Will became older and developed expensive tastes which his mother liked to see gratified. Obliged, more than once, to go in person and extricate Will from some fix or other, Benedict came to wish very much they had been closer, if only because it would have eased the awkwardness of such situations. However, there was no help for it now, and it

105

was between himself and Lady Gerard, always her son's champion, that the sparks really flew. Even Sir William was aware of it.

Still, the sparks couldn't fly in company, the old man told himself. He liked the Whittiers, and young Caroline too: nice girl, no trouble to anyone, took herself off sketching all day long—very ladylike sort of an occupation—pity in a way Clarissa didn't go in for some such thing, might occupy her mind, make her a little less . . . less . . . but loyalty stopped his train of thought at this point. In any case, he promised himself an agreeable evening, and duly enjoyed one.

So too did Mrs Elliott, as she was now recording in her letter.

> . . . and tonight's was a pleasant gathering, although, as we waited in the drawing room for dinner to be served, I must confess I had my fears, for my Cousin Clarissa looked very much out of humour. I'm afraid I chattered away to fill that awkward silence which descends upon company while it is gradually assembling. I wonder why no one has invented some civilised custom to occupy that time, such as the offering of a glass of wine or ratafia to precede dinner? Perhaps I shall invent it myself, when I have my own household again.

This passage was to occasion a mild flutter in Mrs Pauling's romantic breast when the letter arrived in London: 'Oh, John, she *is* thinking of re-marriage! I knew she would come round to the idea in time. See what she says—her own household again! But can it be her cousin William? She does not sound as if she likes him much. Not, of course,' Hetty wisely added, 'that love and liking necessarily go hand in hand.'

'No, and which do you feel for me, eh?' inquired Sir John, leaning over her shoulder to look again at his daughter's letter.

'Both, to be sure, John! Don't be so ridiculous! So I can't wish less for dear Carey, can I?'

'In any case, I wouldn't agitate yourself just yet,' said Sir

John. 'If I know Carey, all she envisages is setting up house on her own.'

But this was so unwelcome a notion to Hetty that she had to shake her head vigorously, by way of dismissing it, before she read on:

So before very long (Carey continued), the Whittiers arrived, besides Cousin Will, looking rather out of sorts as if his mama had ordered his presence upon pain of her displeasure, of which I fancy anyone would go in awe. Hetty will say I am being cattish, but the fact is, Cousin Clarissa has so very good a conceit of herself that it is a little hard to refrain. My newly met Cousin Benedict did incur her displeasure at dinner, for talking to his father about rents and cattle, and so forth. Brave man, he seemed to regard that not at all! He said some things which chimed with what Mrs Hodson had previously told me: how there is a good deal of poverty in these corn-growing parts of the country, in consequence of the fall in the price of wheat since the wars ended, so that many farmers are hard put to it; and where they make mistaken economies there is much discontent among the labouring men. One such farmer, I understand, is a tenant of the Priory's, with a farm at Little Marchingham; a place which still retains the character of a small village, while Great Marchingham is now a market town. This man, a reputed miser, appears to be a source of anxiety to my Cousin Benedict, because he scarcely lays out a penny on improvements if he can help it, and cannot be brought to see that they will be to his own profit in due course. All this was quite new to me, and I thought it interesting, although Cousin Clarissa must have supposed I would not, for she spoke across the table to Will, desiring him to entertain me with something more diverting. Poor Will, of course, was left tongue-tied by this request, so that I felt for him too.

Will was not so much tongue-tied, when required to entertain his cousin, as absorbed in thoughts of his own.

These thoughts were not cheerful. Why must everything happen all at once? Just when that tiresome girl was making such a nuisance of herself, Davy Leigh had to come up to Marchingham and start pestering him too. Not that he knew what he was being pestered for yet, and that was the worst of it—or was it? He supposed he would find out more soon, at the meeting of 'a few good fellows' which Davy had more or less insisted he attend. Will was reluctant; but Davy, dropping some pretty heavy hints to the effect that he had an interesting proposition to put, would not take no for an answer.

'If it's one of your shady pieces of dealing, I won't touch it!' had said Will, suspiciously.

'Shady?' replied Mr Leigh, raising his brows in assumed astonishment. 'Me, shady? You know me better than that, Will. Did you ever hear of *my* being caught doing anything outside the law?'

'Not caught, no,' said Will, morosely, to the bottom of his tankard of ale, only to look up and find Davy's bright gaze fixed disconcertingly upon him. Disconcertingly and—you might almost say—dangerously.

'But I know some who *might* be found to have strayed a little way outside it,' was all he had meditatively remarked. 'Some that ride fine hunters, hunters that cost half what you might expect a man to pay, and all fair and above-board too, nothing wrong with the horse! Well, is there?' he sharply demanded.

'Look here, I bought that hunter from you in all good faith,' said Will indignantly.

'Did you? Did you so?' Davy might have been talking to himself.

'Yes, I did!' Will glared back at him, resentfully. For no one knew better than himself that there must be something odd about that horse. Not the beast itself, no—a fine animal—but Will had certainly feared some hidden fault or vice in him to begin with—going at that price. He had been riding the bay happily to hounds for a whole season's hunting now, without any trouble. But why had Leigh let him have it so cheap? He ought to have made sure of that at the time, instead of shutting his mind to the question. Was the horse by any chance stolen? Might Leigh pretend he,

Will Gerard, had known it was stolen all along? He wished he trusted Davy Leigh, but he didn't.

It wasn't fair, thought Will. It wasn't fair to have London out of bounds to him! What was a fellow to do with himself all day in a hole-and-corner place like Marchingham, outside the hunting season? He didn't see why his mama should be so keen to see him a country gentleman. And to do Will justice, he had no ambitions of his own at all to inherit the Priory, not so long as he was provided with an income. Let Ben have the place and welcome.

Bored as he was, no wonder he had turned to the charms of little Grace Hodson! But he certainly didn't want to marry her. She wasn't even as pretty as she had been—indeed, reduced to a woeful state of tears and pleading, she was hardly pretty at all. He didn't want to marry anyone. Not that he had anything against Cousin Caroline (a hint from his mother before dinner had deepened his gloom), but marriage just wasn't in his line. It was too bad of Grace to be pregnant. If she told her parents and her brothers—a rather muscular set of young men, as Will uncomfortably recollected—well, he would simply deny it. How did he know he was the only man she had been with? He had nothing but her own word for it. Yes, it was too bad of her. And it was too bad of that hunter, so satisfactory in itself, to involve its innocent owner in potential difficulties. It was too bad of Ben to have put his foot down over those few debts; it was too bad of his father not to have stood up to Ben and insisted on the usual allowance; and it was too bad of his mother not to have overruled them both. Devil take the lot of 'em!

He glanced up from his plate to find his Cousin Caroline looking at him in some surprise. 'What was that you said?'

Will's handsome features flushed slightly. He caught the echo of his own voice hanging in the air. Had he actually said, 'Devil take the lot of 'em!' out loud? He must have done.

'Oh, nothing,' he replied, as casually as he could. 'Nothing of any consequence.'

'Are you sure?' She was looking quite concerned. 'You don't seem yourself this evening, cousin.'

'No, well! Ain't,' said Will, succinctly. 'You ever know what it's like to have one thing go wrong after another?'

'Indeed I do. I'm sorry—is that what has happened to you?'

'So to speak. Bad luck all round! Can't seem to put a foot right.'

'Oh, I know the feeling very well!' There was genuine sympathy in Carey's voice and smile, and Lady Gerard, just out of earshot but happening to glance across the table at this moment, was much heartened. 'There are days, or weeks, when nothing turns out as it should, and one is bound to think: "How all occasions do conspire against me!"'

'Aye, that's it. Well said!' Will nodded. 'Cleverly put! Couldn't have put it better myself!'

'Well, I can't take the credit for the felicitous wording,' said Carey, gravely, 'but you should reflect that, as Shakespeare also said: "All may yet be well".'

'I only hope so,' said Will, thinking gloomily of the promise Davy had extracted that he would come to meet those mysterious 'few good fellows', and in no such congenial surroundings as the Rose and Crown in Great Marchingham, but in some God-forsaken barn in the middle of a muddy field. And Leigh wouldn't even tell him the purpose of the meeting, thus keeping him in far from pleasurable suspense.

And now (Carey wrote ruefully), I come to the tale of how I have been inveigled into what I do not like to do, namely drawing figures, or at least sketches: just head and shoulders. It is all my own fault too, for I had idly taken up my pencil while Cousin Clarissa, Mrs Whittier and I sat in the drawing room, waiting for the gentlemen to join us after their port. Mrs Whittier has rather a handsome profile, of a Roman cast; one is inclined to suppose it may have attracted Mr Whittier to her in the first place, since he is himself a passionate classicist, and it seems all her family were classical scholars too. You may well imagine that my sketch fell far short of doing her justice, but nobody else seemed to notice.

Everybody else, indeed, had clustered round to admire. 'Ah, so now at last we have a chance to see your talents in action, Mrs Elliott!' exclaimed the Vicar.

'No, indeed you haven't!' said Carey, horrified. 'When it comes to portraiture, I am the most amateurish of artists.'

'Allow us to be the judges of that, my dear,' said Lady Gerard graciously, and Carey had to bite back an urge to say she could allow no such thing. After all, her cousin meant to be kind. It also struck her that she had better not disclaim any talent in this field too vehemently if she were to make a good case for her desire to paint Grace Hodson. Recollecting this just in time, she casually mentioned her plan: 'I saw Grace today, and it struck me what a charming frontispiece she would make. So it is agreed that I will at least endeavour to paint her—she is the prettiest child.'

Fortunately for Will's peace of mind, he was at the far end of the room, and failed to hear any of this; Carey's eye, however, met that of the elder Mr Gerard, and a conspiratorial glance passed between them.

'So with your kind permission, Mrs Whittier, I will continue to practise upon you!' Carey added, resigning herself, and she sketched on until the light faded, when she laid down her pencil, glad of the excuse. 'There—it isn't finished, but I think that having begun it in daylight, I won't continue by the light of a lamp. I'm afraid it is not very like.'

There was a clamour of protest. Not so! It was like, it was very like! 'Would you not be glad to see it hanging on our wall, my dear?' the Vicar asked his wife. 'I own that I should wish to have it there.'

Mrs Whittier, obviously not displeased, smiled, and said kindly that both her husband and the artist flattered her. 'May we beg you to let us keep the sketch, then, Mrs Elliott?'

'Oh, but it isn't finished yet!' cried Carey, in the genuine dismay she felt at parting with any work until she had done all she could with it.

'Then we will ask you to call and finish it at the Vicarage,' said the Vicar, beaming so hospitably that there was no alternative but to agree.

'Yes, and then, my dear Caroline, you must draw us all!'

added Lady Gerard. It was clear, thought Carey, that her amateurish sketch of Mrs Whittier meant more to her cousin than the flower paintings. 'Such accomplishment! I cannot, I really cannot refrain from asking you to draw Sir William, and your Cousin Will, and even myself, for though nobody cares less for her appearance than I do, I dare say Sir William would like such a picture—' she wagged a roguish finger—'wouldn't you, Sir William?'

Sir William, though somewhat hazy with claret and port, was understood to concur. At least, thought Carey, the two younger Gerards had not added their voices to these embarrassing persuasions. Will seemed to have seized the chance to slip away while everyone else was admiring the sketch, but Benedict now approached to offer her a cup of tea from the tray which had just been brought in.

'I see I have no option but to set up as artist in a line which is not my own!' she said ruefully, sipping tea. '"Oh, what a tangled web we weave . . ."'

'Yes, and you didn't practise to deceive, or not from any base motives,' he gravely agreed, and again offered the unexpectedly delightful smile. 'Will it be a very great imposition?'

'Oh, I don't know that it will.' She began to feel a little less out of temper. 'The thing is, I really have no talent above the ordinary in this field. Anyone who has learnt the rudiments of drawing might do as much. See for yourself.' And she astonished herself by voluntarily offering Mr Gerard her sketchbook.

'I suppose I see what you mean,' he said at length, 'though only because you point out the difference to me. But the flowers are superior, aren't they? Yes, I can tell that they are what you do best. However, you may rest assured that sketches like this of Mrs Whittier will satisfy all but your own exacting self.'

'Well, you almost put me in charity with the notion; and besides making our little ruse with Grace seem more credible, it will be a suitable thank-offering for the kind hospitality I receive here.' Or a form of penance, thought Carey to herself, for my inability to like Cousin Clarissa; she *is* a handsome woman, and I will make amends with the most flattering sketch of her I can contrive. 'I think that once

I have finished Mrs Whittier's picture I will go on to your stepmama's, and then, in any order you please, to Sir William, and yourself, and Will.'

'You may leave me out of it,' said Mr Gerard, looking suddenly quite forbidding.

'Oh dear, can't you spare the time to sit for me? What a pity.'

He smiled again, but with some constraint. 'Well, never mind that. You know, if a really good picture of Grace were called for—for a frontispiece, or any other reason—it occurs to me that Tiberius Taylor is the man to do it.'

'That's Mrs Whittier's brother, isn't it? Such a splendid name! I haven't yet met him: he was unwell, poor man, when we had luncheon at the Vicarage the other day.'

'Very likely,' said Benedict, with what looked like real amusement in his eyes. 'As a matter of fact, he's a painter of some talent, favouring classical figures with a quantity of symbolical imagery.'

'You know, that is not at all a bad notion,' said Carey thoughtfully. 'If two of us were to paint Grace . . . why, that would prolong her convalescence, and she could have the excuse of being paid for acting as model. I am sure we could manage that part of it between us, so that Mr Taylor need not incur the least expense, except that of his time. Would he be willing to paint the girl, do you think?'

'More than willing, I imagine!' The gleam of amusement was still there, and rather intrigued Carey. 'Tiberius would certainly be happy to paint Grace as Flora, or Pomona, or some rustic divinity of harvest, and enjoy every moment of it, for he's a great admirer of the female form, though in the most harmless way imaginable, I can assure you.'

'I own, I long to see his work!' said Carey smiling. 'Though I fancy poor Grace would not wish to be symbolically represented as any goddess of fertility, just at the moment . . . ah, Mrs Whittier!' For that lady was crossing the room, in her stately fashion, to look at the sketch again. 'I only wish it were better, but do remember that it is not finished yet . . .'

And so (wrote Carey, having edited Grace Hodson out of her reasons for embarking on portraiture), I have

113

committed myself to visiting Great Marchingham tomorrow to complete my study of the Vicar's wife. But it may not be a wasted day after all, since Mrs Whittier assures me there are some very pretty flowers growing in the churchyard, just as if it were a country meadow, and she kindly said she would make sure the man did not come with his scythe to mow it until I had looked to see if I wanted to paint anything there. It was thoughtful of her, and I took her at her word. So now I must go to bed, or I shall be fit for nothing in the morning.

. . . I shall be writing this in instalments, I see (she resumed later), and I am afraid you will be paying a fortune to receive it. It is three days since I laid down my pen, and eventful days at that, or so I found them myself, although my Cousin Will, suddenly seeming to wish for a confidante, unburdened himself to me at dinner tonight, asking if I did not find the place a dead bore as well? I feel for him a little, poor fellow. Although if that is his opinion, I cannot think why he remains here, even if his mama wishes him to pay court to me, when luckily neither of us feels as she does in the matter. There does seem to be some other reason, but no one has apprised me of it. I suspect he finds consolation for his boredom in the hostelries of Great Marchingham.

But to pass from Will to his elder brother: I must tell you that I have at last been enlightened as to what is the matter, or supposed to be the matter, with 'poor Benedict'. Really, it is too ridiculous! Such a mountain to make out of a molehill . . . Yesterday, I find myself approached by my Cousin Clarissa, in apologetic mood. She fears I have had a shock. Not at all, say I, more than a little bewildered, what kind of a shock had she in mind? Why, to meet Benedict at dinner without warning! Not without warning at all, say I, for, as I told you earlier in this letter, we had met at Brook End Farm and returned to the Priory together. But still, says she, it must have been a shock. Why, no, I insist, much puzzled: at last, however, after hearing about Clarissa's problems when she married Sir William and found herself with a difficult six-year-old to rear, whom she most sincerely pitied, I discover, from persistent questioning, that the matter is nothing but a slight birthmark the elder Mr Gerard has on one side of his face, which, to be honest with you, I had scarcely noticed until I had been some time in his company. However, Clarissa assures me that the sight of it is commonly 'a shock to persons of delicate sensibilities' —so mine can't be at all delicate; but what a notable anticlimax! I will now own that my imagination had ranged wildly enough, in quite a Gothick manner, but if this is all the mystery, I dare say Benedict gives not a moment's thought to it, any more than anyone who meets him would. If a slight blemish on his face is all that is supposed to keep him from marrying and producing heirs, as Clarissa has been earnestly assuring me he will not, then the only thing I can say, if Hetty will pardon my frankness, is that the business is not achieved with that part of the anatomy!

('Dear me!' said Hetty later, reading this passage, for her own sensibilities were all Lady Gerard could have desired. 'Dear me, she may think begging my pardon makes all well, John, but I wish she wouldn't say such things, all the same!')

I would have told you more of my news (Carey concluded), but I am coming to the end of this sheet, and very soon letters will be taken away for the post, so if this one is to go I must end it now. I will say only that within two days I have made as many new friends. More of that, perhaps, anon . . .

8

Carey made the first of her new friends as the indirect result of Mrs Whittier's invitation to the Vicarage, with the additional inducement of access to the churchyard flowers. As it had occurred to her that she was not required to furnish any pretext for Grace's idleness for a few days yet—not until even Grace's father must be able to calculate that the original, obvious excuse would no longer serve—she availed herself of this invitation directly, and spent the next morning completing her sketch of Mrs Whittier. Both the Vicar and his wife professed themselves delighted, Mr Whittier proposing to have it nicely framed and hung in his study. Taking light refreshment with her hosts, Carey ventured to inquire after the health of Mrs Whittier's brother. Since hearing Benedict Gerard's account of him the day before, she was more curious than ever to meet Mr Taylor, particularly as, looking about her, she could see no work of art upon the drawing room walls which, to judge by Mr Gerard's description, seemed in any way likely to be from his brush. But once again, it appeared, the elusive Mr Taylor was confined to his bedchamber.

'My brother's health,' explained Augusta Whittier, shaking her head, 'has never been robust, and becomes less so with advancing age. Pray take another slice of cake.'

Munching her way through a rather dry slice of Vicarage seedcake, and making polite conversation with the Whittiers, Carey found her eye straying to the pretty houses in New Road on the far side of the churchyard. It was only after she had remarked idly on the well-kept appearance of the house at the end of the row, with its white painted woodwork, polished brass knocker, and the lush green of the creeper growing up its warm red brick, that she realised too late she had been admiring that notorious establishment Number Nineteen.

'Handsome is, they say, as handsome does, and appearances, my dear Mrs Elliott, may be but a Hollow Sham,' said the Vicar's wife quellingly.

'Yes, to be sure,' said Carey, much regretting her *faux pas*. 'Well, I suppose it may be some comfort to you that the house at least appears very pretty,' she feebly suggested.

But it seemed that Augusta Whittier took no comfort at all in the innocuous outward appearance of Number Nineteen, and indeed had no intention of relinquishing discussion of Hollow Shams once the subject had been broached. 'I am sorry to tell you, Mrs Elliott,' she mournfully concluded the recital of her grievances, 'that one may even see the Carmichael woman in church! And her nieces, who are not, of course, her nieces, have been known to attend divine service too!'

'Oh, is that so very bad?' inquired Carey.

She received unexpected support from the Vicar, who suggested mildly: 'Remember Mary Magdalene!'

'So I hope I do,' stated his wife majestically, 'and you know well enough, Theodore, that there is no clear evidence of St Mary Magdalene's ever having been a woman of irregular life. You yourself,' she informed him, 'told me so!'

'How very interesting,' said Carey, thankfully seizing upon this new topic, and applied to the Vicar for further information about the saint, which he was delighted to provide, with many a learned quotation. The time thus passed agreeably enough until Carey could properly betake herself to the churchyard, the mowing of which her hosts had so kindly delayed.

It proved to be all that Mrs Whittier had promised her: a piece of meadowland where the ancestors of the wild flowers now flourishing in it must have grown for centuries. The verger's scythe, mowing the plants down two or three times in a summer, kept them in good health. Carey was pleased to discover, in one corner of the churchyard, a patch of annual vernal grass, rarer and later flowering then the scented variety, and there was a bitter vetch which she would not have expected to find in the eastern counties, and had certainly not seen in or near the Marchinghams before. In no time at all she was installed on her little folding stool among the tall, rustling grass and the flowers, intent upon her work.

She was confining herself to pencil sketches today, since pencil was all she needed to complete the likeness of Mrs Whittier, and she had resolved not to encumber herself with her water-colours. She now rather regretted this decision. However, having recorded their situation and habit of growth, she would pick the vernal grass and the vetch, which were about to be cut down anyway, and take them back with her. Meanwhile her pencil moved over the paper with ease and freedom, and she had little idea how long she had been at work when a woman's voice behind her remarked, 'How very pretty!'

Carey bristled, and was only slightly mollified when the voice immediately corrected itself. 'No, not pretty, or not only pretty: how exact, I should have said.'

If she were not to be downright uncivil, Carey had perforce to turn and reply to this self-appointed critic of her work, and in doing so found herself viewing a most elegant lady. She was clad in a perfectly cut grey walking costume, lavishly trimmed with darker grey braid which matched her eyes, its skirt fashionably wide at the hem and descending no lower than ankle level. 'Of course it is exact, ma'am,' she said prosaically. 'It is the business of my pictures to be exact, since they are for a botanical record.'

'Ah,' said the lady. 'Then you are the Mrs Elliott who has come to Marchingham to paint the flowers and marry Mr William Gerard.'

Carey's momentary ill-humour vanished in her amusement at this succinct statement. 'So I believe rumour has it,' she agreed, returning candour for candour. 'Rumour is right in the first instance and wrong in the second: I am not so very long widowed, and am certainly not going to be married.'

'Very wise,' said the lady, nodding, not specifying whether she approved of the proposition in general or a disinclination to marry Will Gerard in particular. She was now looking at Carey herself with some interest, as if intrigued by her own failure to discompose her. Carey returned her gaze, seeing a face of rather arresting character, no longer young—just how old, she could not be sure, perhaps in the late thirties, but skilfully preserving a youthful appearance. The firm chin, pronounced nose, and those rather cool grey eyes were framed in pale, fair hair, worn dressed in smooth bands with an elegant minimum of ringlets, just enough to soften the severity of the style, and crowned by a very large, dashing hat with a handsome plume of feathers in it.

Carey realised she had seen this face before, and said so: 'In church on Sunday, I believe? But we were not introduced.'

'No,' said the lady, smiling. 'We weren't. My name is Carmichael.' She looked quizzically at Carey. 'I dare say you have heard of me.'

'Yes, a great deal.'

'And nothing to my credit, I'll be bound. I'm afraid that I could not resist stopping to look at your sketch, but now I will take my leave of you, since it will do your credit no good at all to be seen talking to me.'

'Oh, I don't mind that!' said Carey cheerfully, not at all abashed, her pencil returning to its delicate task. 'Though now that I come to think of it,' she added, 'I don't know that I ever did talk to any lady in your line of business before!'

'You are aware of my line of business?' inquired Mrs Carmichael, for the first time showing a little surprise. 'You have heard that I keep the local house of ill fame?'

'Do you know, Mrs Carmichael,' remarked Carey apologetically, laying down her pencil and looking her interlocutor in the eye, 'I'm afraid it is really no use at all trying to shock me!'

Mrs Carmichael laughed outright this time. 'A palpable hit!' she acknowledged. 'Yes, perhaps I *was* trying to see if I could. However, I see that plain speaking is your own forte too. If the facts of the matter are not quite so crude as you have heard, well, they are substantially correct, so I won't draw down opprobrium on you by inviting you to take tea with me, as otherwise I might. I've heard of your painting, of course, and it occurs to me that there's a flower which has sprung up in a corner of my garden that might interest you. I don't know much about such things myself, but I suppose

119

the garden must once have been a part of the same meadow as the churchyard, though my maid Betsy says she has never seen this particular plant there. I believe it may be some kind of orchid.'

'An orchid?' Carey's interest kindled. 'I am rather short of our native English orchids; I've found a few of the later flowering species, but there are some which flower earlier, and are quite rare, and which Professor Lindley, for whom I am doing these pictures, tells me might be found here in the eastern counties on soil that tends to be chalky. It is not chalky enough near the Priory for those particular varieties he suggested I might seek out, but then again, I understand that its constitution can change quite suddenly, almost from field to field; if you please, I should like to see your orchid, if that is what it is.'

Mrs Carmichael hesitated. 'No, but seriously, Mrs Elliott, do think of your credit.'

'Hang my credit!' said Carey. 'There certainly *could* be an orchid here, and any such flowers might well have been picked to death in the churchyard. Pray *do* show me the plant in your garden!' And she was quickly gathering up her little stool, her sketching block and her pencils.

Mrs Carmichael still hesitated, but then shrugged her shoulders and remarked, 'Well, I suppose you know what you're about. After all, they can't have seen us talking from the Vicarage, tucked away here in this corner of the churchyard, with the building itself between us and Petergate. Come along, then! But we had better be quick about the last part of the way, for good Mrs Whittier can and *does* see who goes up and down New Road, and in and out of my own house, simply by looking from her windows.'

'Oh, that's all right; she is out paying calls just now, unless it is later than I think,' said Carey, accompanying her new acquaintance down the churchyard path to the lych-gate. They were making their way through this gate, its intricacies requiring some careful manoeuvring of fashionable skirts, when they encountered another lady about to negotiate it in the opposite direction.

Carey had seen this small, brisk, dark young woman before, and in the selfsame setting. Searching her memory for a name, she said cordially, 'Miss Gage! How do you do?'

To this Roberta Gage replied with only the curtest nod, and a glance of unmistakable dislike. She favoured Mrs Carmichael with an even haughtier look, actually drawing her skirts aside with some ostentation lest they brush the elegant grey walking dress, and proceeded on her way down the path with a firm tread and never a backward glance.

'Goodness me!' said Carey, in mild surprise.

'That was Miss Gage, who keeps the girls' school. She knows better than to speak to me. I did warn you, you know!' remarked Mrs Carmichael. She paused. 'Shouldn't you think better of my orchid?'

'No, no, it wasn't that. She doesn't like me either, though really I can't tell why, since we have met only once, and that briefly,' said Carey thoughtfully, walking on across the road. In a moment both ladies were safely through a little door in the wall and into Number Nineteen's garden. Neither of them missed seeing the little movement at an upstairs window in the Vicarage, as a curtain fell quickly back into place. Carey glanced round with a lift of the eyebrows. 'Mrs Whittier, back from her calls?' she wondered.

'No, only her brother Tiberius,' her new acquaintance reassured her. 'Poor soul; it is the girls he likes to spy on, of course, and he would dearly love to make their further acquaintance, though I believe that painting them in classical attitudes is all he has in mind. But his worthy sister doesn't believe it. I hear he did once try to call upon us, but was apprehended *in flagrante*, or at any rate upon the doorstep! It was a near thing, so I was told by Betsy, who witnessed the scene.'

Carey chuckled. 'I own I should rather like to meet Mr Taylor. I haven't done so yet.'

'Oh, he'll have been kept out of your way,' her companion explained, 'lest he say something shocking: possibly in the classical line, but shocking all the same. He is rather apt to do so, but there's not an bit of harm in him. Now, let me just desire my invaluable Mrs Thompson to make some tea, and while she does that I will show you this flower of mine.'

'Oh yes, you do have an orchid here!' Carey was saying

121

with enthusiasm, a few moments later. 'It's *Orchis militaris*, the Soldier or Military Orchid. They are becoming rarer and rarer, you know. Good clumps may still be found, if you know where to look, but not very many, so Lindley tells me; I am doubly lucky, because this one is flowering a couple of weeks late, no doubt on account of growing in the shade of that little bush.'

'Well, you had better pick it, or dig it up, whichever is best, and take it with you,' offered Mrs Carmichael.

'No, I had better not,' said Carey firmly. 'I mustn't disturb your orchid at all; what I had really better do, if I may, is come back here within the next day or so and paint it just as it grows. I can't do so now: the light will not last very much longer, and I believe I have worked as much as I ought for one day. Would you mind? Since my business is conducted by daylight, and yours, I suppose, is not,' she pointed out, 'I hope I should not be in your way!'

This caused Mrs Carmichael to laugh again, quite heartily, as she led her guest back to the house. 'What a str . . . what an interesting creature you are, Mrs Elliott!' she remarked.

'Strange, you were going to say!' replied Carey, unperturbed. 'Oh, what a charming drawing room!'

This was perfectly true. 'Not what you expected in such a house, Mrs Elliott?' suggested her hostess, handing her a cup of tea. Carey intrigued, noticed, that Mrs Thompson, who had brought in the tea, looked the soul of respectability, like a most superior housekeeper.

'I was going to say no such thing: do not put words into my mouth!' she replied. 'And let us not be so formal: my name is Caroline, or more usually Carey—what is yours? Marie? Marie Carmichael—how romantic; just like one of the ladies in the Scottish ballad!'

'Yes, and both the Marie and the Carmichael are my own, though you will hardly find anyone in Marchingham to believe it. Ah, here is my young friend Miss Polly Brignold!' This as a very handsome, dark-haired young woman entered the room. Carey's hostess cast her another rather challenging look.

One of the nieces, she thought, carefully preserving a formality as decorous as Miss Brignold's own while Polly, too, took a cup of tea and made polite conversation, acquitting herself very creditably under her mentor's sharp eye. After ten minutes or so she rose to take leave of the visitor with admirable social grace.

'I do trust you didn't object? It was good practice for Polly,' remarked Mrs Carmichael. 'She is really coming along very well. A little Norfolk accent remains in her voice, and she must rid herself of that if she hopes to move in the highest of circles—the highest as such things go, you understand. I am speaking of the fashionable *demi-monde* to which the girls who come to stay for a while in my house may aspire by the time they leave it. If she should find her niche there,' she added thoughtfully, 'I am not sure she might not be better advised to change her name, though so far she clings to Polly. Mary or Maria would cause some confusion here, as I have another niece of the same name just now, but later . . . what do you think?'

'She could become a Mariana?' suggested Carey. 'Marietta, even?'

'No, simplicity is best. Nothing too fanciful. Simplicity, restraint, dignity; with those weapons in her armoury, one of my girls may go far. And Polly, I must say, is one of the most promising whose tuition I have yet undertaken. She is naturally ambitious and has intelligence, as well as the necessary good looks, though I have had to tone down her taste in dress a good deal. However, she is a fast learner.'

Carey could not suppress a chuckle. 'I see that this place is not quite what is generally thought!'

'Oh, to a great extent it is, for the girls require some practical experience too, you know,' Mrs Carmichael calmly informed her. 'But we do not accept every gentleman who would like to visit us. For instance,' she added in cordial tones, 'as I have taken a great liking to you—I hope you don't mind my saying so—I am glad to hear that you are *not* in point of fact attached to your cousin Mr William Gerard, who I fear was unable to understand that he was expected to behave like a gentleman to my girls.'

Carey found that she was not altogether surprised to hear it. 'You are right, I am not attached to him, which is lucky. For though you may have heard, erroneously, that he and I

123

are to marry, I do not think that it would be at all comfortable to be married to my cousin Will.'

'No; I suppose I might as well tell you that he has a rather indiscriminate way of conferring his favours, and if, as you surmise, little Miss Gage does not like you, that is why. The fact is,' continued Mrs Carmichael, after a moment's hesitation, 'that Roberta Gage has been setting her ladylike cap at Will Gerard herself, and thought something would come of it, but then he shied away.'

'Goodness me!' said Carey, quite awed to discover these complexities in the social life of Great Marchingham. 'Er—did she tell you of this?'

'Oh no, of course not,' Marie Carmichael smiled slightly. 'Such things become commonly known, you understand, however discreet people believe they are. I can well imagine what direction Mr William Gerard's own intentions took, and that it was not at all what Miss Gage wanted, though if she did but know, she is well out of it. The latest object of your amiable cousin's affections,' she continued, 'is, I understand, a pretty country lass without any sense in her head at all. Dear me, you will say I am gossiping! Of course all the less creditable tales of any neighbourhood do find their way to a place like this, although my girls are strictly trained not to pass them on, and I need hardly say I don't generally do so myself. But I have not forgotten how your cousin behaved to little Jenny . . . well, never mind that; I won't go into detail, but in my view Will Gerard is no great catch for anyone, and I don't scruple to tell you so.'

'Yes, well, I am exceedingly obliged to you,' said Carey. Much entertained at first by the interesting tale of Will and Roberta, she had suddenly sat up very straight towards the end of her new acquaintance's discourse. 'You may well believe that I'm in no danger of becoming infatuated with my Cousin Will myself, but . . . did you say a pretty country lass? Oh no! Can you mean Grace Hodson?'

'I don't believe I ever heard the girl's name, but it sounds likely enough; the Hodsons are a farming family on the Marchingham estate, are they not?'

'It must be Grace!' said Carey, dismayed. 'At least, I fear it must. Oh dear, oh *dear*! How very, very vexatious! And now, after what has happened, what am I to do?'

'Do?' asked Marie Carmichael. 'But how can this girl concern you—if you are not to marry your cousin, I mean? And what, if you don't mind my asking, *has* happened?'

Carey hesitated for a moment, and then briefly told her.

* * *

A little while later Carey was driving herself back to the Priory in the dog-cart. She had much to think about on the way. Trotting along the quiet country lanes in the evening sunlight, she was well aware of having indulged in gossip herself. Though it is a curious thing, she reflected, that when you take to somebody, it feels more like exchanging confidences with a friend: reprehensible, no doubt, but sometimes enjoyable and, as in this instance, useful. Somehow she was sure she could trust Marie Carmichael's discretion over the tale of poor little Grace; without such an instinctive feeling, she would hardly have confided in her new acquaintance at all, though she fancied it would soon have come to Mrs Carmichael's ears in any case.

The question was, what use if any should be made of her present knowledge of Cousin's Will's amorous activities? So far as poor Grace was concerned, of course, the damage had been done, and there was no help for that now. Carey was much inclined to agree with Mrs Carmichael that Grace, and Miss Gage—and indeed any other lady whom Cousin Will did *not* desire to marry—were well out of it! Would it do Peggy Hodson any real good to know the identity of her daughter's seducer? While they had a fair chance of keeping the whole wretched business from the girl's father and brothers, might it not be best if she, Carey, held her own tongue?

She came to the conclusion, however, that she had better tell the whole of her discovery to the elder Mr Gerard, and she was disappointed, to a degree which quite surprised her, to find he was not at dinner that evening. After dinner it was wearisome to feel obliged to begin sketching Cousin Clarissa's patrician features, when she had already drawn so much that day. But at least putting her tired eyes and fingers to the task helped to assuage any remaining pangs of conscience she might feel for accepting the Gerards' hospitality under false pretences, so to speak. At least, she reflected philosophically as she worked, at least I would rather have Clarissa for a subject than Will. I am glad he is not disposed to make me any advances, for I really don't think I could support them with equanimity just now. What on earth could poor Grace see in him? If it comes to that, what on earth could little Miss Gage see in him? She looks as if she doesn't lack for sense.

Will himself, to her own relief and his mother's evident displeasure, had left the family party with a mumbled excuse at an early stage of the evening. I suppose I shall have to draw him sooner or later, she thought. But I *will* do a head and shoulders of Benedict too, let him just see if I don't! Clarissa may even be surprised to discover from such a sketch how little that mark on his face strikes the casual observer. How can she make so much of it? I should not object to drawing Marie Carmichael's face either, or trying to draw it, for it is full of character. Now there, at least, is one interesting new acquaintance I have made since coming to Marchingham, besides the Hodson family and Benedict.

Her second new acquaintance was made the next morning. She had been so tired after the long day, the interesting novelty of her encounter with Mrs Carmichael, and her subsequent puzzling over the question of Will and poor Grace, that she fell asleep as soon as her lamp was out. She slept very soundly, but then woke early. Her mind went straight to the orchid, to which she would return with her water-colours, but not for a day or so; meanwhile, Mrs Carmichael had promised to give the plant protection if the weather should unexpectedly turn stormy.

A glance from her window showed her that no storms threatened at present. Suddenly she was very wide awake. A clock struck in the house below: seven, and a good two and a half hours or more before the family would be breakfasting, although she could hear servants moving quietly and busily around the stairs and corridors. She did not feel like lingering in bed on a fine morning, and as the rays of the morning sun struck across the lawn, glinting on the dewdrops that trembled at the tips of the grassblades, she made up her mind to go out walking.

Hastily washing herself in cold water from the ewer on her stand, she dressed, put on a pair of stout shoes, and, putting a small sketchpad and some pencils in the serviceable reticule she commonly carried with her, set out. On her way she encountered no one but a housemaid, with whom she exchanged smiles, found a side door already unbolted, and made her way out into the fresh, fragrant morning air.

She had the Imperial Promenade in mind as her destination. This grandly named avenue, a kind of scenic folly dating back to the days of Sir William's grandfather, the landscape gardening enthusiast, stretched a good quarter of a mile from a life-sized statue of Artemis at one end to an equally large statue of Pan at the other, and was lined all along its way with the busts of Roman Emperors. What fancy had induced the late baronet to import them from Italy, where he had been on the Grand Tour, into the flat farming countryside of eastern England, no one could now tell, but Carey thought their very incongruity lent them a certain charm. She had found the place not long after she came to the Priory, and it had become rather a favourite resort of hers, partly because nobody else seemed to frequent it.

Her surprise was all the greater at this early hour when, on rounding the tall hedge beyond which the Imperial Promenade lay, and coming within sight of the Rotunda, where she had thought she might sit and enjoy the quiet of the morning for a while, she found that edifice already occupied. The Rotunda partly belied its name: it was a small open building which did indeed have a circular ground plan, but the original little dome (again, commissioned by the present Sir William's grandfather) had been replaced by a squared roof in the Chinese style, made of tiles, tip-tilted at its outer edges and altogether sitting rather oddly on the neo-classical columns pressed into its service. This alteration had been one of the results of Sir William's father's improving fervour, and surveying it, Carey had thought more than once that it was just as well the present baronet felt no desire to outdo his forebears in architectural fancy; Heaven knew what further strange hybrid buildings might have arisen had he not been content (or obliged for lack of funds) to let matters remain as they were.

Though the roof might no longer suit the little building's name, the place was certainly rotund up to the top of the columns. Rotund, too, was its present occupant. Also, as Carey observed with some surprise, he was going about something very like her own business. A small easel stood propped in the grass just outside the steps of the Rotunda, and on the top step, within easy reach of it and palette in hand, sat a small, stout gentleman with a great deal of white hair, wielding his brush with energy and enthusiasm.

This gentleman looked up without any apparent surprise as Mrs Elliott hesitated, waving his brush at her and declaiming: 'Queen and huntress, chaste and fair . . . no, no, we already have Artemis down at the end there, of course! Aurora, perhaps? Rosy-fingered Dawn? Or still better, Pallas! Pallas Athene, you know, or to the Romans, Minerva, commonly considered the goddess of . . .' But here, without warning and in mid-speech, the gentleman suddenly leaned slowly and involuntarily forward, appeared to lose his balance, toppled off the step and fell gently into the grass in front of the Rotunda, to lie recumbent among the buttercups and daisies.

Carey hurried to help him to his feet, but he waved her away, apparently perfectly comfortable. 'No, no, I thank you! I do very well where I am,' he remarked. 'I shall draw strength, like Antaeus, from contact with my mother Earth! As I was saying, Pallas Athene, goddess of wisdom— but without the owl. All hail, Minerva! Goddess fair, all hail!'

'No, I'm Caroline Elliott, and can claim none of Athene's wisdom,' said Carey, smiling at this absurd little gentleman. 'Not even enough to be certain that you *don't* require assistance, sir, whatever you may say. Are you sure you are feeling quite the thing?'

For on coming closer she had noticed a powerful odour about him, which she now thought she identified . . . could it possibly be strong liquor, at *this* hour of the morning? She glanced curiously at the painting on the easel, which, while plainly still in an unfinished state, was wild and grandiose in style, yet in its own undisciplined manner struck her as remarkably good. It showed mountain tops of a pictures-que nature standing boldly out against a tumultuous sky, with some roughly sketched little figures, either Cupids or cherubs, hovering among the light and dark of the clouds. Lower down, amongst the vegetation sketched in on the mountainsides, Carey saw shapes which proved to be several of the Imperial heads that lined the Promenade, peering out from amidst the greenery. She supposed it was to paint them that the artist had taken himself off to the Priory so early in the morning.

'I am perfectly well, thank you,' said the prostrate gentle-man, quite at his ease. 'If not Athene, then perhaps it should be Hera, or to the Romans, as you are aware, Juno. Yes, Hera in the character of Lady of the Flowers—one of her titles, you know. A happy thought!' he congratulated himself. 'For you too, I am told, Mrs Elliott, are a lady of flowers!'

'Must it be Hera? Was she not a rather overbearing female?' replied Carey, smiling. 'I had rather you ad-dressed me as, say, one of the Muses, or some such agreeable figure. However, you evidently know who I am, sir, and I believe I know who you are, too. I fancy you must be Mr Tiberius Taylor, whom I have not had the pleasure of meeting before, though I was calling upon Mr and Mrs Whittier yesterday.'

'I know. Saw you from the window. With the lovely Mrs Carmichael,' said Mr Taylor, a trifle wistfully. 'But mum's the word, eh?' he added, with a trace of anxiety. 'Wouldn't do to let Augusta know I was . . . well, looking.'

'So you *are* Mr Taylor?' Carey deduced.

'Or you may, if you wish, address me as the Sage of Marchingham,' suggested Tiberius Taylor.

'I might indeed!' agreed Carey, 'and I would ask in what field your particular sagacity lies, but looking at your picture—I hope you don't object to my doing so—I take it that you mean in the realm of Art.'

'Of Art, and Knowledge of the World to boot!' announced Mr Taylor grandly. 'You would like to be a Muse? You *shall* be a Muse! I myself,' he added, contriving to prop himself on one elbow and peer up at his painting, 'am a worshipper of the Muses. You shall figure as any of them you please! What say you to Euterpe, and Lyric Poetry? Just *there*, perhaps, in what will be a charming grove at the foot of Mount Olympus, with the Pierian spring.'

'Well, it's very kind of you,' said Carey, rather touched, 'but I'm afraid I have little time for posing as a model. In my modest way I am quite busy with my own work, you understand. On the other hand,' she added, seizing upon this opening, 'if you really want a model for a Muse, Mr Gerard—Mr Benedict Gerard, that is—did have it in mind to suggest to you a fit subject for your brush, though I dare say he hasn't had time to do it just yet.' She paused, eyeing the self-styled Sage a little dubiously. There could be no doubt about it: he did smell most powerfully of brandy. Was he a fit person to be painting Grace? Well, she supposed Benedict knew what he was about. It was a little strange, she owned, to feel such confidence in someone she scarcely knew, but somehow she could not think her confidence was misplaced.

In any case, Mr Taylor had paid no attention to her last remarks, having fallen into contemplation of his own work again from his present semi-recumbent position. 'Observe,' he said, with great satisfaction, 'the grandeur of my design! Mount Olympus to one side, with all the gods assembled. Mount Ida to the other, with the Judgment of Paris. This is only a preliminary sketch, you understand, and upon a small scale, but still, you may gather some idea of the fine conception of the whole! Observe the use that may be made of the native features of our landscape, as the Emperors and deities merge into English flowers and grasses!'

By now Carey was beginning to be a little concerned about the way in which the artist himself was merging into those same flowers and grasses, which must surely still be wet and chilly with dew, and bad for a white-haired gentleman in late middle age. Did Mr Taylor not wish to pick himself up, or was he concealing the fact that he couldn't?

'I may also include this pavilion itself,' he continued, looking up at the Rotunda. 'Pray observe it! A curious piece of Gothick folly, yet pleasing in its way. Observe, too, the

130

fine, spreading trees yonder, fit setting for the demi-gods on the lower slopes of Olympus. This work, you understand, is to be my masterpiece! Only sketches so far, but it is to be a mural. Murals, you must know, are my particular strength, and this will be a mural of the most impressive nature. When completed, Mrs Elliott, when my sketches are transferred to their permanent home, it will adorn the whole of one wall in the Vicarage drawing room.'

'Will it, indeed?' said Carey politely, though the notion struck her as a most dubious proposition, unlikely ever to be realised.

'Oh yes, once I have brought Augusta, and my good brother-in-law Theodore, to see what renown such a work will bring upon their house, it certainly will!' Mr Taylor assured her. 'Or perhaps,' he added, considering, 'I should employ two walls? One for Mount Olympus, one for Mount Ida . . . to accommodate all the figures that must be included. What do *you* think?' Fortunately for Carey, he did not seem to require an answer, but pursued: 'I fancy, Mrs Elliott, it is because Dr Taylor, our papa—Augusta's and mine, I mean—was so much addicted to the classics that I am attracted to such subjects. You understand, Mrs Elliott, that we ourselves were named after the Roman Emperors. I was myself the third child of our dear parents, so that the names of the first two emperors had been used up, so to speak, upon my sisters Augusta and Julia. Therefore, I was left with Tiberius.'

He paused, apparently expecting some response. 'A very good sort of a name, to be sure,' Carey offered, weakly enough, she felt. The Sage of Marchingham had now risen to his feet, thus relieving her of some of her anxiety: he could move if he wanted to. He was, however, swaying slightly, and she prudently took the palette from his slack grasp as he took a couple of very shaky steps, fixed his eyes on the Italian Artemis at the far end of the Promenade, and addressed it in verse. ' "Hesperus entreats thy light. Goddess excellently bright!" No, my apologies . . . wrong time of day,' he added, staggering alarmingly this time, and just managed to utter a final: 'Goddess, all hail!' as he waved a hand in what was evidently salutation to the statue.

It was a mistake: he promptly lost his balance and once

more fell headlong to the ground. This time he lay there motionless, eyes closed, apparently unconscious.

'Oh dear!' exclaimed Carey, dismayed. The artist was breathing noisily: he was certainly not dead, merely dead drunk. However, it could not be good for him to lie there on the wet grass, poor man! Despite his short stature, his bulk made him rather a solid object to shift, and though she was not particularly frail, she found that her efforts at least to haul him up to the dry stone floor of the Rotunda were useless. Carey did not quite like to abandon the Sage here, though she supposed she must do so in order to go to the Priory and fetch help. 'Dear me!' she said aloud, rather crossly. 'Where can he have got the liquor from, and at this hour of the morning?'

'More easily abstracted from the Vicarage sideboard first thing,' said a very welcome voice; equally welcome was the sight of Mr Benedict Gerard's amused face, when Carey looked up from the prostrate classicist at her feet. 'Tiberius, you have made a fool of yourself again,' Mr Gerard informed the unconscious artist. 'This is Tiberius Taylor, by the way—or did he have time to introduce himself?'

'Oh yes, indeed he did,' said Carey. 'And to describe his great work, which he says is to occupy a wall of the Vicarage drawing room. I must say, I rather doubt that. Or it may be going to occupy *two* walls,' she recollected. 'Mount Olympus on one, Mount Ida on the other.'

'Hope springs eternal,' Mr Gerard remarked. 'Poor Tiberius; he will be very much ashamed of himself later. He probably hasn't taken as much drink as you might suppose; I'm afraid that only a very small quantity will get him into this state, as Mrs Whittier is well aware, so she keeps an eagle eye upon him. Two walls, did you say?'

'That's what he said, and he certainly seemed quite lucid, if a little extravagant in his manner of speech,' said Carey. 'Until he collapsed, that is. I do trust he is all right.'

'Oh, he'll do,' Mr Gerard reassured her. 'Come along, old friend!' And so saying he bent and picked up the dead weight of Mr Tiberius Taylor without any apparent difficulty; Carey thought that although her adoptive cousin might not be a particularly large man, there must be a good deal of strength in his lean body. 'Luckily I have the gig not far away. Could you retrieve his things, do you think?' he added over his shoulder, bearing Mr Taylor off.

Willingly making herself useful in this small way, Carey followed. A gig was indeed standing on the bridle path conveniently close to the Imperial Promenade, and Mr Gerard deposited his burden in it. 'Mrs Whittier will be, well, rather displeased to see the Sage back in this state, won't she?' said Carey a little doubtfully, adding, as Benedict raised an eyebrow, 'The Sage of Marchingham: that's what he suggested I might call him.'

'I haven't heard that one before!' said Benedict, smiling. 'A new notion. Myself, I have always pictured sages with long white beards. Mrs Whittier? No, she wouldn't be pleased at all; however, I'm not taking him home, but to the Priory.'

'I find I am for ever raising objections,' said Carey apologetically, clambering uninvited up into the gig too, 'but do you think your stepmama will be any better pleased herself?'

'Oh, she won't know!' said Benedict. 'I told you I have a couple of rooms to myself, didn't I? Not so far from the stable block, in fact, so that I needn't disturb the household by keeping odd hours . . . Tiberius is accustomed to sleep it off there.'

'You mean he makes a habit of this?' said Carey, diverted.

'Within reason, and as I say, I'm afraid a very little liquor will suffice,' said Mr Gerard, letting his horse move on. 'You would like to be driven back to the Priory yourself, I take it?'

'Well, of course. I'm coming to help you get poor Mr Taylor comfortably settled,' said Carey firmly.

'No need for that,' Mr Gerard told her. 'Ministering angels, in this instance, aren't called for; all your Sage needs is a few hours in which to recover.'

However, she was not to be shaken off so easily, saying primly, 'But my dear cousin, this is an adventure such as I am not accustomed to, or anyway not so early in the morning. Surely you wouldn't deprive me of a new and interesting experience? Anyway, you can't carry Mr Taylor and his palette and canvas and easel, now can you?'

A little later, therefore, she was following Mr Gerard as he bore the still limp form of the artist up a steep flight of back stairs. 'How delightfully surreptitious: I am reminded of the times I used to creep down to the kitchen in the middle of the night as a child, just for the fun of doing what I knew I shouldn't,' she remarked lightly, though thinking to herself as they made their way along a corridor, which did not even boast the threadbare carpeting laid down in the grander parts of the Priory, that Benedict appeared to have chosen his rooms in what could not be far from the servants' quarters. 'You live in Spartan surroundings, I see,' she ventured to observe, as he set his burden down briefly to open a door.

Pausing in this act, he looked back at her, unexpectedly favouring her again with that extraordinarily pleasing smile. 'Spartan? No, not at all.' And he suddenly began to laugh: 'I live in surroundings of unparalleled luxury and splendour. Just wait until you see them!'

9

'It was the funniest, and yet in a way the most magnificent thing I ever set eyes upon,' Mrs Elliott wrote to her loved ones in London, a couple of days later. On reflection, she saw that though she had promised them an account of her new acquaintances, she could scarcely go into much detail concerning the interesting Mrs Carmichael. Dear Hetty would certainly be both shocked and anxious, fearing as she always did that Carey would impulsively contrive to ruin her own reputation for ever. And Hetty had had enough anxiety in her life; she would not risk adding to it.

Tiberius Taylor, however, was a different matter: she thought both Hetty and Sir John would be amused by him, and so chose to dwell upon that amiable if eccentric gentleman and his classical art.

Though it is really more in the wild, Romantic style than truly classical (she wrote). The subjects, however, are chiefly drawn from classical mythology and literature. My Cousin Benedict is plainly a kind friend to Mr Taylor, not least in the matter of providing house room for his Art! I like Benedict more and more—he appears, by the way, to undertake most competently the whole work of running the Priory estate, his father being unable and his half-brother disinclined to do anything at all about it. But now, where was I? Of course—in Benedict's rooms—very correctly chaperoned, dear Hetty, by Mr Tiberius Taylor, the Sage of Marchingham himself. Furthermore, the rooms are not at all like anyone's private apartments, but more resemble an art gallery: in promising me splendour, my Cousin Benedict was entirely accurate! Not as regards his furnishings, which were as plain as

135

can well be imagined, for left to himself he obviously has simple tastes. The decoration of the walls of his rooms, however, has been left to Mr Taylor, with the most startling and, it must be confessed, superb results. Such extraordinary effects of light and colour! One would think the pictures almost alive, although the outlines are sometimes imprecise, and hint at the elements of a scene rather than depicting it exactly: one sees no statuesque forms—rather, they are creatures caught in the act of rapid movement, or in the grip of some strong emotion. I should suppose it rather unnerving to wake every morning to such strange scenes—for not all the figures can be quite explained at first sight, and among the familiar characters of myth and legend, odd little creatures appear, sometimes resembling the fauns, satyrs and nymphs of antiquity, but sometimes curiously winged, like and yet unlike angels; nor are they precisely the fairies of our English tradition. However, Mr Gerard, like their creator, seems quite at ease with them all.

'The fall of Troy, no less, facing the window,' Benedict had pointed out. 'I particularly like the Trojan Horse, which has a very baleful look in its wooden eye. I'm told that is Odysseus, deviser of the scheme, peering out through a kind of porthole in the animal's side, but it looks more like a self-portrait of the artist to me. To your left, as you face Troy, we have Aeneas taking leave of Dido, with what I think are the tutelary spirits of Rome hovering above the tragic pair to make perfectly sure Aeneas does as he ought. To your right, Odysseus again, slaying Penelope's suitors. When I was shown the sketch for *that* scene, with Antinous so realistically clutching at his throat in agony, I thought it rather too dramatic for a bedroom and asked to have it in my sitting room here, which of course left me—oh, thank you—' as Carey opened the door of the adjoining room, so that her cousin could pass through and lay the still unconscious Mr Taylor on a bed—'which left me with Odysseus on Circe's island in here.'

'Good heavens!' said Carey, staring in frank astonishment at this last work, which entirely covered the whole of the sizeable wall opposite the bedroom windows. It depicted a crowded scene of frenzied imaginative power, featuring not only Odysseus himself (providently draining a cup of what Carey took to be the infusion of moly root), and the enchantress Circe in all her seductive beauty, but the crew of the hero's vessel being changed into pigs, while other animals with partly human features peered apprehensively from the island's luxuriant vegetation.

'I believe Tiberius included themes suggested by Milton's *Comus* as well,' remarked Mr Gerard. 'Since the poet describes Comus as Circe's son by Bacchus, I suppose it gave him cheering notions.'

'I see; that accounts for all the grapes,' agreed Carey, exploring the details of the picture further. 'And for the "pert fairies and the dapper elves" which I see on the "tawny sands" there. Mr Taylor seems to agree with Comus: "What hath night to do with sleep?" I shouldn't suppose it a very restful picture, is it? At least, I am sure it would keep me awake. And are those Odysseus's other lady loves, languishing rather impatiently out of the main picture, in three of the corners?'

'Yes, that's it,' Mr Gerard agreed. 'Nausicaa, faithful Penelope, weaving away at her web, and Calypso upon her island.'

'Well, at least Calypso had the pleasure of Odysseus's company for nine years when he did reach it, as far as I remember,' said Carey. 'Poor Penelope: one can't help feeling sorry for her. It is reprehensible, really, that one likes Odysseus better than the other Greek and Trojan heroes, on account of his being so much more resourceful! I am sure he was not at all an admirable character, but plainly Mr Taylor shares my preference for him. Unless it is because Odysseus kept company with so many goddesses and nymphs, and that gives him an excuse to paint all those ladies.'

Mr Gerard had by this time settled the artist, now breathing peacefully in what appeared to be a refreshing slumber, as comfortably as he could, and they left him, closing the bedroom door. 'When he wakes up,' said Benedict, 'he will probably spend a happy hour deciding whether Mounts Olympus and Ida should go to the right or the left of Circe.

Unless he really does mean to use both walls: one for Olympus, one for Ida.'

'But then what?' inquired Carey. 'For when next he is visited by a grand conception, he will have run out of space. I suppose he could paint around your windows . . . I must say, I wouldn't give much for his chances of being permitted to have one of these remarkably pagan scenes all over a wall in the Vicarage!'

'Nor would I, though that's always his first intention,' Mr Gerard agreed. 'It shows a very proper kind of family feeling: every one of these murals was originally meant for Tiberius's sister's house. You will be astonished to learn, however,' he added, perfectly straight-faced, 'that Mrs Whittier turned down all the artist's munificent offers.'

'Amazing indeed!' agreed Carey. 'Though you know,' she said critically, scanning the Fall of Troy again, 'the loss is hers. I can quite see it would not do for Mr Whittier's parishioners to be confronted with such a mural, but they really are very good. It's hard to tell, until Time has pronounced its verdict, but I would not be surprised if your friend Mr Taylor were to appear a positive genius in the eyes of posterity.'

'I'm glad you think so; myself, I believe his work very fine, and you know more than I of such things. Certainly I'm happy to give the paintings a home upon my walls.'

'Does my Cousin Clarissa know they are here?' inquired Carey.

'Good God, no!' The smile was in evidence again: I believe, thought Mrs Elliott to herself, that it is becoming an object with me to see if I can lure it forth. 'I confess to inducing Mrs Jackson—the housekeeper, you know—to enter into a conspiracy with me. She has a soft spot for Tiberius Taylor, so although she can make nothing of his pictures, there has been no difficulty. Now I wonder, if I appeal to her again,' he added thoughtfully, as they went down the stairs and out into the yard again, 'whether we couldn't find an empty attic with walls to spare for Tiberius's next few works? There's no immediate urgency. He has Mounts Ida and Olympus yet to complete, and we want to get him painting Grace Hodson, too. Though you might not suppose so from his style of conversation, he is a

138

most meticulous worker: the many sketches he prepares in advance seem to me in themselves very good, and when he comes to the full-scale works, he may spend months upon them. He can't be here painting as much as he would like, either: Mrs Whittier keeps a pretty strict eye upon him.'

'I own, I should like to know more of Mr Taylor's—' history, Carey had been going to add, but she was interrupted by the striking of the stable clock. 'Good gracious, is that the time? We shall be expected for breakfast, and I must say I am quite famished! Aren't you coming?' she inquired, seeing Mr Gerard make no move to follow her round to the front part of the house.

'No, I breakfasted some while ago, and have several things to do before I take the gig over to Little Marchingham, where I have to make some visits.' Mr Gerard paused briefly and then added, 'There's a wood near the village, famous for its wild flowers among the people here; would you care to come with me? I can wait until you have breakfasted, of course.'

'I should like it very much!' exclaimed Carey.

Rather oddly, she thought, Mr Gerard, having spoken as if on impulse, now seemed rather to regret this invitation. 'On the other hand,' he at once continued, 'you might find it a dead bore—and there is nothing to interest you in Little Marchingham itself—nor would you think the Dedmans, whom I particularly want to see, such agreeable folk as Peggy Hodson and her family, or—'

'Oh, never mind any of that!' said Carey, not to be put off now. 'Give me a chance to explore this wood you mention, and I promise I won't be bored, or get in your way either. If you really don't mind waiting while I breakfast, I will be as quick as I possibly can.'

That was not, in fact, quite as quick as she would have liked, for breakfast could not be hurried, and while Clarissa Gerard seemed determined to draw out her son Will into lively conversation, Will himself, never much inclined to lively conversation first thing in the morning, seemed more than ordinarily morose. He looked pale and heavy-eyed, too, as if he had not slept well and had some gloomy matter on his mind. Carey, whose sympathy for a young man dominated by his mother had now largely evaporated, hoped it might be remorse on Grace's account, but doubted it.

She remembered now that she had meant to tell his brother what she had learnt from Mrs Carmichael, a matter quite driven from her mind by her encounter with Mr Tiberius Taylor, and she decided against it after all, at least for the time being. It struck her that the elder Mr Gerard had enough to do anyway, running the estate and managing the Home Farm; she did not see why he should also have to deal with the problems of Will's indiscretions, or not if it could be helped. Supposing, just supposing, Will was beginning to come belatedly round to a more proper way of thinking about Grace, then she need not pass on what she knew to anyone at this juncture. And she didn't know it for *certain*, did she? For the moment, she reflected, drinking tea and waiting impatiently for her Cousin Clarissa to leave the table, she had probably better do nothing and wait to see what happened.

Breakfast had taken so long Carey was afraid Mr Gerard might have left for Little Marchingham without her; but when, having snatched up her sketching things, she arrived back in the yard, there was the gig with a horse between its shafts, and Mr Gerard himself walking over from the cowsheds, contriving to look not at all impatient. Whatever it was that had made him wish to withdraw his invitation almost as soon as he had offered it, he appeared quite reconciled now to her company, and brushed aside her apologies. 'No, no: there's a couple of the calves giving Fowler some anxiety, so I was glad to wait and take a look at them.'

'Well, that's very handsomely said of you,' Carey told him, getting nimbly up into the gig. 'I suppose Mr Taylor's still asleep?' And as Benedict nodded, and turned the gig out into a broad bridle path leading over the fields—'Do tell me why he is so much under his good sister's thumb. For really, when he is so gifted, one might expect him to be more at home in artistic circles in London. His talents are not at all like my own small ones, which do require living, growing plants—that, of course, is why I was so glad to accept Cousin Clarissa's invitation. I can't but wonder what he is doing here in Marchingham, and what his history is?'

'A sad one, I'm afraid. He did live in London until a few years ago, and I understand had a small but growing reputation for his work, besides teaching a number of private pupils—that was until the death of his wife. To hear him speak of her, you would think she was as lovely as Helen of Troy, although the miniature of her he has shown me depicts a rather plain if pleasant-faced woman. Well, she died of a fever, and he went quite to pieces, poor fellow: could not work, fell into debt, and in his search for the consolation of female beauty, I understand he began frequenting—er—houses of which Mr and Mrs Whittier could not approve.'

'Brothels, you mean? Ah, that certainly helps to explain it,' said Carey, adding in reply to a slightly startled look, 'I mean, why it is such a great grievance of Mrs Whittier's that Number Nineteen, New Road, stands directly opposite her own windows. Forgive me—I suppose I oughtn't to mention the place, though it is plain to me that everyone knows about it. I don't *mean* to be improper, but owing to the circumstance of my mama's having died when I was quite a small child, I was brought up very much among gentlemen, except for my dear Hetty, and I am too old now to start searching for euphemisms every time I am obliged to mention something of that nature.'

He laughed at that. 'Yes, well, you are quite right, Tiberius took to visiting brothels. Not for the usual reason: I don't believe he has touched another female since Mrs Taylor died half a dozen years ago. He only wanted to paint the girls, in the *personae* of nymphs, dryads, Maenads, or what you will—unclothed, of course, for you'll have observed that he prefers the female form naked, or only very lightly draped, in his work. The ladies who keep such houses were only too happy to charge him for the privilege of painting his murals upon their walls.'

'What a shame,' said Carey quite indignantly. 'They ought rather to have been paying him.'

'I entirely agree,' said Mr Gerard.

'I am sure Mrs Carmichael would not take such advantage,' she added.

Mr Gerard looked startled again. 'You don't mean to say you have met Mrs Carmichael?'

141

'Yes, she stopped to look at my work as I painted in the churchyard, and so I made her acquaintance; she is a rather remarkable woman, and not at all, I would suppose, in the common run of—of her profession. There, did I not pick that euphemism rather creditably?' she inquired.

'Very creditably indeed,' he assured her gravely, but she was pleased to see that this time the smile could not be repressed.

'I understand,' she continued, 'that it is an object with Mr Taylor to get access to Mrs Carmichael's house—to paint her nieces, that is—and really, I am quite sure she would not charge him, so Mrs Whittier need have no anxiety on that score. However,' she allowed, 'I do see that she has moral objections, to which she has a right, though I am not perfectly sure if she also has the right to impose them upon her brother, are you? But to the rest of your tale—what next?'

'To cut a long story short, poor Tiberius eventually had to be bailed out of a house of ill fame, dead drunk; for while he enjoys a glass of wine or brandy a great deal, he has never, I understand, been able to tolerate more than a very small amount of liquor. I fancy that while his wife lived she kept a careful eye upon him in that respect. He knows his own weakness there—though as you may have noticed, he preserves his good manners even when intoxicated, particularly in the presence of a lady. No doubt he found a decanter upon the sideboard as he stole out first thing this morning. Well, upon that last occasion in London his brother-in-law had to be sent for, and duly came to the rescue, and then it was that the full extent of Tiberius's debts came out. He has no worldly sense at all, poor fellow. Mr Whittier, who fortunately has quite ample means of his own, paid them, and brought Tiberius back to Marchingham. So you see, he really is very much obliged to the Whittiers, and is aware of it.'

'And is made to *feel* aware of it, I am very sure, at least by Mrs Whittier,' said Carey shrewdly. 'Dear me—a sad story indeed. I must say, there is one thing that does trouble me: would he be able to refrain from painting Grace unclothed —I mean by his imagination? Even that, I fancy, would cause poor Mrs Hodson grave anxiety.'

'Yes, it would,' agreed Mr Gerard. 'Never fear, I will impress upon Tiberius the undesirability of any such course. I think he will be willing to do me a favour—'

'I should think he well might, for it occurs to me that you have probably done a good many favours for him.'

'Oh, the gain's all mine, if you mean the use of my walls. In any case, there'll be time to explain to him exactly what is required, especially if you are to make your own study of Grace for a supposed frontispiece to your book; where-upon, you see, Tiberius will happen to pass by, admire it, and you and he will fall into a professional conversation.'

'Excellent!' said Carey, amused. 'What a good conspirator you are, to be sure, Cousin Benedict! I see you have it all arranged. I dare say Mr Taylor may enjoy a little innocent plotting too. Yes, and if we could conduct this solemn professional conversation in front of Grace's father, it would be all to the good, wouldn't it?'

'True, but this is still asking you to give up some of your time to paint a frontispiece which you don't really need at all. That is, if you still mean to do it?'

'Well, of course I do!' said Carey. 'What do you think I am? A female who takes a whim into her head, and then goes back on her word?'

'By no means,' said Mr Gerard, sounding quite contrite. 'I beg your pardon! I think you are—well, never mind that.'

Natural vanity, she told herself severely, was the only reason she wanted to know what else he had been going to say, but really one could not ask. In any event, at this moment they rounded a bend in the path they had been following across the fields, and Mr Gerard said: 'My first destination lies directly ahead. Will you come to Dead Man's Farm with me, or shall I turn off here and drive you to the wood where the flowers are to be found first?'

'No, do take me with you!' said Carey. 'I wouldn't dream of taking you out of your way, and in any case, I have a great wish to see this enticingly named spot. Dead Man's Farm? How in the world did it come to be so called?'

He smiled. 'Oh, there's nothing mysterious about it. It's only that the farmer is a Mr Josiah Dedman, and he and his father and his father before him, and I don't know for how long back before that—we must have a record of it somewhere—the family has leased that farm; so Dedman's Farm, you see, becomes Dead Man's Farm.'

'How disappointing!' exclaimed Carey. 'One might have imagined all manner of Gothick horrors, though I fancy those are far more enjoyable on paper than in real life. Do you know Mr Peacock's diverting tale of *Nightmare Abbey?* It made me laugh so much when I read it some years ago. I was pleased to find that the same author had published another novel last year, which I bought in London and brought here with me, and I'd be happy to lend it to you now that I have finished it. It is very entertaining, if not perhaps so extremely funny as some of Mr Peacock's other works.'

Mr Gerard, it seemed, had indeed read *Nightmare Abbey*, would very much like to borrow *The Misfortunes of Elphin*, and agreed that anything horrid was far more enjoyable in print. 'In real life . . . well, I'm glad to say there are not tales of actual murder attached to Mr Dedman's farm, despite its name,' he said. 'But violence there has been: you have probably never heard of it, but there was rioting in the eastern counties some years ago, when a number of labourers burned ricks and smashed the threshing machines which they believed, and still do believe, deprive them of their usual winter-time work. One such riot was at Dead Man's Farm. Josiah's father ran the place then. Dedman himself is a good enough farmer in his way, but it's a case of like father, like son: he employs as little labour as he can, and at wages as low as possible. With the bad harvests of recent years—and discontent pretty widespread in rural areas—some people foresee further trouble among the agricultural labourers. I would hope to prevent anything of the sort occurring here, but if it should, Dedman's farm is the most likely place. Forgive me—I must be boring you half to death.'

They had turned into a long track leading up to the farm, which could be seen standing in the distance, among the fields. 'No, not at all,' said Carey, honestly. 'I knew nothing about these things before I came to Marchingham, and it is always interesting to learn something new. So Mr Dedman is a tenant of yours—but I suppose that doesn't mean you can force him to pay higher wages?'

'No; one can only try persuasion. We pay our men on the Home Farm above the minimum, as does George Hodson, the best kind of tenant one could have; both he and I find it pays *us*, in the end, to ensure that our labourers are decently housed and fed, and make our economies elsewhere.'

'But tell me about the threshing machines; surely they are a form of progress, aren't they?'

'Yes, indeed—and bound to come into general use sooner or later. It's their widespread introduction at a time of difficulty like this that causes such ill feeling. There again, I'm afraid Dedman causes resentment. He has actually bought one of these machines himself, with a view to hiring it out and making money from it; one can understand his position, *and* that of his men, who see their winter earnings from the old way of threshing dwindling . . . ah, well, here we are. I don't suppose my business will last long. Mr Dedman is not,' added Mr Gerard, with a slightly weary note in his voice, 'particularly talkative or given to changing his mind.'

On coming closer, Carey saw that Dead Man's Farm, true to its name, was a place of distinctly forbidding aspect: the farmhouse was a square, uncompromising, brick-built structure; the farm buildings were foursquare too, and so were the ricks in the rickyard. Carey fancied there was a slightly slovenly air about it; she supposed she was comparing it with the neat yards of Brook End Farm, or the Home Farm at the Priory. The only person in evidence, a huge, broad-shouldered young man who came leading a carthorse out of its stable and proceeded to harness it up to a haywain, did so with a frowning face that brightened, however, when Mr Gerard hailed him by name, introducing him to Carey as Tom Harris.

Leaving the gig in his care, Mr Gerard and Carey went on towards the farmhouse. The master of the place proved to be built on the same foursquare lines as his farm, and did not appear particularly pleased to see them. Mrs Dedman, however, went quite against the prevailing square pattern, being a tiny, scrawny little thing who looked as if she anticipated that the next wind would blow her away, and was thus constantly on her guard. Her voice was an anxious twitter, but she bade them welcome, and seemed quite awestruck by the presence of a lady in her grimly neat parlour; not liking this at all, Carey begged to be allowed into the kitchen with her hostess when Mrs Dedman went to fetch the gentlemen some refreshment, and found it much the pleasanter room. There were several pretty kittens scuttling about the floor, and a shy little girl who apeared even more timid than her mother, so that in putting mother and daughter at their ease and playing with the cats, Carey amused herself tolerably well until the men came down the passage from the parlour. As he approached, Mr Dedman could be heard to state in a hostile, ironic tone that he couldn't pay the handsome wages some could afford.

'Nobody in these parts can afford to pay handsome wages nowadays,' Benedict replied, with the air of a man who has reiterated an argument many times before, 'but I think you would find it worth your while to pay at least a living wage. Well—keep that machine of yours securely locked up, won't you? And you'll send Fowler word about your bull? Good. Then we'll be off.'

Mr Dedman's farewells included a further complaint, to the effect that it was all very well for men with money behind them. 'Though the fact is,' Mr Gerard remarked ruefully, as he took the gig back from the man Tom Harris, 'that I fancy Dedman has more ready money to hand than we have for the Home Farm. However, it's no use trying to persuade a miser that he is really quite prosperous. Thank you, Tom, and how are the twins?'

The twins, it seemed, were sturdy boys of two years old, like as two peas, and young Harris's face cleared amazingly as he spoke of them with paternal pride.

'It must be hard, however, to have two children at once on such low wages as you tell me a labourer like Mr Harris may earn,' Carey remarked as they drove away.

'It is,' said Mr Gerard briefly. 'But now—here is the road to Little Marchingham, which leads us by the wood I mentioned, and if you would like to explore it for any plants that take your fancy, I have to see some people in the hamlet, and will be back again in an hour's time.'

* * *

146

I had not long enough, it is true, to do more than make a couple of quick sketches, and note what plants the wood contains (Carey wrote to London), but it is certainly a piece of old woodland, and will repay a second visit. Little Marchingham itself proves a small, poor-looking place by comparison with its 'Great' neighbour: this, says Benedict, is because of the difference in their sites, Great Marchingham being so much more favourably situated that it grew into the prospering town it is today, while Little Marchingham conversely declined. There is a general impression of discouragement about the straggling little village street. With the difficulty of making a decent living on the land, which Benedict was explaining to me, it is no wonder if the young people pack up their belongings and move away. Indeed, the handsomest building I saw was not in the hamlet at all, but was a huge barn, clinker-built, with a thatched roof, which I spied a field or so away from my wood, and out of curiosity went to look at it more closely. It resembled a great ship turned upside down, with its tarred timbers, but they too turned out to be suffering from decay, and the thatch mouldering, with a fine crop of weeds on it. I looked inside and saw a quantity of decrepit cartwheels, dusty sacks, and the like, and a ladder leading up to a loft, but was not going to risk my neck upon it just for the sake of curiosity. The barn, so I'm told, is known as Platt's Barn, from a small holding called Platt's Farm which once stood there, but Platt and his farm both being gone, the barn has come to be a place of assignation for young lovers. That will account for the many footprints, some of them small and made by women's shoes, in the softish ground outside the barn door, which might otherwise have puzzled me, since the barn is so isolated. Well, I have devoted this afternoon to social calls with my Cousin Clarissa, and tomorrow may turn with a clearer conscience to a particularly fine Military Orchid unexpectedly discovered in Great Marchingham itself. So you see, my life is very full here—fuller, I fancy, than if I had stayed in London this summer.

10

Carey had written more truly than she was aware.

> Yes (she wrote again, a week later), just as you sup-
> posed, we did hear of the King's death last week from
> the newspaper, before your letter arrived; I know it is
> no more than Papa expected, and one cannot but be
> sorry for the poor man, though he plainly did much to
> ruin his own health. The Season can hardly be a
> brilliant one now, and I suppose was not particularly
> merry before. Nor could I properly have taken a very
> sociable part in it myself had I stayed in London, so I
> hope Hetty is satisfied that I did right to come here. I
> am writing to John Lindley myself, but if you see him,
> do tell him that I am amassing a considerable body of
> work to lay before him on my return to London. And
> that, I assure you, is much more to my taste than
> fashionable socialising!

As for unfashionable socialising—well, that was a different matter, she reflected, and rather more to her liking; nor
need she lack for it at Marchingham. There were the
Hodsons, for instance, and the agreeable company of Mr
Benedict Gerard. There was Marie Carmichael, whose dry,
quizzical manner Carey enjoyed; while the nieces rather
interested her, too, for never before, as she told Mrs
Carmichael without embarrassment, had she met and
talked to young women who positively chose such a way of
life.

'It is not by any means every girl, you know, who *chooses*
it,' commented Mrs Carmichael. 'Sometimes they fall into
it, so to speak, out of sheer fecklessness; sometimes they
are forced into it by misfortune; sometimes they are actually

persuaded into it by their loving relatives. For my own part, it is with some care that I select my girls. Some, of course, show more immediate potential than others: Polly, for instance, is a case in point—although she, I must confess, was a rather unexpected find.'

Indeed, as Carey now learned, Polly had met Mrs Carmichael by literally falling into that lady's path as she, Mrs Carmichael, walked down a back street in Norwich one day, *en route* from a call on her attorney to the hotel where she had left her carriage. As she was passing the door of a public house, Polly came tumbling out of it propelled by a muscular arm within. The arm belonged to her companion of the last few weeks, a sturdy drover, with whom she had just had violent words. She sat where she had landed in the gutter, among a number of cabbage stalks which had strayed there from the Market two streets off, giving back as good as she got in the way of abuse, to the general effect that she was damned if she'd go with other fellows at the bidding of such as Joe Johnson, just to get him the money for more drink, she'd bloody well go with whomsoever she pleased, and for her own profit too, and that wouldn't be with Joe Johnson no more neither.

'Quite so,' agreed Mrs Carmichael. 'You are very right.'

Raising her head to see who could have addressed her —a head already spinning from the effects of the drover's blow and the drink she herself had taken—the startled Polly saw that she was sitting at the feet of an elegant creature clad in a walking dress of Prussian blue, with military braiding and frogging in the very latest fashion. Extraordinarily, this lady was smiling down at her with evident approval, a circumstance which made Polly's head spin worse than ever, for she knew very well what a bedraggled picture she must present, and even were she not sitting in the gutter with a black eye coming on, her wild, dark looks and showy dress were not calculated to win the approval of ladies like this one.

Approve, however, the lady obviously did, and now she was helping Polly to her feet, to the detriment of her own immaculate blue sleeve. 'I should have nothing more to do with your friend in there, if I were you,' she added. 'Instead, I suggest that you come back with me to my hotel,

149

where you may tell me about yourself, and we will discuss your future prospects.'

And Polly actually let her new acquaintance lead her off, such was her surprise, although it was as nothing to the surprise of the hotel porter and two chambermaids, past whom and into a private parlour Mrs Carmichael efficiently swept her.

By the time she was seated in a comfortable chair by the fire, sipping hot, strong tea, Polly's native shrewdness had come to the fore again.

'It's one of two things,' she observed, staring challengingly at her hostess. 'One is, you're wanting to put me back in the Magdalen, which if that's it, I won't go! So there!'

'I should think not, indeed. I have the lowest opinion of such places. I take it,' said Mrs Carmichael, smiling slightly, 'you have resided in a Magdalen at some time, and not found it to your liking?'

Polly waxed eloquent upon the characters of those persons who ran the Norfolk and Norwich Magdalen, the disagreeable nature of life in that institution, and her strong disinclination ever to return to it. 'For I won't be preached at!' she concluded. 'I'm goin' to better meself, see? I want to be . . . I want to be *free!*'

'Hm,' said Mrs Carmichael, inclining her pale, elegant head. 'I am afraid that in any walk of life, there is very little chance of freedom.'

'I'll have it, though,' said Polly defiantly. 'You just see if I don't. I'm going to be me own mistress.'

'Ah—now that is a more practical notion,' approved Mrs Carmichael. 'To become one's own mistress is a perfectly feasible proposition, though best achieved, in the first instance, by becoming somebody else's.'

'Here—who be you, anyhow?' asked Polly, abruptly setting down her teacup. By now she was sober enough to feel alarm. Was she about to be spirited off to London, even shipped abroad, and never heard of again? Vague rumours of such tales had reached her ears. 'And that's the other thing' she said, recollecting her original train of thought. 'Maybe you're luring of me into a nasty, low House, and I won't go there neither!'

150

'No, that is not precisely my suggestion,' said Mrs Carmichael calmly. 'But first, to answer your question as to my identity: let us just say that I am at present a woman of independent means, although in the past I have been in a line of business which I assume to be similar to your own.'

Polly's well-shaped but decidedly dirty jaw dropped open. 'But if you ain't planning to sell me to a House—'

'Will you take a little more tea?' Mrs Carmichael inquired, smoothly interrupting her.

Without a word, Polly pushed her cup forward, her mind effectively distracted. Tea was Polly's weak spot; it was seldom that a hot, strong brew as good as this came her way. Tea was elegant. Tea was expensive. It occurred to Polly that a woman of independent means—means such as Mrs Carmichael evidently possessed—would have no difficulty in purchasing a whole pound of tea all at once. A picture formed in her mind's eye of herself, clad with wonderful elegance, sweeping into a shop and buying a pound of tea . . .

'My own business, however,' Mrs Carmichael continued, 'was conducted with a better class of person than your recent friend Mr Johnson, if I caught his name correctly. Independence such as you hope for cannot be easily acquired by consorting with such men. Do you begin to understand me?'

Polly was far from sure of it, but as she certainly had not a good word to say for her recent friend Mr Johnson, she nodded silently.

'Very well; then listen to me carefully. I see distinct possibilities in you, my dear. You say you wish to better yourself: if you care, therefore, to come and live with me in the town of Great Marchingham for a while, I will teach you how to do so. Now, do not be alarmed. I am sure they told you in the Magdalen that you must mend your ways. It is only your manners which I suggest you mend, and I fancy you are a quick learner. If I am right, you may well hope to mix with persons of quality—with *gentlemen* of quality,' she corrected herself, smiling slightly, 'but I imagine the ladies are a matter of indifference to you. And you may also benefit yourself very considerably thereby. For the immediate future: I never have above two or three girls living with

151

me at any one time—we preserve a polite fiction that they are my nieces—and you will be perfectly comfortable in my house.'

'Ho, yes!' said Polly suspiciously, recovering the use of her tongue. 'Work a girl to the bone and take her earnings, is it? Nor never let her out without a keeper, 'case she run off with the clothes on her back. I know *your* game!' And she gulped the good tea rapidly, intent on getting it all safe inside her before she made her escape.

Mrs Carmichael only gave her another small smile, saying appreciatively, 'No, as it happens you do me wrong there, although you are quite right to think of all these things. It shows a quick mind and a sensible eye to your own advantage. Yes, you promise extremely well! My nieces earn a certain amount while they reside with me, but we do not receive *everyone*—oh, by no means! The object,' Mrs Carmichael astonishingly explained, 'is to make sure that you retain and indeed refine your original skills, while training you in all *other* aspects of your profession besides. Such sums as you do earn, I set aside to help equip you when you leave, or as a nest-egg for the future, whichever may seem more appropriate. It is not impossible, for in- stance—'she looked again, consideringly, at the girl facing her—'that you might quite rapidly find yourself a rich protector, in which case you would do better to lay the money aside, as provision for the future. But do remember that if it is set aside, it should remain untouched until you yourself have need of it. The one thing you must never, never do—I cannot impress this too earnestly upon you —is let any man alive get his hands on your money.'

Polly, who had no quarrel at all with this proposition, nodded again, vigorously.

'I do not promise that you will find such a person as I have been envisaging,' Mrs Carmichael carefully added. 'I say only that it is well within the bounds of possibility. There are a number of ways in which, if you learn to employ your skills to good effect, you will find that when you come to be pensioned off—as you may correctly conclude that, in a manner of speaking, I have been pensioned off—you need not descend into the gutter. As, you will observe, I have not done either. Except,' she added, glancing ruefully at the sleeve she had stained while helping Polly up, 'except quite inadvertently.'

'So what's in it for you, then?' asked Polly sharply.

'Another very sensible question!' approved Mrs Carmichael, nodding her neat head again. 'What is in it for me? Well—occupation, I suppose! I am not accustomed to spending my days doing nothing! I own, I had no thought of such an establishment when first I came into the country, but while I would not, precisely, describe myself as a philanthropist, I do not care to see a young woman waste her talents, so that when I meet with a girl like yourself, who would, I believe, benefit by my own experience, I put to her such a suggestion as I have put to you. Now, drink another cup of tea while you make up your mind, and I will order the carriage.'

What with the tea, and the sheer force of Mrs Carmichael's character, Polly found her mind seemed to have been made up for her, so that she was swept off unprotesting to Great Marchingham. Here, cleaned up and well dressed, she soon became one of the ornaments of Number Nineteen, New Road.

'Forgive my asking,' said Carey, after hearing Polly's tale, 'but suppose a . . . a niece of yours decides against such a life—'

'Then she is much better equipped than before for a respectable one,' said Mrs Carmichael briskly. 'Such was the case, for instance, a year or so ago, with a girl called Jane. She had no difficulty at all in getting a position as a lady's maid.'

'How—how did she do for references?' Carey ventured.

'I wrote them for her, to be sure!' said Mrs Carmichael. 'She had sensibly applied for a post in quite another part of the country: Shropshire, I think it was. I am not notorious quite so far afield, you know! But upon the whole, the girls find they can do better for themselves in the less respectable line. It is my aim to make them into young women of style enough to live by granting their favours to one wealthy and reasonably considerate lover, and to be able to pick and choose who he should be.'

Carey thought to herself that she would never discover

more about Marie Carmichael's own history unless she asked, straight out. 'You may think it uncivil of me, but I can't help wondering what in the world ever brought you to a country town like Marchingham! I don't mean to pry, but I will own to being consumed by curiosity.'

'Very natural, too,' said Marie Carmichael, perfectly composed. 'I was, as you might say, handsomely pensioned off when a young thing of sixteen took my protector's eye. An odd word, protector, when one comes to think of it. I for one had made sure I could protect myself, by habits of prudence and careful investment instead of extravagance, and I never cease to recommend the girls to do the same.'

'You ought to meet my former governess,' said Carey, chuckling. 'You would have more in common than either of you might suppose. Were you . . . were you a very long time with this—er—protector person, and was he extremely grand?'

'Oh, extremely: an Earl, no less, though perhaps I had better mention no names, and rich enough to gratify every whim; so if I were to pride myself on such things, I suppose it was no small achievement to have held his interest for ten years.'

'Were you fond of him?' Carey could not help inquiring.

Mrs Carmichael took no offence, but considered the question carefully. 'A little,' she allowed, nodding her pale and elegant head. 'It helps, you know, and I fancy many a marriage has less liking in it than can be found in some such connections, when they last beyond a month or so.'

'I am very sure you're right,' said Carey, reminded of poor Hetty's dreadful experiences. 'And I am sure your Earl soon realised what a mistake he must have made, with his silly sixteen-year-old.'

'If so, he would be far too proud to admit it, least of all to himself,' said Marie Carmichael drily.

'But why come to Marchingham? You still haven't told me that.'

'Oh, more or less by chance, because I knew nobody in this part of the country, and the very handsome sum with which I was pensioned off was conditional upon my living retired, of course.'

'How odious!' exclaimed Carey. 'Does this Earl of yours even know where you are living?'

'I doubt it, and I wouldn't call the stipulation especially odious. I didn't particularly desire to reside in London any longer, why should I? I had made quite enough money not to have to look about me for another protector at my age, thank God! But to tell you the truth, I found I lacked occupation, so that some three years ago, when my attention was caught by the first of my nieces, as it is more convenient to call them, I couldn't resist the temptation to see what could be made of her. Such a lovely creature, but with her looks all going to waste—whereas now she is being handsomely kept by a General, or was when last I heard of her.'

'I tell you what it is,' said Carey, smiling, 'you are a philanthropist at heart.'

'Not a bit of it,' said Marie Carmichael. 'I *could* have lived in a perfectly respectable way here of course, and even been on visiting terms with the Vicar's wife, but that was going to be excessively dull.'

A curious creature, Carey thought; but she liked Marie Carmichael, and despite her disclaimers, she also thought her unusual friend was genuinely fond of the girls, particularly Polly. The pretty blonde looks of Dorothea (or Dolly), allied to a pliable nature, made her, Mrs Carmichael explained, just what many a man required: to add enough sophistication to make her acceptable in the fashionable *demi-monde*, and thus better able to improve her fortunes there, was Marie's present object (and Carey perceived that it was rather hard work, too). Red-headed Molly was quicker to learn her lessons, albeit inclined to be a little sharp of tongue—'No bad thing if she keeps it within well-judged bounds; a spitfire is attractive to some, but she must be careful not to become shrill. That would never do,' pronounced Marie. However, it was plain that she regarded Polly Brignold as the pick of the bunch: Polly, whose desire to better herself made her such a quick learner. To watch her pouring tea with as much elegance as if she had been born to handle the silver teapot and fine bone china cups was, Carey thought, a highly instructive experience.

Her visits to the more respectable household at Brook End Farm had become a regular thing since the moment when she judged the time ripe for her to call upon Grace's services as model. There had been a slight delay (all to the good, Carey calculated, in that it prolonged the period of Grace's clandestine convalescence) caused by the weather's breaking: it rained on and off for some days, and when the skies cleared again, making it possible for artist and model to sit out in the garden, the fields were still too wet for much work to be done in them. Consequently there were frequent interruptions from interested Hodson menfolk, who could not help looking over Carey's shoulder to see their Grace taking shape on paper.

Grace, it had been decided, was to figure as Flora herself, seated under an apple tree; Carey spent quite a while over the painting of the blossom, which of course had fallen weeks ago, but in this good cause she allowed her fancy to supply it. The apple blossom took a good deal of time, and it did not occur to George Hodson, coming by and stopping to smile indulgently at his daughter, that there was no real need for her to sit there at all while this particular part of the picture was completed, and she might just as well be helping her mother about the house. Singly or in couples, Grace's brothers too seemed to find that their way to the farmyard or fields led them through the garden, and during her second day's work on the portrait, when Carey began to sketch in the form of the girl herself, gracefully disposed on a bench beneath the tree, a basket overflowing with flowers on her lap, Hugh Hodson came by with a young man: he was a stranger to Carey, but evidently not to her model, for Grace flushed when he stopped to greet her, saying with some awkwardness but evident concern that he heard she had been poorly, and hoped she was better now.

Not surprisingly, Grace was indeed paler and more listless than before, so that her blush was painfully obvious, and from it Carey concluded that this young man was a suitor, or a former suitor, as Peggy Hodson confirmed. 'Yes, that's Jim Spring, and if it was him she'd fancied, I'd have been happy enough and so would George. He's a place of his own, not very large, but mostly good arable land, over the other side of the Marching River. Still, there it

156

is: she always liked him well enough, Mrs Elliott, but not in *that* way. And you mustn't go thinking it was Jim Spring got her into trouble. I've known him from a boy, and he'd never take advantage of her. Or if he had, he wouldn't dare show his face here!'

Carey, only too well aware of the probable identity of Grace's seducer, had no intention of casting suspicion on young Mr Spring, and hoped aloud that perhaps Grace might now see his worth.

Perhaps, Peggy Hodson agreed; but she still looked anxious, for Grace seemed to take very little interest in anything much nowadays. 'Do you think she's pining, Mrs Elliott?' Pining, in Mrs Hodson's mind, was a mysterious and dangerous activity. She had had a young aunt who was said by some to have pined away and died for love. Other members of the family said prosaically that it was no such thing, but a wasting disease she couldn't shake off. However that might be, Peggy's dimly remembered Aunt Effie had been fair-haired and pale-skinned, just like Grace, except when her cheeks were unnaturally flushed, and over the past few days Peggy had begun to wonder if her daughter might go the same way. 'She's so drawn into herself,' said Mrs Hodson unhappily. 'It's not like her.'

'I think it's only natural, you know, when she has lost a baby,' said Carey quietly, remembering.

'Which it's a mercy she did lose,' said her mother, sighing, 'though it's my belief she regrets the child still.'

As she worked Carey talked to her model now and then, casually, but there was little response from Grace. The faraway look on the girl's face was not unsuited to the character she was portraying: a certain remoteness, Carey thought, suited a goddess well enough. Or was Flora a demi-goddess? She was not quite sure, but Tiberius Taylor, that authority on all things classical, would certainly be able to set her right, and she would soon have the chance to ask him.

By pre-arrangement, Mr Benedict Gerard came driving up in his gig on the third day of her work, ostensibly to discuss farming matters with George Hodson, in fact to deliver Mr Tiberius Taylor for a meeting with his fellow artist. A carefully edited version of Grace's tale had been

157

given to Mr Taylor, mentioning only a 'debilitating illness';
Mr Taylor had paid little attention, Benedict told Carey, to
any of this, but was happy to oblige his friend, pleased to
think of working from a live model even before he set eyes
on Grace, and overjoyed when he did, for he instantly
discerned her natural pretty looks beneath her present
pallor.

'Flora? Nonsense! Venus! She is Venus!' he said simply,
after a few seconds, and only then did he greet Carey. 'I beg
your pardon, Mrs Elliott; how pleasant to meet you again.
Had it not been for my Affliction, I should have enjoyed
further conversation with you when first we met—but
there it is, one cannot, alas, avoid the visitations of such an
Affliction as mine.'

This was said with a solemn little sigh. If by his Affliction
he meant a propensity to explore his brother-in-law's
dining room for intoxicating liquor in the early hours of the
morning, Carey thought he could have avoided its
visitations easily enough, although it must also be up to the
Whittiers to lock their sideboard. She returned his greeting
warmly, but added, 'I don't think Venus will—will be the
thing, you know. I doubt if Mr and Mrs Hodson would
quite like it.'

'He's thinking of Mount Ida, aren't you, Tiberius?' put in
Mr Gerard. 'Can't you do a separate picture of Grace?'

'To be sure,' said Mr Taylor readily. 'And I can put her on
Mount Ida as well. Venus!' he repeated.

'What about Hestia, or Vesta? Goddess of the hearth and
home?' Carey suggested. 'I believe that might be better.'

Mr Taylor thought about this, and hesitated; his dilemma
was that he had an even more suitable model for Venus on
Mount Ida in mind: the lovely blonde girl he had seen
several times going in and out of Number Nineteen, New
Road. He was aware, however, that his chances of painting
her, or for that matter her dark and red-headed colleagues,
were slim indeed. Though what a trio of goddesses they
would make! Nevertheless, for want of them, Grace might
do very well. Eventually Mr Taylor allowed his friends to
persuade him that she should be painted as the domestic
divinity Vesta, and George Hodson's permission was applied for. Although it was plain enough that he considered

158

the painting of pictures a very frivolous occupation, his paternal pride was flattered, and when the persuasions of Benedict in particular were brought to bear he gave his consent readily enough. Asked to look at Mrs Elliott's unfinished 'Flora' frontispiece, however, he allowed that it was 'very pretty, aye, very taking,' before returning to his work.

'He has hit the nail on the head, I think,' said Carey, looking a little ruefully at her efforts. 'Pretty, yes, and that is about all.'

'Not bad, not at all bad,' said Mr Taylor kindly. 'But ah, that basket of flowers on her lap,' he added with genuine enthusiasm, 'now that is excellent!'

'We understand one another, Mr Taylor. Yes, that's easily the best of it,' agreed Carey. 'I am leaving the detail of it till the last; it will take me several days yet, and mind, Mr Taylor—' here she looked around to make sure none of the Hodsons was in earshot—'mind you do not indicate to anyone that I could just as well do those flowers without Grace to hold them.'

'Not a word!' promised Tiberius Taylor, delighted to be part of this innocent conspiracy, hazy as his understanding of it was, and quite unable to refrain from instantly taking out his sketching block and a stick of charcoal, and beginning his own preliminary sketch of Grace, which Carey, glancing quickly at it, saw at once to be greatly superior to her own portrait. She was also relieved to observe that Mr Taylor envisaged Vesta as a thoroughly, if gracefully, well-draped goddess.

They were thus occupied, Carey with the basket of flowers, Mr Taylor with his first sketch, and Grace sitting docile beneath her apple tree, when unexpected visitors arrived. Mr Gerard, who had gone into the farmhouse with Peggy Hodson, now emerged at the front door, and was pausing at the top of the garden path to observe the pleasant picture presented by the artists and their model, when along the lane came Mr William Gerard, driving Miss Gage in his rather dashing tilbury, with Miss Gage's half-brother, Mr David Leigh, riding beside them on a very handsome bay gelding.

'Good gracious!' said Carey in mild surprise, looking up

from her work. 'What a great many callers Mrs Hodson has this morning.' And having fully taken in the identity of two of these three persons—for she did not know the horseman —she glanced swiftly at her model, and her heart sank. The girl had turned even whiter than before, and looked as if she would drop the basket of flowers any moment.

'Pray hold that perfectly still, Grace,' said Carey, in low but bracing tones, and poor Grace, recalled to her situation, righted the basket on her lap and went on staring as her mother hurried out of the house.

Miss Gage, so she said, had heard of Grace's indisposition—wished to call and see how her former pupil did—brought greetings from her mama—Mr Gerard here had been so kind as to say he would drive her over—and why, yes, they would be very happy to take a glass of Mrs Hodson's elderberry wine, and a slice of Madeira cake. The purpose of Mr Leigh's visit, if any, was not explained, but he was duly introduced to Mrs Elliott, and fell into easy conversation with the elder Mr Gerard, evidently an old acquaintance; Roberta, in the meantime, unexpectedly cordial, came to engage Carey in conversation and exclaim over the beauties of her work.

Of which it is plain, thought Carey, she does not know the first thing. She bore these well-meaning but ill-informed comments on her frontispiece with more equanimity than if the *Floral Companion* itself had been the subject of discussion, and uttered civil nothings in reply to Roberta's questions. How did Mrs Elliott like her stay in Marchingham? Oh, very much indeed! Miss Gage hoped she had met some agreeable people. Why yes, to be sure! It then struck Carey that Mrs and Miss Gage had at no point been among those families upon whom Lady Gerard called, and she exerted herself a little more than before to show interest in Roberta, who perhaps felt that she and her mother had been socially slighted.

And yet, she thought, I still have a strong feeling that Miss Gage doesn't like me, so I wonder why she seeks me out now to talk to me? And what, I wonder, is Will doing here, with Miss Gage and her brother?

The immediate answer was that Will was looking most uneasy. He had offered no remarks of his own apart from mumbled greetings, and was now hanging around on the edge of a group comprising Davy Leigh and a couple of the Hodson sons, Sam and Hugh, who had come round to the garden on hearing the sound of the newcomers' arrival. Although they were talking horses, Will, that enthusiastic horseman, took no part, but was looking around him uneasily.

His discomfort was as nothing to poor Grace's. Nobody at all was talking to her, seated under her tree a little way from the rest of the people gathered in Mrs Hodson's garden, and she had gone from white to very red in the face, and was gazing miserably, with far too much of her heart in her eyes, at Will, who for his part was studiously avoiding her gaze. Yes, Will was the father of her child, said Carey to herself, and then glanced at the elder Mr Gerard. He was standing very still by the front door of the house, evidently seeing exactly what she herself saw in the little scene. Oh, thank goodness, thought Carey, as he suddenly turned, took Mrs Hodson by the arm, and said something or other to her which caused her to go indoors with him.

At this very moment Grace uttered a small choking sound, as if the effort of holding back tears had suddenly become too much for her; the basket of flowers on her lap slid to the ground unheeded, all its pretty contents tumbling out, and she began to weep as if her heart would break.

In an instant Carey was beside her, on her knees on the grass and gathering up the flowers. 'Cough,' she whispered urgently. 'Cough, Grace, cough, and nobody will notice.' And taken by surprise, Grace obediently coughed—and then coughed and coughed, genuinely now, and couldn't stop, until at last Carey and Roberta between them supported the pink-faced, gasping girl into the house, where her anxious mother (Aunt Effie's persistent cough springing to her mind) plied her with glasses of water and various cordials, and made her lie down. Grace, it was agreed, was quite done up, and could sit no more for anyone that day.

'So it was Will!' said his brother succinctly, a little later. After leaving Mr Taylor at the Vicarage in Great Marchingham, he had turned the gig, with himself and Carey in it, towards home. She thought his expression remarkably grim. 'I suppose I should have seen it before.'

'I own, I thought it *might* have been Will—from something someone said to me.' He was not a man to pry further, she thought, nor did he. 'I was going to say so to you,' she rather apologetically continued, 'and then it didn't seem as though it would do any good for me to mention the matter, when I couldn't be sure.'

'One can be pretty sure now,' said Benedict, gloomily. 'I suppose—oh, the devil, I suppose I could have prevented this!'

'I don't suppose any such thing. What could you have done?'

'Found the money, somehow, for Will to go to London, as he wanted to, and as he did last year, only—well, never mind that. But it was largely my doing that he didn't go for the Season this year, and if I'd not kept him here, he wouldn't have made this mischief; out of sheer boredom, I rather fancy. So Clarissa would most certainly say.'

'I call that nonsense,' said Carey firmly. 'To be blaming yourself for what your brother does. No, really! You took Mrs Hodson indoors, by the way, just in the very nick of time.'

'I rather imagine *you* did something in the nick of time too, to provoke that coughing fit, didn't you? Well, at least I think Peggy doesn't know; I'm sorry,' he said, awkwardly, 'that *you* have to know.'

'Why?' And after a moment's reflection, Carey added in some indignation, 'Benedict, do not tell me you are *another* misguided person who believes me to have formed an attachment to my Cousin Will. Really, I call that too bad of you. The whole thing, let me assure you, exists solely in my Cousin Clarissa's imagination. How you *could* . . . !'

His face had relaxed a little. 'Good heavens, don't eat me alive! I must admit, I did suppose—'

'That I had no particular fondness for Will? And well you might; after all, recollect his heartless behaviour to my doll! It is all of a piece, if you ask me, with his conduct towards poor Grace, for people don't change so very much as they grow up. Very well, I suppose I had better tell you what really brought me to Marchingham, besides the flowers.'

And she gave a brief account of Mrs Pauling's sad story. 'So you may see that your brother is, if you don't mind my saying so, a matter of perfect indifference to me. I only wish Grace felt the same. I wish—oh, I wish young Mr Spring, whom I met yesterday, had been here today as well. I can't help thinking she must then have noticed his superiority.'

'So you met Spring? Yes, a good fellow, just the man for Grace Hodson, as I know her mother thinks.'

'But then again, she might not have noticed, or anyway not have cared. What a pity it is,' sighed Carey, 'that one tends not to fall in love with those persons with whom it would be *wise* to fall in love.' There was no reply to this; it crossed her mind, briefly, that Mr Gerard's face had darkened again, though she could not think why that should be. 'And another thing I would like to know,' she added, a moment or so later, 'is just what induced Will to accompany the Gages to Brook End Farm today, when one would suppose, if he had learned what happened to poor Grace or even if he hadn't, that it is the one place he would avoid above all others.'

Anyone desirous of giving Mrs Elliott the answer to that question would have had to go back to the evening before the day when, exploring the woodland near Little Marchingham for interesting botanical subjects, she had idly observed a quantity of footprints in the soft ground not far from the door of the great barn, including the prints of a small woman's shoe.

She had thought no more of it, unaware that events in the barn were giving both Miss Gage and Will Gerard a great deal to think about. Not that they actually met there, although it was a close thing. Roberta had happened to be walking in Little Marchingham Wood herself as twilight came on; she often liked to walk on a fine evening, once the girls had gone home and she and her mother had eaten their simple dinner. Then she could escape into the fresh air from what she felt were the stuffy, petty bounds of her school and her dull provincial life. Sometimes it felt as if she would never break loose from them and breathe the freer air of that kind of society where she knew her rightful place lay. She had by no means given up hope of using Will as a

163

means to that end, yet sometimes even she was discouraged. Unused to doubting herself, she did wonder occasionally whether she had been too vehement in her rejection of Mr Gerard's improper proposals. Not that she ought to have accepted them, of course—that would have been fatal, and would quite have defeated her purposes. But perhaps, if she had shown more poise, she thought, relieving her feelings by treading deliberately on the curved, empty, sea-green shell of a thrush's egg that had served its purpose and fallen from the parental nest; perhaps if she had been more sophisticated—cool and indifferent, rather than indignant—it would first have piqued him, and then brought him the more quickly to think of marriage.

And as her thoughts took this direction, she emerged from the wood and recognised the subject of those same thoughts riding across the flat fields down the track that led this way.

He was still some way off, but Roberta knew Will's bearing very well. She stood where she was, in the shelter of the bushes on the outskirts of the little wood. As the horseman came closer, she saw that she was not mistaken: here came her dancing partner of the Assemblies. It flashed through her mind that this was a chance to rectify her mistake, if mistake it had been: she could cross his path as if by accident; he would be obliged to pause and speak to her, or if he looked like being so uncivil as to ride straight by with only a brief salutation, or none at all, then she would have sprained her ankle, and require assistance. Sprained ankle or not, she would impress him by her poise and the coolness of her demeanour: she might make just a passing reference to the Assemblies, but with a smile, nothing to show that she so much as recollected that disagreeable scene which had ended their winter's acquaintanceship.

She was preparing, therefore, to cross Will's path by accident, when she saw him turn off the track itself and strike across the fields to Platt's Barn. This put rather a different complexion on matters. Platt's Barn, isolated and ramshackle, yet still with a roof on it to keep the weather out, was notorious as a lovers' rendezvous. Roberta knew that as well as everyone else in the Marchinghams. Nor was she unaware that Will liked to amuse himself with common country girls, even if it had been surprising and infuriating to find herself relegated to that low category. Suppose he had an assignation with some young woman in the barn?

Roberta thought quickly. Should she thwart any such meeting by simply continuing with her previous intention? No, that would hardly cause him to feel anything for her but annoyance. Quickly revising her plans, she decided to see if she could discover what Will was about. Knowledge, after all, was always a useful commodity.

Dusk was now falling fast, and it was easy to cross the short distance from the wood to the barn quickly and quietly. Slipping in through the door, Roberta looked about her. Well, if it was to meet a girl that he was on his way to Platt's Barn, she had not yet arrived. The place was just as she remembered it from the old days when she and Davy used to play here with other local children. Even the ladder still led up to the loft. Nimbly climbing it, Roberta settled herself among the musty straw and old sacking that lay in the loft itself, and waited to see what would happen.

If Will wasn't coming here after all, she reflected, she would have wasted an opportunity to remind him of her existence, and would feel rather foolish. But next moment she heard the sounds of a man dismounting outside the barn and tying up his horse; soon there were footsteps on the floor below. Will, for sure. He strode up and down for ten minutes or so, impatiently, and the listener in the loft began to be impatient herself. There could be no doubt about it now: he was indeed waiting for someone.

At last her curiosity looked like being satisfied, for another horse approached, halted, and was hitched to a post outside; another pair of feet trod into the barn, but not a girl's feet, though their step was quick and light, and as it soon turned out, was a step that Roberta knew as well as she knew the newcomer's voice. 'Ah, so there you are, Will,' said her brother Davy. 'Not inconvenient to you, turning out tonight, I trust?'

'Yes, it was! Damned inconvenient, if you must know!' Will sounded thoroughly out of temper.

'Sorry to hear that,' said Mr Leigh easily. 'And there was I thinking you must be a trifle short of amusement just now, with Grace Hodson taken ill . . . she *is* ill, ain't she?'

165

'How the devil did you know?' exclaimed Will, sounding disagreeably surprised. 'Anyway, what of it? Yes, my London cousin visited the Hodsons, said the girl wasn't well—Cousin Caroline's painting her, or some such thing—but what's Grace Hodson to do with me?'

'I fancy you know best!'

'Now look here, Leigh—'

'And if I were you,' continued Davy Leigh, unperturbed, 'I'd not boast so freely of your pretty rustic mistresses another time. Or not to me, at all events.' There was something threatening beneath his smooth tone now, and Roberta, up in the loft and listening with mounting elation, wondered just what his purpose was. The information she was gleaning was useful enough to *her*, but what did Davy want of Will Gerard?

'I named no names,' said Will, surly.

'So you didn't, but I can put two and two together as well as the next man. However, little Grace is hardly our business tonight,' said Davy, disappointingly (from his sister's point of view) changing the subject. 'I'll wait for the others before we go any further, though.'

Roberta pricked up her ears again. Others?

Will, however, continued, uneasily: 'Look here, Leigh, what exactly—I mean, I only heard the girl was sick, no more. Grace, that is. What's the matter with her, then? What do her family say?'

'How should I know?'

'Do you think . . . ?'

'Do I think she's really ill? Or prostrate with grief? Or told her father all? It could be any of 'em, or something else entirely.'

'Devil take it, if she *had* to get herself in the family way—' began Will, furiously.

'Did she, indeed? So that's it!' said Davy, with interest. 'Only think—I had no notion of that until now.' Will uttered another impatient sound, presumably, thought Roberta up in the loft, at his own stupidity. Really, she reflected, he *needs* me to do his thinking for him. Fancy letting Davy trick him so easily into giving himself away. But Davy was continuing, ironically: 'Get *herself* in the family way? Clever thing to do, that! Would you count on her father and brothers believing her, if she claimed as much? Or if you denied your part in it, for that matter? Well, never mind, don't take it to heart. It's possible she and her mother will contrive to hush it all up. The mother's a capable woman. By the way, young Sam will be here tonight . . .'

'Sam Hodson?'

'That's it, the clever lad. He's coming with James Pacey; very thick together, they are. Now those two, Will, have some rather fancy notions of the business which brings us here. And it's a good business and profitable—no doubt of that; you'll be glad you came in with me! To old Pacey and young Sam, though, it's a way of standing up for the rights of the labouring man, or some such thing . . . I've heard a deal of talk from the pair of 'em on that subject, and I'll own,' said Davy thoughtfully, 'that if Pacey didn't know so much, and his place weren't so well situated there just above the Marching River, with that fine view of all the traffic going up and down stream, I'd as soon do without the aid of a fellow impelled by the highest of motives. Unreliable things, high motives. Still, I thought I'd warn you about young Sam . . . for if you should do anything to upset *me*, who knows, I might find myself obliged to say what would upset *him*.'

'I've not the least notion what you mean,' said Will, with a creditable assumption of hauteur.

'Oh, I think you have! However, let's turn to more agreeable matters if you like—how's the horse? Worth what you paid for him . . . or more?'

Will swore again. 'And what did you mean by that in the first place? By pressing him on me?'

'Why, to put a bargain in a friend's way,' said Davy, very blandly. 'Surely you must have known his value. You're no gullible dupe, are you?'

'No, but—oh, curse it all!' said Will, suddenly sounding considerably younger than his age, and only too much like a gullible dupe. 'Ever since spring, you've sought me out whenever you came down this way, hinting the beast was stolen; if so, I never knew of it, and it'd be your word against mine, which I should think would bear more weight.'

'Should you?' said Davy, and Roberta, ear now pressed to the floorboards of the loft in her attempt to miss nothing of this interesting conversation, heard a note in her brother's voice which quite surprised her. 'Should you, though? What, your word against mine in a matter of horseflesh? I promise you I could tell a tale to make things look pretty black for you, and leave myself in the clear. And suppose for a moment little Grace had a tale to tell, too . . . but let's not suppose any such unfortunate thing, shall we? For there's something you can do for me, all in the way of friendship—something I fancy that, all things considered, you would *like* to do for me, Will—'

'Mr Gerard to you!' said Will, with a spurt of childish sullenness.

'Just as you like.' David sounded amused. 'As I was saying, something I fancy you would like to do for me, Mr Gerard. Come over this way, will you, while I show you what I mean. Then you may put your mind to likely places at the Priory, and I'll explain the ins and outs of it.'

To Roberta's considerable annoyance, he seemed to be leading Will to the other end of the great barn, where they were too far from the loft for her to hear more than the murmur of voices, the sound of heavy objects being shifted, something chinking on a flagstone—was there, perhaps, a trapdoor in the floor, hidden beneath the old sacks and broken cartwheels? Roberta wondered if she dared crawl to the edge of the loft and peer down. Not a timid young woman, she was about to try it, when she heard a party of other people come in, and stayed where she was instead.

She judged this party to comprise a dozen or so men; there was a good deal of low-voiced discussion, but strain her ears as she might she could make out only a few phrases. This was irritating, but Roberta, who already suspected the nature of her brother's less respectable activities, had also formed her own pretty accurate ideas of the 'business' in which he meant to involve Will Gerard. These were confirmed by the occasional mention of times and dates, and remarks such as, 'That's in autumn, when the keepers begin to watch out more keen-like, you want to be careful,' or, 'D'you mind the constable that asked to see what was in Tom's bag?' This last occasioned quick, loud laughter, as quickly hushed by Mr Leigh. 'The game does well enough in its way, but it's the contraband brings in the real profits, remember,' Roberta clearly heard him say, before he lowered his voice, raising it again, a little later, to add: 'And now we have Mr Gerard here to help us out of our present little difficulty.'

The air was almost tangibly thick with suspicion. 'Oh, aye?' said one man, doubtfully. 'Why would he do that, then?'

'Because he likes a bit of sport, and can do with what it brings in, like the rest of us,' said Davy, with great joviality. 'Now, you won't many of you be seeing Mr Gerard again —only those who bring the goods from Marchingham when they've come that far up river—but you'll know now he's with us. Ain't that so, Will, old fellow?'

Will was heard to mutter what must be taken as assent.

'And what's more—but here's the last two of us!'

The last two of them greeted Will with more enthusiasm, and seemed less intent upon keeping their voices down. 'Mr Gerard! Good, good!' That's Pacey the cobbler, thought Roberta. 'So you're one of us too, sir!' And the eager young voice surely belonged to clever Sam Hodson. 'There you are, Sam—' Pacey again. 'Don't I always tell you, all right-thinking men, the gentry too, will come to see the wicked-ness of a system where a man mayn't take a bird for the pot, unless he's rich enough not to need it, while the excise only bolsters up that system? A system which forbids a man to ask a decent wage . . .' And Mr Pacey launched into an impassioned speech upon social injustice, with enthusi-astic endorsement from Sam Hodson, and occasional murmurs of agreement from the others present.

But in any case, Roberta could not attend very closely to what was being said, for the dust in the loft, particularly in the straw to which her face was pressed, was beginning to tickle her nose in the most unbearable way, and all her attention had to be bent to a desperate endeavour not to sneeze, an endeavour in which she succeeded, but only by dint of uttering a sudden little gasp.

'Shh!' said sharp-eared Davy at once. 'What was that? Is there anyone up in that loft?'

She was lucky, she thought afterwards, that it was Davy himself who came clambering up into the loft, and stopped short at the sight of her. For a split second, brother and sister stared at one another in silence. Roberta found that her heart was thumping most uncomfortably; it was mortifying to be discovered eavesdropping. However, she was prepared to face it out, looking defiantly back at her half-brother, until Davy quietly mouthed the words, 'Get out when you can.' Then he called down to his companions: 'No, all's well, only a rat, I fancy!'

And he was off down the ladder once more. 'Now for the stuff down below—remember there'll be no more brought here; I've reason to believe someone's dropped a hint to the Revenue men, and we'll need a new place. That's where Mr Gerard will come to our aid. He'll be sending you word of where the next lot's to go—and you, Pacey, will pass that word on to whoever fetches the goods when they come up the river. Come along, then.'

And they were gone, Davy cutting short Mr Pacey, who seemed inclined to resume his oratory, by saying it was hands they must put to work tonight, not voices, if all was to be shifted. A moment or so later Roberta, looking cautiously down, saw the barn apparently empty—except for a flagstone that had been moved and was lying above the level of the rest of the floor. As there was no one now in sight, her suspicion that a cellar of some kind lay below must be correct.

Thankful that the coast was clear, she took her chance. In a moment, moving silently, she was down the ladder, out of the barn and safe away.

'Hallo, little she-rat!' Davy greeted her cheerfully, some hours later, slipping quietly in through the schoolroom door. She had set a lamp in the window, to indicate her presence there, and had waited up after her mother had gone to bed, sure that he would call in Saltgate, however late the time when his nocturnal business was done. The wait at least helped her to calm her ruffled nerves, and to recollect that *she* had done nothing wrong, and need feel no awkwardness.

She therefore said rather tartly, having closed the schoolroom door behind her brother, 'Smuggling, I take it. Poaching? Both?'

'Oh, I've a number of irons in several fires, my dear.' Davy lounged in a chair, smiling at her, not at all discomposed. 'Pretty soon, for instance, I must be off for Newmarket and the July Fortnight, where my real business lies—and all open and above-board too, whatever you may think.'

'*Was* that horse you sold Will Gerard stolen?' Roberta inquired.

'Not a bit of it!' said he, cheerfully.

'You certainly let him think so.'

'So I did,' Mr Leigh agreed. 'It did no harm to let Will Gerard think I've a hold over him. And now, d'you see, that comes in useful. I won't ask what you were doing in Platt's Barn yourself.'

'Nothing illegal!' she swiftly retorted.

'Oh, come: there's nothing so bad about bringing goods into the country untaxed . . . landed on the coast, then taken across country or up river. I'm sure it's no news to you that a fair amount of such stuff passes through Marchingham. I trust you, you see, my dear. Fact is, I'd sooner trust you than Will Gerard. You've more brains, for a start.'

'Thank you!' snapped Roberta, unmoved by this tribute. 'I'll keep what I know to myself, if that's what you mean. I don't want to see you disgrace us all—but I will certainly do nothing against the law!'

'Oh, I don't ask you to. But you know, Bertie,' said Davy, head on one side, 'with what you do know, you could make some headway with friend Will, supposing that's what you still want.'

It *was* what she wanted; she could not deny it, but she was not going to admit to Davy that just such thoughts had been in her mind all evening.

'Didn't I say I'd see what I could contrive for you?' he pursued. 'Incidental to my own business, that is! I take it that to hear of Grace Hodson's misfortune did not shock your delicate ears?'

She shrugged her shoulders slightly.

'Precisely so. You'd be a match for him, I don't doubt

171

that. Well, so we've both had an eye on Will Gerard, for one reason or another.'

'What exactly was yours? That I still don't know,' said Roberta curiously. 'Don't ask me to believe you have nothing but my welfare at heart.'

'No: I want the use of the Priory, or some conveniently out-of-the-way cellar or outhouse there, on Sir William's own property. I'm quite the public benefactor, you know,' continued Mr Leigh, blithely. 'Half the countryside does well out of the goods my friends run in off the coast. But now, besides the fact that someone's dropped a heavy hint to the Excise, there's other trouble brewing. I've warned 'em. Nothing to do with the trade, just trouble,' he said thoughtfully. 'I can smell it in the air, you know. The kind of thing old Pacey likes to think of: folk rioting, demanding what they call their rights, that sort of thing. And given there's trouble, constables and magistrates and all must put on a much bolder show of enforcing the law, d'you see? Many of 'em are only too well aware what the uses of that barn are, besides lovers' meetings—good Lord, Bertie, why d'you think it's been let to stand so long? Few of the local gentry are averse to a cask of brandy or so, now and then. No, it's not a place that can be used safely to store goods any more.'

'So you think Will Gerard can find you a better one? I would scarcely,' said the lady who hoped to marry Will, 'place much reliance upon his discretion or abilities.'

'No, to be sure! I think highly of yours, though, little sister!' said Mr Leigh. 'And I'm not asking you to sully your conscience—but look at it this way: you might keep Will reminded now and again that he's in some slight difficulty, if you or I choose to tell what we know of him, or what he thinks we know of him. Drop a hint, for instance, just a hint that you're aware of little Grace's trouble. Mind, I don't know exactly what the matter with the girl *is*, but at a guess, she's lost a baby, and somehow she and her mother have contrived to keep it from George Hodson, or he'd be after her lover's blood—it'd be the talk of the Marchinghams! So drop a few hints to keep Will in line for me; and you're not the girl I take you for if you can't turn it to your own advantage as well as mine. I'm sure you can contrive. I tell

172

you what: I'll put up here for a few nights, and before I'm off again, why don't I tell Will how much you'd like to be driven over to Brook End Farm, to call upon your former pupil? I assure you, he won't be able to resist the prospect of escorting you; I'll be of the party myself, I think, and then he daren't say no! Aye, that should do for a start, and you may make your own way on from there, while you keep an eye on my interests too. Well, is it a bargain?'

'Yes,' said Roberta. She had been thinking hard. 'Yes, why not?'

After that expedition to Brook End Farm, which left Grace and her mother very distressed, and Will Gerard most uneasy, Roberta came home in a state of such barely suppressed high spirits that Mrs Gage, who had been surprised to see Will call for her daughter in his tilbury, felt it her maternal duty to sound a cautious note. 'It was very civil of Mr Gerard, to be sure, but perhaps you should not refine too much upon it, my dear.'

'I don't,' said Roberta, eyes curiously agleam.

'Well, at least,' Mrs Gage ventured, 'I am glad you are not pining.'

'I'm not the pining sort,' remarked her daughter. 'I am not so poor-spirited, Mama, as not to go out and *do* something to get what I want.'

'Oh, my dear!' said Mrs Gage, and bravely asked, 'But—but if you get what you want—I mean, will it make you happy, dearest?'

'Happy?' said Roberta, turning a glance of patent scorn upon her mother. 'Happy? What has *that* to do with the matter? I assure you, Mama, I am going on very prosperously.'

'Oh, my dear!' was all Mrs Gage could say again, and sighed.

11

'And so you see, I am going on very prosperously here!' Carey had closed her latest letter home to London, unwittingly echoing her self-elected rival for the dubious favours of Mr William Gerard. It was true: she was a good deal happier at Marchingham Priory than she had expected to be, or indeed, she reflected, than she deserved, considering her duplicity in accepting Lady Gerard's invitation in the first place. Nor did she know herself so little as not to understand that she derived this happiness mainly from the agreeable company of the elder Mr Gerard. From this, it was but a short step to wondering, as she sat at work on the meticulous painting of her flowers, whether she were not actually falling in love. Such a contingency, she concluded with some surprise, was far from impossible. She had always supposed, realistically, that without ceasing to value Andrew's memory, she might come to love again some day, if not quite so soon. Soon? It was now nearly two years since Andrew's death—but she had hardly expected anything of this kind to come of her *Floral Companion*! There it was, however: if the strong disappointment she felt on a day when she never happened to encounter Benedict was anything to go by, she had certainly, while hardly noticing it, fallen in love.

But did Mr Gerard entertain any such feelings for her? That was another question, and much harder to answer, for at times she sensed a curious drawing back on his part. Without vanity, she felt sure that he liked her; there had been a sense of easy companionship between them from the first. But who knew? Perhaps, to a man, easy companionship was incompatible with love. Certainly there were moments when something warmer than friendship seemed to be hovering in the air, and it was just then that Benedict appeared to raise his guard.

Dear me, thought Carey ruefully, finishing the delicate veining of a leaf, mixing just the right pink for a crane's-bill flower; here's Cousin Clarissa on the one hand, doing her best to push me into the arms of Cousin Will, and myself on the other thinking I would not be averse to the arms of his brother, and neither gentleman showing the least inclination to open his arms to me! At this rate, Hetty need not fear any of those rapacious fortune-hunters she was prophesying.

It was very provoking, she reflected, that a lady, and dear Hetty had certainly done her best to instil ladylike principles into her, could not properly initiate any move in this particular game. Provoking and really quite stupid. Cheerfully casting ladylike principles to the winds, therefore, she buttonholed Mr Gerard after dinner at the Priory when next he put in an appearance there, and declared her intention of beginning her portrait sketch of him that evening.

To this Benedict replied briskly, if not actually brusquely, that he saw no occasion for her to do any such thing.

'Oh, but I do, and so, I am sure, do Sir William and Cousin Clarissa.' Looking to them for support, she got an amiable murmur of assent from the former, and a stiff nod from the latter. She would have been much cheered if she could have read Clarissa Gerard's mind, and thus become aware of the initial surprise and subsequent alarm with which Lady Gerard had viewed the growing intimacy between her stepson and the rich young cousin who would make Will so ideal a wife. 'Having begun the task, I must complete the family gallery. You all overruled my protests at first, so you cannot properly dissuade me now.'

With which she firmly steered him to that end of the drawing room where the light was best, and where, besides, they might talk with some measure of privacy, made him sit in a chair and required him to look towards her. 'Three-quarters profile, I think; that is how I have drawn the others, except for Cousin Clarissa, who has so very handsome a profile that it would have been a pity not to draw it—or at least attempt to draw it,' she corrected herself.

'But—' began Mr Gerard, making as if to shift his position.

'No, no, please don't move, not when I have you so nicely arranged!'

'But—' Mr Gerard tried again, one hand going involuntarily to the cheek nearest her, the one with the birthmark, as Carey, who had chosen that side of her subject on purpose, did not fail to notice.

'Ah, I see what it is,' she said, with mock severity. 'You are vain!'

'*Vain?*'

'Yes, and how ridiculous!' she continued, beginning to sketch. 'I would never have thought it of you.' Although she had, in fact, given the matter some consideration. Unable at first to believe that the mark of which Lady Gerard made so much could be of the least significance to anyone as sensible, in the general way, as Benedict, she had come to suspect that it was, and thought she guessed why: if Lady Gerard, as Sir William's young bride, had been tactless enough on first meeting her stepson to express distaste for the little boy's looks, no doubt he would indeed have developed an exaggerated notion of them. Tackling the subject head on, Carey therefore added, in matter-of-fact tones, 'If it is that mark on your face you don't want shown, I dare say you may be surprised when you see how little it strikes another person.'

'Thank you,' said Mr Gerard drily, recovering his composure, 'but if you insist upon this, then warts and all, if you please!'

'Exactly as I intended! I myself,' remarked Carey thoughtfully, 'was dreadfully conscious, at sixteen or so, of my mole.'

'What mole?'

'There, you see what I mean? The mole down here somewhere, near my chin. It appeared to me enormous. But then somebody told me it was a beauty spot; in fact, as I recollect,' said Carey, blithely inventing this flight of fancy as she went along, 'he offered to write a poem about it, since he was a young man much given to poetry, and had penned several verses already to the charms of other young ladies, but they were so very bad—the verses, I mean

176

—that I begged him to spare me and my mole . . . very well, laugh if you must, though I think it is unkind of you, but do try to keep your head in just that position for a little longer.' And well enough satisfied with the effect of her remarks, she continued drawing, while their conversation turned to other subjects, concluding with an offer from Mr Gerard to drive her to Great Marchingham the next day, so that she could replenish her painting materials at the only shop in the town which sold such things, while he saw to business of his own. Carey accepted this offer with alacrity, and smilingly turned down her Cousin Clarissa's counter-offer of the family's travelling chaise. 'For there can be no need for two vehicles to make the journey, when Benedict is going in any case, and so kindly offers me a seat in his gig.'

She had passed an agreeable couple of hours in Great Marchingham, had bought her paints, and then executed some commissions for Lady Gerard at the linen-draper's, where she had an agreeable chat with Mrs Pacey and her sensible daughter Susan; she knew Susan as the future wife of Hugh Hodson, and liked the girl. Next she called on the Whittiers, and was at last officially permitted to meet Tiberius Taylor; evidently Augusta had discovered that the two artists were already acquainted, and had given up any attempt to shield Carey from her mercurial brother as a bad job. She next called discreetly on Marie Carmichael, going round to the back of Number Nineteen, as its owner stipulated, and spent half an hour there.

It was a sunny, breezy day, very pleasant, if rather cool for the time of year, and with a little time yet to spare before she was to meet Benedict at the Rose and Crown, where he had left his gig, Mrs Elliott strolled along Riverside Road, looking down at the river Marching where it coiled its silvery way through the marshes, the sun glinting off its waters while grey-green flurries of willow tossed on its banks.

In Riverside Road, by a fortunate chance, she met Mr Gerard himself, his own business done, and they leaned comfortably over the low wall that bounded the open side of the street, talking idly. Would she like, Benedict wondered, to go down the hill and see the boatyards and moorings below? Yes, she would like it very much, and let Mr Gerard lead her to a long flight of steps winding in zigzag fashion down to the waterside.

'Isn't it unusual to find such a high hill in this flat part of the country?' she asked, stopping briefly to disentangle her skirts from a briar that grew over the low wall, beside the irregular steps.

'Yes; I imagine that when people first settled in these eastern regions, whenever they set eyes on a place high enough to be defended, they at once and very sensibly laid claim to it by building a church, or a castle, or some such solid edifice on the top, and—wait, be careful!'

His exclamation was just too late. He was going down the steps first, and had felt the brick edging of one of them rock unsteadily beneath his own foot; it broke away entirely as Carey stepped on it after him, throwing her off balance and pitching her some nine inches down, to land against him.

It was the merest stumble, and she would probably have recovered herself, rather than falling to the ground, if there had been no one there to catch her, but there was: Mr Gerard's arms instantly and firmly grasped hers and held her upright, and so they stood very close to one another, in a moment's curious, intent silence, before he let her go again and said prosaically, 'I'm sorry, I should have seen that before we came to it and warned you. Go carefully, I think a number of these steps need repairing.'

'Yes,' agreed Carey, and arrived safely at the foot of the hill feeling more shaken than the little stumble in itself warranted.

The road down beside the river was no such well paved thoroughfare as Riverside Road above, and was in danger of merging with the mud of the towpath between itself and the water. After the rain that had recently fallen it looked something of a morass. Mr Gerard, observing the elegant shoes Carey had worn to pay calls in Marchingham, said apologetically that he would not have brought her down here if he had known it was so wet.

'Oh, never mind that,' said Carey cheerfully. 'A little water won't hurt me, I promise you. I have tramped very happily around your fields when they were wet with dew or rain in search of my flowers. What a number of boats there are tied up here!'

'Yes, the river is tidal up to this point, you see, so the wherries come right in from the coast—large vessels that can put to sea and skirt the shore, or cross right over to the Low Countries. Look, there are a couple of them there!'

'What a size they are!' exclaimed Carey, admiring the handsome ships with their tall masts and furled dark sails.

'They're large enough to be a convenient means of shipping various items—from here, mostly grain. I imagine it was this river traffic that originally made Great Marchingham so much more prosperous than Little Marchingham.' They were strolling along by the moorings as Mr Gerard talked, and here he broke off to say 'Good day!' to a man in the dress of a constable, who had raised his hat and greeted him as he passed. 'And when the wherries run across the North Sea,' added Benedict, 'they sometimes bring in more than the official cargo on the bill of lading! That was Drew, one of the Marchingham constables, very likely going to cast his eye over the riverside taverns. There are several not far off.'

'A pleasing situation for a tavern,' said Carey, looking over the river to the water-meadows, now gleaming in the sun as the tall grasses blew in the breeze, sprinkled with the bright gold of buttercups in flower.

'Yes, it's a pity they are less respectable than those in the town above, and consequently more frequented by persons engaged in smuggling—this one, the Anchor, is pretty notorious in these parts. So I won't offer you refreshment here, but we might take something at the Rose and Crown before we set off home again.'

'That would be pleasant, and—oh! Wait a moment!' exclaimed Carey suddenly, putting out a hand to halt her cousin, who was walking on past the door of the Anchor. The place did indeed appear less than inviting: the door, which stood open, gave upon a murky interior of a dingy brownish colour, where little but the vague outlines of settles and a couple of tables could be distinguished, while the odour wafting out into the sunlight was powerful and unpleasant. A commotion of some kind seemed to be going on inside the public house, but it was one particular voice that had caught Carey's attention, a voice with which she was fairly well acquainted, although it was now speaking in accents considerably less refined than usual. 'You get orf and let me be!' shrilled Miss Polly Brignold. 'I niver wanted to come in here with you, Joe Johnson, nor I ain't going nowhere with you neither!'

'That's as may be, gal!' a deeper and rougher voice replied. 'Run orf just like that, without a say-so, would you? And who with, I'd like to know? Look at 'er, will you?' The speaker was evidently appealing to his interested drinking companions inside the tavern. 'Who's a-keepin' of *you*, then? Done up to the nines, eh? Run orf outer Norwich to live with some feller what said he could give you better'n what I could, would you?'

'Well, and so 'e could, too, Joe, by the looks of it,' suggested some fair-minded bystander.

'I ain't livin' with any feller!' said Polly, indignantly. 'I bettered meself, Joe Johnson, that's what I done! How durst you drag me down them steps, eh? You just wait, I'll . . . I'll . . .' But here she either found herself at a loss for viable threats, or more likely was silenced, for a sudden gasp ended her speech, and Carey was stirred to take action.

'Benedict, it's Polly! Miss Brignold, I mean, who is— well, one of Mrs Carmichael's nieces, you know, and she is in some kind of trouble. We must do something.' And never doubting Mr Gerard's ability to do something, or his willingness to follow her, she walked into the Anchor.

Peering through fumes of tobacco smoke, she was at last able to make out Polly, in the demure walking dress which that young lady now knew was the thing to wear for a stroll in the town if she wished to remain unmolested. In this instance, the propriety of her appearance had availed her nothing. She was attempting to struggle out of the grip of a large, burly, rough-looking man, who was enumerating his wrongs, evidently not for the first time, to his companions.

'Come on 'er walking down the street, cool as you please! Run orf and left me in Norwich, din't she? When I'd a nice little game lined up for 'er, too!'

'For you, you mean!' retorted Polly, with spirit. 'Me to go with the men, you to pocket the money! Well, I've bettered meself, Joe Johnson, like what I say, so there!'

'So I see—ho yes, so I do see!' returned Joe, with heavy sarcasm. 'What's 'is name, then? Let's have it out of you, me girl! Who give you this?' He had a firm grip of the lapels of her neat spencer with one hand, and was eloquently indicating the rest of her costume with the other.

'It was a lady give it me!'

'Now there's a likely tale!' began Mr Johnson, and would have elaborated on this theme, but her eyes being now accustomed to the gloom, Carey stepped towards him and his unwilling companion, saying crisply, 'Why, Miss Brignold! Is this man annoying you, my dear?'

'Mrs Elliott!' exclaimed Polly, with a gasp of relief.

'So this is your *lady*, eh?' remarked Joe Johnson, with much meaning in his tone, and never slackening his grip upon Polly.

Carey felt Benedict, standing just behind her, begin to move forward, and put a hand on his sleeve to stop him. 'Do I understand,' she continued, in as haughty a tone as she could muster, 'that you have obliged my young friend to accompany you here against her will?'

'He did!' confirmed Polly. 'He did that!'

'I fancied that such was the case, my dear,' agreed Carey, addressing Miss Brignold soothingly, 'for as of course you know, these waterside taverns are not at all the kind of place a lady should enter, or so at any rate my cousin Mr Gerard here informs me. I think you had better come with us, and we will see you safely home.'

Comfortingly aware of Benedict's presence, Carey also became aware, as she spoke, of a certain change in the attitude of their audience, who had been rather on Joe Johnson's side hitherto, and were not, of course, acquainted with herself. But several heads turned at her mention of Mr Gerard's name, and when he was seen standing by the doorway of the tavern, there was a certain amount of uneasy murmuring: as Carey had previously gathered, he was a well respected and familiar figure in Great Marchingham.

He was not, however, at all familiar to Joe Johnson, who replied belligerently, 'I dunno who *you* may be, missus, but this 'ere's my gal, and she ain't running orf from me twice, not if I know it!'

181

His grip moved from Polly's spencer and tightened upon her arm, so that she let out another gasp, of pain this time, squealing, 'Lemme go!'

'You ain't a-goin' nowhere, save with me,' said the persuasive lover.

But here Mr Gerard judged it time to intervene, and stepped forward, remarking in steely tones such as Carey had not heard him use before, 'That will be enough. Be so good as to stop molesting this lady at once, so that she may continue her walk with us.'

'Ho, yes! So what's *your* interest?' inquired Polly's captor. 'And who be *you*?' Several helpful voices offered to tell him, but the question had been rhetorical, for he was in no listening mood, and grasping Polly the more tightly as she tried to wriggle out of his grasp, he added, 'You come along with me, Poll, or I'll give you what for!'

'Go you on then, bor!' suggested one or two of those onlookers who had been relishing the scene; but most of them held their peace and looked at Mr Gerard who, observing that Joe Johnson seemed to be shaping up for a fight, moved to make sure that Carey was well behind him, and said more sharply than before, 'Let the girl go!'

'Nor I don't want no gents interfering neither! I got a right to mind me own business, so you mind yours and leave us be!' said Joe Johnson. But he instinctively let go of Polly in order to deliver a more forceful blow, in defence of his right not to be interfered with, and next moment, to his very great astonishment, found himself flat on the floor among the sawdust and other less salubrious items, the sound of hearty laughter from his erstwhile supporters and drinking companions ringing in his ears.

It had been so quick that Carey felt she had hardly blinked once before it was over; as the large, heavy drover put his fists up threateningly, she had felt a distinct qualm of conscience at involving her cousin in the affair, but evidently without cause, for Mr Gerard had floored his opponent swiftly, neatly, and without the least apparent effort. Meanwhile, Polly seized her chance to scurry for safety to Carey's side, and Benedict, remarking merely, 'There, now we will be going,' turned and escorted the two of them out of the tavern.

A subdued and shaken Polly took leave of her rescuers by the churchyard—thanking them, however, quite gracefully in the circumstances. 'Which were very awkward for her, poor girl,' said Carey to Benedict, as they themselves walked in the direction of the Rose and Crown. 'Mrs Carmichael has great hopes, you see, that she may become the mistress of some prosperous gentleman in London, and here was what I take to be a figure from her less respectable past appearing when she least expected it.'

'Less respectable?' Mr Gerard lifted an eyebrow.

'Well, you can't deny that she would be better off as the mistress of one gentleman than in the clutches of persons such as that man in the Anchor. I like Mrs Carmichael, you know, and confess to being intrigued by her own past history; I understand that she considers she has done pretty well and now looks to see her pupils, of whom Polly is the most promising, follow in her footsteps. I don't see anything so very shocking in that; a great many gentlemen do keep mistresses, who sometimes make them rather more comfortable than the wives they may have married for reasons of family or good connection.' Observing the corners of her cousin's mouth twitch, Carey inquired, belatedly, 'I'm not shocking you, am I?'

At this, he laughed out loud. 'No—and I'm past being surprised by you, but you would certainly shock my stepmother with such sentiments!'

'Oh, I know,' she agreed cordially. 'So I will keep them to myself unless and until I positively *wish* to shock her!'

It was now too late for any refreshment at the Rose and Crown, if Carey were not to arouse anxiety by her long absence from the Priory as dinner time approached, so that soon they were trotting out of Great Marchingham in the gig. 'Well, I must thank you for a pleasant day, and more particularly for coming to poor Polly's aid,' said Carey, as they turned in at the Priory gates and began to go up the long drive. 'I still don't know just how it was you knocked that man down, for he was larger than you, and it was all so fast. How did you do it?'

'Caught him off balance, that's all; nothing very clever about it,' said Mr Gerard, briefly, and instantly changed the subject. 'How is your picture of Grace going?'

'As well as may be expected—which is not so very well,' said Carey, ruefully. 'But at least George Hodson is highly delighted with it, and that was our object. Mr Taylor, by the way, has begun to come and make sketches for his picture, which is certain to be a great deal better than mine. But I'm afraid he still has notions of portraying Grace as one of the competing ladies in the Judgment of Paris. I am very much afraid they all appeared before Paris naked, didn't they?'

'Don't worry, I'll remind him to observe the proprieties,' said Mr Gerard. 'Here, let me help you down—and now we had better make haste if you are to be in time to change for dinner.'

'You are not coming in to dinner tonight yourself?' inquired Carey, as they began walking down the path through the shrubbery between the stable block and the front of the house. 'I have yet to finish your sketch, you know; it is so difficult to get hold of you to sit for me.'

'I shouldn't have thought you so anxious to complete a portrait, when you were decrying your own efforts only a moment ago.'

'*Touché!*' she acknowledged. 'But the portrait plan was not my own fault, you know; I was enticed into it by Mrs Whittier, and Clarissa, who can't see how weak my drawing of the human figure is. Plainly, Augusta Whittier doesn't recognise her own brother's great superiority in that respect. I must say, it does seem to me a pity that Mr Taylor's talents were born to blush unseen, as it were,' added Carey thoughtfully, a vision of his sketches, full as they were of vigour and movement, rising before her mind's eye.

'They don't,' pointed out Mr Gerard. 'I see them. They blush, or rather they don't, on the walls of this house.' For the façade of the Priory lay almost ahead of them. 'Still, I see what you mean, and yes, it *is* a pity. But at least his paintings give *him* scope, and employment.'

'If you do have to give the Judgment of Paris a home, with Grace as Venus, I believe you will get young Mr Spring too, in the part of Paris himself,' observed Carey. 'Tiberius Taylor has his eye on him. The only trouble is that Mr Spring can't for the life of him understand what Tiberius is talking about, and in any case he has no time or inclination to set up as artist's model. He is an estimable young man, however, and devoted to Grace. I suppose I should not say it of your brother and my own cousin, but I would have thought anyone must see Mr Spring's superiority to Will.'

'I hope Grace herself may recognise his merits in time. It would be a good marriage for them both, I fancy. I'm glad you like Spring—for you have become quite fond of Grace, haven't you?'

'Yes; I suppose I have! She is a good-natured child, though sadly featherbrained. And it's good to see her recovering—oh, dear me, Benedict, how did you do that?' For as they walked slowly along, talking, she suddenly saw the severely grazed knuckles of Mr Gerard's right hand, which had been hidden from her view on the drive back from Great Marchingham.

'What? Oh, that.' He looked down briefly, following the direction of her eyes. 'While catching Miss Polly's wooer off balance, I suppose.'

'Really, it was too bad of me to have dragged you into the affair,' said Carey, remorsefully. 'But how could I pass by when I heard the girl in trouble? First Grace, then Polly —well, I suppose it was not exactly Polly's fault, but why must she involve herself with such a great brute of a man in the first place? I am quite vexed with her for needing your aid! I tell you what it is,' she added, feelingly, 'you and I seem to be for ever rescuing silly girls from the consequences of their folly. Much more of this, and I shall be tempted to commit some ridiculous folly myself, merely for the sake of a change.'

The curious little silence of that episode on the steps was between them again. 'Shall you?' said Mr Gerard, in a suddenly altered tone. 'Then so shall I!'

Though it was not yet dusk, the sky had covered over with clouds promising rain. They were standing in a secluded spot by a tall yew hedge, and with a number of laurel bushes on the other side of the path, so that it was a little like being in a twilit wood. Reflecting on the matter afterwards, however, Carey felt that the air had suddenly become so charged, it would have made very little difference to either of them had they been standing in the middle of Great Marchingham with market-day crowds bustling around them. She found herself in Mr Gerard's arms, being held close and kissed hard, a kiss which she returned with considerable enthusiasm, some small part of her mind registering surprise at the strength of her own response. As at last they drew slightly apart, she said, breathlessly, 'Do you call *that* folly?'

It was most unfortunate, she later reflected, that they were interrupted just then by the sound of a stable-lad whistling cheerfully as he came down the path towards them. The spell was broken, the moment over. Mr Gerard instantly let her go, and walked on again, returning the lad's, 'Evening, sir!' as they passed. Carey, perforce, followed suit, feeling suddenly shy. It was not a sensation to which she was accustomed.

They stood still together for a moment again as they reached the house itself. Glancing at Mr Gerard's face, she thought it grave; too grave, surely, for what had just passed between them, and she smiled encouragingly at him, calling forth a glimmer of his own smile in return. She must tell him, when she got a likely opportunity, how much she was becoming addicted to that smile. Perhaps she would get such an opportunity next day? 'Thank you again for taking me into Marchingham—and don't forget, I hope to complete my sketch of you tomorrow,' she said, as calmly and demurely as she could manage in the circumstances. She thought she did very creditably, too. None the less, she went upstairs to change for dinner with her thoughts in a pleasing turmoil.

It was all the more provoking, therefore, that nothing went quite right the next evening. Had they been upon such terms of intimacy as to compare notes, Mrs Elliott and Miss Gage might have found themselves in sympathy over the fate of their best-laid plans.

Carey worked hard on her flowers all day, completing another study for the plate showing the wild roses in George Hodson's hedgerow at every stage in their development. How long ago it seemed that the first buds had shown, and yet it was only some three weeks. She could now paint the arching sprays of the rose in full bloom, and pick several flowers in order to dissect them and paint their separate parts; then only the hips of autumn would remain to be shown, illustrating the full cycle of growth. Though she did a good day's work, she was ready enough to pack up her things and return to the Priory in good time to dress for dinner.

She took her time over that operation, choosing a lilac *gros de Naples* gown, with short puffed sleeves and transparent aerophane oversleeves, and a puckered border in a deeper shade of lilac at the hem. She thought it became her. Downstairs, she found her Cousin Clarissa remarkably cheerful, which made conversation at dinner easier. Though she recommended her husband to partake rather less freely of the claret—'For you will do your gout far more good, Sir William, with calomel and rhubarb followed by a black dose a couple of hours later'—such was Lady Gerard's amiability tonight that she did not seem unduly put out when her husband, who knew his own mind on this one point, ignored her suggestion and had his glass refilled by Long yet again.

Carey was not to know that Lady Gerard's good spirits proceeded from the circumstance of Will's having approached her an hour or so earlier, with a request which was as music to her ears. 'Mama, can you contrive it that I'm alone with Cousin Caroline after dinner?'

'To be sure!' said his mother, and was wise enough to say no more.

Contriving it, however, proved a little more awkward than either mother or son had expected. As the two ladies rose to leave the table, Clarissa made a start by suggesting that, if dear Caroline were not too tired to continue her sketches of the family, she might find the light better in the library than the drawing room. To this Carey agreed with alacrity, but before Will, prompted by a glance from his mother, could open his mouth to propose himself as her subject, she had added, 'For I'm determined to complete my picture of Cousin Benedict this evening—shall we try the light in the library, then, Benedict? I'll see you there soon.'

Mr Gerard showed no wish to linger over the port, and followed her before long, so there was nothing for Will to do but remain behind and drink a glass or so of port with his father himself. He would not normally have minded that, but after going to all the trouble of thinking things over, and making up his mind to a certain course of action, he did not like having to wait—even though, when he and Sir William joined his mother in the drawing room, she dropped a word in his ear, to the effect that it ought not to be long before Benedict left the library. Of course not, thought Will; Ben was always busy about estate business of some kind or other, and not inclined to waste time on light conversation.

Nor was he in any mood for light conversation this evening either, as Carey noticed, settling him in the large window of the library at the correct angle for her sketch. The light really was better there, and showed up Mr Gerard's features clearly. 'You look tired,' she remarked. 'But then, I have noticed that you frequently *do* look tired —only if you can help it, you shouldn't do so when you know I want to sketch you.'

Getting no response to this, she worked away for a little while in silence, and then, glancing up, happened to surprise an exhausted, even drawn look on her subject's face. 'You look *more* than tired,' she said contritely, putting her private hopes of this particular sitting behind her. 'I've dragged you here against your will!'

'No: not dragged me, precisely,' he said, with a faint smile.

'You mean, only you're too civil to say so, that I have an overbearing way of making people do what I want. I'm sorry—I'd suggest we leave this for another day, only I have so nearly done now.' And she let her pencil fly on at what, for her, was an unusual speed. 'There! That is finished, or as finished as I can make it,' she said at last, holding it away from her for a critical inspection before putting it down on the small table that stood between them. 'And now you may see it!'

He picked it up, glanced at it, smiled briefly—a reserved smile without much humour in it, not the smile she liked so much—and put the sketch down on the table again, saying only, 'Very flattering.'

'Rather the opposite, I'm afraid,' she said honestly. 'If I *could* have got that smile of yours into it, I would have done so, but I suppose something of that nature can't be conjured

188

up to order, and if I'd asked you to hold it, it would have become a fixed grin instead.'

'Smile?' said Mr Gerard, bewildered. 'What are you talking about? I despair of ever keeping up with your train of thought!' And suddenly, unbidden, the real smile appeared.

'There! *That's* it! You see what I mean? No, I suppose you don't, without a mirror. You don't even know that you do it.' Encouraged by her success, Carey decided to proceed: nothing venture, nothing win, she thought, and nobody has ever accused me of reluctance at least to venture. 'The fact is, it has become quite an object with me to make you smile in that particular way, and you were obliging me quite frequently yesterday. Now, what have I done today that I can't make you smile for me?'

'What have you done? Good God, nothing!'

'Well, I suppose I must have done something, for you were a great deal friendlier twenty-four hours ago,' said Carey frankly. 'Forgive me—I have never been missish, you know, and I don't think I can begin now—but you'll recollect, we were speaking of folly, and . . . well, as regards what happened after that, *would* you have called it folly?'

Mr Gerard had risen very abruptly to his feet. 'Yes, indeed I would,' he said, face and voice both sombre. 'Folly of the worst kind. Not *yours*, no—no, mine entirely.'

'Good gracious me, why?' inquired Carey, in tones of mild interest; drama, she thought, is something we can do without at this juncture. 'Have you a secret wife and large family hidden away, or something of the sort, making it ineligible for you to go about kissing respectable widows?'

'Have I a . . . well, of course not! How can you be so ridiculous!'

This was better; she had almost made him laugh. On her feet too now, she came round the table, both hands stretched out to him. 'Then in that case, I see no possible harm in it. We might try again?'

It was a moment before the look in his eyes changed, and then he did move towards her, his own arms reaching out at last. With the most pleasurable anticipation, she walked into them, closing her eyes as she raised her face for another kiss.

None was forthcoming. Nothing happened at all. Feeling remarkably foolish, she opened her eyes again to see Mr Gerard a good two feet away from her, staring out of the window. 'Benedict . . .' she hesitantly began.

'I do beg your pardon!' he said stiffly, at exactly the same moment. 'A—a misunderstanding. You are very kind . . . and *nothing*,' he added in tones of positive savagery, 'is worse! I was right—an act of folly indeed!' With which he swung round and was out of the room in an instant.

'Oh dear!' said Carey aloud, an exclamation quite inadequate to express her dismay. She was more than dismayed: she was horrified. How could I have mishandled that so badly, she wondered; what did I do that was so wrong? I didn't think the wretched man so short-tempered, either . . . no, let us be honest, it must have been my own doing. I evidently mistook the situation entirely. She had never been more mortified in her life, she thought, as she buried her burning cheeks in her hands.

It was at this unfortunate moment that Mr Will Gerard, on the watch for Benedict to leave the library, entered it himself. 'Cousin Caroline!' he announced. 'Glad to find you alone! Cousin, I have been thinking.'

That was a dramatic announcement indeed, Carey reflected, even in her distress. And Will had indeed been thinking unusually hard, ever since the meeting at Platt's Barn. The drift of his thoughts was that marriage to his cousin might not be such a bad thing after all. Hitherto, an aversion to marriage in general, allied to a small but natural spirit of rebellion which led him to think he'd be damned if he'd let his mother choose a wife for him, had caused him to reject the notion of the match out of hand. Now, however, it began to look like a loophole: a way of escape from all the troubles that beset him. Cousin Caroline was rich, and not at all bad-looking. Yes, there were several advantages to the match. Betrothal to Cousin Caroline would show Grace that blabbing to her father and brothers, if she felt so inclined, was no manner of use. It would also show Roberta Gage, who had been chattering away to him on that shockingly

190

awkward visit to Brook End Farm—in the most amiable way imaginable, but with just the occasional reference to the Norwich Assemblies—that he could look higher than a country schoolmistress when he wanted a wife. And of course there was the money—just as Mama kept hinting —and Will couldn't deny that would come in handy. Best of all, perhaps, if he had independent means he could get right away from Marchingham, and stay away. No more danger of being required to dabble in such shady matters as smuggling. Caroline would want a town house, and they could live in London most of the time. And if she did wish to go into the country, she could easily be persuaded to fancy some other part of it. And once one had gone to town, and got a house there, one needn't spend so very much time with one's wife, after all. She probably wouldn't even want one to: she had been married before.

Will did not stop to ask himself what, in that case, could induce Cousin Caroline to accept him. She had come to Marchingham at Mama's bidding—people generally did do Mama's bidding. He would allow that Mama might well have been right to bring her here. Again, Mama commonly was right. You had to say that for her. Yes, he'd pop the question to Cousin Caroline after all—Mama had hinted plainly enough that she was only waiting for him to speak. And then he could snap his fingers at Davy Leigh, and the Hodsons, and Roberta Gage, and everyone else.

'Yes, I've been thinking,' said Will again. 'Fact is, I particularly wanted to see you in private.' And he looked hopefully for any sign in Cousin Caroline's face that she understood his meaning, since he wasn't much of a hand at proposals of marriage—well, a fellow had never made one before, but very likely she didn't expect much in the way of fine protestations. 'Never mind the sketching,' he said magnanimously, observing the block which lay on the table. 'Dare say you've done enough for one day.'

'More than enough,' said his cousin, in what struck Will as a rather curious tone of voice. However, he pressed on:

'What I was thinking—you know, with your being here at the Priory, seeing you every day and so forth—well, the thought struck me,' offered Will, whose love-making to Grace had also fallen short of eloquence, though that besotted damsel had not minded, 'the thought struck me that we get along very comfortably together—you and I. As a couple, so to speak,' he added, to make all crystal clear. 'I mean, we might get married.'

Gazing at him in sheer astonishment, Carey began to laugh in a manner that, for a moment, quite alarmed her cousin. If there was one thing he had not thought of her, it was that she was the hysterical sort! To his relief, she quickly controlled herself. Even in the present turmoil of her feelings, it was possible to see the extraordinarily inopportune timing of this proposal as a source of future amusement, but it would be most impolite to show that. Wondering what in the world could have brought him to make such a declaration, for she had thought Will could stand up to his Mama in this instance, she replied, with perfect gravity, 'Will, I am overwhelmed. I had no idea you entertained any such notions.'

Rather gratified, Will continued his declaration: 'Well, glad if *you're* glad. Rather thought you would—' But he had just sense enough not to finish his sentence. Naturally Cousin Caroline would be glad of his proposal; Mama said she would. However, it wouldn't quite do for him to say so. 'So let's settle it, then, and fix the day.'

The sight of Will advancing around the table, with the evident intention of sealing his proposal with a kiss, quite banished the momentary amusement Carey had felt. 'No,' she said baldly.

'What?'

'No. No, thank you, Will,' added Carey, minding her manners as Hetty would have recommended, and trying to overcome her vexation. 'I mean, I am very much obliged to you for your flattering offer, but I don't want to marry you, and I don't think you really want to marry me either, so let's agree to forget the matter, shall we?'

'No!' said Will in his turn, quite indignantly. 'Of course I want to marry you!' And indeed, he now felt that he did. Not only was his loop-hole apparently closing again, which made it the more desirable, it was mortifying to be turned down. 'And Mama said—' he unfortunately let slip.

'Will, if Cousin Clarissa said I would be likely to accept a proposal of marriage from you, I'm afraid she was wrong,' remarked Carey, trying to preserve her patience. 'I can't help but be aware,' she continued, more gently, 'that she favours the idea of a match between us—but I think that however much respect we may both feel for her, neither you nor I ought to entertain such an idea merely for the sake of a third party. Even if the affections of neither of us were engaged elsewhere.'

'Oh.' Will grasped at the offered salve for his damaged pride. 'You mean, Cousin Caroline, that your affections are . . . ?'

'Oh, yes,' said Mrs Elliott, gloomily.

'Someone in London, I suppose?'

Biting back a desire to tell him sharply to mind his own business, Carey said, truthfully enough, 'I would rather not discuss it.'

'Of course. Naturally. Well then, there's no—'

'No more to be said,' Carey swiftly and thankfully put in. 'I hope I haven't offended you, Will; I do most sincerely appreciate the honour of your offer, although I cannot accept it. Now, I am very tired, and if you would be so kind as to make my excuses to your mother and father, I will bid you good night.'

Once in the privacy of her bedroom, she was at last able to give way to her feelings. She found herself between tears and laughter. The comical interlude with Will had at least obliged her to keep calm enough for consecutive thought, and consequently, she now found, the worst of her earlier distress could be banished from her mind.

What an evening, though! To receive a proposal of marriage from the brother whom one did not care for, and who she was as certain as she could be did not care for her either; while the brother for whom she *did* care held back from an invitation so open that it would have shocked dear Hetty profoundly, although she was almost certain he *did* in fact return her feelings.

For a little calm reflection had shown her exactly where it was she had gone wrong. She would have done anything to recall that particular moment, but at least Benedict's reaction was no longer inexplicable to her. And surely, a word of explanation would set everything right.

She would have been dismayed anew to know that Will Gerard felt impelled to offer an explanation of his own to account for her rejection of him, and not just to his mother. A little later, working off his bad temper at the setback he had suffered by marching angrily out into the grounds of the Priory, he encountered his half-brother, and unburdened himself to Benedict too: he, Ben, needn't think that he, Will, would soon be handily out of the way, with a rich wife to supply his needs, because Cousin Caroline had unexpectedly turned him down, and it was all because she had never told them before that she, Cousin Caroline, was in love with some fellow in London, which he, Will, now that he came to think of it, considered downright underhand of her.

But fortunately for her chances of the night's rest she so badly needed, Carey was spared the knowledge that this piece of erroneous information, setting the seal as it did on a disastrous evening for herself and both the Gerard brothers, was now in circulation.

12

A word of explanation, Carey had thought, would do it: would clear up the misunderstanding between herself and Benedict. Over the next few days, she discovered it was going to be more difficult than that. She had a very accurate idea of the mistake she had made, so fatal yet apparently so trifling, and a few questions asked of Peggy Hodson confirmed her theory. However, the information she gleaned from Peggy was not a topic easily broached without *some* sort of co-operation on Mr Gerard's part, and that seemed unlikely to be forthcoming. He was perfectly civil when they chanced to meet, but cool in the extreme. Most vexatiously, it seemed that there was to be no resumption even of their earlier friendship. After a couple of days, Carey had to admit that Benedict was avoiding her.

It was also vexatious that Will, apparently undeterred by her rejection of his offer, had taken to paying her marked and unwelcome attentions. Could Cousin Clarissa have been foolish enough to suggest that he persist with his suit? Surely even the besotted Clarissa, to whom Will must have reported the outcome of his proposal, could not suppose that she, Carey, did not mean what she said? It was irritating enough anyway to have Will suddenly dancing attendance on her, and at this juncture too, but when she thought of Grace she found it hard to bear his company with equanimity.

Grace was taking a long time to recover from her miscarriage; the ruse devised to prolong her convalescence, said Peggy Hodson gratefully, had proved a godsend. And George so admired the portrait taking shape under Mrs Elliott's hands, it had been easier than his wife expected to induce him to agree to Mr Taylor's painting another. But the poor child was obviously listless and sad, which re-tarded her full recovery. She would still say nothing about her seducer, and Carey, like Benedict, kept her knowledge to herself. But she found Will's callousness hard to stomach; though she supposed the charitable might call it mere thoughtlessness, she could not.

At least young Mr Spring was assiduously courting Grace, and Carey quietly encouraged him. What a good thing it would be, she thought to herself, if only Grace could come to feel for this excellent young man what she had previously felt for Will. How anyone could take a fancy to Will, indeed, when he could be compared so easily and so much to his disadvantage with his elder half-brother, was more than Carey could understand.

She did contrive to find some small amusement in Will's attentions to herself on the Sunday after his proposal, when on leaving church he attached himself to her like a limpet, conversing with little inventiveness but great tenacity. It was a moment before Carey identified the reason for this earnest courtship in the person of Miss Gage, advancing towards them with the evident intention of addressing them both, an intention which Will was just as evidently anxious to thwart. Carey recollected Marie Carmichael's remarks about Will and Miss Gage, and with a certain amount of malice, she obliged Roberta by entering into cordial conversation with her. So little Miss Gage still had her eye on Will. I wonder, she thought, ought I to warn her what kind of a husband he would prove? For I don't suppose him the sort of man to change his ways after marriage. Well, no: she fancied Will would evade Miss Gage easily enough—and if not, she was pretty sure that Roberta Gage could look after herself.

Really, it seemed that the only satisfactory part of her life at present lay in her work, and that at least was going well, which afforded her a good deal of satisfaction. Even here, however, she felt the annoyance of days when work out of doors was impossible, for the summer was turning out wet and stormy after that spell of fine weather at haymaking time, and George Hodson muttered darkly about the pros-pects for harvest.

Perhaps, thought Carey, I had better leave the Priory.

Cousin Clarissa's pointed hints to her acquaintances about myself and Will are becoming an embarrassment, and as it seems that I had better put that fancy . . . that very considerable fancy, I had for Benedict behind me, I might as well take the paintings and drawings I have done back to London. But will Hetty feel obliged to move back to Chelsea then? And I had thought I might return here in the autumn, to paint later stages in the life cycle of my botanical specimens—I said as much to Cousin Clarissa, and *that* will be a difficulty now, too.

Altogether, her present situation fretted her. But then, one morning, there arrived a letter directed in Sir John's bold hand, which drove everything else out of her mind.

'Good heavens!' she could not help exclaiming aloud. 'Hetty! Oh—good God, at last!' Aware that the sharp eyes of her Cousin Clarissa, and the vaguer gaze of Sir William, were turned upon her, she explained, 'Oh, do forgive me! But I have had a . . . an unexpected piece of news!'

'Not bad news, I hope, m'dear?' offered Sir William; he and his wife were Carey's only company at breakfast today.

'Well, I suppose one ought to say so, but no, I can't. It concerns my former governess Mrs Pauling, of whom you've heard me speak.'

Lady Gerard pursed her lips slightly. She knew well enough who Mrs Pauling was. Not only Caroline's former governess, but her father's mistress, too! Caroline did not scruple to refer to the lady most affectionately, and there had been moments when Clarissa Gerard felt that the impropriety of such a connection for her beloved Will almost—but not quite—outweighed the advantages of a match with his cousin.

'I dare say you may have heard,' continued Carey, who had not failed to notice that pursing of her cousin's lips, 'though it is not a circumstance I myself have mentioned to you before, that she had the misfortune to be married to a gentleman who become hopelessly insane within a couple of years of their marriage, and had to be confined—and at last,' she finished, unable to keep the jubilation out of her voice, unseemly as it might be, 'at last and quite suddenly, Mr Pauling has died!'

197

'Dear me. I am sorry to hear it,' was Lady Gerard's correct if flat response.

'Carried off by a sudden fever,' Sir John had written. 'All that could be done to preserve his life was done, but to no avail. As you will understand, I can only be glad of it. Hetty is a free woman at last.'

'You needn't be sorry, cousin,' said Carey, frankly. 'His condition was wretched—and he had helped to bring himself to it, by his manner of life. I am sure I need not conceal from you that there has long been an attachment between my father and my dear Hetty, and now they may be married.'

Lady Gerard smiled and did some quick calculations in her head. 'How interesting!' said she. 'Mrs Pauling, I take it, is a lady of mature years?'

'Hetty is forty-five,' said Carey, smiling, 'but one would take her for much younger.'

All the same, thought Clarissa Gerard, relieved, the likelihood of her bearing children to cut Cousin Caroline out of her paternal inheritance must be remote. Even without it, Caroline was a catch worth having, solely for what her late husband had left her. At least Will was now trying to fix his interest with her—provoking boy, why had he not done so before, instead of leaving it so late? That first proposal of his had come too abruptly, Clarissa suspected. But would there be time, now, for a more fervent courtship? For she had a very good notion of what Caroline was likely to say next.

Carey had returned to the reading of her letter. 'At the moment,' Sir John continued, 'as you can imagine, poor Hetty is not very well, feeling quite overset and inclined to blame herself, God knows for what! However, I trust she will soon be better. You know Hetty: for ever distressed about matters that are no conceivable fault of hers. I wouldn't wish to cut short your visit to Marchingham, particularly as you sound happy there, but all the same, I know she will be glad when you can return to London.'

'Oh, I must go home at once!' exclaimed Carey, just as Clarissa expected. 'Forgive me, Cousin Clarissa: the last thing I mean is to be uncivil, after all your kindness to me. But you see how it is. Hetty has been almost like a mother to me—and will be my stepmother now! I understand she is in a state of some natural distress, and I must go to her directly. I wonder, how soon will it be possible to hire a chaise in Great Marchingham?'

But Sir William, rousing himself to take a benevolent part in her arrangements, would not hear of any chaise being hired. Caroline must have the Gerards' own travelling carriage: nothing else would do, he wouldn't be happy in his mind otherwise. It was difficult to refuse his kind offer, although once she had accepted it, it turned out that the carriage itself must go to the wheelwright's before it could set off on a long journey, and her departure could not be until the day after tomorrow. 'Which at least, since there is no positive urgency, gives us two more days of your company,' said Lady Gerard. 'And then perhaps you may return in the autumn—did you not say so? To paint the nuts, and berries, and so forth? How glad we should be of that—and so, to be sure, would Will!' said Lady Gerard, managing not to cast a cross glance at the ceiling above which her son still lay in bed.

Carey *had* said so—but before that unfortunate evening in the library. She would much rather have left for London at once, but there was no urgency, so for civility's sake, there was nothing she could do but give way to her hosts' persuasions. She wished Benedict had been there, to add his own, but perhaps he wouldn't have done so. Well, at least she might rejoice in the future happiness of her father and Hetty, and meanwhile, she must just possess her soul in patience for another two days.

In the event, the delay had its uses. There was time for another letter to reach Mrs Elliott, one delivered by hand to her room when she went to change for dinner that evening. 'That come from Great Marchingham for you, ma'am,' said the maid who brought it in, with her hot water.

Carey did not know the handwriting, for she had never had occasion to see it before, but she guessed where the note came from. She recognised the discreet little seal on the heavy, plain white paper: the elegant stamp that had marked the wafer lay on the equally elegant walnut writing table where Marie Carmichael sat in her drawing room, doing her accounts. Carey left it unopened until the maid had gone away, and only then read it.

It was very brief: Mrs Carmichael believed she was leaving the Priory soon, and wondered if she could call at Number Nineteen before she did so, at as early a moment as might be convenient to her?

No further expanation; yet what an extraordinary request for Marie to make. Marie, who had been so scrupulously, ironically careful of Carey's reputation, discouraging her visits if they took place at all openly, was actually asking her to call! Amidst all her other preoccupations, Carey could not but feel a powerful curiosity to know the cause.

Puzzling over it at least helped to while away the tedious evening, and next morning, on the reasonable and indeed accurate grounds of wishing to take leave of friends in Marchingham, she drove herself into the town alone in the dog-cart, left it at the Rose and Crown, and marched boldly up to the front door of Number Nineteen. Never mind now, said she to herself, *who* is looking from the windows of the Vicarage, and almost thought she sensed the wistful eyes of Mr Tiberius Taylor on her back, envying her access to that forbidden abode of lovely nymphs. Well, at least I have provided Tiberius Taylor with a splendid model in Grace, she thought; no one can say I didn't do my best for him.

It was when Marie Carmichael did not so much as remonstrate with her for using the front door, but came straight to meet her saying, 'Oh, how glad I am to see you!' and when Carey saw the unusual gravity of her face, that her curiosity began to be replaced by misgivings. There was no sign of Polly, Dolly or Molly; she and her hostess were quite alone in the pretty drawing room, its door firmly closed. 'Now. Sit down and take a glass of wine,' said Mrs Carmichael, pouring Madeira, 'and tell me, if I may go straight to the point, what is wrong between you and Mr Gerard.'

'Mr Gerard? Why, nothing. I mean, there is nothing of *any* kind between us,' said Carey, puzzled. 'He proposed marriage to me, almost certainly at his mama's bidding, and I turned him down, that's all.'

200

'No, no, I don't mean your cousin Will. I mean his brother.'

'Oh!' She concealed, or thought she concealed, a start of surprise, but some of the Madeira from the glass she held spilled on her dove-grey skirt all the same, and she became very busy scrubbing away at the tiny spot with her handkerchief. 'But I haven't—I mean to say, I have not said anything at all—to anyone! How could you tell?'

'Easily enough,' said Marie Carmichael, with a hint of her ironic smile. 'When someone seizes every opportunity to introduce a person's name into the conversation, well, there is nothing so very clever about guessing the reason. For instance, you have told me a great many things all about farming, which Mr Gerard has told *you*, although if you stopped to think about it, you would have been aware that my interest in agricultural matters is infinitesimal, if not positively non-existent.'

'Dear me!' said Carey, her colour heightened. 'How very impolite of me. And how transparent, too!'

'Oh, the most natural thing in the world,' Mrs Carmichael assured her cordially. 'You made it plain as the nose on your face. Plainer,' she added, surveying that shapely feature.

'Well . . .' Carey took a deep breath. In a way, it was a relief to have a confidante. 'Well, it isn't plain to him,' she ruefully added.

'So I apprehend. Although from all I know of Mr Gerard, I would have thought you admirably suited.'

'What—what do you know of him?' Certain unwelcome notions presented themselves to Carey's mind.

'Oh, not much. Beyond that he is generally liked in these parts, and held to be twice the man his father is or his brother ever will be. Also, you may well have gathered, that he is thought to have set his face against marriage, owing to an early disappointment.'

'I know about that,' said Carey rather grimly. 'From Mrs Hodson. Years ago, some silly chit—influenced, I fancy, by my Cousin Clarissa—was so thoughtless as to laugh at him when, as a very young man, he made loving speeches to her. I call it a *wicked* thing to have done, and so does Peggy

Hodson. It is a good thing all this was so long ago, or I would be much inclined to seek that young lady out and wring her neck! As for the rest, you may be bound it is all put about by my Cousin Clarissa herself, in her strong desire to see Will's children inherit the Priory.'

'Very likely,' agreed her friend, and then paused. 'Dear me, how very difficult this is—and quite against my principles, I do assure you. How can I put it? It will not surprise you, I'm sure, to know that a man who *is* a man does on occasion, if he is unmarried, feel the need to satisfy certain impulses.'

'You needn't be so delicate, or mince words,' said Carey, but with a sinking feeling inside her as the unwelcome notions loomed larger. 'You mean my Cousin Benedict comes to visit your girls?'

'Not often, and certainly not recently,' said Mrs Carmichael, obviously relieved to have had it said for her. 'Not at all recently! Not since before you came to Marchingham, as a matter of fact. And frankly, when I concluded that you and he—well, I hardly expected to see him here again. Very well, I will not mince words with you: I hear, now, that you are leaving for London, and at the same time, I have a—a request from Mr Gerard for an appointment to visit one of the girls tonight.'

It was a shock. She couldn't deny that it was a shock. Unaware that Mrs Carmichael could see this quite easily, from the way in which the colour had drained completely from her cheeks, Carey concentrated on lifting the glass very steadily to her lips and taking a small sip of Madeira without, this time, spilling anything at all. She managed very creditably. Meanwhile, another unwelcome suspicion occurred to her. 'Not Polly?' she inquired, in an admirably level voice.

Marie Carmichael smiled. 'No, not Polly. I heard how the two of you rescued her, of course. No, anyone but Miss Brignold, I am given to understand. I fancy this is no reflection on Polly's attractions, but a preference for some girl with whom he is wholly unacquainted. So now that I have set your mind at rest on that point—well, will you tell me what is wrong? Or is it something you don't know, or can't tell?'

'Oh, I think I know well enough,' said Carey gloomily, and told her. 'And I did it quite without thinking,' she finished. 'Closed my eyes, I mean.'

'Of course you did,' agreed Mrs Carmichael. 'Nine out of ten women commonly do, when about to be kissed. It's the most natural of reactions.'

'No doubt you are right,' said Carey, who had never thought much about the matter. 'But the first time—well, I suppose dark was coming on, and he did not notice. And then the second time . . . when he said something about kindness, *then* I realised what I had done, and how stupid I had been. The thing is, that because he does not speak of it, one assumes he thinks no more of that mark on his face than anyone else would do. But the fact is, if my Cousin Clarissa has been at work for years persuading him that it presents such a disagreeable appearance, it is very hard to disabuse him of the ridiculous notion, particularly as he will give me no chance to explain myself.'

'Interesting. Yes, you are right, I believe,' said Mrs Carmichael, thoughtfully, 'in your explanation of Mr Gerard's conduct. For on the few occasions he has been here, I do recollect that the girls—none of them with me now, by the way—said he had a rather curious requirement that there should be no light or candle in the room. One of them—a vain little creature, though enchantingly pretty —was rather put out, to think her charms should go unadmired. "Nancy", I said to her, "you may encounter much stranger requirements than that, and in the very highest circles of society, and if you cannot make your charms admired in the dark as well as you can in the light, then I have been wasting my time on you?"'

Even in her decidedly shaken state, Carey could not help smiling at this. 'A situation straight from Shakespeare,' she remarked. '*All's Well That Ends Well!*'

'I wish it may,' said Mrs Carmichael, whose practical mind did not instantly run to the works of the poets, 'though I will admit I don't quite see how: men are so provoking, and in general so stupid, and I cannot say your Benedict is any exception.'

But Carey did not hear her. She was listening to the echo of her own voice. She sat there for a long moment, glass in hand, and then carefully set it down. 'Marie, did you hear what I said?'

'You mentioned Shakespeare, I think,' said Mrs Carmichael, bewildered.

'Precisely! I have often wondered, you know, how it could work—if it could work. One can't *help* but wonder.'

'Wonder what? If what could work?' asked Mrs Carmichael. She observed some colour returning to her friend's cheeks, and was relieved, but she also felt uneasily that there was something a little perturbing about the distinct sparkle that had come into Carey's eye.

'Isabella! Mariana, I mean,' said Carey, still leaving Mrs Carmichael far behind her. 'And Helena, and Diana, or was it Juliet? Not Juliet Capulet, the other one. Well, now is our chance to discover if Shakespeare knew what he was talking about. It will be very interesting from a literary point of view, you understand,' she continued, cheering up by the minute, 'besides gratifying my curiosity, and of course preventing me from becoming shockingly jealous of either Dolly or Molly. You do want to help me, don't you, Marie? Isn't that why you asked me to come here?'

'Yes,' said Mrs Carmichael, guardedly. 'Yes, I suppose that was why.'

'Well, then I will tell you how you may.'

'I don't approve of this,' said Marie Carmichael flatly, a little later. 'I don't approve of it at all. It is a most improper notion. And do not say that I am in no position to tell you so, for that is mere sophistry. By the very nature of the life I have led, I know better than most people what is and what is not proper.'

'It's not improper at all,' protested Carey, who had been warming to her scheme more and more as she outlined it. 'It is the most proper thing imaginable. Unless we are much mistaken—and I don't mean to be so conceited as to suppose I must be irresistible to the man of my own choice, but do I understand that you share my opinion of the facts of the case?'

Reluctantly, Mrs Carmichael nodded.

'Very well. Unless we are much mistaken, I am the person my idiotic Cousin Benedict actually wishes to take to his bed. Forgive me, Marie, but you needn't expect me to be mealy-mouthed about it, when as you know I am not a blushing maid, but a respectable widow.'

'Widow, yes. Respectable, after such an escapade as this, no!' Mrs Carmichael pointed out.

'In any event, I wasn't brought up to be prim,' continued Carey, disregarding this. 'Very well. If I am the woman he wants, I am the one he shall get. I feel precisely the same about him, as you have deduced for yourself. Amiable creatures as your nieces may be, Marie, I hope you will allow I have a prior interest?'

By now Mrs Carmichael was observing her acquaintance with mingled amusement and exasperation. 'What a very odd creature you are, to be sure,' she commented mildly enough. 'But my dear, I do not think you have thought out the possible consequences well enough. What if you and your Shakespearian characters are all wrong, and even in the dark, you are recognised?'

'I shall explain,' said Carey, airily enough, though quelling a small voice of doubt which had at last penetrated the euphoria of her scheme's devising. 'I shall explain everything, and we shall at least have made a notable contribution to the study of Shakespeare! Could it be done, or not? I allow, it has always seemed to me improbable, but in the dark it might well be feasible, particularly if one had not previously slept with the heroine of the play—'

'Is that the part you imagine yourself to be taking?' inquired Mrs Carmichael drily. 'It is not the way heroines of drama commonly conduct themselves.'

'No, you're wrong: Shakespeare's heroines do,' rejoined Carey. 'Or the ones with any spirit in them, anyway, and I wouldn't wish to be one of the meek, milk-and-water sort, would you? Marie, do say you will help me,' she added, quite serious now. 'I need your help.' And, as Mrs Carmichael hesitantly nodded—'Good! Then let us work out the details of this plan.'

Severe misgivings beset her as the day wore on. It was a day of partings in any case: a day in which she must say goodbye to the friends she had made in and around the Priory. She found there were so many of them that she barely had time to pick those botanical specimens she intended to take back to London with her, to finish work on them there. Her leave-taking at Brook End Farm was particularly heartfelt, and she was glad that only a day or so before she had put the finishing touches to her picture of Grace, for poorly as she thought of it, it had served its purpose. Peggy, going against the grain of a lifetime's reserve, actually hugged her warmly before she left, thanking her for seeing Grace through the worst of her trouble. And Tiberius Taylor was coming now, to make preliminary sketches, so her mind might be easy there.

But all the time, the implications of what she was doing sank in more fully. As the hours passed by, her self-confidence ebbed with them. Evening came, and she endured what seemed to her a very insipid dinner, from which Benedict, not surprisingly, was again absent. She hardly knew what she would have done if he had been there. Called off the whole scheme, she rather thought; she could not easily have faced him at the Priory and then gone on with her plans. She soothed her nerves as best she might by finishing off a very feeble sketch of Sir William, with which he none the less seemed genuinely delighted, and then, with the hour for her departure next morning fixed, retired ostensibly to bed.

It was wet out of doors, the raindrops drumming against her window pane. The weather seemed a fitting accompaniment to her sombre, nervous mood—but there was no time to dwell on that now. Nothing venture, nothing win, said she to herself once again. She had let herself in for this piece of play-acting—she had persuaded Marie Carmichael, against that lady's own better judgement, to abet her in it—she must and would go through with it now. Carey let herself out of the little side door which she had found unlocked on the morning when she first met Tiberius Taylor on the Imperial Promenade. The wonderfully discreet John Thompson, a broad, reassuring presence, was waiting with Mrs Carmichael's chaise at the place appointed, to drive her the short distance into Great Marchingham.

It was a cloudy night, with no moon: all to the good! However, Carey felt more than a little apprehensive as she let herself in at the back of Number Nineteen—no marching up to the front door on this occasion, even in the dark. It was strange to be seeing Mrs Carmichael in, as it were, her professional capacity, but remarkably unembarrassing: Marie had previously assured her that none of the girls would be in evidence, and they would all be sent off early to bed. Mrs Carmichael herself, having given way to Carey's persuasions earlier in the day, merely looked at her rather searchingly as they went upstairs together, and asked, echoing her own thoughts, 'Are you sure you want to go through with this?'

'Yes!' said Carey, rather more decidedly than she felt.

'Very well. Oh, and by the way,' said Mrs Carmichael, opening a door at the end of the landing, 'this may not have occurred to you, but all financial transactions are, of course, dealt with by myself.'

That aspect of the affair had not, indeed, occurred to Carey, and she only just managed to preserve an appearance of composure as she thanked Mrs Carmichael for the information. 'For I suppose it might have been awkward,' she admitted.

'It might indeed,' said Mrs Carmichael, drily. 'Really, I do not think you are cut out for this line of business.'

'Well, I'm not going in for it, am I?' countered Carey.

'Ah, well.' Mrs Carmichael shrugged. 'At least I think we may be certain you will come to no physical harm.' And she closed the door behind her, leaving Carey alone in a pretty little bedroom, furnished in excellent taste, and lit by a single candle.

Once more, she was disconcerted by Mrs Carmichael's casual remark. She had not supposed she *would* come to any physical harm; it was a shock, therefore, to reflect that there were gentlemen who would treat a lady in one way, and young women such as Mrs Carmichael's nieces in quite another. Still, though she had not previously taken it into account, she, like Marie, did not think one need fear anything of that nature from Mr Gerard.

Here she was quite correct. However, it turned out that there were a number of other factors she had not taken into account either, and when, neat and tidy once again, she stole downstairs in the small hours to find Marie reading in her little drawing room, fresh as a daisy, she was ready to admit as much.

'As for Shakespeare,' she informed her friend, trying for as light a tone as she could manage, 'I do not know that we are much farther on. It does work—and yet it doesn't quite work either—and I have a dismal kind of feeling, Marie, that I may have gone too far!' she confessed, before surprising herself—but not Mrs Carmichael—by bursting into tears.

For one thing—so she told herself later, trying to account for the tears—she had not expected to be overcome by such sudden panic when at long last (or so it seemed even though Mr Gerard was entirely punctual) she heard footsteps come along the corridor. She had begun to shiver so violently that she only just remembered to put out the single candle. He brought none with him; Mrs Carmichael had been confident enough about *that*, but it was a relief all the same. The relief, however, did not stop the shivering. The windows were shuttered, so there was really nothing to be seen, but he must have sensed it as he came closer, for he had said, low-voiced, 'Don't be afraid. I won't harm you.'

After that—and she could remember in the clearest of detail all the extraordinary things that had happened after that—after that, everything seemed to be going to plan, up to a certain point. She had undressed in advance, which she tried to tell herself explained the shivering. Anyway, it soon passed off, for he was being, as she dimly realised even at the time, remarkably slow and thoughtful of her, considering the circumstances. Then things ceased going to plan. She had thought she knew what to expect. Andrew had been a loving husband, and she had quickly learned to enjoy the physical side of her marriage to him a great deal. She was not, however, prepared to find that she would feel so very much more, in every respect, with Benedict. Had Marie given her away, after all? She could not but ask herself this question as she tried to bring the tumult of thoughts and sensations she was experiencing into some kind of order. And then, for a while, she was obliged to give up consideration of the matter, along with all other coherent thought.

Afterwards, she mused on the same question again. Had he known her—with or without a word from Marie? Surely, though the whole extraordinary business had been conducted in darkness and near-silence, there had been mutual wonder and surprise, as well as satisfaction? Dared she, ought she to speak? But so great had been the release of feeling, she realised later, they had both fallen asleep. Not for long, she thought, perhaps it was only ten minutes or so. She woke to feel her lover's arm come round her once more, and was sure she was discovered now, if not before, for he murmured something drowsy and tender, which seemed to be her own name.

And then, next moment she was sure, or hoped she was sure, she wasn't discovered after all. As she moved willingly closer, he suddenly seemed to wake fully, and pushed her quite violently away, leaping off the bed himself in a reaction which seemed very like revulsion. Next moment he was hastily pulling on his clothes. She sat up suddenly herself, clasping her knees, her hair falling forward about her face, on the point of trying to apologise, to explain. In dismay: dismay which was all the worse for the abruptness with which it came upon her. Dear heaven, she thought: what have I done?

Her dismay seemed somehow to communicate itself to him, for before she could speak he paused briefly in his rapid activities to say confusedly, 'I beg your pardon— nothing to do with you. Forgive me. I must have slept—for a moment I took you for someone else.' He was at the door already, then turned, came back and placed something on the chest by the window. 'For yourself, and thank you.' It was said with the most punctilious politeness, and then he was gone as if he could not get out of that room fast enough.

'And what in the world am I to do with *these*?' asked Carey, showing Mrs Carmichael the five gold sovereigns he had left behind him. Her tears were over, leaving her still shaken, but somewhat restored by tea and the small glass of brandy Mrs Carmichael had insisted she drink.

'Perhaps you will find some means of returning them, and explaining yourself,' said Marie Carmichael, smiling slightly. 'They are nothing to do with me; I have explained that to you already. Cheer up! It does not sound to me as if anything at all disastrous happened.'

'I don't know—I can't work it out,' said Carey, 'Marie, you were perfectly right, and I ought not to have done it after all. And in some ways—well, in some ways I can't regret it. But if he did guess who it was—what must he think of me?'

'If he did, he is probably asking himself a similar question,' said Mrs Carmichael, bracingly. 'But I don't think he did. As I have been trying to tell you—only you, of all people, were too lachrymose to listen to me—I was particularly asked to offer apologies to my niece for any abrupt behaviour; there was no wish to alarm her; he had private concerns of his own on his mind. Does that reassure you?'

'I suppose so.' Carey frowned with the effort of thought on top of emotional turmoil and general exhaustion. 'That means—or I hope so—that he woke—and thought for a moment I was myself—and then thought I wasn't. Goodness me, however am I to untangle this coil?'

'Perhaps you had better just make a clean breast of it!'

'It's not so easy.' She brooded. 'You don't know what barriers the wretched man puts up around himself, or the trouble one has in breaking them down. But somehow it must be done now,' said Carey, resolution returning to her manner.

'That sounds more like you,' remarked Mrs Carmichael encouragingly.

Somehow it must be done, she had said—but just how, she had no idea. Driving back to the Priory, slipping in through the unlocked door, lying in bed with her mind racing too fast to allow her any sleep for what remained of the night, she told herself she was too tired to think, and it was useless to try just yet. She was conscious of a strong desire to get up again, make her way through the draughty corridors of the Priory to the rooms so magnificently adorned with Tiberius Taylor's classical murals, and confess her whole scheme, as suggested by Marie Carmichael, under the surely indulgent eye of Odysseus and all his female friends. But she thought she had done quite enough on impulse for one period of twenty-four hours. Even though she was leaving for

London in the morning—perhaps more especially because she was leaving for London in the morning—it would not do to act without proper thought again. Perhaps there would be a chance for a brief word of some kind, when she said goodbye to Mr Gerard.

In the event, there was no opportunity to say goodbye to him at all, for he was absent somewhere about the estate in the morning, or so Cousin Clarissa said when Carey asked straight out. She supposed she might have expected as much, and after a moment's thought, wrote a brief, friendly note of farewell to leave for him.

Lady Gerard's own farewells were prolonged and effusive, and Sir William's hope that she would soon be back sounded genuine. And then, before she knew it, the carriage was ready, and there could be no more delay if she was to reach London that day, as she fully intended to do. Together with all her own concerns, anxiety about Hetty lay at the back of her mind. She well knew how likely dear Hetty was to fall into distress at the loss of her unlamented husband, and one part of her at least longed to be with Mrs Pauling, cheering her and persuading her to make Sir John a happy man at last; for it would be just like Hetty to refuse him now, out of some silly scruple that would occur to no one but herself, thought Carey.

She was in subdued and still shaken mood as the carriage turned out of the driveway of the Priory and set off towards the Great North Road. It was raining again; even though this was only the end of July, the summer seemed over, the flowers she had painted looked bedraggled, sodden with the recent wet weather. Well, I must put the Priory and everyone in it out of my mind for the time being, she told herself firmly. That was easier said than done. By the time she approached the end of her journey, she had come to a different conclusion. If he doesn't reply to my note, I will write to him again, she thought as the carriage drove through grey London streets. Yes, that is what I will do: I will write to him.

And then she was home—and everything else was indeed driven out of her mind by the sight of her father's face as she came in, and read there confirmation of her worst misgivings concerning Hetty's condition.

'Good heavens—what is it? What is wrong?' she exclaimed.

'Thank God you're here, my dear!' said Sir John. 'Hetty is worse—much worse. In such a state of prostration—it's nervous, I think, and so does Halford, who has seen her, but none the less dangerous for that. Anyway, thank God you're here,' he repeated, 'for if anyone can pull her through this crisis, I think it will be you.'

13

'Not a rout, of course,' Lady Saye assured her caller. 'Anything so large would be most unsuitable while we are in mourning for the King. Just a small, select gathering of friends, tell dear Henrietta; a little music, perhaps; an elegant, light supper. I hope she will feel equal to it. I should be so very happy if it were at *my* house that she and your dear father celebrated their engagement.'

'How good you are!' said Carey, touched. 'Well, now that Hetty has at last agreed to let my father send the notice of their marriage to the *Morning Post*, we will make sure it appears on the date of your party. How *very* good you are!'

'Oh no, not good at all, for I am most sincerely attached to Henrietta,' Lady Saye told her, placing a hand upon her bosom somewhere in the region of her kindly and sentimental heart, 'and ah, how I have felt for her in the—the delicate distress she has suffered all these years.'

'Yes, poor Hetty—the strain of her situation must have been greater than even we truly understood, to make her so very ill when the cause of it was removed. For several days, you know, we actually despaired of her life. But she is well on the road to recovery now, thank goodness.'

'Thanks to your devoted nursing, too, my dear.'

'Oh, nonsense!' said Carey briskly. 'I'm no nurse; naturally, my father engaged the very best that were to be had, and very well they tended her.' But it was true enough that at the height of Hetty's illness, she had seemed to take no notice of anyone but her former pupil, and when the crisis was over, leaving her so weak, Carey had spent days talking endlessly: soothing, cheering, and at last persuading her that she owed it to Sir John to get better.

'You are a good girl, my dear—and now that Henrietta

213

and your papa are to be married,' said Lady Saye, suddenly becoming roguish and wagging a finger at her, 'we must see what can be done for *you*.'

Carey bore this well, merely saying with a smile, 'Don't trouble yourself about me, ma'am. My one thought at the moment is to ensure that Hetty enjoys a pleasant convalescence, and can be married in the autumn.'

'It is to Tunbridge Wells you are taking her, is it not?' inquired Lady Saye, with a knowing gleam in her eye at which Carey rather wondered.

'Yes: her doctors thought sea air might be too bracing, and an inland watering place would be best—besides, my father cannot be away from London for a long period just now, if he is to take Hetty travelling on the Continent after their wedding, but he can visit us at Tunbridge Wells more easily than if we were to go to a seaside place like Brighton.'

This consideration, indeed, had been a deciding factor, causing Hetty herself to declare that she felt a positive aversion to the seaside—Tunbridge Wells was just the thing! 'I believe it is a pleasant place, with pure, invigorating air; we may drink the waters of the chalybeate springs, and then I shall be quite well again. I should like nowhere better than Tunbridge Wells.' And there had been a gleam in Hetty's eye, Carey now remembered, not unlike the one she saw at present in Lady Saye's.

She wondered whether Hetty would feel strong enough for an evening party, but Mrs Pauling became quite animated on receiving the invitation, which she accepted with such alacrity as left Carey a little at a loss to account for it. Until, that is, she entered Lady Saye's drawing room with Sir John and Mrs Pauling on the evening of the small, select gathering, and saw that it was all part of a plan no doubt designed by both ladies long before, but necessarily shelved during Hetty's illness.

There were not above ten people present, and all but one of them were known to her: persons of high social standing, if not particularly notable for their liveliness and wit—none of the interesting oddities one might meet in Sir John's own house, but this, of course, was just what would please Hetty most. To be welcomed into such company as Sir John's future wife allayed any doubts she might still feel

214

about her acceptability in society. Carey, admiring the splendour of Lady Saye's enormous, flower-laden evening hat and her sober-hued but lavishly trimmed gown, silently applauded the kind heart that beat beneath all those trimmings.

She also noticed that the dull but impeccably correct company consisted entirely of persons married to one another—except, of course, for the affianced couple, herself, and that one gentleman she did not already know, to whom Lady Saye was quick to introduce her. 'My dear—let me make the Earl of Anderford known to you.' And Carey was just in time to catch the conspiratorial glance that passed between her hostess and Hetty.

Oh, really, she said to herself, it is too bad of them! An Earl, produced especially for my benefit—or perhaps I have been produced for his, if he needs a rich wife. She was between exasperation and amusement, but amusement won the day. How could she spoil dear Hetty's innocent pleasures? Accordingly, she sat down in a chair beside his lordship and began a conversation with him, while one of the ladies present tinkled away in a mediocre manner on the pianoforte.

To do Lord Anderford justice, he seemed no more anxious to ingratiate himself with her than courtesy demanded, and Carey concluded, as they exchanged small talk, that he could hardly be in search of a rich wife, for he plainly owned large estates, and seemed well-informed about them, not like an absentee landlord. In what part of the country, she inquired, did his lands lie? Most of them were in Kent and Surrey. Indeed—Kent? And Carey's eyes strayed once more to Hetty and Lady Saye, as she recollected Hetty's sudden enthusiasm for the notion of a convalescence in that county. Perhaps, she suggested, Lord Anderford had already heard that she and Mrs Pauling were shortly to spend a few weeks in Tunbridge Wells? Or had it been left to herself to impart that information?

His glance momentarily sharpened at the touch of irony in her tone, but he said civilly enough, 'Then in that case I shall hope to see you both at my country house of Elminghall, which is quite near Tunbridge Wells.'

They fell to discussing the scenery of Kent, which Lord

Anderford supposed would appear tame to Mrs Elliott by comparison with India, where he understood she had spent some years.

'Oh no, for I have already re-accustomed myself to English views. I returned to England in the spring, and have been visiting cousins who live in the eastern counties, at a place called Marchingham.'

It was this last word, which, to her surprise, really aroused the Earl's interest. 'Marchingham?' he exclaimed with more liveliness than he had shown in the entire rather tedious conversation up to this point. 'A town by the name of Great Marchingham, do you mean? You know it well?'

'Why, yes, quite well, although my cousins live a couple of miles away, at Marchingham Priory.'

'What a strange coincidence! I have only just discovered —that is to say, I recently had cause to ask my man of business to discover—the present address of someone of my acquaintance, and that was the very name of the town. How curious!' said he, and seemed to mean it.

Now it was Carey's turn to find herself unexpectedly interested in Lord Anderford. Rapidly reviewing her own acquaintanceship in Great Marchingham, and putting two and two together without the least difficulty— 'Good God!' she exclaimed. 'Marie's Earl!'

And for the first time, she scrutinised him closely, seeing a handsome gentleman of middle age, with intelligent eyes, a sensual mouth and a chin of no great strength, but pleasing enough in his person, though obviously possessed of a certain habitual hauteur, which he showed now as he took in her remark, eyebrows raised. 'I beg your pardon?' His tone was chilly.

No doubt if you were an Earl, and used to deference, such a manner came naturally. But Carey was not to be quelled by any display of aristocratic pretension. 'I mean,' said she, 'it sounds to me as if you know a lady called Mrs Carmichael, who lives in Great Marchingham and with whom I'm acquainted myself.'

'With whom you are acquainted?' The tone of hauteur became yet more pronounced. 'I understood you to be . . .' He stopped short.

216

Carey helped him out of his difficulty: 'A respectable and eligible widow? Well, I am respectable, in the conventional sense of that word. However, I am certainly acquainted with Marie Carmichael, and so I collect are you. Does that make *you* the less respectable?' she inquired, carrying war into the enemy camp. 'I suppose you, or any gentleman, would say it doesn't. What curious distinctions exist between the sexes, do they not? No doubt you feel you have been lured here by Lady Saye under false pretences—does it not strike you that I might feel the same?'

For a moment he looked at her even more frostily than before, and then suddenly laughed. 'Forgive me. I own, you have surprised me, on several counts. But I see I must make my peace with you, if I am to ask you for news of my friend Mrs Carmichael.'

'Your friend?' Carey allowed herself to raise her own eyebrows. 'I believe she is well.'

'What did she . . .' He stopped again.

'Tell me about you? Oh, almost nothing. Not even your name; only your rank, and one other fact. You must know Marie well enough to be aware that one may rely on her discretion. I take it that you have, so to speak, lost track of her?' But he *had*, Carey recollected, gone to the trouble of discovering Marie's present whereabouts. There was something else she herself had better discover, before deciding whether or not to inform Mrs Carmichael of this encounter. Besides, she was curious to know herself . . . 'Didn't it answer?' she asked, without preamble.

'I beg your pardon?' said he blankly. 'Didn't what answer?'

'Why, the pretty chit of sixteen. That was the one other fact.'

Briefly, he looked quite furious, which in the circumstances was hardly surprising, and Carey wondered if she had gone too far. It would be too bad of her to spoil Lady Saye's party; she really ought to guard her tongue better, at her age! She hoped she could trust to Lord Anderford's sense of the proprieties to prevent his standing up and walking out, but all the same she was relieved when, once again, he began to laugh.

'No, it did *not* answer, Mrs Elliott. I may say, I had almost

217

forgotten the girl. Along with several others. You must forgive my frankness; I see there is no need to be mealy-mouthed with you.'

'None at all,' agreed Carey. 'I dare say such persons *would* appear rather dull company, after Marie Carmichael.'

'What a very forthright young woman you are!' said the Earl, by now regarding her with considerable fascination.

'Unsuitably plainspoken, you mean. And *not* eligible, whatever you have been told. We have been thrown together, you understand, in order that we may marry each other,' she kindly explained.

'Awkward, isn't it?' said the Earl, gravely.

'Not particularly, I think, because once we have agreed that neither of us wishes to do any such thing, there need be no awkwardness at all.'

At this moment the pianist finished her piece, to a murmur of mild applause, and supper was announced. 'Anderford! Will you take Mrs Elliott in?' Lady Saye swooped graciously towards them with a rustle of silk skirts.

'With the utmost pleasure!' said he, so readily that his delighted hostess whispered to Mrs Pauling, 'I do believe they are quite taken with one another,' as her guests were ushered into the supper room, there to be plied with chicken and lobster patties and champagne, in which the health of the affianced couple was drunk before private conversation again became possible.

'You are quite right,' said Lord Anderford, installing Carey and himself at a small table in the corner. 'One must own that Lady Saye, though well-meaning, is a match-maker, and as I am a distant cousin of hers, considers me fair game. I, however, am not the marrying kind.'

'Do you know, I had somehow concluded that you weren't? To be perfectly frank with you, I am not on the marriage market at all, for excellent private reasons, so you have nothing to fear from me.'

'Plainspoken indeed!' The smile in his lordship's eyes was more pronounced now, and Carey decided that she liked him better than she had thought she would. 'I begin to see it's not so surprising that you should have made the acquaintance of M—of Mrs Carmichael,' he

218

added, 'although, as you must know, such a thing is—well, unconventional!'

'I dare say,' said Carey. 'So is she, if it comes to that, and so am I. I fancy, sir, you are the most conventional of us all.' And the Earl found that he, in his turn, was being subjected to close scrutiny.

He was not used to so obvious an appraisal from a woman, or to receiving the impression that he was being weighed in the balance and found wanting. 'You think me a poorly behaved sort of fellow, do you?' he inquired a little defensively, proffering lobster patties.

She took one, and considered the question. 'Oh, not poorly behaved, precisely. Just conventional, as I said. I should tell you that I have a high regard for Marie Carmichael. You haven't behaved very well towards her, have you? Generously, perhaps, but not well.'

'No, but—'

'But conventionally.' Carey sighed.

'Perhaps,' said his lordship, adding firmly, 'but I am anxious for what news you may have of her, so while we gratify Lady Saye and your future mama by our interest in one another, perhaps you can bring yourself to tell it.'

Gratification was indeed uppermost in the breasts of the two watching ladies. 'They have been getting on famously,' breathed Mrs Pauling to her hostess, as she took her leave. 'How glad I am! It has done me the world of good just to see it.' And her cheeks, Carey saw as they stepped into Sir John's carriage, had indeed recovered some colour, while her eyes were sparkling with more than the glass of champagne she had drunk. All in all, Carey thought, she had done a pretty good evening's work.

But there was more to be done yet, though it must wait until next day, when she could settle down to write two letters, the first of them destined for Number Nineteen, New Road, Great Marchingham.

My dear Marie—I hope you will not be surprised to hear from me. The fact is, you have been in my mind a good deal, and something occurred yesterday which I feel concerns you nearly . . . And so, my dear Marie, do not be too surprised if his lordship should seek you out. I will own that, to some degree, I encouraged him to do so, but I hope you won't think me a busybody, for after all, you can always decline to receive him. However, he was so full of questions about you, I believe it would have been unkind of me *not* to have suggested that if he wanted to know the answers, he might as well go and find them out for himself. Seriously, I think he has been wishing to do that very thing for some time. It is plain enough that the young woman who was the occasion of his rash act in parting from you proved a sad disappointment, and so did her successors, none of whom had had the benefit of an aunt such as yourself . . . I will add, in the language of the nursery, that it only serves him right!

I warn you of this well in advance, for I believe you will have time to think it over. I understood from Lord Anderford that duty calls him into the country next week: not only has he estate business to attend to, but it seems there is some trouble among the agricultural labourers of the south-east: fires started, rick-burning, threats to the new threshing machines which are so disliked—indeed, just the kind of thing I heard Mr Gerard speak of before I left Marchingham—and as a Justice of the Peace of those parts of Kent and Surrey where his lands lie, Lord Anderford thinks it incumbent upon him to be near at hand until any such troubles are set at rest. I own, I thought the better of his lordship for this resolve, and altogether like him more than I would have expected. I repeat, I think he has been regretting you for some little while, and only pride has prevented him from approaching you. What a strange thing is pride . . . and how much more a man is inclined to stand upon it than a woman . . .

With which thought in her mind, and a small, reminiscent smile upon her lips, Carey turned to the writing of her second letter: a letter which she intended to remind the irritatingly elusive Mr Gerard of her existence. Little do they know it, she thought, but I don't need Lady Saye or dear Hetty working on my behalf at all: I am perfectly well able to contrive these things for myself.

. . . I write to say how sorry I was not to have seen you before I returned to London. You may have heard, from Clarissa, of the sad state in which I found my dear Hetty, who is now much better . . . We go to Tunbridge Wells next week, where she will take the waters, and we have hired a house which I am assured will suit us nicely. I will add its address to the bottom of this letter. I am told by a new acquaintance, the Earl of Anderford, that Tunbridge Wells is *quite* safe, and there is no danger of any of the fires that have been seen during the summer in Kent. Lord Anderford, whose own estates are not far away, hopes to show us something of the countryside while we are there. (No harm in stirring up a little jealousy if possible, thought Carey as her pen ran smoothly on.) . . . We now expect my father's marriage to take place in the autumn, and as I have not the least intention of accompanying the bridal pair on their honeymoon, though warmly urged to do so by the bride herself, I hope then to accept the kind invitation of Sir William and Clarissa to return to the Priory, where I may complete work on the study of various plants for my *Floral Companion*. Meanwhile, I have a favour to ask. Will you beg George Hodson for me, when he and his sons are hedging, to spare that corner of the hayfield where the rose bush grows—I mean the bush I was sketching on the day in June when Grace was so ill? I have recorded every stage of its growth except for the fruits, and I should like to be able to paint the identical bush in its autumnal aspect too . . . Do let me have news of the Hodsons; I should like to know how they go on, particularly Grace. And I confess to some curiosity as to the progress of Tiberius Taylor's grand projects for Mounts Ida and Olympus, and the Judgment of Paris. We were at the play the other night —just my father and myself, for Hetty was not quite equal to such excitement as Kean's performance in *Othello*—and it crossed my mind that Mr Taylor may have missed his true vocation: his sweeping brush might be well suited to the painting of stage scenery . . . Should you object if I were to write again? (I must

warn you that I am a prodigious correspondent.) I
hope you received the note I wrote you on leaving; I
would be sorry if you thought me so uncivil as to part
without a word . . .

There, thought Carey with some satisfaction in her own
work, as she sealed her letter: now what can he do but write
back?

He did: on the very day of her arrival with Hetty in
Tunbridge Wells, Carey was gratified to find a letter awaiting her in the pleasant, elegant little house they had taken
near the middle of the town, where they need go only a step
to be able to stroll on the Pantiles. Hetty was charmed with
the place; its atmosphere invigorating, but not too bracing.
She was sure it would do her the world of good. Why, she
felt stronger already!

Carey encouraged her in this admirably positive attitude,
and waited until she was alone to read her letter. It was
quite a short one, and perhaps a little stiffly phrased, but
any stiffness wore off in the course of the further replies
she elicited to her own letters, of which, as she had
warned their recipient, she proceeded to write a good
many.

A curious correspondence, she thought: they were love
letters, surely, yet without a word of love in them. Now and
then Carey took herself severely to task, wondering if she
had perhaps imagined everything. Then, however, she
would think of that extraordinary last night in Marchingham; no, such things one did not imagine.

Truth to tell, she thought a little guiltily, August and
early September would have been rather dull but for two
things, one of them her correspondence with Mr Gerard.
Tunbridge Wells might be doing Hetty the world of good;
Carey found herself a trifle bored there. Her correspondence transported her to another place, and even apart
from her feelings for Mr Gerard himself, gave her news of
people to whom she had become sincerely attached.

. . . Mount Olympus nears completion (wrote Benedict), and is very grand indêed upon my wall: not the

most restful of pictures, what with the almost excessive brightness of Apollo and the particularly ferocious aspect of Mars, but certainly very grand. Mount Ida, however, is still at a comparatively early stage. Since he considers it likely to be his masterpiece, Tiberius is extremely anxious to find precisely the right models for his three goddesses and has not yet succeeded in that aim, partly because, in his quest for them, he ended up badly intoxicated in one of the riverside hostelries, and was returned to the Vicarage in that condition by some kind souls who had also been drinking there. Pointing out the classical nature of his pursuit to Mrs Whittier did not, I fear, induce her to look more favourably on it, and I fancy it will be a little while before he is able to come back to the Priory and continue his work . . . His picture of Grace Hodson, however, is now completed; I think it very fine, and believe you would say so too if you could see it . . .

Grace herself, Carey was glad to learn, had recovered her strength and some of her spirits, and it seemed the courtship of young Jim Spring was prospering in a quiet way.

And though we dissuaded Tiberius from making Grace his Venus (wrote Benedict), I think he has indeed got his eye on Jim Spring for Paris; Spring is certainly a good-looking, well-set-up young man, but if painting from the life is a *sine qua non*, Tiberius will have to abandon the notion. I know Jim Spring well enough to be sure that any suggestion of his posing naked would strike him as very improper.

Hugh Hodson and Susan Pacey were to marry in the spring. Had Carey been aware of the friendship which existed between Susan's father and young Sam Hodson? Not at all an unlikely one except in terms of age, for both were fond of books, and while Benedict himself had often lent Sam volumes from the library at the Priory, he fancied that the works of political theory from which the cobbler liked to quote were more to the young man's taste. However, he had heard of the two of them being seen in public eagerly talking politics of a Utopian or indeed revolutionary nature—which did no harm in itself, and was certainly most innocently meant by both parties, but he, Benedict, was a little afraid lest less innocent persons than James Pacey take advantage of Sam's bright, inquiring mind . . . as his Cousin Caroline would remember, he was perhaps Peggy Hodson's favourite among her sons . . .

The other thing that enlivened the placid existence of Mrs Pauling and Mrs Elliott was the Earl of Anderford's presence in the vicinity of Tunbridge Wells, and the civil attention he paid both ladies. This rejoiced Mrs Pauling's fond heart, for she saw in it a growing attachment to her dear Carey, and she thought Carey was not indifferent to the Earl either.

Here she was correct, in so far as Carey continued to like him more the better she knew him.

I am glad to find (she wrote to Mr Gerard), that thanks to you, I am able to take an intelligent interest in the matters with which Lord Anderford is at the moment concerned. It seems that there have been an unusual number of incidents of arson in Kent and Surrey since the month of June. Barns and ricks have been destroyed, and now they are breaking the threshing machines as well. I knew the causes for the men's disliking these new-fangled machines—which on the face of it sound so admirable an invention—from our expedition to Mr Dedman's farm earlier in the summer; I never did see his treasured threshing machine, though! Well, some of the Kentish farmers, either sympathising with the labourers or, which is perhaps more likely, fearing violence, agreed to discontinue the use of them, but others undid any good that this measure might have done, by seeing it as a chance to be turned to their own advantage, and went on hiring the machines, whereupon several were broken by what are described as large and desperate gangs; Lord

Anderford says, however, that from all he can ascertain on closer inquiry, these gangs are neither large nor particularly desperate, and not as riotously behaved as one might think from some of the reports that are flying about: they make but one demand, that threshing with the machines should cease, and if it is refused, commit the single if admittedly violent act of breaking them. Lord Anderford is a Justice of the Peace, like your father, and taking his duties seriously, sees himself likely to be kept in Kent for some little while, which is unfortunate, as he says he had hoped to be elsewhere by now . . .

A likely story, thought Mr Gerard, upon reading this with all the inward annoyance Carey could have hoped for.

Even to him, she would not betray the confidences of either Mrs Carmichael or the Earl; she had been amused to find herself, during these late summer weeks, cast in the role of confidante to the latter. By now an easy friendship existed between them; she said what she thought to his lordship, so that when she first visited his residence of Elminghall, with Marchingham much in her mind, it was not surprising if on entering its handsome rooms she instantly exclaimed, 'Oh, how I wish Tiberius Taylor were here! What would he not give for one of these walls to cover!'

Picture to yourself (she wrote to Mr Gerard), a fine mansion in the Palladian style, with two wings folded backwards, the whole effect very neat and compact. Within the central part of the house there is a well proportioned hall and a drawing room, with other rooms behind them, leading to a light and airy orangery. In one wing, there is a gallery hung not only with the usual portraits of the noble owner's ancestors, but with other works too, by masters both ancient and modern: a fine collection such as I am sure Tiberius Taylor would appreciate—as I did. In the other wing there is a library. I understand both these are largely the present Earl's own creation. The room in which the library is housed, however, has always had a painting of some antiquity, showing a hunting scene, all along the top of one wall, above the books there: it depicts what I take to be Greek warriors in pursuit of a boar.

Was it, she had wondered aloud, the Caledonian hunt? The Earl had always thought this possible, and pointed out the Amazonian lady aiming a spear who, he surmised, might be Atalanta herself. From childhood, he added, the old picture had intrigued him, and one day he hoped to have the other walls of the library ornamented in a similar fashion.

Hetty, tired after the journey from Tunbridge Wells, was resting in the Orangery, with its pleasant view of the gardens. Carey had therefore been free to linger over the paintings as long as she liked, well aware that nothing could please Mrs Pauling more than to know that she and the Earl were enjoying a *tête à tête* together, and her first thought, on hearing Lord Anderford's plans for the library, was of the charms it would hold for Mr Taylor. Her exclamation was quite spontaneous.

Lord Anderford raised an eyebrow. 'Tiberius Taylor? What a splendid name!' he commented, as she herself had done.

'Yes, and his style is equal to his name . . . if I were to describe his work to you,' said Carey thoughtfully, 'I dare say it might sound a little ridiculous, but when one actually sees it, it is no such thing. I believe he is a true original.'

'And where does this genius reside?'

'Well—in Great Marchingham, but,' said Carey a little doubtfully, 'even if you were to go there when you are able, and seek him out, I am not sure that you would be allowed to see him. He is not exactly a free agent,' she added, thinking of Benedict's account of the artist's recent fall from grace, and the eagle eye kept upon him by his sister Augusta.

'In what way?' asked the Earl, intrigued.

She hesitated, and then gave him a brief account of Mr Taylor's history, which intrigued him further. 'So his works languish on the walls of the back bedrooms of a tumble-down manor house? I shall certainly seek Mr Taylor out

226

when I visit Marchingham. I only wish that might be sooner than now seems likely. These wretched disturbances . . .'

'They are getting worse, are they? As you feared?'

'Yes—but they're not so bad as some people would have one believe—the kind of people who see bloody revolution everywhere, and would have it put down with the utmost severity. There are reports, too, of similar disturbances beginning in other counties: in Hampshire and the west, for instance. I see I shall very likely have to remain here, or not much further away than London, at least until the quarter sessions at the end of October. If you are in Marchingham before me, perhaps you'll tell your friend Mr Taylor—for I trust your judgment in such matters—that I should like to see his work.'

'Nothing could please him more,' said Carey, smiling. Then her smile faded. 'But though Hetty is better, much better, she is still not as strong as we would like—and I can't very well leave her until she is safely married to my father. Goodness knows what whim she might take into her head, fancying it an obstacle to the union. I am afraid you and I are deceiving her a little by letting her think we are becoming fond of each other, you know; but it does her so much good to believe her innocent scheme is working. Once she is my father's legal wife, I trust she will not take such an interest in *my* affairs. Meanwhile, however, I can't desert her. She was so good to me as a child, for so long.' And she sighed. 'So whether I shall be in Marchingham before you, who knows.'

14

Carey had been right to foresee further delay. Mrs Pauling's convalescence was slow: they were back in London and it was early November before Sir John's eminent colleague Sir Henry Halford at last pronounced his patient perfectly well again, and the two medical men, Carey, and Hetty herself all raised a glass of Sir John's excellent Madeira in celebration.

'So now that you are quite better, Hetty,' said Carey, 'you can go away for your honeymoon to somewhere warm, and sunny, and altogether delightful, as Papa has been planning all this time—am I not right, Papa?'

'Aye, I wouldn't take Hetty out of this country before, don't entirely trust medical facilities in the Mediterranean countries, but there can be no objection to our going abroad now, eh, Halford?'

'None at all, none in the world,' agreed Sir Henry affably. 'Where do you mean to go, Law?'

'First, and just for a few days, to my relations—or Carey's, rather, her mother's cousins in the east of the country, where she herself will stay. She paid 'em a visit earlier this year—seems to wish to return,' said Sir John, shooting his daughter a slightly quizzical look from under bushy brows. 'And then Hetty and I will take ship from one of the East Coast ports over to the Low Countries, go on into France, down to Italy, perhaps, even Greece—just as we please.'

He was in excellent spirits. The tedious period of waiting for his bride's full recovery was over now; he had a strong notion that Carey had found it tedious too, even though Hetty was so sure she had been well amused in Tunbridge Wells by the attentions of Lord Anderford. But Sir John had never shared her conviction that an attachment was developing between the two of them, and sure enough, nothing had come of it. His lordship, it seemed, had entertained the two ladies civilly while they were in Kent, then became very busy about his duties as a Justice of the Peace, and after that had gone off somewhere, Carey didn't know where. Nor did she even seem very interested when Hetty anxiously asked her.

'But that might be just pretence, of course, for I am sure she is too proud to show disappointment if her heart had been touched. I do hope,' said Hetty to Sir John, 'that she is not pining for him. How dreadful that would be!'

'Set your mind at rest,' said Sir John, drily. 'Carey's not the pining sort. She found Anderford pleasant company, I dare say, but if you ask me, my dear—and this ought to please you—she has a second husband in mind already, and has chosen him quite by herself.'

Hetty's mouth dropped slightly open as she struggled with her bewilderment. 'Dear me!' she managed faintly. 'But . . . but who could that be? Not Lord Anderford, you believe?'

'By no means. You and Lady Saye will have to admit defeat there. Come, my dear, why do you suppose Carey is so ready to accept a second invitation from a woman whom I know for a fact she does not like, if she hasn't taken it into her head to fall in love with her cousin, the one she keeps talking about?'

'With Mr Gerard? Oh no!' exclaimed Hetty. 'Surely not! Why, she does not like *him* either. I am sure I have heard her say as much a dozen times, and rather more strongly than she ought. Besides having taken him in such dislike as a child, for throwing her doll into the farmyard. And though one must not be uncharitable to a person one has never met, he does sound a—a rather *lightweight* young man, which would never do for Carey.'

'No, no, not that Mr Gerard! The one she keeps talking about, I said. His brother, no real kin of hers,' explained Sir John. 'And not a lightweight fellow at all, by the sound of him. Why do you suppose it's been "Benedict says this" and "Benedict thinks that", ever since she came home? I must own, I feel curious to meet him. For in general, you'll

229

agree, Carey does not rely upon the opinions of *any* gentleman, preferring to form her own. Not that my curiosity will delay me more than a couple of days before I bear you off to the Continent, my dear—but if Carey chooses to spend Christmas in a dilapidated manor, with a set of persons she doesn't much care for, and in what sounds to me like a devilish dull part of the country—well, there is something more than painting hips and haws and blackberries and all that stuff behind it, you may be bound.'

Sir John, no countryman, had but a hazy notion of the exact time when hips and blackberries and all that stuff might be found, or the fact that by mid-November those hedgerow fruits were well past their prime would have struck him as even more conclusive proof of his theory. Indeed, as Hetty's convalescence was prolonged, Carey had given up hope of returning to her subjects in Mr Hodson's hedges, and had been working on the plates for the *Floral Companion* using sketches made at Elminghall, and materials supplied by Professor Lindley. Generally speaking, however, her father's guesswork was fairly accurate, although in supposing Marchingham to be devilish dull he spoke without suspecting what might be brewing there this autumn.

For there was a kind of general restlessness in the air, felt by many, and not always for the same reasons. Clarissa Gerard, for instance, was in a state of happy anticipation. Her reasoning matched Sir John's: there must be some inducement other than autumnal fruits to draw Cousin Caroline back to the Priory, and what could that be but Will?

Fresh hopes revived in Lady Gerard's breast. She knew Cousin Caroline well enough now to be pretty sure she would not mind remaining alone in London, so it could not be just that she wanted some relative to take her in while Sir John and his bride were away. She was also realist enough to be aware that no very great sympathy existed between herself and Mary's daughter. (If it crossed her mind to wonder how she would like to be mother-in-law to so strong-minded a young woman, she dismissed the thought again: Will's interests must come first.) By a process of elimination, therefore, it became clear that Will's belated wooing had done its work, and absence had made the heart grow fonder. Hence Cousin Caroline's proposed return.

She hinted as much to Will, but he had never been very good at taking a hint, and these days he seemed remarkably abstracted, as if he had something preying on his mind. In the end, she had to tell him outright that it looked as if Caroline had thought better of turning him down.

'Oh,' said Will, his gloomy expression failing to clear.

'Is that all you can find to say?' inquired his mother, irritated. 'Now if ever is the time to press your advantage home. Think: her father married, her husband over two years dead—her mind *must* be running on her own remarriage,' said Clarissa, with all the certainty of one who assumed a good marriage to be the goal of every female alive. 'She is certainly aware that you are not a *rich* match, so it must be your *person* that brings her back here. And after all, with that fortune, she may marry for love if she likes. Yes, yes, I know she rejected your offer, but by now, you see, she will have had time to think it over and discover where her inclination lies: why, by coming back here she is as good as saying so, Will, so don't lose heart.'

'No, very well, Mama,' said the ardent lover. Though by now, he didn't really see that marriage to Cousin Caroline, or indeed anything else, could help him out of his difficulties.

He was in too deep, that was the trouble. Only now, when it was too late, did he realise that he need never have begun to give Davy Leigh's friends any assistance after all. If he had taken a firm stand: if he had told Davy boldly that nothing about that horse could possibly be proved against him, that even to accuse him of buying it cheap, knowing it to be stolen, would be as good as an admission of guilt on his, Davy's, part; if he had brazened it out over Grace Hodson, swearing she was not the girl he had mentioned to Davy, and he'd tell her brothers so too if need be, and if he had then stuck to his story—well, if he had done these things, Davy would have had no hold over him, and he wouldn't be in this present tangle. What was almost as bad was that he felt sure Davy knew it, and had probably been laughing up his sleeve the whole time—that would be like him.

231

But now he *had* done things that wouldn't bear much investigation. Many a venturesome young fellow might have seen it as a bit of a lark to help the smuggling fraternity; after all, no one thought it so very bad to bring a few barrels of brandy or crates of tea into the country without paying duty. Will Gerard, however, was not a venturesome soul. And contriving these things was not as easy as Davy had blithely implied. It was all very well for *him* to say there were plenty of tumbledown old outhouses on the Priory lands, places the Revenue men would never think of searching, ideal as a half-way house for the cart-loads that came by night from the coast and up the Marching river. Yes, so there were, but who knew when Ben, with his passion for improvement, might not take it into his head to refurbish the very one Will had chosen?

He thought he was safe so far: three consignments of goods in all had now arrived, to be stored for a few days in the old North Lodge, a cottage surrounded by briars and weeds where no lodge-keeper had lived for years. It stood at the end of the long back drive up to the Priory, and any attempt to maintain this as well as the main drive in good condition had been abandoned some thirty years or more ago. By now it was quite hard even to make out where the back drive ran, so overgrown was it. Will had thought of the disused ice-house, but it had no key, and Davy insisted that the hiding place for the goods his friends brought should be locked. Not everybody involved, said Davy blandly, was as trustworthy as he ought to be. So the North Lodge it must be.

The advantage of Will's own idea would have been that there was no likelihood whatever of Ben's suddenly declaring that funds allowed such a luxury as an ice-house to be put in order and brought back into use. But there was always the chance that the sale of a few cows, or a good price for the harvest, or some such thing, might set Ben announcing that the North Lodge was going to be done up and used to house some deserving labouring family. It was just the kind of thing Ben *would* do, thought Will, as usual blaming his difficult circumstances on the perversity of others. He had a poor grasp of agricultural matters, or he would have known that with so bad a harvest after the cold, wet summer, he need not fear any very sudden access of prosperity.

The consignments of goods did not come at regular intervals, either. That made it worse—one couldn't put the matter comfortably out of mind until next time, if one didn't know just when next time might be. There would be a message requiring Will's presence, with his key, at a certain day and a certain hour. The men who came and left their cartload would tell him when it was to be fetched again, and then he and the key would be required once more. None of the men he saw at either end of the transaction seemed to be local. He guessed, too late, that Davy had summoned him to that accursed meeting at Platt's Barn just so that his involvement *was* known to local men. And every now and then someone who had been there would be so bold as to give him a knowing wink in passing—to which Will replied with as haughty a stare as he could muster.

The worst moment, perhaps, had been when he was waiting in the Rose and Crown for his mother's carriage to be harnessed up and brought round, so that he might escort her home from a round of morning calls, and two of the men from Platt's Barn had accosted him: young Sam Hodson, and that oddity the cobbler James Pacey.

'Sir! Mr Gerard!' exclaimed Sam, approaching him, tankard in hand, and to his dismay, Will saw Pacey closing in on him too.

'I dare say we shouldn't, sir, but I've been wishing to shake you by the hand,' declared the cobbler earnestly, and what with wondering why the devil Pacey should say that, and whether Sam had found out anything about his sister Grace, before Will knew it he was seated on a settle in the corner of the taproom, with a mug of ale hospitably pressed upon him, listening to the strangest stuff he had ever heard in his life.

Sam wanted him, Mr Gerard, to know it was good to see that some of the gentry felt for the plight of the labouring poor. Mr Pacey went on to explain (so far as Will could make it out) that such activities as smuggling and poaching were not, of course, to be pursued for themselves, but in protest against the iniquitous laws passed by the ruling classes for their own sole benefit. 'Where a man can't get a decent wage of two shillings a week if single, or two shillings and sixpence if married, and is forbidden to take a rabbit or a bird for the pot, who's to wonder at it if folk find their patience outworn and take matters into their own hands? Which I hear they're doing in the south–east, and the Midland counties, and you mark my words, sir, we'll be having some of that here before long,' Mr Pacey concluded.

Will had no notion what he was talking about; it sounded to him like a farrago of nonsense, dangerous nonsense too, so that he was heartily glad when he heard the carriage being brought round.

The one person in whose society he found some release from his present anxieties was Miss Gage. He had encountered her a little while ago by chance (a chance neatly engineered by Roberta herself) when she was walking in the town, and she had asked, with a prettily apologetic air, whether he would mind helping her home with her purchases, which were rather more than she could carry. She had been so hoping to meet some gentleman of her acquaintance, and now, providentially, here he was. In civility, he could hardly refuse her request, and he was relieved to find that her manner towards him was pleasant and easy; she seemed to have forgotten that unfortunate misunderstanding earlier in the year, and was not, after all, going to be difficult about it, as he had feared on the day when Davy Leigh *would* have all three of them drive to Brook End Farm together.

Somehow or other—he was not sure just how it came about—they seemed to meet quite frequently that autumn. It could not be said they were on precisely the same footing as at the time of the Norwich Assemblies, for Will was on his guard against giving a false impression again. Besides, there was his mama urging him to resume his suit to Cousin Caroline. But a little undemanding friendliness was pleasant, and he could feel sorry for Miss Gage, with a disreputable fellow like Davy Leigh for a brother; for she was so straitlaced, as he himself should know, that no one could suppose she knew the kind of thing Davy got up to.

Only the other day, indeed, she had ventured to ask, hesitantly, whether Davy had offended him in some way. Something her brother had said when he was in Great

Marchingham recently . . . she let her voice trail away, and Will, struck with the liveliest alarm, looked apprehensively at her. Oh, confessed Roberta, she wasn't sure what it was all about—something to do with horses, she rather thought, which she wouldn't understand—but she would be so sorry if Davy, who had always admired Mr Gerard, were to be the cause of any trouble to him. If there was anything she could do, or say, she would be only too happy.

No, no, nothing, Will assured her, rather touched by this evidence of disinterested goodwill. It did briefly cross his mind that perhaps only Miss Gage could persuade her brother to leave him alone. What a relief that would be! No more hints and threats, no more of those alarming nocturnal expeditions to the North Lodge, armed with its incriminating key. To relieve him of all that was something even Cousin Caroline, with all her money, couldn't do for him. Not that he wished to be married at all, of course. Still, suppose he *were* Davy Leigh's brother-in-law; Davy would have to change his tune then. Mama wouldn't like it either. Will found the idea of doing what Mama wouldn't like rather attractive. On the other hand, he would then be landed with a wife: a less attractive prospect. He dismissed it.

The notion Roberta had planted in his mind remained there, however, biding its time. Taking care not to scan Mr Gerard's face too obviously as he escorted her home to Saltgate (for they had chanced to meet in the town yet again), Miss Gage felt well satisfied with the effect of her remarks.

It was late in November, and not so very long after that little exchange between Roberta and Will, when Mr Leigh paid one of his unannounced visits to his mother and sister —unannounced because, as he airily remarked, he never could tell in advance just when he would have occasion to come to Great Marchingham, or on just what business.

'I dare say not,' agreed Roberta, carefully matching a strand of silk to the piece of embroidery upon which she was working, and with a good deal of meaning in her tone.

He grinned at her, quite unabashed, taking her point. 'And how does your business go on, little sister?'

'Oh, pretty well, I believe.'

'*Very* well, my dear Davy, I am glad to say,' agreed Mrs Gage. 'We have quite as many pupils as we can comfortably take now.'

'Glad to hear it,' said Mr Leigh, 'but that wasn't precisely the aspect of your affairs I was inquiring after, Bertie.'

'Then I'm sure I can't think what was,' she replied, frowning slightly to remind him that their mother was present.

But Mr Leigh took no notice. 'Affairs of the heart, to be sure!' he said blandly.

Mrs Gage exclaimed, 'Oh, hush, Davy!' and shook her head. She thought no one had yet replaced Mr William Gerard in her daughter's fancy, and she had been rather distressed to hear that Roberta had been walking with him in the town recently: that was not the best way to forget someone—no, a clean break was the only remedy for a heartache, as she herself could have told Roberta if Roberta had but asked her advice.

'You don't want me to talk about that tender heart of Bertie's? Then I won't,' said the affable Davy. 'What shall we talk about instead, Mama? The state of the nation? The Tories going out and the Whigs coming in? What's *your* opinion of the change of government?' he gravely asked, a teasing sparkle in his eye.

'Good gracious me, I've no idea, and well you know it!' said Mrs Gage, who was not quite the fool Roberta thought her, and could hold her own with her son rather better than with her daughter.

'The state of the countryside, then? Captain Swing?'

'Captain Swing?' Mrs Gage sounded blank. 'Who may he be? What a curious name!'

'You haven't heard of him? I'd have thought there'd be Swing letters in these parts by now.'

'Oh—I have heard of him,' said Roberta, stitching away, 'or at least read of him in the newspaper, though I believe Captain Swing is thought not to be a real person, but a name to cover a whole quantity of wicked revolutionaries.'

236

'If it's thought wicked for a man to demand a decent wage,' suggested Mr Leigh, 'I expect you're right.'

'I am sure it's wicked to burn ricks, and barns, and other property, in support of such demands, and to break machines too,' retorted his sister. 'Captain Swing is the signature put to those dreadful threatening letters that have been sent to many of the farmers in the southern counties, Mama,' she explained. 'About wages, and the new threshing machines, and so forth. And there have been gangs going about, I believe, extorting money, and threatening violence too.'

'Dear me, yes, that is very bad indeed! I am sure Roberta is right to say so,' agreed Mrs Gage. 'Rick-burning and machine-breaking! I trust we shall hear of no such dreadful things near Marchingham.'

'I wouldn't be too confident,' Mr Leigh remarked. 'Bertie is right: so far, most of this business has been in the southern counties, but the thing is spreading. Some say it's all a cover, mind you, for folk smuggling contraband in from the Continent.'

'Indeed?' said Roberta, looking up briefly.

'But I don't believe that for a moment,' continued her brother, smoothly, 'any more than I believe it's the work of desperate French Jacobins, urging English Radicals on to their ruin. However, I suppose you may have the man in the green gig here in the Marchinghams yet.'

'What man is that?' asked Roberta, curiously.

'Oh, some say he's Captain Swing in person, but I fancy that's all a story; however, they say he goes about the eastern counties in his gig, handing out leaflets and inciting the labourers to violence. In consequence, several perfectly innocent gentlemen, who happened to be going about in green gigs minding their own business, have been summarily arrested and delivered up to the officers of the peace, if they didn't happen to have faces well known in the particular place where they were driving. Well, one can't be too careful, in these dangerous times. Whom would you *expect* to receive such a letter as these supposed epistles from Captain Swing, in the Marchinghams, would you say, if anyone did?'

'Josiah Dedman, of course,' said Roberta at once. 'He has

237

the most shocking reputation for miserliness, and is known to pay low wages, preferring the parish to make up the money to anyone who works for him. At least, that is what I have heard my pupils who are farmers' daughters say of him. Not that I encourage gossip,' Roberta hastened to explain, 'but they *will* do it, and one can't help hearing what they say.'

'Interesting—and *has* Mr Dedman received any threats yet?'

'Not that I know of,' said Roberta, who, as it happened, was less well informed than usual upon this particular point. 'And I hope he won't.'

'Dear me, so do I,' shuddered Mrs Gage. 'Poor Mr Dedman!'

'I take it he isn't poor, but rich—hence his reputation as a miser,' pointed out Mr Leigh. 'Just the sort of person, in fact, who positively invites the attentions of Captain Swing and his followers.'

'I wish you won't alarm Mama,' said Roberta, primly. 'I wouldn't put it past you to paint your own gig green, like the man you spoke of, and travel about with a fistful of blank papers, just for sheer devilment.'

This made Davy laugh. 'I hadn't thought of that, Bertie —it might be a lark, but no, I think I won't.' And he rose to leave, saying he had bought a likely mare at Marchingham market and must now take her home. 'Seriously, though, Bertie,' he said quietly to his sister, as she saw him to the door, 'I'd be on the alert. Who knows what may happen, as I was saying, in these dangerous times? It could be something to your own advantage. Oh, and by the way, do you ever go past the North Lodge at the Priory on those interesting walks you take by yourself?'

She gazed thoughtfully after him as he went away down Saltgate. It was clear enough that she had just received a strong hint, though of precisely what she did not know. None the less, she resolved not to forget that, from the sound of it, the North Lodge was a place now used in the process of moving contraband about the country. She must also, of course, continue to cultivate the company of Will Gerard.

Late in November, too, on a mild Sunday afternoon, Hugh Hodson and Susan Pacey were out courting: that is to say, they were walking decorously along Riverside Road, down the steps to the river and up again, in the approved manner of all engaged couples in the Marchinghams.

Dusk was falling as they climbed back up the steps, and they could see Susan's father through the lighted window of his workshop. He was not working in it, of course, on a Sunday, but was poring over a volume open on his workbench, with an oil lamp set beside it. With his rosy face, white hair and contented expression, James Pacey made a pleasant picture, yet the sight of it brought a slight frown to Hugh's open face. He stopped, causing his sweetheart to come to a halt too, and asked bluntly, 'Susan, what's your Pa about nowadays?'

'Dear me, Hugh, I don't know!' said Susan, puzzled. 'Reading his old books, I suppose, just as he always does when he isn't working, and sometimes when he *ought* to be working too, so Ma says.'

'No, I didn't mean now. That's about Sam, you see,' explained Hugh, his frown deepening a little. 'Always off to Great Marchingham to see your Pa, he is, whenever he's got the time and has taken one of his fancy ideas into his head, which he says he wants to talk over with Mr Pacey.'

'It'll be the books,' repeated Susan. 'He's a great one for books, isn't he, your Sam? Just like my Pa.'

'Yes, I reckon that's all,' said Hugh, moving on again towards the Paceys' door. 'Yes, that'll be just the books, that's all.'

It was also in late November that the Reverend Mr Whittier received a note, delivered by hand from the Priory, asking him, as Sir William Gerard's fellow magistrate, to call at the Priory that day if it was convenient, since Sir William's gout made it all but impossible for him to come out and see the Vicar himself. Not at all averse to a ride on a pleasant autumn day, Mr Whittier at once had his riding horse brought round, and was in the library of the Priory by noon, accepting a glass of claret, shaking hands with Sir William, and greeting the elder Mr Gerard, who saw him comfortably settled into a chair by the fire before broaching the subject to be discussed. 'Good of you to come so soon, sir. There's a matter upon which my father particularly wished to consult you; it's a puzzle and something of an anxiety to him.'

'What's that you say, Ben, my boy?' Sir William had had a couple of glasses of his own excellent claret before his visitor arrived—there was no stinting on the quality of the wine drunk in his house, whatever other economies Ben practised—and consequently he had fallen into a pleasant state of torpor by the fireside. 'Aye, well, a puzzle, yes, that's it. As a Justice of the Peace, and all that, you know, Whittier, it concerns me, eh, Ben? Concerns you too, Whittier. A puzzle and something of an anxiety, that's right.'

'You mean, it has *you* puzzled, Benedict?' said the Vicar, raising a quizzical eyebrow as he took the piece of paper Mr Gerard was offering him.

It was rather crumpled, not too clean, and addressed to Mr Josiah Dedman . . . 'and This,' it proceeded, 'is to Let You No, that if you do Not pay Tow Shilling and Six Pence A Day, And Disist from the Use of the new threshing Machine, yore Yards shall all be burnt to Ashes. Observe what we say, or you are a Dead Man indeed. From your Wel Wisher, Captain SWING.'

'Ah. Yes, I see,' remarked Mr Whittier, having scanned it, and reading it through for the second time. 'Yes, how strange! A *second* letter to Dedman, the only man to have received any such representations, unless you count my-self.'

'I don't,' said Mr Gerard, smiling. 'What you received was a civil request from a deputation of farmers, respect-fully asking whether you would be willing to reduce your tithe so that they could pay their men a higher wage, a request to which you immediately agreed, and I hear that the whole affair was conducted in the most amicable fashion imaginable.'

'Aye, well, that was largely your doing,' said the Vicar, a little ruefully. 'I should have thought of it for myself—can't think why I didn't.'

'You didn't because you never think of money at all, sir. As everyone who knows you is aware. And what could be

240

more fitting, in a clergyman? Though I can tell you, it's not by any means all clergymen who are willing to come to such an arrangement—and if threats are made against them and their property, as is sometimes the case, that's understandable. But where a reduction in the tithe *can* be made, it is an easy way to satisfy everyone. I was very much obliged to you.'

'Easy enough for me,' said the Vicar, waving this aside. 'With a reasonable private income besides my stipend . . . well, it's true that I need not think of these things much, and that's why it did not occur to me before. But as you say, there's been no further threat of trouble, not to speak of—very largely due to your good work again, Ben—isn't that right, Sir William?' he added in a louder voice, observing that his nominal host and fellow magistrate had almost dropped off to sleep again.

'Eh? What? Yes, to be sure,' offered Sir William vaguely.

'So far,' said Mr Gerard, frowning, 'there's been only that one letter to Dedman, some two weeks ago, when I let it get around that I was going to have a word with him.'

'Which I suppose you did, Benedict?' said the Vicar.

'Which I did. At least he had sense enough to promise higher wages, when I explained how it would be for his own good, though I'm afraid he considered *I* was threatening him too, and was crotchety enough about it. But I did get him to understand that it would be more prudent not to use that threshing machine of his this winter. *That* took some doing, since he means to hire it out, a reasonable enough idea in itself, and surely the machines will come into general use,' Benedict sighed, leaning his forehead on his hand as he looked down at the letter on the table again. 'Naturally Dedman doesn't like to see his investment lying idle. But to use it this winter, in flat defiance of the feeling among the labouring men—oh, I don't know, but I thought I'd persuaded him. And I made sure Tom Harris, as the most likely firebrand among the men he employs, knew the substance of our discussion. So why this second letter, now?'

'You don't think Harris wrote the letters himself?'

'Tom Harris is completely illiterate—and no, I don't think he is behind them, either. Nor do I know who is. But

I'm fairly sure they came from different hands. I rather suspect this one,' said Mr Gerard, 'of being a fake, and written by someone who is only pretending to be ill-educated.'

'Yes, I see.' Mr Whittier pointed a finger to the penultimate sentence. 'The writer couldn't resist that play on words—Dedman, Dead Man—and suddenly the orthography is much improved.'

'Exactly! It *is* puzzling—and when I had hoped that the Marchinghams were quiet, and when you, and almost all the local farmers too, had acted with such good sense and humanity. I'm hoping,' said Mr Gerard, 'that this is a mere hoax—written for a whim, or to see what kind of mischief can be made. But if it isn't, sir, I thought that as my father is your colleague on the Bench, you should see it at once, in case any further action has to be taken.'

They turned to glance at the Vicar's colleague on the Bench.

'Further action,' murmured Sir William, 'has to be taken . . .' And as his son quietly escorted the Vicar from the room, he fell asleep, with a comfortable sense of having done his duty and dealt very properly with a shocking riot, or something of that nature.

That same day, and indeed just as Mr Whittier arrived home from the Priory, a gentleman's carriage of remarkable elegance, with a coat of arms traced in gold on its doors, drove into Great Marchingham and drew up outside Number Nineteen, New Road, under the fascinated gaze of all those residents of Petergate, on the other side of the churchyard, who happened to be looking out of their windows at the time. They promptly drew their curtains sufficiently to remain unobserved themselves, and continued to look out. A gentleman whose elegance was quite equal to that of his carriage stepped down from it, and was saluted civilly by Mr Whittier as he dismounted from his hack, for the Vicar used to pass the time of day with all and sundry as he rode or walked about his parishes. Encountering a well-spoken personage whose clerical bands proclaimed his calling, the elegant gentleman saluted him in return. None of this was lost upon the spectators. Nor was the assured way in which the elegant gentleman walked boldly up to the front door of Number Nineteen—in broad daylight, too!—knocked and was admitted. Those of the audience who had particularly good eyesight, and could see into the interior of a dark hall on the opposite side of the road, swore that Mrs Carmichael's surprisingly respectable housekeeper had offered the visitor a smile of recognition and welcome.

'How d'you do, Mrs Thompson?' said the Earl of Anderford. 'A nice little house you have here, I see.'

'Very nice indeed, my lord,' agreed Mrs Thompson, closing the door behind him. 'I will announce you, sir, as John is out at present.'

'Don't bother,' said his lordship, and looked around for a likely drawing room door. 'Shall I find her in here?'

But the lady of the house herself, coming out into the hall at that moment, rendered any answer superfluous. 'Oh!' said the normally imperturbable Mrs Carmichael, visibly perturbed now, despite her forewarning.

'I thought,' said his lordship, 'that I would like to see how you went on, buried in the depths of the country.'

Three interested and strikingly pretty faces appeared in the doorway behind Mrs Carmichael. She became aware of them. It would not do to neglect all her own precepts concerning etiquette. 'My lord,' she said, formally, 'allow me to present my three nieces. Miss Polly Brignold. Miss Dorothea Jameson. Miss Mary Holt. My dears, let me make you known to Lord Anderford.'

The girls' eyes popped slightly, but she was glad to observe the very proper manner in which they acknowledged the introduction.

'Your nieces?' said he, obviously amused as he worked it out. 'I see—at least, I think so. I should like to hear how you came by all these young relations. Er . . . if you should invite me to stay for a while, are they my nieces too, I wonder?'

'What exactly,' inquired Mrs Carmichael, careful now not to betray the fact of her forewarning, 'has brought you here?'

'Oh, a number of things, all of which I hope to accomplish before I must return to Kent in mid-December—there has been some sort of rural rioting there, you see, a great bore—but the upshot is that I've to sit on a Special Commission in the middle of the month. Meanwhile, I have more important matters to attend to. For instance,' said Lord Anderford, letting his gaze stray out of the window of the room into which his hostess had ushered him, 'I believe there is an artist of genius residing within a stone's throw of you. I am in urgent need of an artist of genius, and am anxious to make this gentleman's acquaintance.'

'Tiberius Taylor, you mean!' exclaimed Mrs Carmichael. 'Good heavens!' she added, as the various possible implications of his lordship's arrival in Great Marchingham opened up before her inward eye. 'If you are going to seek out Tiberius Taylor, and from *this* house, you will be putting the cat among the pigeons indeed. Well, well . . . how amusing that would be!'

15

Lieutenant Frederick Davis did not like the eastern counties. He thought Marchingham as unattractive a place as he had ever set eyes upon. Nothing but a waste of flat, muddy fields, stretching in every direction under the bleak December sky. No real prospect of action, either . . . he was feeling increasingly pessimistic about his mission here. It had *sounded* well enough, when Colonel Brotherton of the 16th Lancers sent him off, with a couple of dozen men, to put down riots in this area. However, there were no riots to be put down, or at least not yet. Apparently Marchingham had been rife with them when there was trouble in the countryside some years ago—fire-raising, rick-burning, that kind of thing—so the Colonel had supposed it a likely spot for rioting again. Some years ago, Lieutenant Davis gloomily reflected, was not now. Other officers had been sent to places such as Ixworth in Suffolk, or Attleborough in Norfolk, where there were genuine rioters to be dispersed —but not Fred Davis.

He had muttered something about hotbeds of sedition as he rode around the Marchinghams, but even to his own ears it sounded unconvincing, and it had earned him an ironic smile from his companion, Mr Benedict Gerard. Mr Gerard made haste to suppress the smile, and suggested, soothingly, that very likely it was the presence of Lieutenant Davis and his men that kept the peace: Lieutenant Davis had still seen his amusement. Nobody likes to be laughed at, and the Lieutenant felt ruffled.

No, he didn't like the eastern counties, or keeping the peace either. Dash it, he *was* a military man! Fifteen years since Waterloo, and not a bit of action to be seen. This was not what his adventurous spirit had craved when he persuaded his father to buy him a commission. Boney might be dead and buried, but some other ogre was sure to come along in due course, requiring Fred Davis's heroic opposition in the field. It was just his luck that now, when action of some kind had looked likely, he should have ended up in what appeared to be a backwater of peace and calm surrounded by rioting, rick-burning and machine-breaking, all of it just outside his province and within that of other of the 'small, mobile forces' (Colonel Brotherton's own description) dispatched to deal with the trouble. And what was more, sitting at dinner in Marchingham Priory's decidedly draughty Old Refectory, he was obliged to echo the cautious satisfaction with this peaceful state of affairs expressed by the rest of the company.

This comprised, first, his host Sir William, an amiable old fellow who liked his claret too much, and Sir William's wife—a handsome woman for her age, but rather uncomfortably like his formidable future mother-in-law. Then there were Sir William's sons, the younger a good-looking nonentity, while the elder, his companion of that afternoon, had an irritatingly prosaic, dampening way about him. Finally, the Gerards had some guests: a tall, imposing Scotsman, introduced as Sir John Law, with his second wife and his daughter by his previous marriage, Mrs Elliott, a handsome young widow to whose artistic talent reference was made from time to time.

Lieutenant Davis, who liked a good-looking woman, had hoped to be placed beside this lady at dinner, and was not disappointed, but unfortunately she did not seem especially impressed by a military uniform. However, he prided himself on his understanding of the fair sex, and observed before long that while she talked civilly enough, she had eyes for no one but the elder Mr Gerard, he of the prosaic manner, and that although they were not seated close together, the feeling was apparently mutual. Well, no accounting for tastes! But there was nothing for Fred Davis here in the fields of either love or war, and he really began to wish himself back in Norwich, which at least had its amusements. He might as well take what advantage he could of such amusements before next spring, when he was to marry a young lady of moderate looks but handsome fortune.

Dinner was over at last; port was drunk, they had joined the ladies. The prospects of any entertainment in the Marchinghams appeared slender indeed. Lieutenant Davis thought wistfully of a certain pretty little doxy he had visited in Norwich a couple of days ago, and wouldn't mind visiting again. All that kind of thing was going to be more difficult once he was married to his Cassandra. Was it true that a woman always grew to be like her mother . . . ?

He became aware that someone—Mr Benedict Gerard —was asking him a question. How long did Colonel Brotherton mean to remain in Norwich?

'As long as it takes, sir, to quell these shocking riots.'

'Yes, very right, very right,' contributed Sir William from the depths of his chair, which had a stool in front of it to support his gouty foot.

Mrs Elliott, who seemed to know something about the present disturbances, took up the subject. 'I understand that there has been some difficulty in deciding just *how* the rioting ought to be dealt with.'

All eyes were turned towards the Lieutenant. It is never disagreeable to have a number of people hanging on one's words, and he launched into a disquisition largely gleaned from what he had heard Colonel Brotherton say, although he made it sound his own.

Yes, Mrs Elliott was right: the local magistrates—he bowed towards Sir William—had only a few constables to enforce their authority in rural areas, since most of the old Yeomanry and militia corps were disbanded after the French wars. London had its new police force, the 'Peelers' or 'Bobbies', but of course these riots did not occur in London. Sir Robert Peel himself, until recently Home Secretary, after whom the London force was named, had begun sending troops of cavalrymen to the worst affected areas in the middle of November, and though Lieutenant Davis was a Tory he could not but applaud the resolute stance of Lord Melbourne, who had taken over at the Home Office towards the end of the month, when the Whigs came in. It was at Melbourne's instigation that Colonel Brotherton, the distinguished Peninsula veteran, had come to

Norwich to supervise the movements of troops in the eastern counties. Hence his own presence in the Marchinghams. Had anything, he wondered, been done here about Colonel Brotherton's recommendation to enrol volunteer 'specials'?

Sir William was plainly incapable of supplying this or any other information, and he was answered briefly by the elder Mr Gerard: yes, but he was happy to say their services had not yet been required. Only one small dispute had occurred, and that was easily settled.

'Indeed, sir?' remarked the Lieutenant. 'Recollect, it doesn't do to be too soft with violent men. The Kent magistrates quite failed to deal with certain of the rioters as they should, you know, at their recent Assizes. A lamentable business, that.'

'I am quite well acquainted with one of those magistrates,' remarked the handsome Mrs Elliott, with a certain coolness in her manner.

'Yes, well, nothing can excuse the behaviour of the Kentish labourers, but I dare say the magistrates there did not quite see what would come of leniency,' the Lieutenant suggested, to mollify the lady, but he found himself taken up by Mr Gerard.

'I can't agree with you, sir: in many cases excuses can be found. Life is not easy for the labouring poor, and I believe you'll find that many of the magistrates who know the working men well feel sympathy for them. Our own Vicar has voluntarily reduced his tithe, which in itself makes riots a good deal less likely in the Marchinghams.'

'Aye, well, I hope you are right,' said the Lieutenant sceptically.

'Oh!' exclaimed Lady Law. 'I am sure Mr Gerard is right. We would not like to think of Caroline's remaining here, you know, if there were the least danger, while we ourselves go jaunting off out of harm's way.'

'Certainly there is no danger!' pronounced Lady Gerard. 'The labouring poor of Marchingham, I am glad to say, know their station.'

They would, thought the Lieutenant gloomily. He wondered about the chances of finding a good class of girl in a dull spot like Marchingham. I might ask the younger fellow, he mused, Mr Will Gerard; he seems pretty much as bored as I am by this evening's entertainment, and I fancy he's not so stuffy as that brother of his. But such a question could not be put in present company, and Lieutenant Davis was obliged to wait until he was taking his leave to ask it.

Still, perhaps he had made a hit with the handsome Mrs Elliott after all, which did his self-esteem good. For on parting, she gave him a warm smile, saying, 'Good night, Lieutenant Davis. I am *so* glad you are here.'

'Yes, indeed,' agreed Lady Law cordially. 'With the military in Marchingham, dear Carey, I am sure you will be perfectly safe.'

'There—I was right, wasn't I?' demanded Sir John of his bride, when they were alone in their bedchamber.

'Of course you were right, dear,' Hetty readily agreed. 'About what?'

'About Carey and Mr Gerard, you featherhead,' said Sir John, affectionately. 'Obvious, isn't it?'

'Well, not so very obvious, John,' Lady Law ventured to suggest. 'I thought he was rather avoiding talking to Carey than otherwise.'

'Yes, yes, but did you see them look at each other? That's what gives it away,' said Sir John, indulgently. 'I wonder if I'm to be asked my permission before we leave? I don't mean to delay here too long: Clarissa's as trying a woman as ever she was, and if Carey is able to endure much of her company she has strong reasons indeed for wishing to be here, so *that* proves it too. But never mind the rest of 'em now.' And he proceeded to give Lady Law some very cogent reasons for paying no heed to anything but her own newly married state, which still bemused and enchanted her.

Carey had meant what she said to the Lieutenant; she *was* very glad he was there, for his presence at dinner made it impossible for Benedict to absent himself from that meal for the second night running.

It had been disappointing not to see him on her arrival, when she was so impatient to do so—though she felt a little natural apprehension too, which was soon dispelled; as their eyes met, she could not help being aware that he was very glad to see her. So *that* is all right, she said to herself, and though it may take a little while to bring him about, I mean to do it in the end. I suppose I may have to confess the whole of my Shakespearian stratagem—well, I *must* do so some time; it would be very underhand of me not to. Besides, I have five sovereigns to return to him.

But there was no opportunity yet for private conversation, and she found herself envying the conceited Lieutenant Davis, who had been riding around the Marchinghams with Benedict most of the day. She would not let *that* circumstance mortify her, however. It was plain that Mr Gerard had recently been extremely busy making intensive efforts to prevent just such riots as the gallant Lieutenant and his men had arrived on purpose to put down; riots which, as she knew from Lord Anderford, tended to be contagious, spreading from village to village. She was only sorry that Benedict's efforts had made him look so careworn.

Will too, she thought, looked careworn, and she wondered why, but was not disposed to spend much time puzzling over that particular question.

Will had received a note, just such a note as he dreaded. With the most dismal sinking feeling, he had felt it was only too likely to arrive at this, the worst possible time, when the place was swarming with military men. He felt too wretched even to take his mother's advice and make up to Cousin Caroline. In the circumstances, what good would it do him even if she *had* changed her mind?

And his own mind came round, once more, to Miss Gage—the one person who might, just might, be able to help. Suppose, for instance, he simply ignored Davy's message—could Roberta shield him from the consequences?

And if she could, and did, what price would he have to pay?

It was as much as he could do to be civil to that jackanapes Davis when the Lieutenant, on leaving, drew him aside with many a nudge and wink, to ask if there were any good, clean girls to be had in Great Marchingham. Will himself, he gloomily reflected, was finished with all *that*. How pleasant, how easy, to have gone into the Army, and be free to lounge about all day indulging your appetites. He gave the Lieutenant the only possible answer to his question, and hoped, morosely, that Mrs Carmichael and her nieces at Number Nineteen, New Road, would find one of their inexplicable reasons for showing him the door.

He had followed his father's example and consumed a good deal of strong liquor that evening, hoping it would cheer him up, or at least cause him to forget his difficulties. So far, it had not, but it was the sole remedy that occurred to him, and put further out of humour by his brief exchange with Lieutenant Davis, he did not go straight upstairs like his parents and the Laws, but instead resorted to the library, where he well knew his father kept a surreptitious supply of brandy in a cupboard. He was taken aback to find his Cousin Caroline already in that room, searching not for brandy but for books.

'Oh, Will, you're tall enough, aren't you, to reach me down *The Bride of Lammermoor* and *Ivanhoe* from that shelf? Then I needn't fetch the steps. Thank you. I wonder which would be best to re-read, on a winter night? she mused. 'What would *you* say?'

She seemed quite glad to see him, thought Will. Now if ever was the time for amorous dalliance, yet he hadn't the heart for it. Quite unable to answer her literary query, as he had never read either of the novels she named once, let alone twice, he mumbled something, and sat down. He couldn't very well search for the brandy while Cousin Caroline was there.

Carey looked at him in some concern. Yes, he *did* seem hagridden, poor Will! Her conscience urged her to discover if there was anything she could do, or say, to help him. 'Is something the matter?' she gently asked. 'You don't seem yourself, Will; I've thought so ever since we arrived.'

He roused himself sufficiently to assure her that it was nothing.

'But it *is* something, I am sure,' she persisted, and after a moment added, a little hesitantly, 'Will, you mustn't think that because you once asked me to marry you and I said no,

251

there need be any awkwardness between us. We are cousins—do think of me as a friend, and tell me if there is anything I can do to help.'

'Nothing, I tell you!' Will repeated quite savagely, but seeing Carey's look of surprise, for she had chosen her words as well as she could, and meant them, he recollected himself and apologised for speaking so brusquely. 'It's just that—oh, well, one thing and the other, you know.' And then, suddenly overtaken afresh by a sense of the injustice of it all, he let his most recent complaint burst out, entirely disregarding its unsuitability for Cousin Caroline's ears. 'As for that cockscomb Davis, asking me if I knew where he could find a good, clean girl—as if I'd nothing else to think of.' Her glance, again, was startled, and he apologised once more. 'Sorry, didn't mean to say that—you wouldn't know what I mean, of course.'

Carey said soothingly that it was of no consequence, and he waited for her to leave the library. However, as she made no move to do so, but seemed inclined to settle down by the dying fire with her books, there was nothing for it but to retire without the brandy he had come to find, muttering under his breath something which sounded like, 'Devil take Davy Leigh!'

Lieutenant Davis had gone straight from the Priory to his lodging in Great Marchingham, knowing that Sergeant Cooper (who, with the men, was less comfortably billeted in a corn-chandler's empty warehouse) would come for him there if he were needed in the night, but his rest was undisturbed. As the Sergeant cheerfully reported next morning, there was no trouble at all brewing in the Marchinghams, so far as he could see.

'Don't be too confident,' warned the Lieutenant, but he resigned himself to another tedious, uneventful day.

Mrs Elliott and the Laws were in the town that morning too, a clear indication that no one at the Priory expected any trouble, for Sir John would not have taken his Hetty, easily alarmed as she was, anywhere near the least hint of a riot. It was therefore fortunate that the first person from the Priory to receive any indication to the contrary was Carey, who was not easily alarmed at all, and that she received it only

252

after parting from Sir John and Hetty, whom she had taken to see the Vicar and his wife.

As she had expected, her father got on famously with Mr Whittier, and Mrs Whittier took an instant liking to Hetty, whose gentle, engaging ways were exactly what would endear her to the forceful Augusta. It had been the same, Carey was amused to note, with Lady Gerard, who for all her previous disapproval had actually said graciously that Lady Law seemed a most amiable person: high praise indeed, from Clarissa.

Carey had also hoped to make Sir John and Hetty known to Tiberius Taylor, but he was not in evidence, and an inquiry after his health produced only the frostiest of glances from Augusta Whittier. She concluded, sadly, that poor Mr Taylor was in disgrace again. She felt no qualms in absenting herself to call on other friends in Marchingham, for she left Sir John deep in discussion of Ovid with the Vicar, and the two ladies equally deep in discussion of the relative merits of black and green tea, with a plan that they would all go round the church and have luncheon together later. Carey's idea was to go the long way round and present herself at Mrs Carmichael's back door. To do this without being seen from Petergate, as she supposed Mrs Carmichael would prefer, she must first go a little way along Riverside Road, and seeing the door of Mrs Pacey's shop ajar, she thought she would look in and pass the time of day with the good lady.

Mrs Pacey, however, was not there. Instead, Carey found that very sensible young couple, Susan Pacey and Hugh Hodson, engaged in earnest conversation. She was about to withdraw and not disturb them, when Susan, looking up at the slight sound of the shop door, saw her.

'Oh!' she exclaimed, in tones of some relief. 'It's Mrs Elliott! Oh, ma'am, I heard you were back, and I'm glad as I can be to see you. Hugh, I'm sure Mrs Elliott will know what's best to do.'

Carey, who had no notion what Susan was talking about, was going to demur, but when the normally imperturbable Hugh turned to look at her with eyes very like his mother's, his face was so troubled that she bit back her disclaimer and asked, 'Whatever is it? Are you in some sort of difficulty?

253

Goodness, Hugh, you do look grave; surely it can't be as bad as all that.'

'It is, ma'am; that's about as bad as it can be,' said Hugh heavily.

'Now, now, you stopped him,' said Susan, consolingly. 'You kept him at home, Hugh, and you got it all out of him—that's something!'

'Kept whom at home?' asked Carey, bewildered. 'Stopped whom?'

'Sam,' said Hugh. 'My brother Sam. That'd just about kill my mother, I reckon, to think Sam was up to no good. Sam's always been her favourite.'

This was true; if Sam Hodson, clever, industrious Sam, the apple of her eye, had indeed been up to no good, Carey dared not think of the effect upon Peggy, and when she had quite recently suffered such distress over Grace, too. 'What exactly has Sam done?' Carey asked.

'That ain't so much what he have done, that's more what he was aiming to do. And the rest of 'em. Including Susan's Pa,' said Hugh.

'At his age! Would you credit it?' said Susan, sounding exactly like her own mother. 'Well! We had a word with Pa just now, Hugh and me. He won't be gallivanting around the countryside with that blackguardly set, or he knows well enough I'll tell Ma.'

'That all come of books, and learning,' said Hugh morosely. 'Books, and learning, never did a working man a bit of good. There won't be no books in *our* house, Susan,' he added, glaring at his betrothed as if she had just proposed the purchase of a gentleman's library on the grand scale.

'No, no, Hugh dear,' said Susan, soothingly—really, she is an admirable girl, thought Carey. 'But we've still got to think what to do. I say we tell Mrs Elliott the whole, and see what she thinks. You don't mind, ma'am? Mrs Elliott's a friend to your family, Hugh, you know she is.'

'Of course I am!' said Carey quickly, seeing and understanding Hugh's hesitation. 'I assure you, anything you tell me will be in confidence. Isn't your mother here, Susan?'

'No, she's gone out, thanks be! And I've promised Pa, if

we *can* keep it from her, so we will. I don't reckon there's going to be many customers along this morning,' said Susan, pulling the shop door to and putting a notice inscribed CLOSED, in Mr Pacey's very best lettering, in the window. 'Would you step in here, ma'am? If you'll excuse the muddle.'

They duly stepped into the little cubbyhole behind the shop which was dignified by the name of 'Susan's sewing room' when Mrs Pacey wished to impress customers who might order one of Susan's dresses. It was cramped, and full of the tools of the dressmaker's trade: pins, needles, scraps of fabric, reels of thread, pinking shears, paper patterns of Susan's own making. Susan's natural neatness, however, was evident, and the place was by no means in a muddle. Carey was going to say so, but the young couple had more urgent matters on their minds; Hugh still seemed doubtful of the wisdom of confiding in Mrs Elliott, but Susan had obviously made her decision, and as soon as the door of the little room was closed behind them, she pulled a crumpled piece of paper out of her pocket and handed it to Carey.

'There—that's what Hugh found in his brother Sam's room.'

Carey studied it, bewildered. It was a long-winded document, setting forth, in a rational enough if rhetorical way, matters pertaining to the 'State and Condition of the Labouring Man', and the Labouring Man's case for getting, as the writer put it, his natural rights: if the Labouring Man did *not* get them, it would be a standing reproach to the recipient of this letter, and all such as thought like him, so that they would incur the general reprobation of all honest men; the rights mentioned above comprising higher wages, lower tithes or none at all, honest work available to the Labouring Man at all times, freedom to take, for the nourishment of his family, the bounty of God's earth . . . 'Poaching, that's what that means,' observed Susan tartly, her own finger travelling down the lines as she read the thing through again over Carey's shoulder.

'He don't mention the smuggling, do he?' remarked Hugh, witheringly.

'No, on account of gentlefolk not minding a bit about the smuggling,' retorted Susan.

The really puzzling thing was that the whole effusion was addressed to Mr Josiah Dedman. Carey, who had met the man, could hardly think of a person less likely to care about incurring general reprobation, and so forth. It would have taken a textual scholar of some expertise to perceive in this the first draft of the letter that had eventually found its way to Mr Dedman, and thence to Marchingham Priory to be laid before the vicar. But—'Just turn it over,' said Susan, and Carey did so.

On the other side ran a revised and much shorter version: 'Dear Mr Dedman, this is to let you know that if you do not pay your men two shillings and six pence a day, and desist from the use of the new threshing machine, your yards will all be burnt to ashes. With respect, from your well-wisher, Captain Swing.' The original text was perfectly spelt. Several words had been crossed out, and ill-spelt versions written in over the top. Not the most expert of textual scholars could have deduced from the evidence, however, the amount of laughter with which Mr Leigh and his cronies had read the first version, before returning it to its authors with a terse request that it be made less correct and more to the point.

'A Swing letter?' said Carey. 'But—you found it in *Sam's* room, Hugh?'

'That's right,' assented Hugh, gloomily. 'When I was looking for a book, on account of my mother said she'd fancy a read of the *Pilgrim's Progress* off Sam's shelf. Books,' he reiterated, 'mean nothing but trouble. Tucked in among Sam's books, this was. So I waited for him to come in. Well, says I, so you think you'd figure well as Captain Swing, do you? And I got it all out of him.'

'Don't ask me,' Susan chimed in, 'what they thought they were up to, my Pa and Sam, if they thought at all, but they did it between 'em, you see, ma'am. My Pa says he wrote *that*'—and she turned the page over to the original version again.

'With Sam putting some of the extra bits in,' added Hugh.

'And then they were asked to change it,' proceeded

Susan. 'And then Sam took it home to write out the way it was wanted, because try as he might, my Pa said, he couldn't help but write a fair hand.'

'I reckon,' said Hugh, with a sudden spurt of fraternal loyalty, 'our Sam won't have found that easy, neither.'

'Your Sam's young,' said Susan, tolerantly. 'It comes hard to older folk, Hugh, changing their ways. Though goodness knows, I hope Pa's going to change his, for his own sake. Oh, if Ma should hear of this!'

'But,' said Carey, trying to make sense of it all, 'it sounds like a Swing letter, threatening a Swing riot, and there *are* no such riots in the Marchingham area.'

'Yet!' said Hugh, succinctly, and Susan elaborated:

'But there is to be one, ma'am, and it's all planned for today. A gang coming down out of Norfolk, and gathering men as they go along, and making for Dead Man's Farm —as I reckon they still will, even if we've kept my Pa, and Sam Hodson, from joining them and coming to I don't know what sort of harm—transportation very like, if not worse!' She had obviously been facing a family crisis of the utmost gravity: Carey's opinion of Susan Pacey rose by the minute. 'And all to cover up something else. For you can be sure, if it's planned ahead it's no real riot such as they've had up north of us, and down south. No, it's to cover up something else, that's what it's for,' said shrewd Susan.

'Good heavens!' said Carey, rapidly digesting all this information as it poured out. 'What else?'

'Smuggling, I reckon,' said Hugh. 'Smuggling, most like. Only don't know too much about that. *That's* not what interests Sam,' he said with heavy irony. 'Rights of the labouring man, that's our Sam's line. Nor he wouldn't say who was behind it all, neither, but I've a pretty good notion! I reckon that's Davy Leigh.' And as Carey looked blank, 'Brother to Miss Gage, that keeps the school.'

'Oh.' She digested this too. Vaguely, she remembered Mr Leigh; that dark, sprightly, youngish man she had met once at Brook End Farm. 'Miss Gage's brother? Well, you do surprise me!'

'That'd be partly for devilment, you can be sure,' said Hugh. 'Devilment, or what the gentry would call sport, maybe, as well as the profit. He's kind of half and half, Davy Leigh: half gentry, and some folk would say half gypsy. What's more, he can slide out of anything, that's his way. Leaving the likes of Sam, and Mr Pacey, and God knows who else may join 'em, to bear the blame. Sam says that's no such thing, but then Sam's a fool. Clever with books and figures, and that, but a fool.'

'Oh,' said Carey again. 'Yes, I see. You mean there is a gang of some kind which means to comport itself like a band of men agitating for the labourers' claims, though it isn't?' Susan and Hugh nodded. 'On its way here now?' The young couple nodded again. 'And going to Dead Man's Farm as a kind of diversion, while something else, which you believe to be a smuggling operation, occurs elsewhere . . .' Carey concluded. 'Where?'

'I'd have beaten the living daylights out of Sam to get him to tell me,' said Hugh, 'only I reckon he didn't know much about it himself. And my mother wouldn't have liked that, if I did him any harm,' he added, as an afterthought.

'No. I don't think she would,' Carey gravely agreed. 'But what is the trouble now, do you think? I mean, you have induced Sam, and Mr Pacey, not to take part in this undertaking, which of course was your first concern. Is there so very much danger to others, who may become involved out of misunderstanding rather than anything else?'

But she had thought of the answer before Hugh gave it—stupid not to have seen it at once, with all she had endured of Lieutenant Davis's conversation the night before.

'There's the soldiers here, ma'am,' said Hugh. 'Soldiers just on the look-out for any trouble. It couldn't be worse, not if you wanted to make folk look black. Mind, I say anyone that gets taken up has only himself to blame, and seeing we've got Sam and Mr Pacey out of it, let 'em hang!'

'Tell me,' said Carey, 'does Mr Gerard—I mean Mr Benedict Gerard, of course—know anything about this?'

The young couple looked at one another, and shook their heads this time.

'Very well, then. Hugh, I suppose you made sure Sam keeps well out of harm's way?'

'Sam's locked in his room,' said Hugh, grimly.

'Good—then will you go and find Mr Gerard, wherever he may be, and tell him this news? And tell him too, from me, that I believe I know a way in which I can divert the attention of the soldiers—or at least their officer, and it is he that matters most—from whatever may happen today—or anyway delay them a little.' For she had been thinking rapidly, weighing up various considerations in her mind: what she knew of Will, and his remarks made in her hearing last night; what she guessed of Roberta Gage, half-sister to the engaging rogue Davy Leigh who, if Susan and Hugh were right, was going to undo Benedict's best endeavours to keep the men of the Marchinghams on the right side of the law. Roberta, who had her own eye on Will Gerard . . . 'I am going to see someone—perhaps two people—who may be able to help. And if after all nothing happens,' she meditated out loud, suddenly smiling, 'well, I suppose no harm is done.'

Hugh and Susan nodded. She thought, with some alarm, that they were looking at her as hopefully as if she had the answer to everything. She wished she could have gone to find Benedict herself, since he was far more likely than she to know what to make of this situation, but for that very reason she ought not to keep the news from reaching him until she and Sir John and Hetty had made their leisurely way back to the Priory. 'And Hugh, could you leave a note at the Vicarage for me first? I must tell them there I am delayed.' She scribbled it, hastily. 'Now, see if you can find Mr Gerard. I am sure we can safely leave it all to him; but I will do what I can, too.'

16

Susan had told her where to find the Gages' school, but in all the agitation of the moment, neither of them had stopped to think that both Mrs and Miss Gage would be busy in the schoolroom with their pupils at this hour of the day. However, that intelligence, conveyed by the little maidservant who opened the door, did not delay Mrs Elliott for long: requesting pen and paper, she seated herself at a small table in the hall, drew off her gloves, and wrote a couple of lines which caused Roberta Gage to leave the pupils to her mother and come out to her.

You could not have told, from looking at Roberta, that her heart had given a sudden thud of excitement when she received the note in Mrs Elliott's hand. *I'd be on the alert*, Davy had said, dropping that hint about the North Lodge. Hints were more in Davy's line than direct information, and she doubted that she would hear any more; it was up to her to take her chance when it came. Ever since, therefore, she had been waiting for something unusual to happen, but life had pursued its even course as before. A call in the middle of the day from Mrs Elliott, so recently back from London, *was* unusual, though. And Mrs Elliott meant the Priory, and the Priory meant Will, and the North Lodge too.

She offered no very effusive greeting to her visitor, saying merely, 'Mrs Elliott? So you are back.'

'I am,' agreed Carey. 'I dare say you're surprised to see me, Miss Gage, and at so inconvenient an hour. I'm sorry for that, but I believe the matter is urgent.' For her part, she was looking at Roberta with more attention than before. A steely-willed young woman, she suspected: was it kind to poor Will to let her have him? On the other hand, Roberta would stand up to his mother for him; somebody would have to do that, if he was ever to have any chance in the world at all, and it was not going to be herself, Carey Elliott. 'And I think you may be able to help me.'

Roberta raised her eyebrows. 'I am sure I do not know how.'

'Let's say, then, that you may be able to help my cousin William, whom I think you know quite well, and may wish to know better.'

Roberta stiffened. 'And what do you care for your cousin?' she inquired, in very chilly tones indeed. 'Somebody has been indulging in idle gossip, I see.'

'Well, no; I made my own observations during the summer,' said Carey briskly. 'I won't fence with you, Miss Gage; this is the time for plain speaking. I take it you do want to marry my cousin Will?' There was only the faintest query in her tone, and this time Roberta remained silent. 'Good! I can assure you that I don't want to marry him, as you may once erroneously have believed. I wouldn't have him if I were you—on the other hand, Will might think himself very lucky to get you. For my part, I am anxious to spare a number of other people a good deal of trouble. Quite by the way, that will spare Will some difficulties too. I dare say he might be glad to think that you had been of use. Your brother—half-brother—is Mr David Leigh, isn't he?'

'Y . . . yes,' said Roberta slowly, sitting down opposite Carey.

'I think your brother has been rather busy, Miss Gage; whether out of mischief or malice, I don't know, but there are parts of this business upon which I fancy you may be better informed than I am. I suggest we pool our knowledge, to our mutual benefit.' Whereupon she launched into a rapid account of what she had learnt from the worthy young couple in Mrs Pacey's shop. 'And I feel sure,' she concluded, 'there is some connection between Will and your brother. "Devil take Davy Leigh!" he said last night, quite distinctly, in my hearing, and he is certainly in some kind of trouble. *Now* will you tell me what is going on?'

Deciding on an alliance of expediency, Roberta told her.

A little later—and considerably later than she had originally planned to arrive there—Carey was approaching

Number Nineteen, New Road, taking Roberta Gage with her.

Mrs Thompson let them in, greeting Carey as if she were no stranger—something which surprised Roberta almost as much as had Carey's announcement of their destination. There was a good deal else to surprise her too, not least her own presence in this notorious house. She looked about her in some confusion, which she managed to conceal tolerably well. Like every other respectable lady in Great Marchingham, Miss Gage had been wont to refer to Mrs Carmichael in hushed, horrified tones, if at all. The interior of her house, Roberta had automatically assumed, would resemble a den of iniquity . . . as to the precise appearance of dens of iniquity, she was not too sure, but would scarcely have been startled to find that their furnishings included garish scarlet wall hangings, turbaned servants with curved daggers, strange, heavy perfumes of incense and sandalwood, and dim lighting even at noon. Instead, she was ushered into a very pretty white and gold drawing room, illuminated by the ordinary light of day and containing furniture of the utmost elegance and propriety, an elegance and propriety echoed in the quiet but obviously expensive morning gowns worn by the three young ladies who were clustered around someone sitting comfortably in a corner, sketching block on his knee, his pencil flying over the paper. He tore off a sheet and flung it carelessly to the floor to join several others even as the two callers entered the room.

'Goodness me!' exclaimed Carey. 'Mr Taylor!'

The artist leaped to his feet, more sketches flying from their precarious perch on the little table beside him. 'Mrs Elliott! My Muse!' he exuberantly exclaimed. 'Now, *which* Muse was it? Did we say Calliope?'

'No, we didn't! We have been through all that before, Mr Taylor, and you may remember that I didn't wish to be anybody's Muse,' said Carey, picking up one of the dropped sketches. 'Anyway, I can see you are very well provided with Muses here.' For the sketch showed Molly, the redhead, caught on paper in the act of dancing, filmy classical robes which featured only in Mr Taylor's imagination (for she was clad in a becoming but demure gown of blue challis) floating around her, head flung back, ringlets whirling. 'That's very good,' she said. 'Terpsichore, or some other Muse?'

'Oh, never mind Muses, just as you say,' replied the artist, looking happily at the three girls. 'Muses are all very well in their way, Mrs Elliott. But here—here I have my three goddesses. Juno—' he waved a hand at Polly, who had come forward, poised and smiling, to greet the new arrivals. 'And Minerva!' A gesture towards Molly this time. 'And this, of course, is Venus!' He proudly indicated the lovely blonde Dolly. 'Not that there is anything to choose between you, my dears,' he added. 'It is only that one thinks of Venus as divinely fair.'

'Molly and I won't take offence, Mr Taylor,' Polly assured him.

'I should think not,' said Carey. 'You will probably never have an artist like Mr Taylor to paint you in your lives again.' It was true; the sketches she had picked up from the floor had a wonderful energy about them, a sense of movement and form which showed Tiberius Taylor at his best. 'But Mr Taylor—how do you come to be here?'

'Murals,' explained the artist, simply.

'Murals?' said Carey. 'What, here? I know Mrs Whittier doesn't care to have them in the Vicarage, but . . .' She looked doubtfully around the room: it was the largest in the house, but not of those extensive proportions which would suit Mr Taylor's style.

'No, no! For my Patron!' continued Mr Taylor, with a grand wave of his hand. 'Why should I mind what Augusta cares for now? I have a Patron, my dear Mrs Elliott! And unlike the late Dr Johnson, I am fortunate in my Patron. I may snap my fingers at Augusta, and so I will,' he concluded, with what Carey felt was pardonable glee.

Thus prepared, she was not very much surprised to see the Earl of Anderford enter the room next moment, to be introduced gravely by Mrs Carmichael. 'Mrs Elliott, I know, has met my kinsman already. You have not, however, Miss Gage; pray let me make you known to Lord Anderford.'

'Mr Taylor,' explained the Earl, picking up another of the sketches that littered the floor and scrutinising it, 'is coming to stay at Elminghall, where I have a great many plain, white, undistinguished walls, crying out for his work to embellish them. I am much indebted to you, Mrs Elliott, for telling me where to find him. Murals are the very thing for my house, don't you think? And Mr Taylor's murals are the murals for me.'

'By a stroke of great good fortune,' the artist explained, 'I had not yet quite begun on my great picture of Mount Ida and the Judgment of Paris when Lord Anderford called to discuss the matter with me, so it will be the first of the many fine things I have in mind for his lordship's house; and while we are still here, I am making sketches of these delightful young ladies, to figure in the painting. They may then visit us for further sittings at Elminghall. Look at these, if you please, my lord. What do you say to these, Miss Gage?'

And he fell to searching frantically among the sketches on the table, until he was able to produce what he wanted and display it in triumph.

'Remarkable!' Roberta Gage managed to say, seeing some comment was expected of her. 'I have never in my life known anything like it,' she added, and whether she meant the sketches, or the house, or the company she found inside it, was hard to say. Out of sheer curiosity, she would have liked to see more of Mrs Carmichael's unexpectedly refined and apparently respectable nieces, but at an almost imperceptible sign from the lady of the house herself, the girls seemed to have melted tactfully away.

'Isn't Mrs Whittier angry?' Carey asked Marie Carmichael, low-voiced.

'Furious, but really, there is nothing she can do about it. Mr Taylor is a free agent. Anderford can be quite formidable when he likes, you know, and is well able to deal with Mrs Whittier. He has struck up a friendship with the Vicar, too. Mr Taylor will accompany us when we set out for London and thence to Kent, in a few days' time.'

'We?' said Carey, and almost thought that Marie Carmichael blushed. 'I am lucky to find you still here, then, Marie,' she added, recalled to the business of the moment, 'because the fact is, we need your help. Miss Gage and I, that is. It is to do with this stupid Swing business, and the trouble that a few foolish persons may be in. And to do with

Miss Gage's brother, and several other people, and the soldiers who came here a couple of days ago, and now that I know all about it—or if not all, a considerable amount—I have formed a plan.'

She stopped, looking a little doubtfully at Lord Anderford.

'You are quite right, Mrs Elliott,' said he, accurately guessing her thoughts. 'Perhaps I'd better not hear your plan, in case there is anything in it to which I ought to object.'

'Very true,' agreed Mrs Carmichael. 'He has probably taken all sorts of oaths, you know, as a Justice of the Peace.'

'Yes, I hadn't thought of that before,' Carey acknowledged.

'Never fear,' said the Earl, affable as ever. 'I am now about to go across the churchyard to call on the Vicar and his wife, and Mr Taylor may come with me, to break the news that he is going to leave them.'

'What an excellent idea! And you will find my father there, and my new stepmother, only don't say that I am here, will you?' Augusta Whittier can't speak her mind to Tiberius Taylor in very strong terms if she has callers, thought Carey, watching the two gentlemen cross the churchyard and rather wishing she could be present at that scene. But there was no time for entertainment now. One thing, however, she had to know, even before disclosing her plan. 'Marie, are you going to be married to him?'

'Oh dear me, no,' said Mrs Carmichael mildly. 'Neither of us, you know, is the marrying kind. We find we still deal extremely well together, but marriage would never do. In any case, I fancy we both prefer the *demi-monde*, he and I.'

Though everything seemed to be all topsy-turvy in this strange place, Roberta Gage, with some difficulty, was beginning to regain her sense of moral values. 'If this improper conversation is to continue,' said she, acidly, 'I might as well return home.'

'Well, it isn't,' said Carey, 'because we have business to discuss, and you are right to remind us of it, Miss Gage, though as for *propriety*—well, never mind that. Now, Marie, let us tell you what this is all about . . .'

By the time Lord Anderford returned from the Vicarage with an elated Tiberius Taylor, Carey and Roberta had left again, and Mrs Carmichael was seated in the drawing room in conference with Polly, Molly and Dolly. 'Ah, there you are!' said she. 'Do you know, Edward, nothing could be more opportune than your being here at the moment after all.'

'Now that,' said the Earl, much moved, 'is a touching tribute. I had rather thought it was suggested I was *de trop*.'

'Never fear, nobody asks you to know what you ought not, but—'

'I thought there'd be a but,' said his lordship.

'But I believe you're the very person to be of real assistance. You and Mr Taylor too. All we want is for you to help us *embarrass* a military man, to such an extent that he will be glad to go home again without the trouble of arresting anybody. I am about to compose him a note.'

Hugh Hodson had returned to Brook End Farm in the family's gig—not a speedy vehicle, particularly on muddy December roads—and had then saddled up a horse and set off once more, not stopping even for a word with his delinquent brother Sam, something he was to regret, though the fact was, he didn't trust himself to set eyes on Sam at present. All the same, by the time he eventually tracked Mr Gerard down on the far side of the Home Farm, where he was looking at a fence that needed mending, he was only just first with the intelligence he had to bring. It was then about the middle of the afternoon, and even as Hugh, hurriedly dismounting from his cob, stood talking urgently, while Mr Gerard's expression grew steadily darker, a lad came racing up from the direction of the farmyard, panting out that they reckoned, back up to the Farm, Mr Gerard ought to know. So out of breath was he after imparting this information, that it was a little while before he could say precisely what it was reckoned Mr Gerard ought to know, beyond gasping the word, 'Mob!' from time to time. Eventually, he managed to make himself clear: there was a dangerous mob, said to be coming down south towards the Marching River, demanding beer and money and threatening to break machines, and gathering more men in every parish it passed through.

'The devil it is!' said Benedict, his mouth tightening as he looked around at the flat and peaceful fields, where—as it was a clear, fine winter's day, with the sun now sinking lower in the sky—one could see the roofs of Great Marchingham in one direction, the sparse, poor cottages of Little Marchingham in the other, and the shapes of a few farmhouses here and there on the horizon. 'It sounds as if you're right, Hugh. I *knew* there was something wrong about that letter. Damn your brother! Well, no—I suppose without him we'd have had no warning. But damn Davy Leigh, if he is the author of this. And with soldiers already stationed in Great Marchingham, too.'

At this, Hugh remembered to deliver Carey's message, but Mr Gerard, unable to think what she might mean, puzzled over it only briefly, and then put it out of his mind. 'Will you come with me, Hugh—you and Jack and Bob? Good. I'll get a horse, and meet you at your own place.'

When Mr Gerard arrived at Brook End Farm, with the least possible delay, it was to find that Sam had after all eluded his brother's vigilance; Hugh came to meet him swearing he'd tear the young fool limb from limb when he caught up with him. 'Must've got into the big beech outside of the windows somehow, and climbed down,' said he, ruefully. 'I never thought of that! What's come over young Sam?'

'A misplaced sense of loyalty. Let's hope we catch up with him on our way, and no more harm's done. You say your mother and father didn't know before?' said Benedict. 'Well, not a word to them now, then!'

The briefest of explanations served for an alarmed George and Peggy Hodson. They and the rest of their family were gathered in the comfortable kitchen of the farmhouse as the early December evening came on, and it was with difficulty that Mr Hodson himself could be prevented from joining Mr Gerard's party, of which he evidently assumed young Sam was a member. By a fortunate chance, however, Jim Spring had dropped in—for a word with Mr Hodson, he said, although all the family who were present had smiled knowingly and allowed him to make his way to the window where Grace sat sewing in the fading daylight. Mr Spring, volunteering to ride over the fields with the Hodson brothers, was a welcome auxiliary.

'Where are we going, sir?' asked Hugh, as the five of them set off.

'Dead Man's Farm, of course,' Benedict told him. 'And I hope we can get there before the soldiers, though by now I rather doubt it.'

However, when rumours of the approach of a dangerous mob reached the soldiers in Great Marchingham, who had come there for the express purpose of dealing summarily with any such thing, the officer commanding them had for some little while been incommunicado behind the firmly closed door of Number Nineteen, New Road.

What with the inactivity of the last two days, the extremely boring air of normality that prevailed in the streets of Great Marchingham, and Mr Gerard's dampening assurances that no rioters were likely to wreak havoc in this neighbourhood, Lieutenant Davis had just about resigned himself to the probability that his mission would prove a fiasco. The delivery, by some person unknown, of a note addressed in an elegant and unmistakably feminine hand, was an intriguing diversion. He was even more intrigued when he opened it. Mrs Carmichael, of Number Nineteen, New Road, opposite the church, had heard from a mutual acquaintance that Lieutenant Davis would like to visit her house, and would be happy to receive him. The sooner the better, she delicately indicated, in order to arrange an appointment for a later hour. Would between one and two o'clock suit him?

Torn between duty and inclination like any hero of romance, the Lieutenant chewed his lower lip thoughtfully. Will Gerard had indicated that Number Nineteen was as exclusive a house of ill fame as you could hope to find outside London. A preliminary visit just to arrange an 'appointment'—that was putting on airs indeed. Lieutenant Davis's curiosity was aroused. It would certainly be a pity not to try the place. That would be something to boast of to his friends, and might help to gloss over the unfortunate fact that he had not put down any riots. For if there was no trouble soon, the men would have spent several days and nights here idle, and he would have to take them back to headquarters and report the area quiet. So it was now or never for Number Nineteen.

He read Mrs Carmichael's note again. Well, if this was the way they did things in her house, he supposed he must keep up the pretence of a polite social call. Making up his mind, he told Sergeant Cooper he was going to stroll about the town a little, just to see how the land lay. He would be back, he assured the Sergeant, almost directly.

Half an hour later, he was seated in Mrs Carmichael's drawing room, drinking a glass of wine. His surprise at the elegance of his surroundings was similar to Roberta Gage's earlier that day—and he, unlike Roberta, had been in such establishments before. He would scarcely have known Mrs Carmichael for what she was, so little hint did she give of her calling as she sat talking pleasantly and stitching at a piece of fine embroidery.

The girls were very refined, too—and remarkably pretty. Yes, it had obviously been worth his while to come, even if he was becoming a little restive at the time it took to come to the point, when he only wanted to pick a girl for tonight. Should he have Dolly, the lovely blonde, or the pretty redhead Molly?

All three ladies were not just well-spoken, but plied him with flattering questions about life in the Army and his opinions on various subjects, so that it was difficult to find a gap in the flow of their conversation when he could come to the point. He found it at last, however, and before his views could be sought on the acting of Kean, the works of Thomas Moore, or any other such irrelevant matter, he seized his opportunity: 'And now to business, ma'am! I must be going before long!'

'Business?' said Mrs Carmichael. She sounded surprised. 'Oh, pray don't go just yet. You haven't met my other niece, Miss Brignold.'

'I thank you, but let's make it Dolly or Molly here. A bout with either of these young ladies will do very nicely for me,' said the Lieutenant, and laughed in an extremely jovial manner.

Next moment he wished he had not. Three pairs of eyes

269

were turned wonderingly on him, as if he had committed some solecism.

'Dear me!' said Mrs Carmichael, in dulcet tones. 'A bout? What can you mean, sir?' And without appearing to, she glanced at the little clock on the mantelpiece. Time was passing in a very satisfactory way. She had raised her voice in mentioning Polly, who was waiting in the next room, promptly made her entrance upon this cue, and began performing the part in which she had just been swiftly coached.

Polly's education, Mrs Carmichael reflected complacently, could be considered a success. Polly did her mentor the utmost credit. She was a lady from top to toe, exquisitely dressed, her voice retaining no trace of country accent. Fortunately, she had contrived to learn her letters even before coming to Mrs Carmichael's, sensibly recognising literacy as a useful skill for one who wished to better herself, and if at first she had been rather reluctant to read the books Mrs Carmichael gave her, she had quite taken to the habit after a while, and was now as well informed as any lady need be. She was also stunningly beautiful.

The Lieutenant was dazzled. The thought of holding this glorious creature in his arms—and doing more into the bargain—was irresistibly exciting. In any other establishment, he would have drawn the woman in charge aside and suggested the encounter take place now, at once . . . yet something about the demeanour of Mrs Carmichael (who had fairly accurately read his thoughts) prevented his doing so. Instead, he must sit and converse with Polly as if she were a young lady of quality—or at least a London courtesan of the highest class, in the Harriette Wilson mould.

If Polly had a fault, it seemed to be loquacity. She rattled on guilelessly: about the walks she had taken in Marchingham while staying with her aunt; the history of the place, from a little booklet written by the Vicar, the Reverend Mr Whittier; the novels of Sir Walter Scott, which she thought very grand. Here she proceeded to tell Lieutenant Davis, who had unwisely admitted to ignorance of it, most of the plot of *Rob Roy*.

And after a while, as he sat listening to Polly's artless prattle, a suspicion that he might have made a terrible mistake began to creep into the Lieutenant's mind. Had he been wrong in assuming this to be a superior brothel? Were these ladies perfectly respectable after all? Had Will Gerard, for mysterious reasons of his own, been leading him up the garden path? If so, it was a devilish good thing he had not managed to say more about his business here. Very likely he had said more than he should already. He searched his memory with some trepidation.

Polly was now describing parties she claimed to have attended in Norwich. 'And my dear, kind aunt,' she added, with a pretty, sparkling glance at Mrs Carmichael, 'says she will take me to London next Season.'

Mrs Carmichael smiled upon her highly satisfactory niece, leaned towards the Lieutenant and confided, in a whisper, that his lordship had a most eligible *parti* in mind for dear Polly. (And we *will* find her one, too, she thought; if ever a girl deserved to be kept in style it's Polly).

'His *lordship*?' queried the Lieutenant.

'Why, yes, didn't I mention that my kinsman, the Earl of Anderford, is staying in Marchingham himself at present?'

Or perhaps, thought Lieutenant Davis wildly, perhaps he had wholly mistaken the purport of Will Gerard's remarks? He did not know what to think, and was cast into further confusion by the entrance into the room, at this moment, of a gentleman of obvious elegance and distinction, with another, smaller gentleman who carried a large sketching block.

'And here he is now!' cried Mrs Carmichael gaily. 'Allow me to introduce Lieutenant Davis, Edward! He is making sure we are all safe from these shocking riots! Lieutenant Davis—Lord Anderford and Mr Tiberius Taylor, an artist of great genius, whom Anderford has engaged to paint murals in his country house in Kent.'

'Where our riots, I believe, have been a good deal worse than they are here,' said the Earl, amiably shaking hands and becoming as prolix upon the subject of the Kentish riots as Carey herself could have desired.

Prolix he might be, but there could be no doubt about it, Lord Anderford knew what he was talking about. Lieutenant Davis did not for a moment doubt his identity. He was not used to mixing with Earls, and did not know how in the

271

world to extricate himself from the company of a nobleman who seemed so full of questions, so anxious to impart information, and so interested in what he had to say. Murmurs to the effect that he really must leave, having other business to attend to, went unheeded.

He did have other business to attend to, had he but known it: it was about this time that Sergeant Cooper began searching the town for his superior officer, who had now been gone a full hour. For news of a mob had reached Great Marchingham, and the Sergeant was cursing himself for his improvidence in not discovering just where Lieutenant Davis was going.

Oh, so Lieutenant Davis knew Colonel Brotherton? The Earl was pretty well acquainted with Thomas Brotherton himself. He supposed Lieutenant Davis was aware that certain gentlemen, including Lord Suffield in Norfolk, and the Duke of Wellington in Hampshire, had raised what amounted to private armies of their own in order to put down the rioting? What did he think of such measures?

Meanwhile, Mr Taylor had settled himself into what was now his accustomed chair in the corner of Mrs Carmichael's drawing room, and was busily sketching away. As a pause in the conversation threatened, he glanced up, saying, 'Pray don't move, Lieutenant! I must get you down on paper in *just* that pose. Yes, that's it! Paris! What do you say to Paris?'

The Lieutenant confessed that he had never been there.

Mrs Carmichael uttered a pretty trill of laughter. 'No, no, sir, I fancy you have made a mistake.' (The Lieutenant himself was sure of it by now.) 'Mr Taylor means Paris of Troy. He is to paint scenes from the Homeric epics in Lord Anderford's house. I am sure they will be very fine! My nieces are to figure as the goddesses in the story—the Judgment of Paris, you know: Juno, Minerva, and Venus.'

The unhappy Lieutenant managed to croak out an attempt at a compliment, wondering desperately how much longer he must stay. It was mortifying to have made such a mistake, and he wanted nothing more now than to get away from this house.

But he was not to make his escape so easily. 'You have no objection to Paris, I trust?' said Lord Anderford.

'The pose is almost right; if I might trouble you to bend your knee a little?' suggested the artist. 'As if you were kneeling before Virtue, Wisdom and Beauty! Now, an apple! We require an apple!'

The maid Betsy was rung for, sent to the kitchen for an apple, and returned with two: a russet and a golden pippin. Choosing between them took some time. Mr Taylor did not like the colour of the russet; he preferred the golden pippin, if only for the gold in its name. After some ten minutes or so of sketching, however, while Lord Anderford talked on and on, Mr Taylor announced that after all the pippin was too small.

'It is commonly thought,' said Mrs Carmichael, 'that smaller fruit have the better flavour.'

'Flavour, ma'am, has nothing to do with it,' said Mr Taylor firmly. 'The flavour of the apple is not of the slightest consequence! We are not to suppose that Venus *ate* the apple awarded to her by Paris.'

'What *are* we to suppose she did with it?' mused Mrs Carmichael. 'What is your opinion, Lieutenant? I think artistic licence is called for, don't you? A turnip, now, is larger than an apple, and might serve. I am sure Mrs Thompson has plenty of them in the kitchen.' And Betsy was summoned again, to be sent for turnips.

It took another fifteen minutes to choose the right vegetable; to re-position Lieutenant Davis, who had seized this opportunity to stretch his limbs; to place the turnip in his hand in the most graceful way. They would none of them even listen to his protestations that his duty lay elsewhere. Oh no, cried Mrs Carmichael, everyone was sure there would be no riots in Marchingham. The girls laughed, and said he couldn't leave now! He thought of simply walking out, but the idea of offering such incivility to ladies—in the presence of an Earl who knew his commanding officer well, at that—prevented him. One by one, the girls peered over the artist's shoulder, assuring Lieutenant Davis that the portrait really was very like. That, he thought, was a matter of indifference to him.

It was an hour before Sergeant Cooper could get any notion of his whereabouts, and then by chance: the Lieutenant's rakish inclinations were common knowledge, and after trying the more respectable parts of the town, in vain, for any trace of his missing officer, Sergeant Cooper began making inquiries in the riverside taverns. There, somebody suggested Number Nineteen, New Road. Dubiously eyeing its position opposite the church, the Sergeant wondered if his informant had been trying to fool him, but as he crossed the churchyard he caught sight of his quarry through the drawing room window of Number Nineteen. Lord knew what Lieutenant Davis thought he was doing, half kneeling on the ground in a very strange attitude, and holding aloft what looked like, but surely couldn't be, a turnip!

Sergeant Cooper went round to hammer at the back door, where he encountered John Thompson, very large, leaning in the doorway and affecting deafness and slowness of understanding for some ten minutes, after which Mr Thompson judged it time to send a message through to the drawing room. Mrs Carmichael glanced at her clock, and nodded; it would have been pleasant to let the game go on a little longer, but there were limits, and she fancied the Lieutenant might not stand for any more of it. The girls exclaimed: what a pity he must go so soon! Oh, but he *must* look at Mr Taylor's beautiful picture before he went away!

The Lieutenant looked, and was transfixed by horror. He had been unable to see the sketch while Mr Taylor was at work, because of the angle at which the artist held it: all he could see was Mr Taylor's own bright eye glancing up from time to time, to rest upon his face—or upon the rest of his person. Lieutenant Davis only wished he had read some warning in those latter glances. For in the artist's imagination, Prince Paris of Troy appeared stark naked, with only an antique helmet upon his head. The face was like Fred Davis, very like, just as the girls had said, and the expression on that face did not quite match the heroic headgear: it was a look of the utmost anxiety, so that the general effect was ludicrous, particularly as Mr Taylor, his sense of artistic licence deserting him, had not even portrayed the turnip as an apple. A turnip it realistically remained. As the drawing was passed from hand to hand, the girls' giggles swelled to delighted laughter. Lord Anderford refrained from comment, but his lips visibly twitched.

'An excellent likeness,' cooed Mrs Carmichael. '*Anyone* would recognise you, sir.' The Lieutenant feared this was only too true. 'You are going to sign it, aren't you, Mr Taylor?' she added.

'And date it, oh yes, to be sure!' agreed the artist, and inscribed along the bottom: 'Lieutenant F. Davis, taken by T. Taylor in Mrs Carmichael's house, 19 New Road, Great Marchingham, 16th December 1830.'

Lieutenant Davis longed to snatch the dreadful thing and tear it to shreds, but had to stand by and watch it added to the pile of sketches lying on the table by Mr Taylor's hand: then, and only then, was he at long last able to make his escape, and learn from the Sergeant, waiting by the back door, that a mob of men on the move had been sighted. The latest intelligence was that they looked like avoiding Great Marchingham itself, and were sweeping round in a wide arc to the south and west of it.

'Are they, though?' said Lieutenant Davis grimly, his glance defying the Sergeant to ask what he had been doing in Number Nineteen. 'Then let's go after them! And at once!'

Roberta Gage's part had been to wait. She did not like inactivity, but it could not be helped: what Will Gerard would surely be expecting this evening could hardly arrive before dark. So she waited all afternoon, concealing her impatience, but when the girls had gone home, and twilight came on, she put on her warmest pelisse, a pair of stout shoes, took her muff, and told Mrs Gage she was going out to drink tea with a friend.

She was a strong walker, and before the last of the light was gone she had reached the North Lodge, where she hid herself among the tangled shrubs. It was cold, but there was not long to wait now; Will Gerard came riding up the neglected drive when she had been there not half an hour. He unlocked the door of the little building and went inside. Another half an hour passed, and several dark-clad figures arrived over the fields with a cart, its wheels muffled, unloaded what appeared to be a quantity of casks, carried them into the North Lodge, and drove away again. Ten minutes more, and Will emerged, locked the door behind him, and set off to find the horse he had left tied up to a tree.

His heart lurched uncomfortably as he saw someone standing beside the animal. He could not see the face in the dark, but he instantly recognised the voice which addressed him by name. 'Mr Gerard?'

'Miss Gage—thank God, it's only you!' Unflattering this might be, but the relief in his voice was plain.

'Don't be alarmed!' said she swiftly. 'I have guessed it all!'

'You have?' said Will, not in the least reassured by this remark.

'Yes—and I fancy Davy has left *you* to bear the brunt of it, hasn't he? Oh, I see just how it was! Even I can't deny that Davy is—is *devious*!' said Davy's fond sister. 'He has taken advantage of you, Mr Gerard, as I am sure you must suspect by now. Only your own good heart, your sincere sympathy for the lot of the poor, has led you into this.'

'Er—has it? Yes, I suppose so,' said Will, floundering.

'Of course you were not aware,' continued Miss Gage, 'that Davy was going to use those poor men as a cloak for his other business—for that.' She indicated the building behind them. 'But listen: there is a mob on the move, and the military after them. Suppose the soldiers should come here? Suppose they should take the men who were here just now, or whoever comes to fetch what they brought again, and you were by? Do you know when that's to be?' she briskly inquired.

'About five in the morning,' said Will, ideas crowding in upon him too fast for his bewildered mind to deal with them. Chiefly, however, he was aware that Miss Gage seemed to have the situation in hand, although how she had found out these things, he could not imagine.

'Then there is no time to be lost. Now, listen carefully. We were here in the grounds of the Priory and saw those men come, so we watched and—let me see—they had with them the key to this lodge, and left it there under a stone, for whoever was to fetch those casks. Brandy, I suppose —but plainly contraband. So we decided that it was best to take the key and go to—to the Vicar, perhaps, and tell him to send some men with a cart to take the casks away. Yes, the Vicar will do admirably, and he can send word to the Revenue men.'

This part of Roberta's plan was her own work, owing nothing to Davy, who was not going to like it at all. But there really would be nothing he could do. She wondered whether Davy had stopped to think what excellent weapons for blackmail he had handed her. Probably not: devious he might be, but she was much the more ruthless of the two of them.

'And there will be no need to explain anything to anyone beyond that,' she pursued. 'Certainly not to Davy. I can deal with Davy, never fear! Only your good heart has led you to this pass, Mr Gerard, and I don't see why you should suffer for it, although you did not previously see how to extricate yourself without harming those for whom you feel so sorry.'

'Yes,' Will cautiously agreed again. His spirits were beginning to lift a little, sufficiently for him to see one or two objections. 'But, Miss Gage, how did we come to be here together at all?'

'Why, we had an assignation to meet near the North Lodge, of course.'

'And—and why don't we go straight to the Priory, and tell someone there? Ben, for instance?' Not that he *wanted* to try this tale on Ben, thought Will. He had a notion that Ben might see straight through it.

'Because your mother does not approve of me, to be sure,' said Roberta, in tones of wistful regret. 'Now, can you take me up on your horse with you? I am not very heavy. Then we may get to Great Marchingham all the sooner—and you will spend the rest of this evening with Mama and me, won't you? Because we are so afraid of the mob, if it should come into the town.'

Will was about to say that he didn't see any real need for that, he was sure Miss Gage and her mother would be quite safe, when Roberta delivered her clincher.

'And then, of course, I shall be able to say you were with me *all the time*, and nobody can ever hold you to blame for anything.'

17

Carey too had passed an afternoon of enforced inactivity. She, her father and Hetty had driven back from Great Marchingham, and seen no sign of riotous mobs or any other kind of trouble. Perhaps there wasn't going to be any after all? Perhaps Hugh and Susan had not understood everything perfectly? Well, if so, all the better. But as she sat indoors talking to Hetty and Clarissa, she could not help wondering what was happening now.

After a while, it occurred to her that she might be of use at Brook End Farm, for clever, silly Sam was surely in some distress, and if Hugh had felt obliged to tell George and Peggy the tale of his errors, in deep disgrace too. Slipping on a pelisse, she stated her intention of walking in the grounds, and left the two older ladies to their talk, Clarissa expressing a parting hope that she might meet Will and walk with him.

She would rather have met Benedict, but knew that to be unlikely. However, on reaching Brook End Farm to find everyone but George, Peggy and Grace gone from the house, she heard that she had missed him there by only half an hour—and that there was indeed news of a mob. Mr Gerard, and Jim Spring, who had been here when the news came, said Peggy, were off somewhere along with Hugh, Bob, Jack and Sam.

'*And* Sam?' said Carey.

'Why, yes!' There was some surprise in Mrs Hodson's voice.

'Did you see him go—I mean, isn't he in his room?' How strange the question must sound! 'There was—was something I particularly wanted to say to Sam,' she lamely added.

Peggy looked at her a little oddly, but went upstairs to see. No, Sam wasn't in his room. Now she came to think of it, most likely he'd gone out ahead of the rest of them; she hadn't seen him leave with his brothers.

So Hugh *had* reached Benedict with his news; it was plain, too, that he and Susan had *not* been mistaken, and the famous mob was on its way to Mr Dedman's farm. It was also plain that Sam's parents did not know what Sam had been up to, and Carey was not going to tell them. She would have liked to know what Benedict had in mind, and whether Marie Carmichael had managed to delay the soldiers long enough to give him time to disperse what was surely a largely spurious mob. However, she supposed she must possess her soul in patience. Accordingly, she set off to return to the Priory.

The lane which ran between Brook End Farm and the Home Farm was full of December mud now; she had come the longer way round, by the road—by no means dry, but less of a quagmire—and she started back the same way. It was sheer chance that she left the farmhouse when she did, and so encountered a vehicle coming the opposite way, out of Great Marchingham, which drew up as she approached, and proved to be a gig driven by Mrs Carmichael's stalwart retainer John Thompson. She shouldn't be out, said Mr Thompson: the mob was said to be moving this way, and he was sent by Lord Anderford to let Mr Gerard know the soldiers had been delayed for an hour or so but would be on the road soon. It was nearly dark, and he was looking about him, rather dubiously, at the uniformly flat and featureless fields. 'You don't know where I might find Mr Gerard, ma'am?'

'Indeed I do,' said Carey, delighted by this happy coincidence. 'Let me come up with you, and I'll show you the way.'

Mr Thompson demurred, but she was having none of that, and was up in the gig in an instant. 'Come along, then!' said she, briskly.

'Where to, ma'am?'

'To a place called Dead Man's Farm,' said Carey. 'With luck, if Lieutenant Davis is delayed, there's not too much hurry.'

But they were only about a mile from Mr Dedman's farm, just approaching the hamlet of Little Marchingham, when a sudden flower of orange flame blossomed in the dark sky.

She remembered the way to Dead Man's Farm quite well, and was able to guide John Thompson, who was now driving the gig as fast as it would safely go: who knew what that ominous fire meant? Its glow remained in the sky as they turned into the straggling hamlet of Little Marching-ham, which this evening appeared quite uninhabited: hardly a light showed in any of the cottages, and Carey wondered whether the people had shut themselves in-doors, determined to remain there and avoid trouble, or joined the mob bound for Mr Dedman's farm on purpose to court it.

No further flames showed, however, and as they approached the four-square farmhouse Carey saw that the fire came from a rick standing on its own to one side of the yard, without any near neighbours. The rickyard was out-side the farmyard proper. Some twenty yards from the track leading to the farmhouse and the burning rick stood a group of about fifteen men, whom Carey took to be the dangerous mob. They were not doing anything much, just looking at their handiwork with a somewhat hesitant air. Certainly they made no attempt to stop the gig as John Thompson drove it briskly into the farmyard and drew to a halt there.

There was no air of hesitancy whatever about the Hodson brothers, who, Carey saw, had formed an efficient chain to the burning rick from the farmyard well, and were taking buckets of water from one another and conveying them to the fire. There they all were: the large figure of Hugh Hodson nearest to the stack and the mob, and going back from him to the farmyard, in order, stood his brothers Bob, Jack, and—

'Sam!' exclaimed Carey, jumping down from the gig.

Beyond Sam, again, she saw Jim Spring and Benedict, who was vigorously working the handle of the farmyard pump, and to whom she made her way.

'Good God, what are you doing here?' said he, abruptly, pushing the hair back from his eyes and keeping the pump handle in movement. He did not sound pleased to see her, but then she had not expected that he would.

'Didn't you get a message from me? Well, perhaps not —never mind that. I came because of Sam—and I met John Thompson, and the soldiers are very likely on their way by now. It's no good being angry with me, Benedict, because I *am* here, so losing your temper is simply a waste of effort,' said Carey reasonably. 'But what *about* Sam?'

'I can see you're here! You shouldn't be—but thank God, I doubt if there's any danger. I don't suppose this charade is going to last very much longer. As for Sam, Hugh Hodson may not be as clever as his brother, but he's a biting tongue in his head when he wants!' She was pleased to see the faint shadow of Benedict's smile, the one she liked so much. 'I had something to say to Sam myself. I suppose he climbed out of his window to join his friends from a sense of loyalty, and then found that most of them weren't his friends at all, but a set of strangers out for what they could get, where- upon he very sensibly joined his brothers instead. Here, Dedman, you can take this pump over,' said Mr Gerard unceremoniously.

Looking around, she saw the dour Mr Dedman standing in his farmhouse doorway, arms folded, apparently taking no part in the proceedings at all, while his little wife twittered anxiously beside him. Reluctantly, however, he obeyed the command, and came to the handle of his own pump.

The rick was burning low now. 'So that's the mob, is it?' inquired Carey, looking with interest at the rather subdued party standing by the embers. 'It's rather small, is it not? For a mob, that is. Not that I have much experience of such things, but I had always supposed a mob to be much larger, and altogether more alarming.'

'It is rather small,' agreed Mr Gerard, and she saw the smile involuntarily appear again. 'It was larger when it arrived here, and I understand from Sam that a number of its members decided they had done enough before they got as far as this, and went away again. Nasty-looking cus- tomers, he called them, and city folk too, judging by the way they talked among themselves. In fact, Sam has been pretty thoroughly disillusioned by this day's work! And thank God for that, if the military are going to turn up—you say they're on their way?'

'Yes.' John Thompson, seeing where a strong arm was needed, had gone straight to join the chain of men with buckets of water, so it was left to her to give his information.

'And they were delayed? A message from Lord Anderford?' inquired Mr Gerard, puzzled. 'Surely you wrote to me of him, in Kent—but how the devil . . . ?' With one eye on the sullen group of men watching the Hodsons put out the fire they had lit, however, he could hardly spare time for such questions now.

'Well, as to that,' said Carey, 'it is quite a long story, and I don't know just how it worked, but it evidently did—the idea, I mean: we enlisted the help of Mrs Carmichael, and her nieces, and—oh, I shall have to tell you all that later! Who are these men—the dangerous mob, I mean?'

'A few people just out to make trouble, I think; and local men come along partly out of curiosity, and all Dedman's own labourers,' said Benedict, sounding rather grim again. 'The latter two categories probably with a good deal of drink inside them—Dutch courage. Poor Dedman: he'd agreed to most of the changes asked, even if he was slow to put them into practice; he doesn't deserve this, nor do his men. I want to get them home again before the soldiers arrive. I wonder what the chances are?'

She could not answer that. Looking around, she now saw a vaguely familiar face in the forefront of the mob, and identified it after a moment as that of Tom Harris, the man she had spoken to in the summer, who had the twin boys. He was clutching a piece of board on a stick. It bore the words 'BREAD OR BLOOD', lettered with care and as suspiciously well spelt as the first letter to Mr Dedman. Sam Hodson's work again, Carey suspected.

The fire was nearly out, the men in the yard had slackened the speed with which they filled, passed, and emptied their buckets, and the mob seemed to think it was about time something else happened. One of them had a horn with him, and now blew it, with a certain shaky defiance; a couple of others, obviously the bolder spirits, moved forward and began to chant the words on the placard. 'Bread or blood! Bread or blood! Bread or blood!' And then, above the others, rose Tom Harris's own voice. 'Let's break the bloody machine, then! Over in that there shed!'

The men, gathering courage from their chant, began to move towards an outhouse on one side of the farmyard.

Dedman dropped the bucket he had been holding and moved quickly between the mob and the place that housed his precious machine. 'That you don't! You leave that be, and be off with you!' As if he had been holding his temper on a short rein for some little while, he began to shout: 'Tom Harris! Dixon! Smith! Be off with you, and don't none of you never come back no more! Oh, you'll be sorry for this, that you will!'

He was no coward, thought Carey, but his intervention had been unwise. It by no means halted the surge towards the outhouse pointed out by Tom Harris, and suddenly —where it had come from, Carey could not have said, for she was sure there had been no sign of it a moment ago—suddenly, instead of the placard he had been holding, Tom Harris had a shotgun in his hands, and was pointing it at Dedman.

'Don't be a fool, Harris!' said Benedict sharply, moving in front of the farmer, who had stepped back smartly. 'Put that down, and listen. Mr Dedman has already come to a sensible decision regarding wages, you can see for yourselves that your recent companions have gone off, leaving the rest of you to take any blame—and I will tell you now, I have just had word that the soldiers from Great Marchingham are on their way. No doubt the fire you lit will help to guide them here. For heaven's sake go home, all of you, as fast as you can, and we'll say the fired rick was an accident.'

'Who says the soldiers is coming?' asked a sceptical voice.

'Common sense, and Mr Thompson here, who has driven from Great Marchingham on purpose with that news. Take his advice and mine, and go home.'

The large figure of John Thompson himself had by now moved up to Benedict's side, to be joined by the four Hodson brothers and Jim Spring. The mob visibly hesitated. They outnumbered the defenders of Mr Dedman's threshing machine, but not by so very many and, taken as a

283

body, the Hodsons and their allies looked rather formidable. All the same—'We'll get that bloody machine first!' shouted Tom Harris, defiance suddenly flaring up again, and the men moved forward.

It was most unfortunate, all agreed later, that just at this moment Mr Dedman chose to defend his own property by snatching up a pitchfork, lunging forward with it in a very sudden manner, liable to unnerve a man who had already had to fortify himself with strong liquor for this expedition, and shouting, 'Oh no, you won't, Tom Harris, and come what may you can get out of that cottage of yours this very night!'

The shotgun went off. Whether by accident, or design, who could say? Tom swore later it was accident, and if not, either he was simply unhandy with a gun, or he had been impeded by the other men standing so close. In any case, it was Mr Gerard, moving instinctively forward to stop him, who suddenly staggered backwards, to lean against the farmhouse wall, clutching at his shoulder.

Carey was beside him at once, an arm reached out to support him, and at that precise moment a roar of flame went up from the rickyard as a second stack blazed into the sky. They supposed, afterwards, that a spark must have jumped from the first fire, had lain there smouldering, and only now caught properly.

The mob stopped in its tracks, looked from the injured man to the blazing rick, and seemed about to turn and flee, but was deterred by one or two who stood firmer than the rest; Tom Harris no longer among them. He was staring, horrified, at Mr Gerard, and there was no need for his nearest neighbour in the mob to adjure him, righteously, to look what he done now. One of those bolder souls, however, set up a new cry: 'Give us some money and then we'll be gone!'

'Aye, let's have five shilling apiece!' suggested another, daringly.

'Somebody bring me a light,' commanded Carey urgently. She was trying to discover how badly Mr Gerard might be injured, but though he had been holding his left shoulder as if in some pain, he pushed her hand away as she attempted to undo his coat, only to clutch the shoulder

284

again, saying between his teeth, 'The idiots! Let it be—I'm all right. Buckshot, was it, Tom? No, really, Carey, many a man gets as much as that on the Scottish moors.'

'I never meant . . .' stammered the unfortunate Tom.

'Keep still, Benedict; it can do you no good to move about,' said Carey. 'You must come inside and sit down. Mrs Dedman, find some linen, and hot water, and two of you—' turning to the Hodsons and their companions—'can you help him into the house?'

'Not yet,' said Benedict, though breathing rather hard, as Hugh and Jack Hodson went to do her bidding. Meanwhile, some of the hopeful rioters, their imaginations caught by the boldness of the demand, were still calling for five shillings apiece, although several men had taken Mr Gerard's advice and left when the second rick began to burn.

Despite Carey's efforts to stop him, Mr Gerard was doing his best to push himself off from the wall against which he was leaning. He looked at the blazing stack, which threatened the others in the rickyard. 'Hugh, see to putting that fire out, will you? Carey—can you look in my pocket?' He was still clutching his shoulder, and evidently did not like to take the hand away. 'See if there's anything we can give them, to make the fools go home. I don't think I have much money on me, but it may do.'

'Don't worry; I have something,' said Carey. For so indeed she had. 'Really, it is quite providential,' she added, half to herself, as she took out the little purse she had been carrying ever since her return to Marchingham, undid it, and shook the coins it contained into her hand. She then rose to her feet and walked towards what remained of the mob. 'Here,' she said in a firm voice. 'Here are five sovereigns. Divided between you, I think that will come to what you are asking, or more! Now do as Mr Gerard says, and go away directly. You don't want to end up on the gallows, or transported, I suppose? Very well, then—that's the very thing Mr Gerard has been trying to prevent. So will you now please *go home*?'

She uttered this speech with some trepidation—which she hoped did not show—for after all, she had never before faced a mob, however uncertain of itself, and then found that she had not faced it on her own after all: while the Hodsons obediently turned their attention to the second burning rick, the reassuring figures of John Thompson and Jim Spring had come up behind her, Mr Spring calling to several of the men by name and offering to knock them down himself if they didn't do as the lady said directly. The mob, if it could be so styled any longer, melted away, dispersing in different directions and leaving behind only a considerable area of trampled mud and straw, and the two ricks that had been fired.

The second fire was coming under control more easily than the first; perhaps the rick might not burn right out. Mr Thompson and Mr Spring, having helped Benedict to a settle in the farmhouse kitchen, assisted Carey in getting his coat off, a process which obviously caused him some discomfort, and then went to join the Hodsons, leaving her to cut away the sleeve of his shirt and investigate the damage. 'I told you it was nothing,' he said drawing in his breath a little sharply all the same as she dabbed carefully at his shoulder with the cloth provided by Mrs Dedman, who was twittering more anxiously than ever. Carey waved the poor woman away again.

There was a little bleeding, but not much. 'You've got several pellets in there, I think; my father will take them out for you, which I'm afraid will hurt, but there's no help for it,' she said, matter-of-factly. 'The Hodsons are getting on quite nicely with the fire out there, so that's all over, and you had better just rest for a little.'

'Damn nuisance!' said Mr Gerard, obviously more irritated than anything else by his mishap. 'Thank you, though,' he added, a little tardily. 'I should have said so before, shouldn't I? I'm afraid I snapped at you when you came here, but it was you sent them safely off home in the end.' He managed a rueful smile. 'I'll return you your five sovereigns, of course, as soon as we are back.'

'Well, as to that . . .' She thought for a moment, but it wouldn't do to think too long; take the bull by the horns, she told herself. 'Well, as a matter of fact, they were yours anyway; I was going to return them, when there was a convenient opportunity; that's why I had them with me.'

'Mine?' He sounded puzzled. 'What do you mean? I don't think I ever lent you any money.'

'This is more than a little awkward, but—but I have something particular to say to you. I thought it was going to be very, very difficult, and I see it still may be, but—well,' said Carey, as she concentrated on dressing the injured shoulder, speaking rather rapidly in an attempt to hide the fact that her usual self-possession had quite deserted her, 'I *told* you I had become friendly with Marie Carmichael, didn't I? You must remember how we rescued Polly between us. And she—Marie, that is—guessed my feelings for you. So that when you—when she told me—well, the fact is, it was all my own idea, and she did not like it at all. Only I thought, perhaps, I was the one you really wanted, and to tell you the truth I was jealous. Very jealous. I did *not* see, if I was right, why Polly or one of the others should —oh, and then there was Shakespeare; of course, it was his idea in the first place. I mean, it was Shakespeare who put it into my head. Oh dear, I am not saying any of this very well at all. I would have contrived to tell you sooner, only I was obliged to go away the very next day, and then, later, it was not a circumstance one could easily put into a letter . . .'

'Could you stop talking for a moment, do you think?' inquired Mr Gerard, which was just as well, for at this point her voice failed her entirely. 'Good God!' he added, quietly. Only a little way into her remarkably incoherent speech, he had sat up very straight, despite the injured shoulder, and begun listening intently. He had turned rather pale too, but that might be the effect of being peppered with buckshot at close range by the now repentant Tom Harris. 'Are you telling me it was you? What must you think of me?' But his uninjured arm was held out to her.

She let out a huge sigh, and settled thankfully into it. Everything was going to be all right. 'I think, rather, it's a case of what you must think of *me*. But you were being so reserved, and cool, and wouldn't even kiss me a second time . . . There, you see!' she added, emerging from his embrace a moment later. 'You did it yourself!'

'Did what?'

'Closed your eyes, of course. Almost everyone does so

287

when they are kissing, or so Marie Carmichael says, and you will allow that she ought to know. Try it again, and you will see what I mean.'

This invitation met with a response which was all she could have desired: the one drawback was that when she opened her own eyes again, it was to see several Hodsons who had meanwhile entered the farmhouse kitchen, with John Thompson and Jim Spring, and were waiting until Mr Gerard might be at liberty to attend to them and their news of the soldiers' imminent arrival. 'We heard a bugle, sir,' said Hugh, 'and there's horsemen with lights coming— only a mile or so off along the road, I reckon!'

'The devil they are!' said Mr Gerard, recalled to a sense of his surroundings.

'Glad to hear it,' commented Mr Dedman, at last showing some animation as he hurried to his doorway to look out for the approaching soldiers. 'Glad to hear it. They'll be in time to go after that set of blackguards. Just wait till I tell 'em what's been afoot here,' he added, vengefully.

'Dedman,' said Benedict, quite quietly, but in a tone that made the farmer hesitate on his threshold, and reluctantly turn back to listen. 'You'll do no such thing. You know well enough this was no true riot, but a put-up business, and I can guess who was behind it too . . . well, never mind that for now. Are you surprised your men were gullible enough to join in? If you'd been quicker to do as you told me you would, you couldn't have been made the excuse for what happened here tonight. I haven't gone to all this trouble to see a few poor dupes suffer for expressing a grudge against you—and nor have the Hodsons here, or Mrs Elliott, who probably saved your threshing machine for you. I'll just add that if we all say there *was* no riot, and only you say otherwise, you will not be believed.'

'Aggie there'll back me!' remarked the farmer, jerking his head towards his wife, who hovered in the background, beyond even twittering by now, although at this she did utter a squeak of alarm.

'Naturally she would,' said Carey. 'She is a good wife to you—now please don't distress yourself, Mrs Dedman.' Rather reluctantly, she had left her position beside Mr Gerard, and gone to comfort the woman. 'You would not wish to see poor men and their families suffer unnecessarily, I know, but don't concern yourself, Mr Gerard will make everything right.'

'Ho, yes? And how,' snapped the angry Mr Dedman, 'd'you think all *this* can be explained to the soldiers, then?' He indicated the remains of the two ricks, one still smouldering, while clouds of vapour rose from the other where the Hodsons had thoroughly drenched it in water, and pointed to the many footprints that had trampled the muddy yard. 'Anyone can see there's been a crowd of folk around the place.'

But here they all fell silent, for the sound of horses' hooves was heard approaching, and sooner than might have been expected.

18

'Not enough of them to be the military, surely?' said Benedict.

He was right. Next moment there drove up an elegant, if sadly mud-splashed carriage, from which two gentlemen got down, and picked their way rather carefully across to the lighted farmhouse doorway.

'Your father!' exclaimed Mr Gerard as they approached, and—'Lord Anderford!' cried Carey, at the same moment.

'Lord Anderford of whom you wrote to me so often?' inquired Benedict, 'The gentleman in London to whom you were—to whom I *supposed* you were attached?'

'No, no, he's attached to Mrs Carmichael—or rather, he is *again* attached to Mrs Carmichael, whom he has known for a very long time, and he is staying with her in Great Marchingham . . . but Papa, Lord Anderford—what *are* you doing here?'

'That,' remarked Sir John drily, 'is what I might well ask you. It occurred to Hetty and Clarissa, you know, to become a little concerned when you failed to return from your walk. Particularly when it was learnt that there was a mob roving the countryside. Even more particularly when Anderford here came driving out with his cousin, Mrs Carmichael, and Mr Taylor, to inform us that Davis and his men were riding off to disperse it, and to put his experience of this kind of thing in Kent at Sir William's disposal.'

'Came driving out with Mrs Carmichael? Good gracious,' said Carey, 'where is she now?'

'At the Priory, of course, with Hetty and Lady Gerard, who believed that you were very likely in safe hands with your Cousin Will somewhere, and was thus less agitated than Hetty, who didn't believe any such thing. Where is the

290

mob?' inquired Sir John, looking around him. 'I can see it's been here, and the fires it lit guided us, but where has it gone? Davis will be on the spot before long; we could hear his men riding up by the road while we took the bridle path ourselves—which can't have done the springing of Anderford's carriage any good, but the way looked shorter. I don't see this famous mob of rioters, though.'

'No, there wasn't one, sir,' said Benedict, who, Carey observed, had been thinking hard. 'What you see is—is the result of an accident which occurred during some rustic merry-making. That should serve.'

'There is a great deal to tell you, Papa, and Lord Anderford may have told you some of it—oh, this is my Cousin Benedict, Lord Anderford—but will you back us up?' said Carey swiftly, for the sound of a considerably greater number of horses was now beginning to be heard. 'About the rustic merry-making . . . what *sort* of rustic merry-making, Benedict?'

'A mumming . . . yes, I think that will do. A Christmas mumming.'

''Tain't Christmas yet,' pointed out Mr Dedman, morosely.

'It's near enough,' said Benedict firmly, 'and Mrs Elliott wished to see one—no, even better, Sir John wished to see one. You have never seen a Christmas mumming play in the country, have you, sir? St George and the dragon, and so forth? I thought not—and you are going abroad within a few days?'

'To be sure. I have the greatest curiosity to see a mumming play,' said Sir John, obligingly. 'I suppose somebody will tell me why, some time. But you are quite right, I am leaving in a day or so.'

'Exactly—so it was now or never to see such a play, and Mr Dedman's men very kindly offered to show you one. But the ricks accidentally caught fire, from a torch carried by one of the mummers, careless fellow—that was you, Tom. Do you understand? You were very sorry, naturally, to see what you had done, and while the other men all went away, you stayed behind to help put out the blaze, lest it spread to the other ricks.'

It said much for Tom Harris, thought Carey, that he had

291

in fact stayed behind, displaying a pathetic anxiety to atone for the accident that had really happened, and he now nodded vigorously.

'And the Hodsons helped to put out the flames too —that's true enough,' continued Benedict. 'Dedman, let's have a barrel of your best home-brew broached, and quickly.'

'What for?' growled the farmer.

'For verisimilitude,' snapped Mr Gerard, 'and for refreshment to offer the soldiers, and because the men who've saved your rickyard deserve it.'

Ten minutes later, when the first of the cavalrymen rode up the lane from the main road and dismounted at the farmyard gates, the scene inside the farmhouse was one of restrained conviviality as the firefighters refreshed themselves after their labours, and Carey, having taken swift instruction from Mr Gerard in the nature of a Christmas mumming play, prepared to give Lieutenant Davis a detailed account of that ancient form of entertainment, and the unfortunate way in which tonight's performance had ended.

'Ah,' said Lord Anderford, strolling out of the farmhouse door as the Lieutenant marched up to it, jaw grimly jutting. 'So here you are at last. And after all, it seems, there was no mob; I am afraid you have had your ride for nothing.'

The Lieutenant could never afterwards be quite sure what had or had not happened that day; he was only certain it had been a disaster for himself from beginning to end. He had to believe Mr Gerard's account of things, of course . . . yet wasn't there something odd about those smouldering ricks? He and the men had seen the glow of the first fire in the sky while they were still a long way from Dead Man's Farm, and the second flared up when they were a good deal closer: proof positive that this was the scene of the rioting. So perhaps he did not entirely believe Gerard about the mummers. But why should he tell a tale which wasn't true? One which was also backed up by Mrs Elliott and her father. It was odd, too, that Mrs Elliott seemed to keep looking anxiously at Mr Gerard, as if her mind were on something quite other than the story of the mumming and its unfortunate end. (He was correct, and her anxiety was caused by Mr Gerard's pallor; a shoulder peppered with buckshot did not quite seem to fit the tale of a mumming, so it could not be mentioned, and she was wondering how much it hurt him now he had his coat back on over it.)

Then again, the tale was borne out by Mr Dedman the farmer, though he was obviously a man of few words, and did not look at all happy. Still, by accident or design, he *had* lost a rick and had another drenched with water and rendered useless. However, the threshing machine which might have been supposed to be the prime target of any rioters was untouched, standing in its shed, as the farmer, at Mr Gerard's urging, proved to him.

No, Lieutenant Davis was at a loss, and what cast him into the greatest confusion was the wholly unexpected presence of the Earl, together with a large man identified by Sergeant Cooper as the manservant at Number Nineteen, New Road, who had been so slow to let him deliver his message to his superior officer. And Lord Anderford knew how long he, Fred Davis, had been in the house when his sergeant was searching high and low for him. Almost worse, although Lord Anderford had not been present while Tiberius Taylor made his sketch for Paris of Troy, his lordship was staying in that house, and the damn sketch was still to be found there. Who knew, he might have seen it, if Mr Taylor was such a protégé of his. A new and dreadful thought occurred to Lieutenant Davis: suppose his likeness, naked but recognisable, ultimately figured in one of Lord Anderford's murals. The notion made him so very anxious to be out of his lordship's company that he could only mutter assent to Anderford's bland assurances that it was all exactly as Mrs Elliott, Sir John, and Mr Gerard said, and then give permission for his men to accept the draughts of ale so hospitably offered them.

Nor, subsequently, could he quite work out whether Number Nineteen was or was not what it seemed. Altogether, it was a day which Fred Davis did his best to expunge entirely from his memory; though on the credit side, perhaps, was the fact that it made him more appreciative of the virtues of his Cassandra, who might not be the most beautiful or witty of young ladies, but in whom there was certainly no deception or deviousness at all.

'I have seldom,' said Sir John, still chuckling reminiscently from time to time, 'enjoyed an evening so much in my life. No, no, Hetty, I assure you, nobody was hurt at all except Benedict here—bad luck, that, but he'll do well enough.' For when he, the Earl, Carey and Mr Gerard had arrived back at Marchingham Priory in Lord Anderford's carriage, his first action had been to take Mr Gerard upstairs and dig the shot out of the injured shoulder. Both gentlemen had firmly refused Carey permission to be present during this operation, which was not a pleasant one, but their being alone together enabled Mr Gerard to ask Sir John a question which did not surprise the physician at all, and to receive a satisfactory answer.

Carey had therefore gone to her room to change her dress and repair some of the ravages to her appearance caused by a walk in the Priory grounds, followed by a drive in an open gig on a December evening, and subsequently by attendance at an unsuccessful riot and an imaginary mumming, and was astonished to find, when she came downstairs again, that it was now about ten o'clock in the evening.

'Good gracious!' said she. 'This is quite a party!' And indeed, the drawing room of the Priory was unusually animated for that hour. Assembled there, she saw, were the entire Gerard family, with Sir John and Hetty, the Earl of Anderford, and Mr Tiberius Taylor, who had attached himself like a limpet to his patron, perhaps lest Mrs Whittier deprive him of his new-found independence at the last moment, and was sketching busily away in a corner as usual. Besides all these, the Earl's alleged kinswoman Mrs Carmichael was present. So were Mrs and Miss Gage from the girls' school in Great Marchingham.

How it was that they came to be part of the company, Carey did not know, but supposed she would discover in due course. Lady Gerard—seated beside Sir William, who himself appeared unusually lively—was casting dark glances now at Mrs Carmichael, now at the Gage ladies. The only person who seemed to mind them was Mrs Gage; she quailed visibly when such a glance came her way.

294

Roberta, Carey now saw, was sitting next to Will, who did not look especially happy. Mrs Carmichael, a picture of composure, was sharing a sofa with Hetty, who until Sir John and Benedict came down, just after Carey, had been talking to her—trust Hetty!—with the utmost amiability.

Tea, and coffee, and stronger liquors than those, were laid out to one side of the room, and Carey, helping herself to a welcome cup of tea, went to detach Roberta Gage from Will. 'Miss Gage! I hope you have not been unduly alarmed, in Great Marchingham, by unfounded rumours of rioting?'

'Oh, indeed we were!' Roberta looked demure. 'In fact, my mother and I *dared* not stay there alone tonight, without a man in the house. But your cousin, who happened to be with us, was so kind as to suggest he brought us both back here with him. Was not that good of him?'

'So kind as Mr Gerard has been tonight. Dear me, have you heard, Mrs Elliott, of this dreadful smuggling business?' put in Mrs Gage. 'Roberta and William, as I suppose I must now learn to call him, found out about it all, and told the Vicar, and the Vicar sent to tell the Revenue men—only think, however, what a shock to Roberta! And then, when news of the riots came—why, I do not know *what* we would have done without William tonight!' And Mrs Gage turned to address her effusions of gratitude to Will in person, so that Carey could move a little way aside with Roberta.

'So your part in the business was satisfactorily concluded?' she inquired. 'I fancy your brother is the only person missing from this interesting gathering, and I don't suppose he is likely to put in an appearance.'

'Oh, but he *has* been to see us tonight in Saltgate, although he could not stay.' Roberta allowed herself a small smile. For unwittingly, Davy had done her a good turn at the last moment, turning up just when Will, having spent a decidedly awkward evening in the company of Miss Gage and her mother, seemed to feel all danger to himself was now over, and stated his intention of going home. He had not been very ready to credit Roberta with such alarm as she then expressed at the notion of hypothetical rioters roaming wild in the streets of Great Marchingham, and he was almost relieved to see Davy Leigh come in: he wanted no more to do with Leigh, but at least he could now decently go away and leave the ladies to him, if they really required protection.

But no. Davy, it appeared, could not stay. Davy, it further appeared, thought—or pretended to think—that he, Will, had in some way compromised his sister, and ought to be protecting her. 'Though whether you're a fit person,' said he so softly that Mrs Gage could not hear him, 'who is to say? *I* could say, perhaps, if I wished . . .'

And just as Will thought he was free of all that. But Davy had reckoned without Roberta, who, prettily smiling, had said, 'Oh, Davy, of *course* he will protect us. Why, I am sure I could say all sorts of things too, if I wished.'

She had then raised her head, and brother and sister stared hard at each other for some seconds. Will had a confused impression that a great many things were being said in that silence, and in the end it was Davy Leigh who remarked, shortly, 'Very well. I see. I'll wish you joy, then!'

And that was that. All through the evening, it had been lurking at the back of Will's mind that he had accepted Roberta's help, had been glad to have it, and there would be a price to pay. So now it must be paid. He took a deep breath and did as he knew he must. 'Don't go for a moment, Leigh. I want to say I hope your sister will agree to be my wife.'

There was to be no maidenly hanging back from Roberta at this point. 'Oh Will, yes!' said she softly, in front of both her mother and her brother; there could never be any denying the fact that he had made this proposal. Roberta had more sense and more worldly wisdom by far than Grace Hodson. 'For we deal extremely well together, do we not? I remember so clearly how our steps matched at the Assemblies, last winter.'

'It was there,' said Will, with a very respectable attempt at gallantry as he accepted his destiny, 'it was there that I first knew you were the wife for me.'

'Precisely so!' Roberta had agreed, drawing his arm through hers. And now, to Carey, she said quietly, 'I must tell you that I am engaged to be married to Mr William Gerard.'

'I wish you both well,' said Carey, and dismissing Will

and Roberta from her mind she went to urge Benedict, who was still looking a little pale, to occupy a small sofa with her, where they were soon deep in a private conversation, conducted in low voices and very pleasing to them both.

'There, ma'am!' Mr Taylor, heedless of all but his art, had torn yet another sheet off his sketching block, and was handing it to Lady Gerard. 'See your picture! When I have completed my grand mural of the Judgment of Paris on Mount Ida, I am planning a series of works on the subsequent history of the Siege of Troy, and I shall beg your leave to depict *you* as the noble figure of Hecuba. The Fall of Troy I have already painted, but that picture must remain where it is, and there is no reason why, after I have finished my series on the Trojan War itself, I should not treat that epic subject again.'

'The Trojan War lasted nine years, didn't it?' observed Carey, catching this remark and allowing it to distract her, briefly, from conversation with Mr Gerard. 'Have you got enough walls, Lord Anderford?'

'Oh, any number of them,' said he. 'A lucky circumstance!'

Lady Gerard, receiving the sketch of herself from Mr Taylor's hands, was surprised but not displeased. 'Very nice, Mr Taylor,' said she graciously, handing it back to him. One could not have told from her manner how bewildered Clarissa Gerard felt. She was wholly unable to work out the connection between Mr Taylor, Lord Anderford —greeted by Lady Law as an old acquaintance—and the notorious Mrs Carmichael. It was all quite, quite extraordinary, and as for Mrs Carmichael's being his lordship's kinswoman, she did not believe a word of it. Augusta Whittier, she thought, will never credit it that I have received the woman in my house. I would never have credited it myself. But how could I refuse to admit her, when Lord Anderford introduced her here? And then there is Augusta's brother, who mercifully is not making any of those improper remarks of his tonight, and who seems so well acquainted with them both. Even Cousin Caroline greeted the woman as if she had met her before. I do not know what to think, Lady Gerard concluded. I really do not know.

Carey had not only greeted Marie Carmichael, she had seen Mr Gerard's glance fly briefly to that lady and then return to herself again. A little colour came to his face, which was all to the good, but she was quick to say, 'I told you, it was entirely my notion, and I had to *make* Marie help me. And I had always wondered, about Shakespeare.'

She spoke just loud enough to be overheard by Sir William, seated nearest to them. 'Shakespeare?' said he, feeling that in all the confusion of this evening, which he had given up trying to understand at all, it was about time he said something, and here at least was a name he recognised. 'Shakespeare? Eh, what? What has he to say to anything?'

Receiving his picture of Lady Gerard back, Tiberius Taylor had risen to his feet and was now strolling around the room, as if to fix upon the next subject for his pencil. 'A great deal. sir. A great deal,' he assured Sir William earnestly. 'The Swan of Avon—always a great deal to say on *any* subject. When I have completed the Trojan War, it is possible that I may turn my attention to scenes from the major works of the Bard.' And he continued on his perambulation about the room, stopping briefly to look at a surprised Roberta Gage, shake his head, muttering obscurely, 'Cressida? Rosalind? Goneril? No, no, not quite!' and pass on.

'I mean *Measure for Measure*, and *All's Well*, you know,' Carey was continuing, to Benedict, in whose eyes she was glad to see more amusement than anything else. She spoke lower now, though it was doubtful whether anyone else could have understood the tenor of their conversation. 'Whether they could have brought it off successfully— Isabella, and Helena, that is. And then I was not sure; that is, there was a moment when I thought you knew me; only you went away so suddenly, almost as if you were angry.'

'I *was* angry,' said he, holding her hand rather tightly. 'With myself—for finding I could—as I thought—take such pleasure when . . . well, never mind that, and all the time it *was* you . . .'

'Of course,' recollected Carey, mentally reviewing the works of Shakespeare, 'the two cases were not quite the same, because in *All's Well* it was Helena who wished to

supplant that other girl with Bertram—Diana, wasn't it?
—while Isabella was anxious to substitute Mariana for
herself, with Angelo.'

'Did it occur to you,' inquired her love, 'that nobody
would much relish figuring as Angelo, or Bertram?'
However, she saw he was smiling.

'Angelo? Bertram?' inquired Sir William, catching these
two names as well. 'Don't know anyone called Angelo.
Sounds like a foreigner to me. Knew a Bertram once,
though. Bertie Partridge. Don't believe you ever met him,
Ben. Before your time.'

'No, sir. We were only discussing Shakespeare,' said Mr
Gerard.

'Well, I wish you would stop it. I still do not see what
Shakespeare has to do with us,' said Sir William, a little
fretfully.

'Shakespeare has to do with everything!' cried the enthusiastic Mr Taylor.

'I should take no notice, William,' Sir John advised his
host. He observed that Lady Gerard's eye had now fallen
upon the clasped hands of the couple thus engaged in
literary criticism. 'It's simply their way of billing and
cooing, I imagine.'

'Billing?' inquired Lady Gerard, frostily. 'Cooing?'

'Yes, we are going to be married, Cousin Clarissa,' Carey
told her. 'Benedict has just asked me—with my father's
permission, which he did not really *need*, as I am my own
mistress, and have control of my own fortune. But in any
case, we are all quite of the same mind about the marriage.'

She was interested to note, from the expression on Mr
Gerard's face, that in all the confusion of this evening's
events, the existence of her fortune had obviously slipped
his mind entirely. And indeed: 'I had forgotten about that,'
he said, sounding stricken.

'Please!' begged Carey, low-voiced again. 'Do not, for
goodness' sake, begin to have more misgivings, of a different order this time. I have had more than enough of that
sort of thing. Cousin Clarissa, I assure you, will be very
happy to see me marry a Gerard.'

'You are going to marry *Benedict*?' said the astonished
Lady Gerard, struggling to take it in.

'Ah! Good notion. Been thinking so for some time,' offered Sir William, unexpectedly.

'But . . .' said his wife, and then found herself at a loss for words.

'You won't object to having me for a daughter-in-law, Cousin Clarissa?' inquired Carey, looking very straight at her.

'But Will . . .' began Clarissa Gerard, and once again fell silent.

Into her silence, Miss Gage spoke up, in a voice of crystal clarity. 'And we have something to tell you too, Lady Gerard—Sir William.'

She turned expectantly to Will.

'Er . . . yes, yes, to be sure. Going to be married,' he said, swallowing hard. 'Miss Gage and I, that is.' And he and his bride-to-be looked at one another.

The revelations of the last few minutes had been something of a shock to Roberta too, although she concealed it better than Lady Gerard. Forced by circumstances into alliance with Mrs Elliott today, she had found herself entertaining a certain unwilling respect for her, and it was clear enough by now that Mrs Elliott had never after all wanted to marry Will. But that the heiress might marry the *other* Mr Gerard had somehow never occurred to her, since she had unconsciously absorbed all Lady Gerard's own opinions on the unlikelihood of Benedict's marrying and producing heirs to the Marchingham estate. As she found him rather alarming, with an uncomfortable way of looking at one as if he guessed just what one was thinking, it had not previously struck her that Lady Gerard might be wholly mistaken on this point.

But now, it seemed, her prize was not quite so rich as she had supposed. Will and his children might not inherit almost everything after all! This was a shock, but Roberta was not a young woman to be easily discouraged. As she had made her bed, so she must lie on it, and she would ensure that it was as comfortable a bed as she could devise. Casting a practical eye upon her prize, who was making a better hand of meeting his mother's questions than might have been expected, she began to devise ways of making the best of *him*, too. Lady Gerard would be glad to have her

300

for a daughter-in-law in the end. And she began by easing Will's path at this difficult juncture with mention of the grand Gages of Dullerton at judicious intervals, and by setting herself to charm Sir William, who, genuinely pleased with the turn events seemed to have taken this evening, was very ready to be charmed by any future daughter-in-law who cared to try it.

'"Jack shall have Jill",' observed Mr Taylor, still wandering around the room under the spell of the Bard and paying only the slightest attention to what was going on around him, but vaguely aware that there was talk of marriage in the air. '"Nought shall go ill, the man shall have his mare again and all shall be well." I should also like to paint *this* gentleman,' he added, coming to a halt in front of Sir John, 'though in what character, I am not yet sure. Nestor, perhaps?'

'Nestor be damned!' said Sir John, outraged. 'I'm not in my dotage yet! Why not make it Methuselah and be done with it?'

'Hm.' Tiberius Taylor stopped to consider this. 'I had not yet thought beyond the Judgment of Paris and the Trojan Wars, to be followed by the Shakespearian episodes . . . but perhaps you are right, and I should subsequently turn my attention to the Old Testament. After all, Methuselah must have been a man of great vigour, to live so long.'

'I think it's time we turned our own attention, and our carriage, towards Great Marchingham again, Taylor,' remarked Lord Anderford. 'Lady Gerard, Sir William, now that the alarms of this night have been brought to a happy conclusion—several happy conclusions, as Mr Taylor here has poetically pointed out—we must take our leave. Mrs Gage—Miss Gage—as there are no riots after all, would you care to return with us too? I believe there would be room for us all in the carriage?' But there was a reluctance on Miss Gage's part to accept this offer, and civility constrained Lady Gerard to protest that bedrooms had already been prepared for the ladies, when they came seeking safety from the mob, and they must have no more travelling tonight.

'Quite so!' agreed his lordship. 'Well, are you ready, Marie?'

'Certainly, Edward!' And Mrs Carmichael, who had said very little throughout the evening, but sat listening to everything with the utmost interest, and with bright amusement in her grey eyes, rose to make her farewells in a very correct manner, appearing not to mind or even notice the cool nature of Lady Gerard's response. Her own parting embrace of Carey, however, was a warm one.

'Are you going to spend the night at Number Nineteen with us, Taylor, or would you rather we attempted to rouse them at the Vicarage and let you in?' inquired the Earl, as they moved to the door.

'I would prefer the former alternative, my lord,' said Mr Taylor fervently. 'I would *much* prefer it!'

'I wonder how Tiberius will go on, in Lord Anderford's house,' said Carey.

'Admirably, I imagine. Just the place for him,' said Mr Gerard. 'A cultivated, easy-going atmosphere, from all you say, and I am sure Mrs Carmichael will see to it that he has pretty girls to paint. He will be as happy as the day is long.'

'Mrs Carmichael says she is to leave these parts too,' remarked Hetty, who had lingered for a moment beside the dying fire to felicitate the newly engaged couple. 'Such an agreeable woman.'

'Yes . . . yes, indeed,' said Carey, glancing a little askance at her stepmother. For in all their acquaintance with the Earl during the summer, she thought he had never mentioned Marie Carmichael to Hetty, and certainly she had never done so; she wondered what opinion Hetty had really formed of that lady. 'You liked her?'

'Oh yes,' said Hetty firmly. 'Very agreeable. Most lady-like, too, all things considered—and entertains the friendliest of feelings towards you, my dear. And of course, she is the Earl's kinswoman as well. Quite unexceptionable!' she pronounced, and went upstairs to join Sir John, leaving Carey for once unsure of the extent of her dear Hetty's knowledge of the world, or indeed her own knowledge of Hetty.

'I suppose,' said Carey rather later, to Mr Gerard, after an interval of a very pleasing nature, 'I suppose that now some person or persons of the first respectability will come along and buy the house at Number Nineteen, and Mrs Whittier's days will be sadly dull. Speaking of houses, I don't think I would particularly care to live here, Benedict; we shan't have to, shall we?'

'Certainly not; we can find somewhere else that I hope you will like. You won't mind living in the country?'

'I shall like it very much. I can paint the flowers that grow on my own doorstep, and go to London now and then to see my botanical friends, and ask them here too, if you have no objection. But I don't really think I want to reside under the same roof as my Cousin Clarissa. She ought to be satisfied, you know,' added Carey pensively, 'because she did want me for Marchingham Priory, and she has got me, after all. I believe, however, I would rather leave it to Roberta to be her *resident* daughter-in-law. And that will be interesting, as well. Won't you be sorry not to have Mr Taylor's magnificent murals to look at any more, though?'

'I should much prefer,' said he, 'to look at you.'

There was another interval, of as pleasing a nature as before.

'And we could always commission him to come and paint us some more,' he added later.

'You know, the other thing about Number Nineteen,' said Carey thoughtfully, 'is that after this, when Mrs Carmichael is borne away by Lord Anderford—while the nieces, I suppose, will find the most distinguished protectors imaginable—well, no one is ever going to be quite sure just what kind of an establishment Number Nineteen really *was*. For those who really know, beyond any shadow of doubt, are the least likely of all to speak up and say so.'